Praise f...

"If you're into Austen retellings, ... you like talking dragons with your regency romance, or if you're just looking for an upbeat, light-hearted change to your fantasy routine, *Heartstone* is for you."

—The Book Smugglers

"Wow, where do I even start? I *must* address the stunning world-building that lies within these pages. This is White's debut novel, but her imaginative and addictive world feels as if it was written by a seasoned writer. Elle Katharine White is an author to watch."

—The Speculative Herald

"Somehow though, Elle Katharine White has managed to blend the classic elements of *Pride and Prejudice*—the characters, the social commentary and financial issues, and the conflict between Lizzie Bennet and Mr. Darcy—with wonderful, monster-filled fantasy. It has all the lovely romance with a hint of heartbreak from the original, but combines it with fantasy in a way that feels utterly unique."

—All About Romance

"Honestly, pick up and read *Heartstone*. Even if you don't much like *Pride and Prejudice*, this fantasy retelling is accessible, does a very nice job creating a fantasy world, and has a fine analogue Elizabeth Bennet in the form of Aliza Bentaine."

—Culturess

"It is a truth universally acknowledged that adding dragons to *Pride and Prejudice* is the best idea I've heard in a while."

—B&N Sci Fi and Fantasy Blog

DRAGONSHADOW

BY ELLE KATHARINE WHITE

Heartstone
Dragonshadow

Dragonshadow

A HEARTSTONE NOVEL

Elle Katharine White

HARPER Voyager

An Imprint of HarperCollins*Publishers*

DRAGONSHADOW. Copyright © 2018 by Laura Katharine White. All rights reserved. Printed in the United States of America. No part of this book may be used or reproduced in any manner whatsoever without written permission except in the case of brief quotations embodied in critical articles and reviews. For information, address HarperCollins Publishers, 195 Broadway, New York, NY 10007.

HarperCollins books may be purchased for educational, business, or sales promotional use. For information, please email the Special Markets Department at SPsales@harpercollins.com.

Harper Voyager and design are trademarks of HarperCollins Publishers LLC.

FIRST EDITION

Designed by Paula Russell Szafranski

Title page and chapter opener art © Mathee saengkaew

Library of Congress Cataloging-in-Publication Data has been applied for.

ISBN 978-0-06-274796-9

18 19 20 21 22   LSC   10 9 8 7 6 5 4 3 2 1

For Leanna,
Ahla-Na set Sorra-d'ei-Aliana

DRAGONSHADOW

CHAPTER 1

THE SILVER BOX

I woke to an animal growl in the predawn dark.

Dreams lingered along the edge of perception, shapeless, terrible dreams of monsters and gaping earth and a pyre that would not go out. Blankets that had once comforted me turned suffocating; I clawed them aside and sat up, clutching handfuls of coverlet like an anchor against the horrors in my head.

Breathe, I told myself. *It isn't real.* Slowly, breath by breath, my heartbeat steadied and the tightness in my chest eased. *You're safe. He's safe. We're all safe.* The words tumbled together in my mind in what had become my waking prayer. The Battle of North Fields was won, the War of the Worm was over, and we had nothing to be afraid of.

The growling resumed just beyond the curtains surrounding our bed.

Or . . . maybe we do. I reached for my husband's side of the mattress, expecting the reassuring touch of warm skin and sleep-tousled hair. Smooth sheets, cool and unoccupied, met my fingers. I squinted in the dark. "Alastair?"

No answer. He was gone, and I was alone with the creature.

The drapes around the bed parted and I snatched up a pillow, holding it in front of me like a shield as something black and snarling leapt onto the bed, all furred fury and glowing yellow eyes.

I yelped as four stone of angry stoorcat landed on my chest. "*Ow! PAN! Get off!*"

Pan the stoorcat retracted his claws and glared at me. Stoorcats weren't *Shani*, those ancient creatures of Arle who counted humans as allies, nor were they *Tekari*, our sworn enemies. Nor, as far as I could tell, were they *Idar*, those creatures indifferent to humans. Stoorcats were simply very large, very intelligent, and very vindictive house pets. Pan made a sound in his throat, half whine, half snarl, and pawed at the blankets.

"Can't you find someone else to torture?" I said. He meowed, and I shoved him toward my husband's side of the bed. "He's up. Go bother him."

His ears flicked toward the opposite side of the room. Muscles tensed beneath that glossy fur, black as a rat's nightmare, as he made himself comfortable on my chest.

"You—are—*impossible!*" I grunted, trying to dislodge him. It would've been easier to move the Dragonsmoor Mountains. He returned to glaring and I slumped back on my elbows. "You know, if it were up to me and Julienna, you'd be on the first boat back to the Garhad Islands," I told him sternly.

He looked smug.

"Yes, well, you're lucky Alastair likes—"

At the name *Alastair*, Pan yowled.

I sat up. Nightmare shadows crept back into the room. "Is he all right?"

Pan stopped howling. Slowly, solemnly, he put his head to one side and meowed.

I rolled out from underneath him, leapt out of bed, and threw on the first dressing gown I saw, playing out every explanation for the stoorcat's behavior in my mind's eye. Each grew more far-fetched than the last. Pan might hate me, but his affection for Alastair was unquestionable. Whatever had driven him to me must've been something terrible indeed: the Greater Lindworm's army risen again, House Pendragon under siege, *Tekari* at the gates . . .

I shook my head. If I valued my sanity, I couldn't let myself think like that, and in any case, Alastair's leather armor still hung in its place on the wooden manikin next to the wardrobe. He and his younger sister, Julienna, usually rose early for their morning exercises, but she had been away in Edonarle for the last few weeks. *Whatever called him away wouldn't be too dangerous, surely?* The thought withered in my brain almost as soon as it flowered. My husband had once put the solitary tracking and slaying of mountain gryphons down as "casual exercise." *Please, please, don't be hunting gryphons, Alastair,* I thought as Pan bounded toward the opposite end of the room. *Not on our honeymoon.*

Our bedchambers opened out onto a shuttered balcony with stairs leading down to the Sparring courtyard below. It was brighter outside where the first streaks of true daylight fell in silvery patches across the stone. Old fears crowded into my mind, staining memory with images of Alastair as he lay dying in the lodge at North Fields, his face bloodless, the whites of his eyes veined with black from the poison of the Greater Lindworm. Pan meowed again.

I looked down—and breathed out a white-cloud sigh of relief. Alastair sat on the ground in the center of the courtyard, shirtless and unmoving but otherwise unharmed. I followed Pan down the stairs, feeling foolish for my panic and wishing all sorts of ills on my guide. Alastair was fine, House Pendragon still stood, and the stupid stoorcat had robbed me of three hours of sleep.

At the bottom of the stairs I paused, much to Pan's displeasure, which I ignored. Marriage had brought me many titles: Lady Daired, mistress of House Pendragon, and wife to the foremost Rider in the kingdom, but I was an artist first and forever, and Alastair Daired was worth a moment of silent admiration. He sat cross-legged on the pavement, head raised a little toward the mountain peaks beyond the high walls of the house. A breeze moved the Rider's plait that hung over his shoulder, night-black against warm-brown. Shadows fell along his back where scars both new and old textured his skin, white lines and red burns and one yellowish crescent curving just under his shoulder blade. Memories of battles won and lost, they told the stories of years, each scar tied to an adventure and at least one dead *Tekari*. I'd already memorized the patterns. More than once since our marriage I'd woken in the middle of the night with a pounding heart and a scream in my throat, fighting off imaginary lamias as I waded through the ruins of Merybourne Manor, ankle-deep in blood. Almost two months now and the nightmares still plagued me, and though adjusting to the waking world had gotten easier I still found myself turning to Alastair on those nights. Odd as it was, his scars comforted me. I'd trace the patterns and contemplate the man sleeping next to me—warrior, dragonrider, hero of Arle—and marvel at the fact that, not only had he survived, but he was mine.

And on the nights my stirring had woken him, Alastair lost no time in assuring me in gentle yet undisputable terms that such a conclusion was absolutely and entirely correct.

My pulse quickened. I looked around the courtyard, pleased to see that Alastair was the only one in sight. As if he'd read my thoughts, Pan head-butted me in the shin. I smiled. All was right in the world again.

"Alastair, I'm sorely tempted to ship this cat of yours off to Nordenheath on the next available boat," I said.

"Mikla save us." He didn't turn around, but I heard the smile in his voice. "Is Aliza Daired awake before noon?"

"Against my will, I promise. Your cat has a lot to answer for."

He glanced over his shoulder. "Pan, I told you to leave her alone."

Pan shrank under his master's stern look and dashed off into the tangle of rhododendrons hedging the courtyard. The greenery in close proximity to our chambers had grown unruly in the weeks following our wedding, no doubt a result of Alastair's instructions to the household staff regarding interruptions. They were simple: *don't.*

"What are you doing out here dressed like that?" I asked as he stood. He wore nothing save a pair of breeches and the heartstone I'd given him on a chain around his neck.

"Finishing my morning exercises."

"In the freezing cold?"

"Cold is clarity."

"Cold is *cold*. And likely to give you one."

He smiled. It brought out the tiny dimple below the scar on his cheek, and it was devastating. "There are ways to remedy that, *khera*," he said, using what I'd quickly discovered was my favorite Eth word. *Beloved.* He reached for my hand.

From the edge of the courtyard, someone coughed. It was the cough of a well-trained servant who'd weighed his master's orders to be left alone against some news that warranted an interruption, and decided it was in everyone's best interests to be brave.

Alastair closed his eyes. "What is it, Barton?"

The steward of House Pendragon stepped out from the hidden archway. I avoided his gaze. "Begging your pardon, my lord. My lady. Sir, the lord general and several of his attendants have just arrived from Edonarle. I've settled them in the east parlor."

Alastair's eyes snapped open. "What?"

"The lord general and—"

"Lord Camron came *himself*?" Alastair asked.

"Indeed, sir. He'd like to speak with you at your earliest convenience."

There was a pause, and in those few seconds I saw the last of the sand trickle through our honeymoon hourglass, draining away along with the playful light in Alastair's eyes. "Tell him I'll be with him shortly," he said.

"Very good, sir." Barton turned to me, seemed to think better of it, bowed, and went back into the house.

Alastair rubbed the scar above his collarbone. Its white and knotted contours were the only remnant of the Greater Lindworm's sting and the poison that had come so close to killing him.

"It's over, isn't it?" I said quietly.

"What?"

"Our honeymoon."

His shoulders sank. "Soon, yes. I'm sorry, Aliza. Akarra and I have already gotten more contract offers than we know what to do with. If Lord Camron has a commission, we can't put it off any longer."

"Aye, I understand. *Tey iskaros.*"

"*Tey iskaros.*" He repeated the standard of House Daired with the solemnity of a prayer. *We serve.*

I cast around for something to take our minds off the invisible cloud that had settled over the courtyard. "Does the lord general often visit?"

"No. The last time he came to Pendragon was when my father was alive. I hear Camron's been escorting ambassadors in the Garhad Islands for the past few years." He looked out over the distant foothills and rubbed his shoulder again. Birds wheeled over the nearest mountain peak, their slow circle sealing the doom of some small creature below.

"Do you think something's wrong?" I asked.

He shook his head. "If there were real trouble, Camron would've had his people battering down our doors, not sending messages through my manservant."

"Still. You shouldn't keep him waiting." I nudged him toward the stairs. "But please put some trousers on first."

"I will." There was a pause. He didn't move, only looked at me with a strange little smile.

"You're not going," I said.

"No, I'm not."

"Didn't we just decide you shouldn't keep the lord general waiting?"

Alastair took my hand. "Camron was a newlywed once. He'll understand."

It was unfair, his ability to disarm me with just a few words and a smile. I gave in and let him draw me closer, savoring his warmth as I laid my hand on his chest. My fingers came to rest on his scar on his shoulder.

It was as if the sun slipped behind a cloudbank. Again I saw the smoking ruin of Cloven Cairn and the blood-soaked battleground so close to my old home. The Greater Lindworm and its army of *Tekari* had taken much from us, and the Battle of North Fields had left deep wounds in its wake, some more obvious than others, but all painful. The heartstone Alastair wore around his neck had crystallized from the last drop of lifeblood of the Worm, and every glimpse of it reminded me not only how fortunate we were to be alive, but also how close we'd come to losing each other. A breeze knifing down from the mountains set me shivering again and I closed my eyes. *Blood for blood.* Charis Brysney's battle cry still echoed sometimes in my dreams. Her sacrifice had brought down the Worm and saved Arle, but it had also cost Alastair one of his dearest friends.

"Aliza? Are you all right?"

I opened my eyes. We had mourned, we had wept, we had grieved, and now the War of the Worm was behind us. It was time, as my sister Leyda had once said, to live. "Aye."

Alastair tilted up my chin so our gazes met. There were stories behind his smiles, and like an apprentice bard I'd spent the last few months learning them hungrily. When required in polite company, he wore a tight-lipped smile that spoke of duty. With fellow Riders like Charis's twin brother, Cedric, there was a wry grin, often hiding, as I'd learned, a surprisingly wicked sense of humor. But this smile was my favorite. His eyes crinkled at the corners when he was truly happy, and just for a moment the stern, steel-edged Lord Daired was lost in the unselfconscious joy of a child. I wondered if he knew how irresistible it made him.

"We'll finish this conversation later, yes?" he asked softly.

There was only one sensible answer. I kissed him. For a minute or so we both forgot about Barton, the lord general, the kingdom, and indeed, about breathing as well. "Yes, we will," I said and drew away. "Go. You're needed."

He rested his forehead on mine. "Blast Camron, *khera.* I need *you*," he said in a low voice that was nearly as irresistible as his smile.

Nearly. I ducked beneath his kiss. "Later."

As one of the few people in Arle who could tease a Daired

without consequence, I'd determined almost as soon as we were married not to let that opportunity go to waste. It had become my second-favorite pastime with him. His shoulders slumped in exaggerated disappointment as he backed toward the door. "Don't forget, you promised," he said.

"Aye, I promised. Now go!"

His grin returned as he hurried into the house.

I didn't follow right away. Beneath the empty sky the quietness of the courtyard without him seemed deeper, magnified somehow, and for no reason I could put to words I wished Alastair's dragon was nearby. Akarra had left to visit her Nestmother in the Dragonsmoor eyries after the wedding festivities. "To give you privacy," she'd said with a knowing smile, and until now I hadn't realized how much I missed her. I glanced toward the Dragonsmoor Mountains. The sun's light fell across the peaks beyond the western wall of the house, and above the mountains the last few stars winked out of sight.

A shadow drifted across the courtyard. I shaded my eyes and looked east, prepared to wave hello, but it wasn't Akarra or any other dragon I knew. Just another bird. This one flew apart from the rest, a buzzard by the wingspan, or some other kind of carrion eater. It widened its circle without flapping its wings, a somber stain against the sky. The wind ruffling my hair carried with it the creature's cry. I started toward the stairs, chased by queasiness I couldn't explain, and wondered what had died.

I didn't make it far. With a yowl Pan sprang from the bushes and skittered across the stone between the stairs and me. "For the love of all—what do you *want?*" I cried.

He crouched and twitched his tail, mouth open, claws extended.

"Don't make me call Alastair."

Canines showed against his lip, the fangs so white they were almost blue. He padded closer.

"Pan, stop."

He bounded past me and disappeared beyond the curtain of chain mail that separated the Sparring courtyard from the rest of the house. A moment later his head reappeared and he meowed again, staring at me with an air of extreme vexation.

I frowned. "Are you trying to show me something?"

He let out a short, guttural yelp. With a sigh, I followed him inside.

Despite having called it home for weeks, the majority of House Pendragon was still a mystery to me, which spoke more to its size and complexity than lack of curiosity on my part. I counted corners as Pan led me through corridors and vaulted galleries, skirting the reception halls and parlor where the lord general and his embassy waited. I heard voices as we passed and for a second I was tempted to peek inside and see for myself what news Lord Camron thought important enough to deliver to the lord of House Pendragon in person, but an impatient stoorcat guide, the possibility that Barton was hovering nearby, and the fact that I wore little more than a dressing gown made my decision. Alastair would tell me what they discussed later.

Pan stopped halfway down the hall that led to the servants' wing and clawed at the doorjamb of a plain wooden door, unremarkable save for the fact that, unlike most of the other wood furnishings within the house, this had no fireproof veneer of silver or tin. I knocked. There was no answer. Pan twined around my legs. I knocked again, louder this time.

"Hello?" Nothing. I pushed the door open.

For one fleeting instant I entertained the thought of making myself a cozy stoorcat stole for the winter. By the ledger on the side table and the general quality of stewardishness about the room I guessed it was Barton's study, and Pan had led me right to it. Really, it was almost as if he knew the man had been looking for me.

When no steward descended to politely but firmly insist I review the household accounts with him, I heaved a sigh of relief. Barton's study, yes, but no Barton. Instead, scores of parcels and packages, boxes and chests lay around the room, some wrapped in paper, some decorated in gold and silver gilt. Piles balanced on the desk, chairs, and floor formed a precarious labyrinth around the study. Pan leapt for the first pile on my left, swerving out of the way just before it collapsed. In a moment I lost sight of him.

A long roll of paper curled atop the nearest stack, written all over in a neat, looping hand. My curiosity got the better of me and I picked it up.

- FROM: *Lord Hatch, the sum of one (1) set of silver dinnerware with dragon engravings, with deepest gratitude and congratulations to Lord and Lady Daired (see attached card)*
- FROM: *Magistrate Holm on behalf of Village Lambsley, the sum of five (5) bolts of fine white wool and three (3) fattened rams for Lord Daired's dragon, on the hoof (must have a word with Master Groundskeeper)*
- FROM: *Lord and Lady Selwyn of Castle Selwyn, Lake Meera, the sum of one (1) pearl necklace for Lady Aliza Daired and one (1) pearl-handled dagger for Lord Alastair Daired, with respectful regards*
- FROM: *A Minister of the Ledger, in recognition of bravery against the old, deep things of the world, the sum of one (1) cask of Garhadi ale (no name?)*

"Oh! Your Ladyship, you gave me a start!"

I almost dropped the list. The plump, motherly figure of the Pendragon housekeeper stood in the doorway, her arms filled with more parcels. "Sorry, Madam Gretna," I said. "I just happened to peek in. What *is* all this?"

She deposited her parcels on a chair by the empty fireplace and mopped her forehead with her hand. "Wedding presents, Ladyship. They've been coming for weeks. I think those there should be the last of them now. Ah, I see you found the list."

I let the paper unroll. The bottom brushed the floor.

"That's just half. I hope you don't mind. I know Master Barton's been asking for you, but I told him, I said, let the two enjoy their wedding weeks! And I didn't want to bother you and the master until you were ready, so I thought—"

"Yes, yes, it's all fine." I pointed to the fourth item on the list, the one without a name. "Madam Gretna, where did you put that?"

"The Garhadi ale? Locked that straight in the wine cellars, Your Ladyship. Didn't want to leave it lying about in the warm."

"Good." In my entire life I'd only met one minister, the Shadow Minister of Els, and the memories of our encounter in the abandoned gallery in Merybourne Manor were not pleasant. Wedding gift or not, I didn't trust anything associated with that creature. "Do me a favor, will you? Don't open it without letting me know."

She gave me a curious look but didn't ask for an explanation. "While you're here, would you like me to fetch the other list? It's nearly done."

"Aye, do," I said, and she bustled out. A stack of gifts on the other side of the room gave a treacherous wobble. "Pan!" I hissed. "Get out of there!"

His only answer was a growl. I followed the sound to a pile

of small boxes, some enclosed in gold-brushed paper, some tied with silken cords, some not covered at all. One box stood a little to the side, the plainest of the bunch, wrapped in an oilskin still dusty from the post carriage and tied shut with rope. Pan circled it, every hair on his body standing on end, his tail like a bottle-brush sticking straight up.

"What's this?" I asked, reaching for the parcel.

He arched his back, let out a bloodcurdling howl, and streaked away. A vase on the table by the door swayed perilously as he dashed out of the room.

I looked at the package. There was no note or giver's name. Cautiously I touched it. Nothing happened, though what I expected to happen I couldn't say. The bindings had been loosened, either by the road or by Pan's nosing, and it didn't take much to undo them. The oilskin fell away with a tired crinkle.

Inside was a box. A silver box no larger than my two fists, plain and unimpressive. There was a square of parchment wedged in one corner, written over in an uneven hand.

> To Lord & Lady Daired
> Keep this safe at all costs

I lifted the box. It was lighter than it looked, cool against my fingers, and though there were clasps there was no keyhole. I tried opening it. The lid wouldn't budge. *Odd.* After a moment's hesitation, I folded the note, picked up the box, and slipped them both into my dressing gown pocket.

Very odd.

CHAPTER 2

A MESSAGE FROM LAKE MEERA

I nearly crashed into Madam Gretna as she bustled back into the study, another long sheet of parchment fluttering from her grasp. "Thousand apologies, milady," she muttered, and shoved the list into my hands. "What you asked for. If you'll excuse me." She bobbed into a curtsy and rushed out again, her face pinched with worry.

"Thank you. Madam Gretna, is something wrong?" I called after her.

"Lord Alastair's asked the lord general to stay for lunch," she called over her shoulder. "And the dining room in the east wing hasn't been cleaned yet today!"

I tucked the list in the pocket with the silver box. Chasing after a mad Pan in the early morning hours was one thing, but I'd not risk stumbling into the lord general of Arle's entire royal retinue wearing nothing but a dressing gown. I hurried back to our chambers.

The size of the house wasn't the only thing I'd had to get used to when I took on the Daired name. It still mildly surprised me each time I opened the wardrobe and realized all the clothes

14

within were mine, not hand-me-downs from my older sister, Anjey, or misplaced from my younger sisters' room. It was a nice change, but there were mornings when I missed the ritual scuffle over who would get to wear the gown with pockets. After the wedding Alastair had smiled but passed along my requests to the Daired seamstress without comment, and when my new dresses were returned to our chambers, even he had to acknowledge the practicality of pockets on each side.

I slipped my hand into the pocket of the gown I'd chosen and pulled out a small book, bound in leather with crisp, unmarked pages of remarkably high quality. A pouch in the back held three sticks of charcoal, finer than any I'd ever owned before. The only writing was on the front page.

> *To Aliza, from Henry Brandon. For all your adventures to come.*

Tears had started in my eyes when my friend had presented it to me at the wedding banquet. Henry had once told me there was little fortune in being a bard; the tales must be their own reward. Commissioning the sketchbook would've cost my friend a great deal. I'd promised him then I'd carry it with me always, and today I had plans to put it to good use.

On more than one occasion since our wedding Alastair had started to show me around Pendragon to get to know it, as he said, "like a Daired." We'd never managed to go far before our attention was otherwise engaged, but on one such excursion we had made a cursory circuit of what he had called Story Hall. It was a long corridor on one of the upper floors, bright and quiet and full of sunlight, with thick-carpeted floors and walls decorated with the most exquisite murals I'd ever seen. It had annoyed me how little Alastair seemed interested in it, intent as he was on showing me the enormous statue of Edan Daired and his dragon Aur'eth the Flamespoken that stood guard at the end of the hall. This tribute to his distant ancestor and the founder of Arle had received my obligatory admiration, but it was the murals that had lodged in my mind.

Today the corridor was empty. I settled down on the floor in front of the widest section of mural and set my sketchbook on my lap. I could almost hear Henry singing "The Lay of Saint Ellia of the Shattered Bow" as I traced the contours of the image with my eye, marking out the bounding lines on my paper. There was Ellia, robed in white and gold and green, the colors of her father's kingdom. On her right stood Saint Marten and his wyvern, protecting their princess from those creatures who refused an alliance with humans. On her left sat her other guardians: the silver dragon Sanar and her Rider Niaveth Daired, chronicler of the saints' story and no doubt the one who had earned the mural a place in House Pendragon. Around the three writhed the monsters that refused Ellia's Accord of Kinds and would forever afterward be known as *Tekari*: gryphons, direwolves, valkyries, sirens, sea-serpents, even the great sphinx that guarded the Silent Citadel of Els.

"But that was *before* it was called Silent," Henry always added when he reached that part of the story, pressing a hand to his forehead. "And gods damn the day that drove the saints to those fateful shores!"

I smiled at my friend's imagined theatrics as I sketched out the outlines for Niaveth. The Daired features had run true for hundreds of years, and it was fascinating how much of Julienna I could see in her face. An older, battle-hardened, bitter Julienna, maybe, but without a doubt the Blood of the Fireborn.

"Aliza Bentaine."

I started and looked around. The silent, sunlit gallery looked back, empty as it had been since I came in. Dust stirred in eddies around me, hanging like minuscule moths in the bars of sunlight falling from the windows.

"Alastair?" I called softly.

The dust motes moved as the air shifted. A draft fingered through my hair, playing across my face with the cold, acrid smell of steel and old blood. The hair rose on the back of my neck.

"Lady Daired?"

I sprang to my feet and whirled around. A maidservant stood twisting her hands beneath the gallery arch. She ducked into a curtsy the moment I stood.

"B-begging your pardon, milady," she said. "I—"

"How long have you been there?" I demanded.

The maid trembled. "Only a moment."

"Did you say my name?"

"Sorry?"

"Did you say my name?"

"I-I called for Lady Daired. I didn't . . . I don't . . . I'm sorry, milady?"

I picked up my fallen sketchbook and drew in a long breath. The draft and the strange smell had vanished, the sound of my whispered name fading like the distant memory it was. *The wedding gift.* It had to be that. Seeing the Elsian minister's name again attached to that cask of ale had stirred up old fears and set them running wild through the hallways of my imagination.

"I'm sorry. I didn't mean to snap," I told the poor girl, who looked at me with the terror of a cornered mouse. "You just startled me." When she made no move to relax, I tried a different avenue. "What's your name?"

She blinked. "Um. Milena, milady."

"Miss Milena then. You have a message for me?"

"Oh. Ah, aye. I just come up from Madam Gretna. She told me to tell you that, er, Lord-Daired-is-waiting-for-you-in-the-East-Hall," she blurted, fell into a curtsy, and scuttled out.

Splendidly done, Aliza. First ignoring the household accounts, now yelling at the servants. Some mistress of House Pendragon I was turning out to be.

THE LORD GENERAL OF ARLE WAS NOT AT ALL WHAT I imagined. From the Merybourne gossip and the comments of my aunt Lissa and uncle Gregory I'd gotten the impression of a stern old fighter, grizzled and battle scarred from his years in command of the king's army. The man Alastair introduced me to in the East Hall looked less a grizzled old warrior as an apple-cheeked grandfather with a fondness for sweets, and the scars running from brow to chin looked more like the signs of an ill-behaved pet cat than the marks of battle. He swept the papers he and Alastair had been studying aside and stood as I entered the hall.

"Shield and Circle, Alastair, is this your new bride?" he boomed.

"Indeed it is. Aliza, this is August Camron, lord general of Arle and an old family friend," Alastair said. "Camron, my wife, Aliza Daired."

I curtsied as he came forward. "Your Lordship."

"There are songs about you in Edonarle, my lady," the general said. His eyes fell to the bloodred brooch at my shoulder as he kissed my hand. "The part you played in the death of the Greater Lindworm has not been forgotten."

"An honor to meet you, sir."

"No, no, the honor is mine," he said slowly, his eyes never

leaving the heartstone brooch. After a moment just half a heartbeat past comfort, he released me and turned to Alastair. "Yes
indeed, lad. Your father would approve, Thell give him rest. *Nakla*
or not, any woman to earn a verse in the same ballad as Charis
Brysney has certainly proven her worth."

It shouldn't have stung so much. That he meant it kindly I had
no doubt, but even Alastair had not used the Eth term for non-
Riders since before our wedding, and for some reason it struck me
more than it should have, a quiet reminder of all that I lacked in
the eyes of the world. Compounded with the comparison to Charis
and I no longer wondered at Lord Camron's deserving of the title
"general." If his arrows found their mark the way his words did,
he'd be a fearsome warrior indeed.

"There's none like her." Alastair smiled at me over Camron's
shoulder. "Shall we eat?"

The general returned to his seat as Alastair rang the bell for
the meal. I tried to get a better look at the papers they'd been
poring over, succeeding only in deciphering the outline of a map
before Lord Camron finished clearing them away.

With practiced alacrity, servants in the gold and crimson livery of House Daired emerged from the doors opposite and set
the dishes on the table. I looked around at the place settings.
There were only enough for the three of us.

"What about your retinue, Lord Camron?" I asked.

"Your people are seeing to them. No need for extra ears in a
conversation between old friends, eh?"

Into which you are invited by merit of your husband's name alone. I
heard it in the space between his words, saw it now in the angled
placement of his and Alastair's chairs pulled close together with a
third added to the end of the table like an afterthought. I squared
my chin, dragged the chair directly across from theirs, and sat with

what I hoped was Daired-like dignity. Another smile touched Alastair's lips. If the general noticed, he gave no sign.

"What brings you to Pendragon?" I asked Lord Camron after we'd filled our plates.

"My apologies, my lady, I'd thought you'd heard. I was sent to deliver the royal wedding present."

I looked to Alastair. "A pair of Pelagian mares," he said. He pulled a letter from his pocket and pushed it across the table. The waxy remains of the royal crest still clung to the edges of the paper. I unfolded the letter and read.

> To the honorable Lord Alastair Daired and Lady Aliza Daired,
> House Pendragon, Dragonsmoor:
> Greetings.
>
> It gives us great pleasure to extend our sincere congratulations on the occasion of your wedding and to offer these mares as tokens of our esteem and regard, with best wishes for the continued health, happiness, and loyalty of House Daired.
>
> Sincerely,
> His Majesty King Harrold IV of Arle
> Her Highness Queen Consort Callina I of the Garhad Islands
> His Highness Prince Darragh III of Arle
> Edonarle, Late Summer, 1061se

I blinked at the paper in my hand. The words didn't change. *Good gods.* The royal family knew my name. For a few seconds it was the only coherent thought I could form. "That's, ah, generous of them." I folded the letter and handed it back. "Thank you, Your Lordship."

"Terribly belated, I know," Lord Camron said. "The king and queen consort wanted me to relay their apologies. After word of the Worm spread, it was all we could do to convince even the Garhad ships to keep coming in. The Pelagian horse traders were twice as nervous. The Garhadis wanted proof—physical proof!—the Worm was dead before they'd let one of their own on Arlean soil." He gestured angrily with his fish knife. "What do you think of that, Alastair?"

Alastair studied the wine in his glass. "Their merchants are no warriors. They wouldn't have helped us."

"Maybe not, maybe not. But it would have been a damn fine show of solidarity." The general snorted. "Turned from us in our hour of need, they did. And now they wonder why we're looking toward Els!"

I set down my glass. Cold sweat started at my temples. The ghastly blue light of the Shadow Minister's conjured flame danced before my eyes. "What's that about Els?" I asked.

"There's talk in Edonarle of an official trade agreement," Alastair answered. "Lord Camron says Els has offered to open their ports."

I recalled all I knew of our relationship with the Silent Kingdom and the other nations to the south, realizing then how pitifully little it was. "Haven't we always gone through the Garhad Islands?" I asked.

"For near two hundred years," Lord Camron said, and turned back to Alastair. "You'd think that'd buy us some loyalty, wouldn't you? Well, now we know where they stand, so what's to stop us from taking Els up on their offer? Or going straight to the Principalities? I tell you, lad, if we hope to—"

"What made the Silent King change his mind?" I said. This time both Alastair and the general looked at me. I reminded myself to apologize later. This was important.

"No one's, ah, sure, Lady Daired," Lord Camron said. "Perhaps wiser heads prevailed among his council. Or perhaps his court was as shaken by news of the Worm as we were, but even they must see the value in an alliance. After all, they have Elsian steel, and our defenders need more weapons."

"Those of us who are left," Alastair said in a quiet voice.

"Too true," Lord Camron said. "Speaking of which, when do you and Akarra begin your rounds again? And where is she? I thought we might have seen her riding in."

"She's visiting her Nestmother in the eyries. She'll be back soon."

"Best not wait much longer. The Worm may be dead, but the *Tekari* are still out there. We're hearing reports of direwolves savaging flocks as far south as Westhull, and banshees are creeping out across the plains at Middlemoor. My people and the Free Regiments are doing their best to take care of the smaller incursions"—he spread his hands—"but frankly, lad, my soldiers don't ride dragons."

Alastair frowned. "Julienna and Mar'esh have been in Edonarle these past few weeks, haven't they?"

"They have. And doing a fine job of guarding the roads around the capital, though of course . . ." He trailed off and busied himself with cleaning his plate. In the sudden absence of conversation, I became aware of a faint whistling sound, as if someone nearby was breathing sharply through parted lips. It rose and fell at uneven intervals before ceasing altogether. The others didn't seem to notice.

"Yes?" Alastair asked.

The general chewed his last bite with a thoughtful expression. "Well, your sister's dragon is rather, er, earthbound."

The clink of crystal on the polished oakstone surface of the table hung in the air like a well-mannered gasp. Alastair looked away, and I saw at once the strength of the friendship between the lord general and House Daired. Little else would weather such a comment. Julienna's dragon Mar'esh had a maimed wing, a gift from the accursed Ranger Tristan Wydrick, and though both Mar'esh and his Rider were deadly warriors, Mar'esh could not fly. Wise Arleans, however, didn't mention that in the hearing of Julienna's older brother. Alastair had killed Wydrick at the Battle of North Fields in retribution for what he'd done both to Mar'esh and to my younger sister Leyda. Even now thoughts of Wydrick still made me angry, yet whatever fury I felt I knew Alastair felt it ten times over.

"Not to say she and Mar'esh didn't take their fair share of *Tekari* heads," Lord Camron added after an awkward pause. "Of course. And Lady Catriona and the Drakaina and your cousin have been helping secure the southern coast, naturally, but—"

I held up a hand. "Forgive me, Lord Camron," I said. "Alastair, do you hear that?" The whistling sound had started again. "Listen."

We listened. From the distant depths of the house it came a third time, less like a whistle and more like a screech. I remembered Cedric Brysney's arrival at Pendragon just a few months before and his wyvern's scream, announcing the approach of the Greater Lindworm and the end of Arle as we knew it. A sick feeling settled in the pit of my stomach and I was halfway to my feet when the door at the end of the hall flew open.

"Barton?" Alastair asked. "What's going on?"

Barton's usually impeccable suit was disheveled and his breath came in gasps as if he'd just run the whole length of the house. "You have—you have—forgive me, my lord—you have a visitor," he wheezed.

"For Thell's sake, man, catch your breath," Alastair said.

The steward straightened his jacket. "Apologies again, my lord, my lady. It's a messenger—most urgent."

"Whose messenger?" I asked.

"From the north. Castle Selwyn on Lake Meera," Barton said.

"Lord Alastair, he asked to speak with you immediately. Says it's a matter of life and death. Madam Gretna and Master Nettlebaum are with him in the summer parlor."

"Nettlebaum? Is someone hurt?"

"Not exactly, sir. Madam Gretna merely thought it prudent to summon a physician just in case. The young man was quite wild."

"We'll be with him in a moment," Alastair said. Barton bowed and hurried out.

"Life or death, eh?" the general said.

"I'm sorry, Camron. We weren't expecting any other visitors today," Alastair said.

Lord Camron shrugged and pushed back his chair. "You have duties, just as I have. I won't keep you from them. In any case, the king expects me back in Edonarle soon. We'd better be off. Thank you for lunch." He bowed and touched four fingers to his brow in a fourfold farewell. "Shield and Circle keep you, lad."

Alastair returned the gesture. "And you, my friend."

Lord Camron turned to me. "Lady Aliza, it was a pleasure. I hope I will see you both again in Edonarle soon. No, no," he said as Alastair moved for the bell to summon a servant. "No need. I know the way out. Go. See to your visitor."

WE FOUND MADAM GRETNA AT THE DOOR TO THE SUMmer parlor giving orders to a handful of maids. "Oh! My lord, my lady, I'm so glad you've come," Madam Gretna said. "He won't speak to anyone else. He's inside."

A young man, who escaped the title "boy" only by virtue of the patchy beard clinging to his chin and cheeks, lay on a sofa pulled close to the fire, attended by Master Nettlebaum, the Pendragon physician. The young man wore the formal livery of a lord's messenger, a surcoat in deep navy with the wheel-and-trident crest of

Lake Meera on his shoulder. His face was pale and sheened with sweat but I saw no injuries. A hooded gyrfalcon stood guard on the back of the sofa, talons sunk deep into the upholstery, jesses jingling an agitated rhythm. When we entered, the bird let out a piercing cry, loud enough to make Madam Gretna jump. The messenger opened his eyes. When he saw us, he struggled to his feet.

"Lie down, boy!" Nettlebaum said, but the young man pushed him aside.

"Jen T-Trennan of Castle Selwyn, Lake Meera," he said, each word clipped by the steel edge of a Noordish accent. A shock of fair hair flopped into his face as he bowed, overbalanced, and caught himself. He held out a letter to Alastair in one hand. With the other hand he twisted a button on his surcoat. "Lord Daired, I bring a message from Lord Selwyn."

"Begging your pardon, sir, but the boy needs quiet." Nettlebaum slid between them as Alastair took the letter, doing his best to herd Trennan back toward the sofa. "It was a tomfool thing to do, ride without resting like that."

"I had my orders—"

"Three days, he says, my lord!" Nettlebaum said. "Three days' hard riding from Hatch Ford with hardly a pause for breath, let alone food or sleep, and that on top of the ride from Lake Meera! Nearly falling out of the saddle, he was."

"Was something chasing you, Master Trennan?" I asked.

He looked from my face to Alastair's and back. If possible, he grew paler. "I don't—I don't know, milady," he said.

"You don't *know?*" Alastair said.

"I never saw anything, sir. Not so much as that. But there was a feeling . . ." He shook his head and thrust the letter once more toward us. "I'm sorry, Lord Daired, but my master gave me strict orders. I'm to make certain you read this at once."

I leaned over Alastair's shoulder to read as he unfolded the paper. It smelled of wax, ink, and sweat, both human and equine. However hard he'd ridden, however fast he'd run, Trennan had kept his master's message close to him the whole way.

To the honorable Lord Alastair Daired,
Keeper of the House and Bloodline of Edan the Fireborn,
Protector and defender of Arle, dear to Mikla and to Thell:
Greetings.

Sir, please allow me once again to offer my congratulations on your recent nuptials and wish you and your new bride every manner of happiness the Fourfold God can bestow. I trust you received our small token of regard, though I am certain your fighting skills are worthy of a finer blade, just as I am sure your lady's beauty outshines even the finest Lake Meera pearls.

I write on a business matter of the utmost seriousness. Not long after the death of the Great Worm (for which all of Arle owes you and your dragon our profound gratitude), strange things began to happen in the vicinity of Castle Selwyn. First it was no more than missing livestock, sheep and chickens and the like. Then the people of the lake towns began to find bodies lying along the shore—not human bodies and not their missing livestock, but Idar. The first was a young troll, beheaded. Soon after it was a gale of pixies, their wings twisted off and their bodies strewn across the beach. Most recently was a second troll, an adult this time, stabbed through the eye. All the slain Idar had one thing in common. No matter how they died, the killer or killers had cut open their chests and removed their heartstones.

I have spoken to the local contingent of Vesh and lithosmiths. They are as puzzled as I am and swear none of their people are responsible. However, last week it was not only livestock or Idar that went missing. A young girl of the town nearest to Castle Selwyn vanished during her evening chores. She has not been seen since. As yet no one has been able to discover what happened to her, but we are prepared to accept the worst, that this killer has taken its first human life.

Lord Daired, I would like to make a formal petition for the services of you and your dragon with the purpose of seeking out this killer and removing it before it causes further harm to the people of Lake Meera. I have also secured the services of a beoryn Rider, one Theold Gorecrow of Selkie's Keep, and his beoryn Chirrorim, to pursue this monster in whatever form it takes, be it Oldkind or human. It was Master Gorecrow who recommended you to me as a partner in this hunt. I understand you are old acquaintances.

Should you accept this commission, I beg that no time be lost. Winter is approaching fast and the passes to Lake Meera may be cut off if you do not leave before Martenmas. The hunt too will prove treacherous should you wait until the snows come. Please, sir, take my advice: do not wait.

In recognition of the swiftness with which my request requires, I am prepared to offer you whatever bond-price you will name, up to one hundred gold dragonbacks.

Please send your reply posthaste with my messenger.

Respectfully,
Lord Niall Selwyn
Keeper of the Lochs and Lord Sentinel of the Lake
Castle Selwyn, Lake Meera, Arle

Alastair folded the letter.

"Will you take the commission, sir?" Trennan asked. "Will you come help us?"

"My dragon and I will discuss it," Alastair said.

Trennan's face crumpled.

"Yes, yes, very well," Nettlebaum said. "Now *please*, if you don't mind, Lord and Lady Daired, the boy needs to rest. If he hopes to sit in the saddle again any time this month, he needs to get his strength back. So, with all due respect, *out*."

I caught a glimpse of Trennan's expression over Nettlebaum's shoulder as he swept us toward the door. Delivering the message hadn't seemed to ease his anxiety. He watched us leave, face pinched with worry, fingers still plucking at the thread on his jerkin. He'd twisted the button clean off.

CHAPTER 3

DUST AND DARKNESS

Later that afternoon Alastair and I headed for the stables to see the mares Lord Camron had delivered. Our shadows stretched out behind us as the sun slipped toward the mountains to the west, an extension of the dark mood that had descended again after Trennan's arrival.

Lord Selwyn's letter weighed heavy on my mind, stirring questions like broken wings inside my head. What monster would kill *Idar* and cut out their heartstones? And why turn suddenly to hunt human children? *A young girl attacked during her evening chores, panicked and alone, running toward safety that was just out of reach . . .* My heart grew cold and I forced aside the image, still so fiercely clear, of my little sister Rina's body broken over the stone wall of the south pasture at Merybourne Manor. A *Tekari* would think little of killing either humans or *Idar*, but that didn't explain the heartstones. There too was what Trennan had said about being followed. I hefted my cloak around my shoulders as a new thought shot through me, sharper than the wind from the mountains. *What if it followed him here?*

I looked up along the nearest slope. Edan Daired had built the

first wing of what would become House Pendragon on an outcrop
of the Dragonsmoor foothills, high enough to see any enemies approaching across the moors and buttressed by a wall of mountains
at the back. Ancillary buildings had sprung up around the main
house, from stables to storehouses to the family's own private
smithy. Paved walkways and covered colonnades connected them,
the starkness of the marble mellowed by climbing vines and the
golden light of evening. Dim against the blue sky, the dark shapes
of vultures circled overhead, fewer than this morning but still an
ominous shadow over the otherwise peaceful scene. Dried and dying leaves lined the path to the stables, stirred into piles by the
recent passage of Lord Camron and his retinue. Alastair walked a
little ahead of me, hands clasped behind his back, head bowed in
thoughtful silence.

"Will you take the contract?" I asked.

He looked up. "Hm?"

I slipped my hand in the crook of his arm. "You're miles away,
dearest. You have been all afternoon."

"Have I? Forgive me. Just thinking."

"About Selwyn's contract?"

"And other things." He paused beneath the arched doorway to
the stables and felt in his jerkin. I heard the crinkle of paper and
he withdrew a letter in his hand. He handed it to me. "Barton said
this came just after Trennan arrived. Tell me what you think."

I recognized the sailing ship crest of the southern city Wain-
on-the-Water from the broken seal. I skimmed the letter's contents.
*"Blessings and congratulations on your marriage, Lord Daired, favor of the
gods, etc. etc. . . . our city has been beset by more than the usual amount of
Tekari since the death of the Great Worm . . . unfamiliar beasts, creatures
we've never seen before . . . living in a state of great unrest . . . we'd sleep easier
knowing there was a dragon guarding our borders . . . yours faithfully, etc."*

I handed it back to him. "They're scared and they're asking for a Rider's protection. What's so intriguing about that?"

"'*Unfamiliar beasts?*' I've fought many *Tekari* in my time, Aliza, but never one that no one's seen before. And it's not just Wain-on-the-Water. Nearly every request I've gotten in the last fortnight has said something to that effect."

"Have they said anything about murdered *Idar* and missing heartstones?"

"No, thank the gods," he said, "but it still worries me. If there's new evil abroad in Arle, we Riders need to know about it, and Akarra and I can only take so many contracts at once."

He lapsed into silence again as we drew near to the stable. A wave of warm air rolled out over us, homely with the snuffling of horses and the smell of hay. The door swung open just before we reached it and a slight woman in plain, practical riding leathers came out to greet us. She bowed and touched four fingers to her forehead.

"Ah, Horsemaster," Alastair said. "Aliza, I don't know if you've been introduced. This is Horsemaster Ramsrath."

I returned her fourfold greeting. "Pleasure to meet you."

"My lady," she said. "I assume you're here to see our newest additions, my lord? Beautiful creatures. Pelagians of the First Pasture with sealed pedigrees. Ready for breeding." She gestured to the middle two stalls with proprietary pride. "A boon for the Pendragon stock, Lord Alastair. You couldn't ask for finer."

They were indeed beautiful beasts, a blood bay and a liver chestnut with a reddish mane and tail. The bay stared at us suspiciously from the far side of her stall and refused my offered hand, but the chestnut was friendlier. She thrust her head over the stall wall and sniffed my fingers with equine politeness. Alastair leaned against the edge of the stall and inspected them with a critical eye. "Are you in contact with the Royal Master of Horse, Ramsrath?"

"Of course, sir."

"Good. Write to him tonight and find out if they have any studs available. There's a letter of mine going to the palace on the next post carriage. Tell Barton to send yours with it."

The way he said it made me smile. This was his "Lord Daired" voice; for all its politeness, all its understated courtesy, it was a voice used to commanding absolute respect. It struck me as Ramsrath bowed that, to the majority of his household staff, and indeed to most of Arle, this was the only Alastair Daired they knew.

"When were you going to tell me that your family bred horses?" I said when the horsemaster had left us.

"When you asked," he said with a smile as he extended a hand into the bay's stall. The mare watched him without moving. "Daireds have bred them for generations. The name *Pendragon* means a lot to the horse traders in Pelagios."

"You sell them?"

"Sometimes."

I frowned as the bay sidled up to the front of her stall. After a little doubtful nosing, she lowered her head with a grunt of contentment and allowed Alastair to stroke the white star on her forehead. I searched for the right words to the next most obvious question. "Do we . . . er, need the money?"

His laughter cut like a sunbeam through the gloom of his former attitude. "*Khera*, you don't think Pendragon was paid for by our bond-prices alone, do you?" My sheepish silence was answer enough. No doubt Barton would have told me as much if I'd worked up the courage to review the household accounts with him, but I hadn't. Alastair's smile turned thoughtful. "Akarra and I bring in dragonbacks, yes, and so do Julienna and Mar'esh, but House Daired has interests in all corners of the kingdom. Beyond it as well."

I thought of the conversation over lunch. "Even in Els?"

"No, not so far, though if what Camron says about a new treaty comes to pass, that might change."

Along with what else? "I think you've been claimed," I said as the bay closed her eyes and snuffled happily. "What are you going to call her?"

"*Eshya,*" he said after a moment's thought.

"That's pretty. What does it mean?"

There was a pause, not long, but just long enough to notice. "'Four-legged wind,' in some dialects of Eth."

I raised an eyebrow. "And in other dialects?"

"Ah, 'horse,'" he said.

The chestnut jerked away from my sudden snort of laughter. "You can't name your horse 'Horse!'" I said when I'd gotten control of myself again.

"Why not?"

"You just can't—ow!" I fell back, and there was a tiny tearing sound as I yanked free, a mouthful of my dress still in the chestnut's mouth. She tossed her head and struck the side of her stall with her hoof. I glared at her. "What was that for?"

"Are you all right?" Alastair asked.

I examined the tear. One side of my left pocket flapped free, not more than a few stitches' worth but now noticeably uneven as the pocket's contents tugged it down. *Wonderful.* "Aye."

He chuckled. "You should call her *Vheeke.*"

"What does that mean?" I asked, reaching for whatever I'd stuffed inside. My fingers closed on something cold, hard, and angular.

"It's Eth for 'trouble.'"

"That's odd."

"I think it suits," he said.

"No, not that," I said, pulling the cold shape from the torn pocket. It was the silver box from Barton's study. "This."

"Something of yours?"

"Yes. Well, no. Ours, I suppose." Briefly I told him about Pan's strange behavior and the note that had come with the wedding gift. "Only I could've sworn I left it in our room when I changed."

He shook the box. Whatever was inside made no noise. "It didn't say who it was from?"

"I must've looked through the wrappings a dozen times. There was no name and no maker's mark. The maids I spoke with don't remember if it arrived with anything else."

"It's light for solid silver."

"That's what I thought too."

He tried to pry off the lid. After several attempts he gave up and tossed the box back to me, sidestepping the newly christened Vheeke's attempt to follow it with her teeth. She shook her mane at both of us and wandered to the back of her stall.

"Maybe there's an apple inside," Alastair said. "I'll have my smith look at it. He might be able to get it open."

"Yes, do," I said, and tucked it into my right pocket, "but never mind that now. You didn't answer my question."

"Which one?"

"Will you take Selwyn's contract?"

"Do you think we should?"

"No one else sent their messenger racing halfway across the kingdom to deliver it. Whatever's happening at Lake Meera scared Master Trennan. It's still scaring him."

He looked at me seriously. "Is it scaring you?"

I folded my arms and moved to the door. Clouds were gathering along the northern horizon, bringing on an early dusk. The vultures had moved on. "Selwyn's letter said a girl is missing."

"*Khera*, that doesn't mean for certain she's dead."

I closed my eyes. All the battles, all the bloodshed I'd seen in the past year had stained my memories red beyond cleansing, and still it was my little sister's face at the bottom of all my nightmares. The gryphons had left her body in the open for us to find, a gruesome taunt to continue the battle that had been raging between human and *Tekari* for centuries. Now it was happening again to another family in another part of Arle. Would it ever end?

"Yes, she is," I said quietly. "I know too much about this world to think otherwise, but that doesn't mean you can't avenge her."

Alastair drew me close and kissed my forehead. "Then we'll take it."

I wrapped my arms around him. For a while we stood there together silently, listening to the shuffling of the horses and feeling the weight of the decision we'd made: heavy at first, then oppressive, then suffocating. I had just sent my husband away for gods knew how long, to face dangers neither of us fully understood, in a cold and barren corner of Arle hundreds of miles from Pendragon. *What if*s crowded into my mind thick and fast. What if this monster was too much for him? What if there was more than one? What if Akarra got lost? *What if . . . ?*

I looked up at him. "Shouldn't you talk to Akarra first?"

"Of course, but she won't disagree. And that reminds me." He turned for the door. "Come with me. There's something I want to show you before it gets dark."

WE STOPPED BY OUR CHAMBERS BEFORE HE WOULD TELL me where we were going, advising me only to wear something warm. "I'd rather not climb a mountain before bed if that's all right with you," I said, snatching up the old winter cloak I'd brought from Hart's Run.

"We're not going up, not yet. We're going down." He led me down the hallway to the kitchens and entered Barton's study. I shied back at first when I realized where we were going. It was empty; Madam Gretna had cleared away the last of the gifts, and with the floor bare of parcels I noticed a trapdoor in the corner, bound in iron and fastened with a padlock. Alastair unlocked it with a key hanging from a chain on his belt. The trapdoor swung up on oiled hinges, revealing a staircase leading into darkness. "We'll need a lantern," he said.

I took the lamp from Barton's desk and handed it to him. "What's down here?"

"Wine cellars."

"Any particular reason the entrance is in Barton's study?"

"He's very protective. Have you spoken with him, by the way? He's been eager to review the household accounts with you."

It was suddenly vital that I inspect the quality of my boots. Like my cloak they were tokens from home, worn but well made and, while quite capable of protecting my feet, they remained unable to deflect my shame. "Yes, we've spoken," I lied.

"Good. Mind your head."

I followed him down the stairs, trailing my fingers along the walls as we descended. Moisture beaded on the stone where I touched it, cool at first, then cold. By the time we reached the bottom of the steps I was glad of the cloak. The smell of fermented drink hung in the air along with the white clouds of our breath. Alastair held up the lamp, its light flickering over rows and rows of wine casks, kegs of beer, ale, and honey-sweet mead.

"Through here."

"Alastair, wait." I paused at the newest cask of ale, its wood untouched by the patina of years. Emblazoned on its lid was the Garhadi dolphin crest, branded over with the roaring sphinx of Els. "Have you got a knife on you?"

"Of course. Why?"

"Give it here a moment. There's something I need to do." He handed me his dagger. I dug the tip of the blade into the cask's seal and pried it free. He leapt back as the ale poured out.

"Aliza! What in *Thell's* name are you doing?"

"Protecting us." As succinctly as I could I explained my past interactions with the Shadow Minister as we stared at the dark stain sinking into the earth. It may have been my imagination, but I fancied I could hear a faint sizzle as the dust drank the minister's gift. Alastair's expression grew grave as I told him about the Merybourne steward's debt to the Silent King, and the sacrifice his daughter Gwyn had made to buy more time for both of them.

"Has this Master Carlyle repaid this minister yet?" he asked when I finished.

"Gwyn didn't say anything about it at the wedding. If he hadn't, she would've told me," I said, yet even as I said it, doubt tangled through my words like a stray thread and pulled my voice taut. *She would, wouldn't she?*

"Your friend is your business, Aliza," Alastair said, "but let me suggest you find out, and soon. How much does Carlyle owe?"

"Gwyn never told me."

"If money is an issue, I'll have my people send whatever she needs."

An instinctive, Hart's Run–bred answer started to my lips. I reeled it in. The Gwyn I knew at Merybourne Manor would never accept such charity for her father's sake even if it came from a friend—but we weren't in Hart's Run anymore, and the Gwyn

I knew might no longer have a choice. After her marriage into a magistrate's house, the minister had named her Carlyle's surety and promised new terms when he returned from his master in Els, but of those terms she had told me nothing. "I'll write to her tomorrow," I said as the last drops fell from the cask. "Now, what did you want to show me?"

He scanned the barrels lining the far wall and crouched beside an old one near the bottom of the stack. Dirt and grease tinged the wood deep brown, obscuring all but the faint outline of the dragon crest branded on the lid.

"Something Julienna and I found when we were children. Hold this." I took the lamp. He seized the rim of the cask and turned it to the left. With a groan of ancient timbers the nearest section of shelves swung out, barrels and all, sending me backward with a little yelp. Alastair grinned. "My family has been building here for a thousand years. Did you really think no one would add a secret passage?"

"I was actually wondering what you and Julienna were doing poking through casks of wine in the first place."

"We were looking for it, of course."

Lantern light danced on the rough-hewn walls as we ducked into the passageway. The air was even colder here, and stale, though the roof of the tunnel rose high enough above us to turn the lamplight into a muddy twilight. Not a breath of wind stirred the carpet of dust covering the stone beneath our feet. The ground sloped downward.

"How far underground are we?" I asked. "And how *old* is it?"

"Below the foundations. Akarra thinks they must've dug these tunnels when Edan Daired settled here."

He raised the lamp, throwing a circle of light onto the walls. Carved in bas-relief in the rock face was a depiction of the Fourfold

God, robed and crowned with the gods' sigils: Odei-Creator with his lightning-pierced diadem, Janna-Provider and her beech leaf, the shield of Mikla-Protector, and the empty circle of Thell-Unmaker. Gingerly I touched the wall beneath the feet of Janna, master of earth and growing things. Stone dust caked under my finger.

"Look behind you," he said.

More carvings filled the opposite wall, the familiar figures of the Oldkind, from valkyries, centaurs, and trolls to forge-wights, wyverns, and even a few hobgoblins, all dancing together around the contours of a great stone dragon. Flames flickered along its spine. Whoever had labored in the darkness to create the frieze had great skill. Even from below I could see the veins pulsing through the membrane of the dragon's stone wings, the individual scales on its horned head, and the—

"Has anyone else been down here recently?" I asked.

"No. Why?"

I reached up as far as I could and ran my finger along the dragon's claw. It came away clean.

"That's odd." He moved closer and peered up at the carving. "Barton, Madam Gretna, Julienna, and I are the only ones with the keys to the cellar, and I don't think the servants know about these tunnels."

I looked down. No footprints but ours showed in the pressed earth. "Does anyone else know about them?"

His hesitation lasted only a fraction of a second, but it was long enough. A shiver danced across my skin, like the ghost of every spider I'd ever killed.

"No," he said, and then added in a low voice, "no one living."

The cold, still air seemed suddenly stifling, weighted down with memories of the long dead. "Let's keep going."

After a minute the ground began to slope upward again. The

ceiling dropped and the carvings gave way to rough rock that snagged our sleeves and forced us to mind our heads. Moss grew in patches on the surface, flooding the tunnel with a damp, rich, rotten smell. In another minute I noticed the darkness lessening until, with a sigh of relief I hadn't realized I'd been suppressing, we stepped into the open air. Juniper branches shielded the mouth of the tunnel. Alastair pushed them aside and helped me climb out.

We stood on a circle of pavement tucked into the slopes of the mountain. High above us rose the Dragonsmoor peaks, their summits dyed scarlet by the approaching sunset. Pillars cracked and crumbling with age surrounded the pavement, and a stone hut stood at the north side of the circle, its walls covered in lichen and ivy, its chimney blackened from long-ago fires. House Pendragon spread out below us. My hand crept toward my sketchbook in my pocket, itching to capture the scene, dank tunnels and misplaced dust forgotten.

"Alastair, it's *beautiful*."

"This was my favorite place as a child." He scanned the horizon with eyes I sensed saw less of the landscape as it was and more of what it had been. "My father taught me swordplay here."

"How could you concentrate on fighting with a view like that?"

"A few flats to the shin teach you to pay attention."

I had to turn around a few times to take it all in. Swallows darted above us against the darkening roof of the sky. There were no other living creatures in sight.

"Alastair?"

"Yes?"

I moved closer and wrapped my arms around his neck. He looked surprised but made no move to draw back. I smiled. "If this is our last night together before you have to be a Rider again, then gods help me, I'm going to make sure it's a memorable one."

"Here?" he said between kisses. *"Now?"*

I pulled him closer until our bodies were flush. "Here. Now."

"Aliza, there's no . . . it's not exactly . . . *comfortable.*"

With the hand I could spare I unclasped my cloak and let it billow to the pavement. "There," I said, and drew him to the ground with me, "we'll make do."

He couldn't argue with that.

CHAPTER 4

THE RED AND THE GREEN

Never before had I so severely overestimated a cloak. I woke cold and stiff with a runny nose, a crick in my neck, and the promise to myself to never, *ever* do that again. We'd lit a fire on the hearth after retiring to the comparative comfort of the hut, but it'd long since burned out, and I stirred the embers in the vain attempt to draw out some warmth. Alastair shifted onto his back next to me, his fur-lined cloak draped over his chest. Sunlight crept over him with the rosy-gold tint of just after dawn. His tunic, hauberk, and sword-belt lay scattered across the hut floor. I smiled. It hadn't *all* been unpleasant.

I tugged my dress over my chemise and, after tucking my cloak around my shoulders, I slipped outside. If I had to be awake at this hour, I'd at least make the best of it. Outside, mist wandered in fleecy shreds down the mountain slope. High overhead a pair of choughs chased each other, crying out their chirruping screeches as they rode the updrafts.

"Up early again, *khera?*"

I turned just in time to see Alastair stumble out of the hut,

42

one foot halfway through his trouser leg, which quite ruined the impact of his sultry "good morning."

"I didn't actually plan on us spending the night," I said.

"Do you regret it?" His gaze locked on mine and I blushed.

"Not in the least."

"Good." He smiled and pulled on his tunic. "Because while we're here there's one more thing I want to show you."

After dressing he led me up a narrow path behind the hut, well disguised by a rambunctious growth of juniper. The path twisted back on itself twice before depositing us, breathless, at a second stone circle, this one a third the size of the Sparring place below. The pavement here was rougher and weeds grew up through the cracks in the stone. The only other thing of interest was a series of shallow steps carved into the slope on the west side of the circle, terminating at a flat stone the height of a troll and several strides across. A ram's horn curled out from the stone a few feet above the ground as if it had grown there.

"What's this?" I asked.

In answer, Alastair stepped up to the horn and blew. No sound came out. He continued blowing. Only when his face was red and the veins were standing out on his forehead did he stop. "Lysandra's Horn," he said, stepping away and wiping his mouth. "Lysandra Daired built it three generations after Edan Daired settled here. It sounds in the eyries." Grimacing, he spat into the overgrowth at the edge of the circle. "It's been a long time since anyone's used it to summon their dragon."

I shielded my eyes against the sting of morning sun on the snowy slopes above. "How long will it take Akarra to get here?"

"If I know her, she's already on her way, but it'll take some time to navigate the summit winds."

I gave him a sideways glance. "How much time exactly?"

The dimpled smile slipped out when he saw my expression. "Long enough to help you get warm again, *khera*."

"Now that you mention it, I do have some ideas."

He came closer. I held his gaze, relishing the heat in it. It no longer astonished me why Pan adored him so. Alastair may have had dragonfire in his blood, but he moved like one of the great cats. The rapidly decreasing sliver of me unaffected by his presence watched with a sculptor's appreciation for the long, lean lines of his body, graceful despite its strength, capable of bearing all the righteous rage of a warrior and the tenderness of a lover. My very own Fireborn.

"Do you?" he said softly.

"I do." I rested my cheek against his, breathing in the warm, smoky scent that was uniquely his, and whispered, "Breakfast."

AKARRA RETURNED JUST AS ALASTAIR HAD SAID, HER welcoming trumpet and column of dragonfire igniting the sky outside our breakfast room just minutes after we'd sat down. Alastair leapt up before he'd taken a bite. "She'll want to know about Trennan right away." He stooped to kiss my cheek. "I'll let you know what she says."

"You—aren't you going to eat?"

He stopped at the end of the table and snatched up a roll before hurrying out.

The click of the door as it closed after him hung in the air, echoing with ominous finality. I set down my fork. The chair creaked beneath me. On the other side of the room a grandfather clock scythed away slivers of time with each swing of its polished brass pendulum. Sunlight fell in bright bars over the table, gilding the flatware with lines of gold. Everything was quiet, sunny, and peaceful.

He's really leaving.

I felt like a sleepwalker shaken awake in the dark halls of my own home, dropping me scared and disoriented into a world I knew yet didn't understand. Alastair was leaving.

But then, why shouldn't he? He was heir of House Daired and I was a *nakla* nobody from the hills of Hart's Run. Against all odds we'd found each other, faced our enemies, won our heartstones, and earned the bliss of the last few weeks together. But now the morning had come. The heady dream would end, *was* ending, and I was left with the closed door, the empty room, and the viper's sting of loneliness.

Well, what did you expect? My inner voice did an excellent impression of Aunt Lissa at her sternest. *Did you think the two of you would spend the rest of your lives lounging around House Pendragon, drinking wine and making love? He's a Rider and you're not. He couldn't stay forever. And in any case, you told him to take this contract.*

I pushed my breakfast plate aside. Of course I'd known it would end, but knowing our honeymoon would end and accepting it were not the same. It was one reason I'd avoided Barton for so long. Every reminder of our encroaching responsibilities had made me push away the inevitable.

My appetite gone, I left the silent breakfast room and headed back to our chambers. They too were empty. A wave of homesickness swept through me, and I dug out a sheaf of paper and bottle of ink from the writing desk in the corner. I wrote first to Gwyn, then to my family, then to Aunt Lissa and Uncle Gregory in Edonarle. Imagining my aunt's response to my letter improved my mood considerably. Among other things I felt certain she'd be anxious to inquire whether her embarrassingly exhaustive advice before the wedding night had done any good, and I composed my reply in my head as I gave my letters to Madam Gretna to post. *That, my dear aunt, is none of your business.*

THE AFTERNOON SUN SLANTED DOWN THROUGH LAT-
ticed skylights as I wandered back from delivering my letters. In
the space between my study and the housekeeper's rooms my dark
mood had descended again. It fed off the silence of the house, its
emptiness, and the weight of years that hung in its corridors like
some solemn perfume. Pendragon *breathed* history. I was astonished I'd not yet seen any ghosts. Pillars rose on either side of the
colonnade like tree trunks, their marble surfaces worn smooth by
generations of passing hands. Hallways branched from the corridor
at regular intervals, leading to chambers and passages and court-
yards and balconies and gods knew what other secrets a thousand
years of Daireds had tucked away in their family fortress.

Lost in the contemplation of the immensity around me, I almost missed the footsteps until it was too late. Just in time I pulled
away from the corner as Barton's familiar shuffle sounded from
the adjacent hallway. *Blast.* I ducked down the corridor to my left
and prayed he hadn't heard me. *This has got to stop*, the rational side
of me panted as I took refuge in the Mural Hall. It was a child-
ish game, but the thought of sitting down to the real business of
the thing, with all the sundries and inconveniences of the ancient
house laid in my lap while Alastair was off being a Rider, made the
sweat start on my forehead.

The footsteps from the adjoining hallway faded. I leaned back
against the wall, feeling the disappointed gazes of Ellia, Marten,
and Niaveth on my head. Someday I would face it, someday I must
face it, but not today. Today my stoorcat-and-mouse game with
Barton would continue. *Just a little longer—*

I straightened. *Why shouldn't I go with Alastair?*

The thought shocked me into stillness. For a moment I stared
at the mural without seeing it. *Absurd!* The idea was absurd. I put
it out of my mind.

It snuck, Pan-like, back around the other side. Was it really?

Completely ridiculous. I hurried from the hall but the preposterous idea followed me like a bee, forcing me to strap on every buckler of argument I had against its stings. No matter how much I disliked it, a contract was Riders' work. I was a *nakla*, and not only a *nakla*, but a *nakla* who hated flying and felt sick at the sight of blood. Never mind that I'd killed a gryphon in the Witherwood, or that I'd maimed a direwolf in the Battle of North Fields, or that I'd bargained with the Broodmother Crone of Cloven Cairn, or for that matter if I'd stood my ground before the Drakaina Herreki's red-hot rage and lived to speak of it. The dangerous games of the guardians of Arle were none of my business anymore.

Weren't they?

No, of course not. I was settled now. I had a title, and responsibilities, and a household to manage, and accounts to examine, and . . . and . . .

A minute later I was back in front of the mural.

Could I join Alastair and Akarra on a contract? Excitement and trepidation tumbled through my head, leaping and dancing in terrified *what ifs?* Once more I studied the painted figures of Marten and Ellia. They stood so proud, so heroic next to each other. Servant of Janna and sword of Mikla, lovers fighting together for something beyond either of them, their memory now preserved for all time in the hearts of every Arlean. It had been done before, hadn't it? Logic came puffing along behind excitement to offer its grudging support. Fortified walls would stand between danger and me if I accompanied Alastair to Lake Meera, and Selwyn had not mentioned any monsters within his castle. What skills I lacked with weapons I could make up for in other ways, surely. Few people dealing with the ravages of roving *Tekari* would turn away a trained herbmaster. Warrior and healer together again, the red and the green.

And then I knew. The last bastion of resistance threw down its flag in the face of the simple truth: if I stayed behind this time, I would always stay behind. What we decided in the next few days would set the precedent for the rest of our lives, and if I knew nothing else, I knew I didn't want to grow old and die within the walls of House Pendragon, buried in trivial household concerns while the people I loved fought the battles that truly mattered. I'd already lived long enough shut up behind closed doors and bolted windows, hiding from the dangers of the world and watching them creep through anyway. *Nakla* or not, I wouldn't do it again. I couldn't. One way or another I'd be going with Alastair on his next contract.

Now I just had to convince him of that.

I BROACHED THE SUBJECT THAT EVENING AT DINNER. "What did Akarra say?" I asked as we sat down.

"She agrees with you. We've decided to accept Selwyn's offer."

"When will you leave?"

"If we want to miss the first snows, it'll have to be soon. Tomorrow, or the day after at the latest."

Oh. "So quickly?"

"Selwyn wasn't making light when he spoke of the dangers of northern winters. I've seen ice storms scour the skin from Riders' faces, and that was only in Selkie's Keep. In the mountains around Lake Meera it'll be even worse. We need to leave while there's still a chance to miss the snows. That said," he added with a smile, "we won't be going anywhere tonight. Our honeymoon doesn't have to be over quite yet."

"Alastair . . ." *Red and the green, green and the red.* I reached for the certainty I'd felt in the Mural Hall and found only fear, pacing around my convictions like a pack of hungry direwolves. Safety was here, and comfort was here, and quiet and peace and everything I should want. *Except him.* I raised my chin. "I want to come with you."

His smile vanished. "What?"

"I want to come with you to Castle Selwyn."

"Aliza, no. You know that's not possible."

"Why not?"

"It's dangerous."

"We live in Arle, love. Waking up is dangerous. Walking outside is dangerous. *Everything* is dangerous."

"Not like this. It'll be a long trip over wild country with a *Tekari* hunt at its end and a northern winter hanging over our heads. Anyway, don't you hate flying?"

"Aye, but—"

"Then why do you want to come?"

Reason and logic, my once reluctant friends, turned traitor and ran. I took a deep breath. "Because I'm a *nakla* who married a Daired. If I'm to live the rest of my life between the two titles, then I need to determine what that looks like."

"It's not that I don't admire your courage," he said carefully, "but that doesn't change anything. It's still dangerous. I can't promise I'll always be able to protect you."

"Then teach me how to protect myself."

A shadow of a grin started again, not on his lips, but in the corners of his eyes. "Last time I brought that up you said you weren't interested in killing things."

"I wouldn't mind mastering the basics of . . . incapacitation. As a last resort." I folded my arms. "Look, Alastair, I'm not asking to go hunt this creature by myself. I only want to come with you to

Lake Meera. Once we're there I'll stay safe inside the castle walls. I promise."

"No."

"If you—"

"No, Aliza." His expression hardened. "I will not take you with me on a contract."

"Don't I get a say in this?"

"Not when it's life or death."

"That's quite gallant of you, but it's my life we're talking about. I'm not asking if Madam Gretna or one of the stableboys can tag along. I know the risks."

"Aliza, we'll be crossing the Old Wilds. There are things there even Akarra and I have never met before. And this monster killing *Idar*, who knows what kind of fight it will put up? I don't want you caught in a war that's not yours."

"I'm not looking to fight anything. I said I'll stay in the castle."

"Lord Selwyn didn't invite you. He may not want you in the castle."

My cheeks burned. I opened my mouth, thought better of it, and said nothing.

"It's not that I don't want you with me," he said after an uncomfortable pause. He reached for me across the table. "I always want you with me."

I took his hand and held it. There were moments I wished he wasn't so good. My fingers ran over the calluses on his palm as I weighed my words, turning them over, tasting them like bittersweet wine, choosing the ones that best captured how I felt. "Then let me come with you." I hesitated. "Please."

He drew back as if surprised, but it was not surprise in his face so much as pain. "Aliza, don't make this difficult. There's nothing I'd like more than to have you at my side on a contract—"

"Then it shouldn't be difficult at all."

"But this is about more than what either of us wants. Whether you're willing or not, it's wrong to put you in danger. I won't do it."

"You and Akarra put yourselves in danger every day."

"Yes, but you're not—" He broke off and looked away. "You shouldn't come to Lake Meera, Aliza. Please don't ask again."

He stood and left the room before I could reply.

OUR CHAMBERS FELT EMPTIER THAN USUAL THE NEXT morning. For a long while after waking I sat on the edge of the bed trying not to look at Alastair's side of the mattress, but the more I tried, the longer I looked and the more cross I became. I knew he was only in his study putting away contract offers, or perhaps in the Sparring courtyard trying not to freeze, but for some reason no logic could explain, the folded blankets and neat stacks of pillows on his side of the bed seemed dreadfully final. I pulled down one corner of the coverlet, arranged the pillows in a haphazard manner across the bed, dressed, and went downstairs.

From a chambermaid I learned that Madam Gretna and Nettlebaum had moved Trennan to one of the guest rooms in the servants' wing. I found the room without much difficulty. "No, you are *not* fit for traveling, young man. Sit down!" Nettlebaum's voice came pinched and irritated through the door.

There was a crash from inside. "I'm fine, you pickled *gimmel-schang*!"

I knocked. A moment of frantic silence resolved itself in the bearded, glowering face of the physician as he opened the door. "Yes, what do you—? Oh! Begging your pardon, my lady."

"Master Nettlebaum, is everything all right?"

"Quite all right, quite all right."

"In that case, I'd like a word with Master Trennan."

Nettlebaum debated for a second before throwing his hands up. "Oh, as you wish. I'll be just outside if you need me." He glared at Trennan with a look that said *mind your manners* and bumbled out, leaving the door open.

Trennan stood by the fire, dressed for riding with his falcon on one gloved arm. Despite Nettlebaum's protests he did look much improved. He bowed. "Milady."

"How are you feeling?"

"Better, thank you. Ready to return once Lord Daired gives me his answer."

"So soon? Master Trennan, didn't you say something was following you?"

The color came blistering into his cheeks. "I said—I'm sorry, milady. I wasn't entirely in control of myself when I arrived. I misspoke."

I frowned. "So you weren't followed?"

"No." It came out a little too quickly. He bowed again. "As I said, only by my duty. My master gave strict orders to make haste. I wished to arrive before Lord Daired was summoned elsewhere."

I considered. His account made sense and his words had the ring of sincerity, but there was still a shiftiness to his manner that made me wonder how much of the truth he was hiding. I set one line of inquiry aside and took up another. "Won't it take you several weeks to make it back to Castle Selwyn? Lord Daired might arrive before you do."

"That's why I brought Tatterdemalion." The bird on his arm let out a squawk. "She'll take his message back to Lake Meera quick as you like. I'll follow and—sorry, do you mean Lord Daired has accepted?"

"He has."

Relief rolled off him in a wave so strong it was almost tangible. His expression cleared. "Thank you, Lady Daired, thank you!"

"And so have I," I added.

Ever so slightly his grin faltered.

"Lord Selwyn won't object, I hope?" I said, and dropped my eyelashes in a gesture I trusted looked more demure than desperate.

"Er, no," he said. "Not at all. And, ah, Lady Selwyn will be delighted. Good morning, milord."

I leapt to my feet. Alastair stood in the doorway, a letter in one hand. "Good morning, Master Trennan," he said. The words came out clipped, elegant, and cold as ice. He handed the letter to Trennan without breaking my gaze. "As Lady Daired said. My official acceptance."

"Thank you, milord! I'll send Tatterdemalion off right away." With that, he rushed out.

"Aliza, I thought we settled this," Alastair said.

Lead bricks might've fallen less heavily than those syllables. I steeled myself for battle. "We just did."

"Do you truly not understand how dangerous this contract might be?"

"I do understand, actually. Which is why I don't want you to go alone," I said. "Alastair, I'm a healer. I can help you."

The vein above his temple ticked faster. "You still talk as if you know what it's like."

"Know what what's like?"

"Flying cross-country over the Old Wilds. Hunting *Tekari* on the borders of the Northern Wastes. Being a Rider."

Being a Rider. The words fell like a whip across my ears, and I replied like any wounded creature, with more anger than sense. "And you have no idea what it's like being a *nakla*! When's the last time you were afraid to go outside, not for someone else's sake, but for your own? When's the last time you wondered if you'd be killed going to the market, or that your little sister would have her throat torn out by gryphons while she was picking flowers? When's the last time you felt truly helpless? You and your family have spent your lives learning how to face the dangers of the world. I've spent my life hiding from them. And I'm *tired* of it, Alastair. I'm tired of being afraid."

Silence gaped between us like a wound, scabbing over in the seconds that passed with a thousand words unspoken, with ten thousand feelings we could not, dared not, or simply did not know how to share. He looked at me like he'd never seen me before.

"I know it's dangerous," I said. "Really, I do. You forget I've been in battles too. But if there must be danger, this time let me choose to face it. For once in my life let me pick my own battle-ground." I took a breath. "A chance. That's all I'm asking."

"Aliza," he said after a moment, "I need you to see something."

I didn't argue, didn't fight him as he led me from the servants' quarters. My anger was spent, years of frustration and the quiet despair I'd never realized I'd been holding back released in a single torrent of words. Its passing left me feeling empty inside, but clean too, and clearheaded enough to listen.

He led me to a long, vaulted gallery overlooking the Great Hall. Paintings of humans and dragons lined the walls. I recognized the style of the portrait he stopped in front of before I recognized the subject. It was a Tornay, done by the master of the Artists' Guild of Edonarle and one of the finest painters in recent memory. She'd employed all her skill here. I felt the tension in the Rider's muscles, felt the weight of his armor and the shimmer of heat over his dragon's neck. One glance at the man's face made the name plaque below unnecessary; his identity cried out in the slant of those imperious black eyebrows, those high cheekbones, and those eyes so like Alastair's, dark and beautiful despite their severity. I read the inscription anyway.

ERRAN DAIRED
Lord of House Pendragon
AH-NA-AL JESHKE-HESHEK'AN-KAHESET
He-Whose-Breath-Ignites-the-Morningstar

"My father," Alastair said. "I wish you could have met him. He was everything I wanted—everything I still want to be. He loved my mother very much."

The Rider in the portrait beside Lord Erran's wore an amused smile, as if she knew all the secrets of the world and had just decided not to share them. One hand rested on the hilt of her sword, the other on the neck of a gray wyvern. Beneath it was a second inscription.

ISOBEL ORANNA-DAIRED
Lady of House Pendragon
GREYTHORN GRIMSPIKE

"You've never spoken of her before," I said quietly.

"We weren't close. She was never home long enough."

I ventured carefully into the obvious question, hoping he'd intended to tell me anyway. We'd talked of life and death, shared pleasure and pain, but when it came to things like this, it struck me that we still knew so little about each other. "What happened to her?"

"She brought home a fever from the Fens near Cloven Cairn. Julienna was still a baby, so Father sent us away to stay with Aunt Catriona at Edan Rose until Mother recovered. Only she didn't."

Beneath his parents' painted gazes, his voice came faintly, as if from a distance that had nothing to do with proximity. "She died a month later. Losing her broke my father in so many ways." He turned to me. "Ways I couldn't understand until now, Aliza, I don't fight you on this because I think you're wrong. I know what you did at Cloven Cairn. I know I owe you my life, and I know you've seen enough of the battlefield to appreciate the danger." He gave a faint smile. "And who knows? If you found yourself up against the *Tekari* of the Old Wilds, you might even manage to reason with them."

I gave him a small smile in return. "Aye, I just might."

"You've been lucky. Extraordinarily so. Thell take me if I ever doubt your courage, but even the best luck can't last forever."

I hung my head. He was right. Of course he was right; I'd known that from the beginning. Gryphons and direwolves and lamias notwithstanding, I was still a *nakla*. Now and forever.

Alastair sighed. "Listen, *khera*. I'm no bard. I've no head for poetry. The only songs I know are those that can be sung with steel"—he tilted my chin up—"but when I call you my beloved, I need you to know that I mean it. What my mother was to Father so you are to me, and I can't—" He drew in a shuddering breath. "Call me a coward, but I can't lose you."

The shield-wall around my heart trembled and retreated. With my eyes I traced the scars along his brow, his ear, his left hand, spelling out his rank and title and calling in letters that could never be unwritten. *Nakla*, I knew, came from the Eth word for "defenseless," but looking at my husband now, seeing the weight of responsibility not only on his shoulders but also on his heart, I wondered if "untroubled" was a better translation. He had taken on the burden of the kingdom and asked so little in return. How could I not offer to share it?

"Alastair Daired, I would never call you a coward."

There was a pause. "But you still want to come, don't you?" he said.

"I do."

"Mikla grant I never meet an enemy as stubborn as my wife. Fine. I'll think about it."

"Tha—"

His kiss left my *thank you* unfinished in a very satisfactory way.

HSSSSST.

Lamias curled through my sleep, hissing, scratching, reaching for me with their war-scythes. I saw the split skull crown, heard the Broodmother's cackling laughter, felt the licking flames of dragonfire. My shoulder burned. *Khera?* The flames moved to my cheek. I rolled, batting them away with a whimper of terror. Cloven Cairn spread before me in a pit of writhing darkness, but this time Alastair was there too. The Broodmother had him in her coils. Her scythe blade rasped along his armor as she raised it to his neck. I tried to run, to help him, but something dragged me backward. *Alastair!* I screamed, but my voice made no noise. He looked at me sadly as the blood began to flow.

Goodbye, my love, he whispered. *I'm sorry.*

Hssst!

I jolted awake to find Pan's face inches from mine. I swore and freed my arms from sweat-drenched sheets, pressing a hand to my chest as if it could somehow slow my pounding heart. *Just a dream.* I slumped back onto the mattress and buried my face in the pillows. *You're safe. He's safe. We're all safe.*

Pan pawed at my shoulder.

"For gods' sakes, Alastair, call off your *bloody* cat," I muttered. There was no answer. I rolled over. Moonlight streamed in through the cracks in the curtains and across his side of the bed. It was made, the blankets folded and pillows tucked against the headboard. There was a sheet of paper on the topmost pillow. The gnawing dread from my nightmare leapt to life again as I sidled into the nearest moonbeam to read it.

> *Aliza,*
>
> *I thought it over. As much as I want you to come with me, I will not, I cannot put you in danger. Forgive me for not telling you sooner, but it may be better this way. Mikla willing, I'll see you in a few weeks.*
>
> I love you always,
Alastair

No. He didn't. He wouldn't. I looked across the room. His armor was missing from the manikin, as were the leather panniers he'd packed the night before. My heart plummeted. He'd left without me.

CHAPTER 5

BROKEN THINGS

Alastair, no! Angry tears blurred my vision. Pan meowed and nipped the edge of the note, his whiskers smearing ink across the paper. *How could—?*

I blinked. *Wet ink?*

I sprang out of bed and kissed Pan's head, forgiving him every annoyance he'd ever inflicted on me. *Please gods, say they haven't left yet!*

There was no dragon in the Sparring courtyard or in the garden beyond. At the gate I stopped as sense overtook panic. I'd never find them in time, running around in the dark without direction. I forced myself to breathe quietly and ignore the feeling of betrayal that settled deeper in my gut with each heartbeat. *Think!* Where would he be? When he wasn't exercising or spending time with me, Alastair had spent most of our honeymoon in his private study poring over something he'd called his family's *Chronicle of Foes*, or taking weather readings in the southern tower. Neither of those helped me now. I would've passed him in his study and a glance at the darkened upper windows ruled out the tower. I turned toward the mountains. *The hut on the slope?* If Akarra had met him there, they could leave without waking anyone in the house. I started for the western gate, but just then I caught the rise and fall of voices from the front portico. One was hushed and hurried; the other was accented in fire. I ran.

Golden torchlight spilled over the porch. Akarra sat across the front steps, ready for flight with her war-saddle secure between her shoulder spikes. Alastair worked with his back to me, head bent, fastening his pannier to the saddle. He wore his armor and his sword strapped in its harness at his back.

"Ah, Aliza!" Akarra said. "Come to wish us off?"

Alastair whirled around. Our eyes met. He didn't say anything, and neither did I. At last he set the pannier aside. "I can explain," he said.

"Were you not even going to say goodbye?" The words came out hard, flat, and calm, not in the angry torrent I expected.

"Aliza—"

"You didn't tell her we were leaving this morning?" Akarra cut in, looking at me, then at him.

"I did!" he said. "And, Aliza, I did say goodbye."

The dream replayed itself in my head, giving new shape to the words I thought I'd imagined. My face grew warm. "Why didn't you wake me?"

"I tried. You pushed me away."

"You could have tried harder!"

"I thought this might be . . . simpler."

"*Simpler?* Simpler than what? Telling me the truth?"

"Alastair, what's going on?" Akarra asked.

"Would you give us a moment?" he said.

"No, *khela*, this is important. Why wouldn't you tell her we were leaving this morning?"

"Because he knew I wanted to come with you to Lake Meera," I said.

"And I said no."

"You said you'd think about it!"

"I have thought about it, Aliza, and I can't—"

"Why shouldn't she come?" Akarra said.

We both turned to her: Alastair aghast, me hopeful. "Akarra, it's *dangerous*," he said.

"Do you accept the risks?" she asked me, and I nodded. "Then it's her choice."

Alastair growled something in Eth.

"No, Alastair," she said in Arlean. "I won't play this game. Aliza is your wife, not your servant. You can't dismiss her and you certainly can't slip away in the night without telling her. Frankly, I'm a little ashamed to see you try."

"Are you?" he asked with a fierce frown. "And what happens when we meet the *Tekari* of the Old Wilds? What happens when the swords are drawn, hm? The battlefield is no place for a *nakla* and you know it."

"If Aliza had held to that custom at Cloven Cairn, you'd be dead and Arle would be overrun with *Tekari*, so don't try that argument now."

"This time it's different."

"How?" Akarra and I asked together.

"We . . . we don't know everything we're up against."

"You think leaving me behind will make things clearer?" I said.

"It's easier to face an enemy when I don't have to look after someone else."

"What do you imagine I'll be doing while you're fighting?" Akarra said. "Chasing marshlights? I'm not going to leave Aliza to fend for herself."

"We both know you can't protect everyone on the battlefield," he snarled.

Akarra drew back. Her wings twitched up, then fluttered tight against her body, her eyes wide. Insects chirped. A night bird cooed from the eaves of the portico. The wind rustled the leaves of a nearby bush.

"I'm sorry, Akarra," Alastair said in a quite different voice. "That's not what I meant."

She didn't look at him, raising her eyes instead to the mountains beyond the walls of the house. "Isn't it?"

"What happened at North Fields was not your fault."

There was a long moment of silence.

"'*Shurran kes-ahla ahla-na set khera,*'" she said at last, and for once I needed no translation. The bridegroom's vow had been repeated in some variation at Arlean weddings for hundreds of years. *Honor her who is your beloved.* "You made a promise," Akarra continued. "Honor Aliza with your trust, my *khela.* She certainly deserves it."

"And if I don't deserve hers?" he asked.

"Then now is the time to earn it."

Defeat settled over him like a visible thing. His shoulders slumped as he undid the buckles that bound the saddle to Akarra's back. It slid sideways onto the tiles with the thud of tired leather.

"Fine. We'll leave tomorrow morning."

"All three of us?" she asked.

Alastair looked at me. Even the wind and the insects held their breath.

"Yes."

"Good." Akarra stretched her wings. "*Now* I'll give you two a moment. I expect you'll need it."

IT WAS NOT A MOMENT WE NEEDED. IT WAS A WEEK, A month, a year, a small lifetime to sort through all the little rules and sundry inconveniences that came with learning not only to love but also to live with someone else. Unfortunately, we only had a day.

Neither of us said much as we went inside. Pan greeted us at the door to our rooms, or rather, he hissed at me and followed Alastair with kitten-like devotion. Whatever goodwill had inspired him to wake me early had run out, and we were back to comfortably hating each other. Alastair sat on the edge of the bed and Pan leapt up next to him, purring with enough force to set the canopy trembling. He stroked the stoorcat's head. "You're angry with me," he said as I shut the door.

"No. Not angry."

"You're not happy."

I lit a lamp. The dam holding back the torrent inside me still held, but I felt it flagging. "I'm surprised. I didn't think you'd be so—"

"Weak?"

"Manipulative. All those things you said last night in the gallery. Was that only to put me off while you prepared to leave?"

"I wasn't trying to deceive you. I said I'd think about it and I did."

The lamp came down hard on the bedside table. "But you were going to leave this morning anyway. Without telling me."

"I *did* try to tell you."

"That doesn't count and you know it!"

"Fine, all right?" He passed a hand over his forehead. "Fine. I was going to leave without telling you."

"*Why?*"

"Because if you asked me again, I knew I wouldn't be able to say no." His voice was taut.

"Is that really so terrible? I've told you I'm ready, and Akarra agrees—"

"It's not you. Aliza, it was *never* you." He stood, spilling Pan onto the floor. In one motion he released his scabbard from its harness and drew his sword, both hands clasping the hilt. I tried not to stare. The three fingers remaining on his left hand had regained some dexterity under Nettlebaum's ruthless care, but they were still stiff and uncooperative. He swung the sword in an arc in front of him. Beads of sweat stood out on his forehead as he brought it back to guard position. "That's why."

"I don't understand."

"I'm not as quick as I was before North Fields," he said. "Maybe you can't see it, but I can. My whole sword arm feels different."

"Sore?"

"Pain I could handle. This is something else." He held out his right arm and sighted along the blade. The point wavered in the air. "It feels heavier. Slower. Like it's unlearned everything my father ever taught it."

"You're still healing. It'll come back."

"And if it doesn't?"

I looked at him. It might've been a trick of the light or my own weary eyes, but he seemed smaller, shrunken somehow, even under his armor. His shoulders stayed stooped and there were dark circles beneath his eyes. The angry waters receded a little.

"It will."

"How do you know?" he asked. "Have you treated many injuries like this before?"

"No," I said truthfully, "but I've also never heard of anyone surviving a lindworm's sting. Give it time."

He sheathed his sword. It took two tries. "I don't know if we have the time."

"Why not?"

"Because in a few days you'll be deep in *Tekari* territory with a Daired who can hardly hold his sword for five minutes without shaking. You're putting your trust in a man whose mistake at North Fields could have killed him, that *should* have killed him, and he's not—" He faced the wall, one fist pressed to his lips. "He's not sure he can do this."

It was as if he'd driven a battering ram straight through the base of the dam, but instead of anger, understanding poured out. "Alastair. Look at me, please."

He turned back. His eyes were wide and red-rimmed. "I'm not the Rider you met a year ago." *And that wasn't the man I fell in love with,* I longed to say, but he continued. "If I misstep in the Old Wilds, or if I can't be fast enough, or strong enough, you'll be the one to suffer for it, and gods help me, *khera,* I won't make you pay for my mistakes. Not again."

A lump settled in my throat. "Let me see."

"What?"

"Your shoulder. Let me see the scar."

He looked reluctant but didn't argue. One by one he shed pieces of his armor: scabbard and harness, hauberk and bracers, sword-belt and chain mail shirt. I grunted as I helped him pull off the mail shirt. It fell at our feet with the clatter of a dozen iron-shod horse hooves. I wondered it didn't rouse the whole house.

"How on *earth* do you move in that?" I said, trying for a light tone I didn't feel. "It must weigh as much as you."

He didn't smile. "Better than a knife through the heart."

Beneath the mail shirt were two tunics: a heavy, woolen one for warmth on long flights, and a lighter linen one because, given the evidence, I assumed Riders had an aversion to wearing any less than four layers. I brushed aside my heartstone on its chain around his neck and folded back the collar of the tunic. Just above his collarbone was the circular scar, large as my palm and veined with white. I traced the cold, dead skin, a jarring absence against the warmth of his chest, and felt him shiver. "Does that hurt?"

"No. Aliza . . ."

"Can you feel this?" Gently I pressed down.

"A little."

"Hallowsweed is good for scar tissue. Madam Gretna has some in the larder, I think. I could make a compress."

He covered my hand with his. "Later."

"Why not now?"

"Because right now it doesn't bother me."

"But you just—"

"Aliza."

"What?"

"I'm trying to say I'm sorry," he said, and leaned close, and kissed me.

It was true what they said about the Daireds. The blood of the Fireborn flowed in their veins, a quiet power rarely seen but always felt, like the first crackle of lightning from a thunderstorm still many miles away. Alastair practically sang with it. I tasted dragonfire on his lips, breathed in the scent of it, spicy and wild and intoxicating.

"Am I forgiven?" he asked softly when we separated.

I tried for a stern look but only made it halfway to annoyed before his uncertain expression stopped me. We still had many things to learn about each other, but there was one thing I'd never let him doubt. I entwined my fingers with his. "Always," I said and claimed his lips again.

NEWS TRAVELED FAST THROUGH HOUSE PENDRAGON. IT seemed everyone in the house knew of my plans to join Alastair almost as soon as we'd made our decision. Madam Gretna offered to help me pack and Barton deposited a second pannier in our rooms after breakfast with his best wishes for a safe journey and a tacit nod in my direction, conceding defeat.

I sat on our bed and examined the leather article. It would hold about the same as a small carpetbag. Less, if you didn't count the three front pockets. Since they were inconveniently narrow and dagger-shaped, I didn't. "Er, what am I supposed to fit in there again?"

"Everything," he said. "Clothes, weapons, anything you think you'll need."

"Oh."

"Which is why you'll want to wear most of it."

I looked down at the only pair of trousers I owned. They were thin linen, worn at the knees and the thighs, and eminently unsuitable for a cross-country flight. "I don't have many riding clothes."

"Don't worry about those. Pack what you think you'll need and I'll see to the rest."

Speaking of which . . . "Before we go, I want to read that book you're always talking about. What do you call it, the *Chronicle of*—"

"—*Foes?*" He looked puzzled but not displeased. "Whatever for?"

"You said it's a record of your family's encounters with *Tekari*, right?"

"Yes, but—"

"Then it might help me understand what we'll face in the Old Wilds."

He rubbed his temples. "Aliza, we can't wait for you to finish it. We have to leave tomorrow."

"Is taking it with us out of the question?"

"It's larger than your luggage and weighs half a stone." One eyebrow crept upward. "And it's chained to a pillar in my study, so yes, taking it with us is out of the question."

"Oh." *Blast.* I did some hurried calculations. *Just how many pages is a book that weighs half a stone?* I wondered. "Well, I assume you've read it."

"You don't take your first contract as a Daired without finishing the *Chronicle*."

"Then you can show me where the best parts are."

"You . . ." He paused and considered. "Oh, all right. Come with me."

He beckoned for me to follow him deeper into the private wing of the house, to a tiny room off his personal study I'd seen before only in passing. It was small and round, walled in undressed marble, lit by the guttering light of a lamp that needed its chimney cleaned, and thick with the smell of old parchment. A writing desk and an armchair, whose better days had been years ago, sat next to a stone pillar, on which was chained an enormous leather-bound book. Ink stained the cracks along the binding. I brushed my fingers across the spine before opening the cover. The first pages were so brittle and yellowed by age I could barely make out the writing, though some of the drawings of *Tekari* were still clear. Stuffed between the pages were notes on newer sheets of paper with dated entries going back several years.

"It looks like a journal."

"Some Daireds did use it as a diary of their contracts. Some added their notes later, after they had hung up their swords."

"How old is it?" I flipped to the second page and heard Alastair wince.

"Old as our family, so please—"

"Aye, I'll be careful." He pursed his lips and said nothing. I rolled my eyes. "I will! I promise." With exaggerated care I turned to the next page and squinted at the faded ink. "When you say 'old as your family,' you mean that was written—?"

"By Edan the Fireborn?" He rested his hand reverently against the edge of the plinth. "We think so."

Good gods. "My sister Mari would give up her entire library for a single hour with this."

"She's welcome to come and visit when we get back from Lake Meera." He glanced at the page I'd opened to, frowned, and gingerly flipped to a latter entry in dark brown ink. "Start there. Do you have paper?" I fished in my pocket and pulled out Henry's sketchbook. "Good. Take notes; there's ink in the desk."

"Where are you going?" I asked as he started for the door.

He smiled. "It's a surprise."

After pulling suitable writing utensils from the drawer and arranging them on the desk, I settled down with the *Chronicle* in my lap. It took some maneuvering to find a comfortable position that allowed me to turn the pages without tearing them. Keen to avoid the ghostly wrath of generations of dead Daireds and the disappointment of one live one, I was glad Alastair had guided me to the newer pages first. I dove in.

It wasn't an easy read. There didn't seem to be any rationale to the entries; one entry in a fine, looping hand would end halfway down the page as the Daired described the best way to take down a charging centaur (*"a single spear-thrust to the chest before diving out of the way, and pray you have good aim"*) and a new one would pick it up in a spiky hand with advice on how to recognize the ancient ghast-ridden (*"dead yellow eyes, split voice, given to fits of senseless violence"*), before a blocky script took over the page with tips on differentiating between wulvers and direwolves (*"the former can take on human-shapes at will and often guard the gates of mountain towns; the latter have only one form and will try to eat you"*).

Over the next few hours I took notes, filling the pages with all the information I could find on each type of *Tekari*. As much as I hoped I'd never need the knowledge, it was comforting to learn the fatal blow to a valkyrie was more effectively struck from above where their talons couldn't interfere, and that a small vial of bees-wax was a vital part of all Riders' armor, lest they meet a ban-shee or siren unprepared. I nearly dropped my quill when Madam Gretna knocked on the door and announced dinner. It came as a shock to my cramped and aching muscles to realize that I'd spent the better part of the day in the *Chronicle* room.

Alastair met me in the dining room. Even on questioning he refused to say anything about his surprise, asking me instead what I'd learned from the *Chronicle*. "Don't make a Daired angry," I said, and he laughed.

"*Tekari* of the Old Wilds be warned: Aliza Daired is no one to trifle with. But tell me, in case they fail to take warning. What do you do when you see an oncoming gale of nixies?"

I shuffled back through my notes until I found the pages marked *NIXIE*. "Find low ground, keep quiet, and hope they haven't already seen you."

"And if they have?"

"Use fire."

"If there's no fire on hand?"

I glanced down. "Stay low and cover your head and neck."

"How do you tell the difference between a pixie and a nixie? No notes this time."

"One is *Idar* and likes to keep out of sight. The other is *Tekari* and will try to kill you if you disturb them. And . . . nixies like water, pixies don't?"

"Correct. Which means we're more likely to see some when we cross the Widdermere Marshes."

The finger holding my notes open slipped. The pages fluttered shut with a papery sigh. "We're crossing the Widdermere?"

"We will if we want to get to Lake Meera before the first snows. It's the fastest way through the Old Wilds if we don't want to cross the Barrens."

I swallowed. I couldn't help it. "And Rushless Wood?"

"We might pass over the southern border." He looked up. "You're not having second thoughts now, are you?"

"Of course not. I've just, um, heard things." Henry Brandon had often plied us Manor-folk with tales from the wild north as we gathered around Midwinter fires on the Long Night. "The Merybourne bard used to tell us stories about the area around the Marshes. He said even Riders avoid the Wood."

He shrugged. "That's because there's nothing in Rushless Wood worth fighting. There are no cities between Selkie's Keep and the Hollow Hills, and if there are any Oldkind in the Wood, they keep to themselves. Now, what about trolls?"

I didn't need the *Chronicle* for that. "Walk, don't run. Do you expect we'll meet many trolls on the way?"

"Between Harborough Hatch and the Marshes the chances are slim. The deeper we go into the Old Wilds, the more likely it is. The more likely anything is."

"How long will it take to get to Lake Meera?"

"A week to the northeastern mountains. A few more days to get to Castle Selwyn if the weather holds, and we'd best pray it does. Yes, Barton?" The steward came forward and whispered something in his master's ear. "Thank you."

"Would you like me to bring it down, Your Lordship?" Barton asked.

"No, we'll come up."

"Very good, sir," he said.

Alastair waited until he had gone. "When we're done here, *khera*, I have something for you," he said.

"Is this your great secret?"

"You'll see."

We finished quickly and went back upstairs. Lights blazed in our chambers and I smelled fresh beeswax. A silk-wrapped bundle lay on the bed next to our panniers, Alastair's still packed, mine almost empty. He pulled away the silk wrappings and held up a shirt of close-fitting leather plates. It was a smaller version of his everyday armor, worn and gouged in places but well tended. Every inch of exposed leather had been polished to a russet-red sheen. Folded beneath the hauberk were padded trousers and a pair of iron-shod boots.

"I know you don't like flying, but this might help make it a little more comfortable." He clasped his hands in front of him, then behind him, then changed his mind and began fiddling with his leather armbands. Unexpected tears started in the corners of my eyes as I felt again how little I deserved this man. His thoughtfulness undid me. "Do you—like it?" he asked when I said nothing.

"Alastair, I love it." His look of schoolboy relief made me want to laugh and cry all at once. "But where did you get all this?" I traced the Daired dragon crest engraved in the plate that would cover my heart. "Your armorer couldn't have possibly made all this in a day."

"They're old pieces of Julienna's. I had my man alter them."

"He did a good job." *As did you.* By the look of it he'd delivered my measurements to his armorer with astonishing accuracy. "She won't mind?"

"No. She has others. And it's just riding gear, not war armor, so it won't do much in the way of protecting you in a battle."

"Better than nothing." The last time I was on Akarra's back I'd shredded my trousers in at least three places, though in fairness I'd also been fleeing from a lamia coven, sliding headfirst down the slopes of Cloven Cairn, and racing against the poison of the Greater Lindworm, none of which had done any favors for my wardrobe. Nevertheless, it comforted me to know there'd be more between the Old Wilds and me than a pair of trousers and a tunic.

"There's this too."

He pulled a bulkier parcel from beneath the silk wrappings. A magnificent cloak tumbled out, its outer layer of oiled wool shining silvery-brown in the lamplight. Fur lined the inside, dense but surprisingly light. I felt warmer just looking at it. I clasped his hand. "It's *beautiful*. They're all beautiful. Thank you." I folded the cloak, tried to fit it in the pannier, and gave up. "Are you sure you don't have anything bigger?"

"We'll tie our cloaks to the saddle when we're not wearing them. Besides that, bring only a few spares of what you can't do without. Underclothes, socks, that sort of thing."

I went to the wardrobe, mentally sorting the necessary from expendable. It no longer astonished me that Riders wore their armor everywhere. Practical, efficient, left no one in doubt of their rank, and simplified the washing.

"One more thing," he said. "Do you still have that knife that Cedric gave you?"

"Aye, I think I have it somewhere." A few drawers sacrificed their contents to the floor before I found it, still bright in its black leather sheath. "Here."

"Good. Bring it."

AND SO, IN THE COLD DARK BEFORE DAWN THE FOLLOWing day, I found myself dressed like a Rider, dagger at my hip and cloak around my shoulders, trembling in my iron-shod boots in a clearing just above House Pendragon. Akarra stretched her wings as Alastair checked the straps that bound the panniers to the saddle, making sure they were evenly weighted and tied shut lest we lose half our baggage over the Arlean countryside. I sensed only a tremor of tension between them as they worked together. None of us had forgotten the events of yesterday, but it seemed for the moment that they'd reconciled, or at least put off their argument until later. When they were both satisfied everything was in order, Akarra extended her foreleg to me and smiled in what I imagined she thought was a sympathetic manner. It wasn't.

As I stepped closer I couldn't help but notice the paper-thin hide spanning her wing-bones, mark the narrowness of the saddle, and imagine how long it would take to hit the ground if I were to slide off. Every instinct in me screamed to stay earthbound.

"I'm glad you're coming, Aliza," she said.

I chose this. This is what I wanted. The words spun in my head like a prayer to whichever facet of the Fourfold God looked with pity on idiots.

"Er, me too."

"I'll fly low and slow today," Akarra said. "You'll be on the ground again before dinner."

"Thank you."

Alastair helped me into the saddle. "Wedge your toes under her—"

"Shoulder spikes. I remember." The words came out more snappishly than I intended. My stomach bucked and reared like an unruly centaur colt and I swallowed hard to keep it under control. "Sorry, yes."

He climbed up behind me and wrapped an arm around my waist. "Ready?"

"Aye," I lied.

"Akarra, *quret!*"

Her muscles coiled beneath us and with a joyous snort of dragonfire she dove off the slope, caught an updraft, wheeled, and turned north, toward the Old Wilds and Castle Selwyn and the mysteries that awaited us there.

CHAPTER 6

HUNTER & QUARRY

Akarra kept her promise. It did me little good. The padded breeches and iron-shod boots protected my legs from chafing but did nothing to mitigate the queasiness as I watched, or tried not to watch, the ground rush by beneath us. Around noon we stopped to eat our lunch of bardsbread and dried fruit on a wild, windswept stretch of the moors, and only Alastair's suggestion that we were still close enough to Pendragon to send me back convinced me to climb into the saddle when we were finished. Never mind that I was stiff, aching, and one unexpected dive away from throwing up; I said I was going to Lake Meera and gods help me, I'd see it through.

The trouble with that attitude, I realized that evening as we started our descent toward a village called Shepherd's Vale, was that it saddled the Fourfold God with a near impossible task.

Akarra landed in a field outside the town wall, scaring the wits out of a herd of grazing sheep. Alastair swung down with the ease of long experience and I couldn't resist a little retaliation as he offered me his hand. I caught his arm and brought us both down onto the grass. "You said these clothes would make it *comfortable*," I hissed. "I won't be able to sit for days."

He laughed and sat up, pushing me upright without releasing his grip so that I ended up sprawled awkwardly on his lap. "I said they'd make it *more* comfortable," he murmured in my ear. "You did fine for your first flight."

"It's hardly my first."

"Your first as a Daired then." He stopped suddenly and smiled. "You've no idea how long I've dreamed of this."

"What, seeing me limp?"

"Flying with you again. Holding you like this. I've dreamed of it since we faced those gryphons in the Witherwood, *khera*."

I arched an eyebrow, a coy reply on my tongue, when I felt a touch on my shoulder. Akarra hung over us, lips twitching. She withdrew her wingtip. "While I in no way disagree with either of you, this may not be the place to discuss such . . . things. You have attendants."

We unsprawled enough to look where she pointed. The town of Shepherd's Vale was a small settlement, the cluster of wood and brick houses surrounded by a wall topped with thorn bushes to discourage attacks from roving *Tekari*. A few men and women jostled at the gate for a glimpse of us. A whisper rippled through their ranks. I heard a giggle.

We jumped to our feet and brushed away bits of sod and dirt and clinging embarrassment. Alastair went forward to meet them with a face that might as well have been carved from stone, if stone could blush. He dragged Akarra's saddle and one of the panniers after him. I shouldered the second pannier and followed, doing my best not to walk bowlegged.

An elderly woman stepped out from among the townsfolk and returned his fourfold greeting. "Come in, come in, my lord and lady! Riders are always welcome here." Her eyes wandered from my lack of scabbard to my unplaited hair. "And Riders' . . . companions."

The innkeeper, as she turned out to be, led us down the single street of the town to her establishment. With its walls of warm brick and heavy wood furniture, the inn reminded me of Merybourne Manor, and I pushed away the thick feeling in my throat as she showed us to the guest chambers, which were just being vacated by a pair of maids with empty pails. Alastair thanked the innkeeper and counted out ten copper trills, which she took with a curtsy and followed the maids out.

He noticed the tub in the corner at the same time I did. He raised a hopeful eyebrow, but I shook my head.

"Don't be ridiculous. It's hardly big enough for one."

"We could call for something larger," he said.

"And scandalize the maids?" I laughed and pulled the bathing screen across the corner. "Not tonight."

"If you insist," he said, "but, Aliza, you'd best not get used to regular baths. After we pass Harborough Hatch we'll be fortunate to find a town most nights. A dry place to camp may be a luxury by the time we reach the northern lakes."

I poked my head out from around the screen. "You mean we'll have to sleep outside?"

"We might. Does that bother you?"

"Depends."

"Have you ever tried it before?"

"I seem to recall we both did a few days ago."

"We had a roof over our heads," he said, but couldn't keep from smiling. "That doesn't count."

I thought. "What about hunting moon-moss with my uncle in the wilds of Edonarle?"

"I'm afraid not."

"We had to stay in the Royal Park all night," I tried. "It was very uncomfortable."

"Were you being chased by *Tekari?*"

"Only the City Watch."

He smiled. "I admire your willingness to face the elements, but spending a night in the Old Wilds is not going to be pleasant."

I slid into the lukewarm water. "In that case, I suppose we'd better enjoy this while we have it."

He muttered something in Eth but otherwise left me to bathe in peace. When I finished, he took his turn, eschewing the screen altogether, but my weariness cheated him out of some much-deserved admiration from me. I fell asleep almost as soon as I touched the mattress.

WE LEFT EARLY THE NEXT DAY. FLYING DIDN'T GET ANY easier but as the hours rolled by it became familiar, and in that, a little more bearable. Alastair sat behind me, arms wrapped securely around my waist, our hands interlaced. For a few miles I shifted around in an effort to find a position in which the buckles of his sword-harness didn't dig into my back, only to realize after a while that there was no such position. I gave up with a sigh and focused on the scenery, or what I could see of it through wind-stung eyes. Akarra flew low over yellowish moors, broken here and there by hollows dark with heather. The wind blew cold but the sun shone across the rocky highlands, gilding the landscape. Alastair and I didn't try to talk. Besides the fact that it'd be hard to hear each other, the task of making sure I didn't fall to my death kept us both too busy to bother with conversation. We stopped again around noon for our lunch. As dull as the flat, hard loaves of bardsbread might've been, they held infinite more appeal than Akarra's meal, which she brought back after a brief hunt in the Dragonsmoor foothills. The carcasses she grasped in her talons were blackened and charred but still recognizable as rams. She laid them out on the ground and, seeing my look, ducked her head as if embarrassed.

"Wild ones, I promise."

I chose a grassy patch facing away from her as we set into our respective lunches. Alastair pointed out landmarks as we ate. "See that peak to the north?"

I nodded, my mouth full.

"That's *An-Edannathair*," he said. "'The Foremost.' We call it Edan's Crest."

I swallowed. "Is that where Edan met his dragon?"

He nodded, a faraway look in his eye. "The Vehryshi say they sparred together for three days before Aur'eth declared Edan worthy of his loyalty. That was where he agreed to fight for humankind against the first *Tekari*."

"Sorry, the *who* told you that?" I asked.

"Vehryshi," Akarra said. "Keepers of the Sacred Hearth and the most honored of dragonkind. And it's not *supposed* to be where Edan Daired met the Flamesire, *khela*," she added, and crunched something bony, "it *is* where they met. The Vehryshi would not be happy to hear a Daired say otherwise." Another crunch, followed by a short blast of dragonfire. "You can turn around now if you like, Aliza. I'm done."

"Thank you. I'm, er, sorry."

"You know, that's something that's always puzzled me about you," Alastair said. "I wouldn't have thought a healer would be so squeamish."

"I didn't used to be." I looked away, trying not to think of my little sister's face and the southern pasture at Merybourne Manor where that had all changed. "And there's a difference between an herbmaster and a surgeon."

"No need for apologies," Akarra said. "Anyway, Alastair's

hardly one to talk. I assume he's told you what he did after he made his first kill?"

He glowered at her as I leaned forward. "What did he do?" I asked.

"Akarra, you said you wouldn't bring that up again," he muttered.

"To your casual acquaintances, maybe," she said with a toothy smile, "but you should keep no secrets from your wife."

"I threw up after I beheaded my first gryphon," he said. "There. Laugh if you must."

"How old were you?" I asked.

"Twelve."

I thought of the gryphon I'd killed. It had been more than a year since our battle in the Witherwood but I could still feel its body twitching beneath me, still hear its dying screams. What must it have been like to go through something like that as a child, to know only the world of blade and blood? A passage from the *Book of Honored Proverbs* came to mind and I no longer wondered at the truth of it: "*Hardest of all is the service of Thell, to whom no one bows without first having been broken.*"

"I would never laugh at that," I said quietly.

"Then you're kinder than most dragons," Alastair said with a last glare in Akarra's direction. "How many more hours to Claykeep?"

"Two or three if the weather stays fine," she answered.

"Is there no chance of making it to Hatch Ford today?"

"Doubtful. The borders of Harborough Hatch are the better part of a day's journey beyond Claykeep. We could try to make it to the Ford tonight, but we'd be flying long after dark. Are we really in such a rush?"

"You may enjoy flying in a blizzard," he said, "but Aliza and I'd both prefer not to get frostbitten crossing the Langloch Mountains in the middle of a storm."

"Oh, we'll be fine. Winter's still a good month away."

"All the more reason to get there quickly."

"How long do you think the hunt will take?" I asked.

"Mikla willing, we'll be back at Pendragon in time for Martenmas." He scratched his nose and stood. "But for now, I'd rather not be in the air after sunset. We'll stay in Claykeep tonight. Besides," he said, pulling a dagger from its sheath on his calf, "that gives us some time to practice. Draw your knife."

I blinked. "What, now?"

"Yes, now. You wanted to learn how to protect yourself, and I'd rather show you in Dragonsmoor than in the Widdermere."

"But I'm not . . ." My mind raced, supplying excuses I'd never thought of before. *Is it wise to fight on a full stomach? Shouldn't we wait until we're safe indoors? Those clouds in the west look ominous; what if it starts raining? All right, it's sunny now. But isn't that too much of a distraction?* "I mean, shouldn't we work up to it?"

"If we wait until you feel ready, we'll never start at all."

My cheeks grew warm. Something about the way he said it made me suspect he'd heard every excuse I hadn't said, and probably even those I hadn't thought of. *This is what you agreed to,* I thought, and drew my knife.

I really hated my past self.

"No, hold it like this." He adjusted my grip. "You're not stabbing your enemy with a paintbrush. Don't be afraid to hold it firmly."

I clenched my fist around the hilt.

"You're not holding a blacksmith's hammer either. Strike a bone while holding it like that and your whole arm will go numb."

"Firmly but not too firmly, loose but not too loose?" I said.

"That's simplifying it, but essentially, yes."

"I suppose I should stay close to my enemy, but not too close?"

He nodded. "And strike but not strike? Maybe kill it, but not really?"

Akarra's laughter rumbled behind us. Alastair furrowed his brow. "Are you taking this at all seriously?"

I relinquished my attempt at levity, astonished at how naked I felt without it. When it came to war, it was not Alastair who fought, or at least not the Alastair I'd gotten to know over the last few months. Put a blade in his hand and he was Lord Daired the Rider, and the Rider didn't have quite the sense of humor as my husband. Perhaps it was just as well. Only the madman laughed on the battlefield. I gave a few experimental thrusts.

He murmured something in Eth. "We'll . . . work on that. Perhaps more basic, then. First lesson: know your weapon. Look at your dagger and tell me what you see."

"It's, um, a long knife. Double-edged. The leather around the grip is worn, but there's—" I looked closer at the hilt. "There's a pattern worked into the steel." Chips of colored stone and enamel glinted in the sun, tiny waves and spirals of white and yellow and blue. I'd never noticed it before. "It's quite pretty, actually."

He pinched the bridge of his nose. "Keep looking."

I stared at the knife, willing it to reveal its secrets. "Oh, I don't know. It's sharp and shiny. Alastair, what am I looking for?"

"Hold it out."

"Yes?"

"Think, Aliza." He circled me, staying just out of reach of the knife's point. "Pretend I'm a *Tekari*. What do you see now?"

I followed each footstep. "I . . . oh! I see."

"There. If I attacked you, you'd have only an arm's length to defend yourself. Whatever strike you decide on, you must make it count the first time. You may not have a second chance."

"So if I'm attacked by, say, a rampaging gnome, I'll be all right?"

"You're the expert on garden-folk. You tell me," he said. "But you understand the principle. A dagger is for close-range combat only."

"I could throw it."

"Then what would you use to defend yourself? Only let go of your weapon if you have no other choice. If you're in danger, your first options should be run, hide, or both."

"What if you need help?"

If possible, he grew even more serious. "You're the bravest person I know, Aliza, but the Old Wilds is no place to prove yourself. If there's danger, run. Don't hesitate, and whatever you do, don't wait for me. Akarra and I will handle the fighting."

"But what—"

"No," he said flatly. "There's no debate. Either you promise me this or we take you back to Pendragon right now."

"Fine."

"Give me your word."

"Aye, I promise."

He parried my dagger easily and closed the distance between us. For an instant the Rider's mask slipped and he was my Alastair again, his voice gentle, his presence warmer than the sunlight falling over his shoulder. "If you want to help me, then protect yourself. As long as you're safe, there's no *Tekari* I couldn't face."

"All right." I moved closer. There didn't seem to be any other sensible option. He glanced down with an expectant look, which rapidly crumbled into disappointment. "What?" I said.

"If you were hoping for the advantage, that was it."

I followed his gaze. The knife hung in my grip like an after-thought, tilted away from his exposed side at the most nonthreatening angle possible. He'd handed me victory and I hadn't even noticed. I glowered up at him. "You did that on purpose."

"Did what?"

"Distracted me!"

"*Myet av-bakhan*," he said with a grin. "It means 'be on your guard.' If you're going to fight, you must learn to see the world as a Rider sees it, and to us the battle is never over. We must always be ready. So should you. Seize every opportunity, every advantage. Mercy has its place, but distraction is death." He moved my hand so the tip of the knife settled in a chink of his armor. "This would give a clean kill. One good thrust up through the ribs and into the liver. I'd bleed to death in minutes." He drew my hand across his body. "If you wanted me to suffer, aim here."

"Stomach? Why?"

"That's not as quick. If you manage to pierce your enemy's stomach, they may ask you to end them before long."

"All this applies to Oldkind anatomy as well, I hope," I said, suddenly uneasy at the realization that Alastair was teaching me how to kill another human.

"Most living things, yes. Your safest bet will always be the head, neck, or heart." He stepped away. "Raise your knife."

For the next hour he taught me the basics of knife-work, how to move like the dagger was part of my arm, how to think on my feet, how to shift and dodge and make myself a more difficult target. It wasn't easy. I lacked his natural grace, his sixth sense for the blade, and frankly, his stamina. Despite Akarra's occasional words of encouragement, my arm ached and my lungs burned after forty-five minutes, most of which was spent diving out of the way as he showed me new angles of attack. How anyone could stand to fight in full armor, with a longsword in their hand, against an opponent who knew what they were doing, was beyond me. When Alastair sheathed his knife and said we were finished for the day, I was almost relieved to climb back into the saddle.

Almost, but not quite. I wasn't *that* exhausted.

THE SUN WAS SETTLING BELOW THE MOUNTAINS BEHIND us when we saw the first glimmer of the torches burning on the walls of Claykeep. The city sat on the edge of a vast, darkened pit—the oakstone quarries, Alastair had told me earlier. Akarra landed outside the city. Cold, sore, and hungry, I wasn't in particularly good spirits as we trudged toward the gates, which promised less protection the closer we got. Mortar crumbled between the bricks and the spikes sticking out from along the top of the city wall were rusty or missing. Alastair banged on the postern with the heel of his hand. There was a scrape, a flare, and the oily reek of a lantern, and a square of light fell onto us as the guard shoved aside the sally port hatch. "Eh? Who's there?"

"Travelers."

"Travelers? Wot business you got in Claykeep at this hour?"

"What do you think?" Alastair growled. "We're looking for lodging. Open the gate."

With a creak of rusty hinges, the door swung open. The guard held up his lantern and peered at us from under his hood. "It's a rare day we see travelers of any sort out this way, 'specially after sunset. Er, Lordship," he added at the sight of the Daired crest. "Can't blame a body for being too careful, wot with all those *Tekari* roaming about. Why, just yesterday—"

"Yes, thank you," I interrupted and asked for him to point us toward the nearest inn before he could begin recounting his adventures as the gatekeeper of Claykeep. He jabbed his lantern toward the center of town and shuffled back to the gatehouse.

What started as a main street soon devolved into a spindling alley lined with quarry refuse and ropes of laundry. Children wielding the long poles and torches of lamplighters swarmed up the walls to light the public lamps with the agility of squirrels. They whispered to each other as we walked by. Alastair snagged one of the girls by the arm as she passed.

"Oi, wotcher!" she cried.

"Where's the nearest inn?"

The girl looked up at him, her face soot streaked and sullen, and didn't answer.

"The inn, girl."

"Yeah? What'll you gimme for it?"

"Oh, for gods' sakes." I fished a copper trill from my purse and handed it to her. She snatched it and stuffed it somewhere among her clothes.

"Righty, milady. Go straight on till the street dust turns white. That's Mason's Alley. There's a halfway-decent inn 'round the corner from there." Alastair released her and she scurried off.

"No need to be so rough," I said as we started off in the direction she'd indicated.

"It worked, didn't it?"

"Our money worked," I added under my breath, but I was too tired to argue.

The inn was more or less where the girl said it was. A sign swinging above the door announced it as HUNTER & QUARRY. The front parlor was empty, save for a thin man with sagging features sweeping the hearth. He stopped sweeping when we entered.

"Do you have a room available?" Alastair asked.

He stared at us. At our repeated entreaties, a twig-bearded gnome peeked around the corner, much to my astonishment. One glance at Alastair and he hurried out, wiping his hands on his apron and giving us a greasy smile as he leapt atop the nearest table. "Gracious me, is this honest-to-gods Riders in my establishment? What brings you out this way, friends?"

"Looking for a room," Alastair said and held out a silver half-dragonback.

The gnome brightened. "Hal! Fix up the south chamber!" he said to the thin man, who scurried up the stairs like a dog with its tail between its legs. The gnome took the coin reverently and tucked it away in his pocket. "We'll see you done right, milord. This here's the best inn in town. Please, sit! Set your bags down. Would you like some dinner, perhaps? Something to refresh yourselves?"

Alastair tossed our bags below the table and ordered whatever the innkeeper could prepare fastest. The gnome bowed again and rushed off to what I assumed was the kitchen, hopping from table to table the whole way. He left tiny footprints on the wood. I touched the table in front of us. A fine layer of quarry dust had settled over everything in sight, including us.

Alastair brushed his armor clean with one hand as he sat with a few words in Eth that did not sound complimentary. A few minutes later an equally dusty maid appeared with a pot of stew, which she ladled for us in return for, as she swore was the innkeeper's orders, five copper trills. It was a shameless cheat, but we were too tired to care. At that point I would've parted with a handful of gold dragonbacks for a chunk of bread and a decent pillow.

The room she showed us to when we finished wasn't much larger than our wardrobe at Pendragon. A few green logs smoldered in the grate, coughing coils of smoke up the chimney, and a black bearskin lay draped over the narrow bed, moth-eaten and missing patches of fur. There was neither bath nor washbasin.

"Charming," I said.

Alastair threw himself onto the bed with a sigh of long-looked-for relief. The mattress sent up a fine cloud of dust and creaked under his weight. "You didn't have any objections spending the night in significantly less hospitable locations. 'We'll make do,' I believe your words were? A sentiment I still admire."

"If somewhere in there is your offer to take the floor, I won't object."

"What's wrong with the bed?"

"It's tiny."

He smiled. "Precisely."

I shed my Rider's gear and curled up on the other side of the lumpy mattress. Despite my protests it did fit both of us. Barely. As if he'd read my mind, Alastair brushed the hair away from the nape of my neck and began rubbing the tension from my shoulders. "Ah, *thank you*," I murmured.

He slid down the straps of my chemise. "Aliza?"

"Hm?"

Slowly he ran one finger along my right shoulder blade, following the scar I'd earned at the end of a lamia's war-scythe. "What happened in the Cairn?"

A word. One word and it began again: the pressure on my chest, the rapid heartbeat, the struggle to breathe normally. *Please, no. Not in front of him.* I buried my face in the pillow but could not shut out the memory. The Broodmother's grinning skull crown swam before my eyes. Blood trickled hot and sticky down my back. I heard the rush of flames. Ashes coated my throat, tasting of dragonfire and death, and I had to swallow twice before I could speak.

"You know what happened."

"Akarra told me what she knew, yes. I need to hear it from you."

"Why?" I hated that my voice shook.

He stroked my hair, his fingers gentle, insistent, persuasive. Akarra's dragonfire had seared off my braid at Cloven Cairn, and the shortened fringe still only brushed my shoulders. "You have dreams about it, don't you?"

It was too much to hope he'd not noticed. "Aye."

"It's nothing to be ashamed of. We all have them."

But I'm not like you, remember? A fleeting anger possessed me at the thought, not at him, but at the world that had made us so different. I was too much a *nakla* to share the honor due a Rider, yet not enough to keep from sharing their nightmares. "I just want to forget."

"Then let this be the last time we talk of it."

"Why do you want to know?"

"Because there's something I want to—something I must tell you, but first you need to tell me what you saw."

I had done it in truth; it could hardly take more courage to do it in memory. I closed my eyes and forced myself back to that gaping black crevice in the side of the Cairn. In a monotone I recounted the whole story, from my sister Mari's assurance that the lamias knew how to survive the poison of the Great Worm, to my entrance to the coven, to my audience with the Broodmother Crone, to my miraculous escape. He listened without interrupting. When I opened my eyes, his face was grave.

"She wore a skull as a crown, didn't she?"

I shuddered. "Yes. It was human."

"I know." He turned away. "I think that was my father's skull."

A chill settled over the room. I sat up, clutching the heart-stone brooch at my shoulder. The words he'd spoken on the hill at Hunter's Forge lay distant and buried but not yet forgotten. *"This is the heartstone I cut from the Broodmother Crone of Cloven Cairn on the darkest day in my memory . . ."*

"Alastair, no."

"I told you what happened to my mother," he said. His voice held the heaviness of years, of grief tamped down, buried, only to spring up in bitter shoots through the cracks. "That fever she'd contracted in the Fens consumed her, and my father had to watch. He said it was like losing her every day. When it was over Father blamed the lamias. He said they poisoned everything around them, that if it weren't for them, she'd have lived. He made me promise that someday we would go to Cloven Cairn together and avenge her. I grew up with that promise. Trained for it. Looked forward to it, even. On Midsummer's Day five years ago we flew to the Cairn and declared war on the coven.

"The coven was smaller then. It was easy at first. I thought we were winning, that we'd killed the last of them, but the old Broodmother—I didn't see her. I should've. It was a mistake." Sheets crumpled in his clenched fist. "She beheaded my father in front of me."

I touched his arm, searching for words and finding none. What comfort was there for a memory like that?

"She paid for it with her life. I ran her through and cut that heartstone from her chest, but it didn't matter. Father was gone."

"Dearest—"

"I couldn't go back for his body. I should've, but I couldn't. By the time I'd killed the Broodmother the young lamias were emerging from the spawning pits, so I ran. I couldn't face them without him." He cleared his throat and looked away. "His dragon never forgave me for that. Kaheset wouldn't even stay for the honor pyre."

"You did all you could." It was a weak sentiment, thin even to my ears, but old horrors saturated that silence and I could not bear it. I had seen Alastair unclothed; this was the first time I'd seen him naked.

"No. Not yet I haven't. Someday I'll go back and finish what we started. For what the lamias did to my mother, my father, and what they did to you, I'm going to make them pay. By Mikla-Protector and Thell-Unmaker I swear it."

Alastair falling beneath a writhing mass of snakish coils, his sword broken, his heartstone shattered, blood pouring out on the foul stones . . . I closed my eyes as if that could block out the images from my nightmares. *It's not real. It will never be real. You're safe, he's safe, we're all safe. Let the past be past.*

A door closed somewhere downstairs. Alastair stirred as if newly woken. "It's late. We should get some rest," he said, and he rolled to his side before I could make any more clumsy attempts at comfort.

That night the heartstone brooch weighed on my mind like lead. Even on the nightstand it painted my dreams in strokes of crimson and gold, accented in the distance by a sharp, piercing green.

THE NEXT MORNING DAWNED BRIGHT AND SUNNY, which made up for our breakfast of cold toast and tea dropped on our doorstep by the sag-faced Hal. Alastair did not mention his father, or the lamias, or Cloven Cairn, and I was content to leave those words locked away in the candlelit darkness of last night.

We met Akarra outside the city walls and she listened with amusement as we told her about the innkeeper's cutthroat hospitality. "You should make sure everything in your purse is accounted for, Alastair," she said as he slung the saddle over her shoulders. "The good gentlegnome sounds like a sticky-fingered fellow."

"It's all there," he said. "I checked."

"It helped that you slept with your dagger under your pillow," I said.

There was a metallic snap and Alastair swore. I looked over Akarra's shoulder. One of the pannier buckles had broken, leaving the leather pouch swinging free at her side. "You did bring spares, didn't you?" she asked. "Tell me you didn't forget."

"Of course I brought them," he grunted, as he fished in the pocket of the pannier. "They're in—" He stopped and frowned.

"What's wrong?" Akarra asked.

"I'm . . . not sure." He turned to me. "Aliza, you didn't bring any of our wedding gifts, did you?"

"Of course not," I replied, puzzled. "Why do you ask?"

He withdrew. "Neither did I."

In his hand was the strange silver box.

CHAPTER 7

THE HALF CITY

None of us knew what to do with the box. Alastair paced around the mysterious gift as if it were a wounded *Tekari* that hadn't died yet.

"There was no name? Nothing at all to show who sent it?" Akarra asked.

I told her about the note. "You don't sense anything, do you?" I asked, thinking of both Pan's and Vheeke's reactions to the gift.

"I'm not sure what you think I should be sensing, but no, I don't."

Alastair stopped pacing. "Then you're sure it's safe?"

"Well, I'm *fairly* certain it doesn't contain a murmur of ghouls, if that's what you're asking," she said. "Maybe Madam Gretna slipped it in and forgot to mention it. There are many things in the world I don't understand and I'm not prepared to lose another few hours of flying time in worry over a box."

In the end we packed it away again, wrapping it in one of Alastair's spare tunics, burying it at the bottom of the pannier, and hoping it stayed there.

94

THE DAY PASSED MUCH AS THE LAST FEW HAD, IN A FLURRY of wings and patchwork scenery. The wind picked up as we approached the rocky shelf that rose along the border of Dragonsmoor. Akarra soared over the edge, caught an updraft, and banked, first one way then another as we started our descent into Harborough Hatch. Below us the dun color of the highlands faded to a drab olive, then to a light green, then to the rich green as the moors fell away into the lowlands of Central Arle. Woods tinged with the rusts and ambers of autumn crept up the slopes of hills, and as evening cast a violet shadow over the land I saw the sparkle of water winding its way through the landscape. The sight made me forget my sore muscles and queasy stomach. The hills and valleys of Harborough Hatch looked almost like home.

Akarra swooped low over the river and the illusion shattered. Beyond the next hill the city of Hatch Ford came into view. Compared to Edonarle and coastal trade centers like Hallowsdean or Westhull, Hatch Ford was a small city, but much bigger than Claykeep and certainly larger than anything Hart's Run had to offer. On the side of the city that bordered the River Hatch great mule-drawn barges inched southward, their timbers creaking and groaning under piles of uncut stone and timber. Carts clattered along cobbled streets. Vendors in the market square pointed and waved as we passed, but their movements were restricted to the eastern shore. The western half of the city was quiet. Where the Worm had passed through Hatch Ford only destruction remained, its path a streak of gangrene through the city. Streets were clogged not with carts but with fallen stone and brick. Buildings lay flattened or crumbling. Closer to the river the banks were broken by a wide ditch that crossed the Ford, leaving water to pool outward, sloshing through fields of rotting corn on the far side of the river and washing around broken docks on the near side. The beginnings of a dam had been built up on each bank, but it seemed to have been abandoned.

The path of the Worm continued from the place it had broken ground north of the city, gaping like a raw wound in the green of the hills. Trees lay splintered in ruts clogged with mud, and boulders the size of cottages lay tossed aside like pebbles where the monstrous creature had shoved them out of its way in its campaign south. The army of *Tekari* that had joined the Worm would've swept through Hatch Ford in its wake, killing at will. I touched my forehead, lips, and heart as Akarra descended, a helpless but heartfelt prayer for the dead.

Movement among the ruins caught my eye as I looked up. "Are there people over there?"

"The *Vesh* are still picking through the dead," Alastair said through gritted teeth. "*Ah-na'shaalk.*"

"What?"

"Cowards," he muttered.

I wondered at the disdain in his voice. Heartstone hounds operated somewhere in the gray space between respectable and unsavory, and most Arleans held to the unspoken agreement to look the other way where they were concerned. After all, they were responsible for providing even the most reputable lithosmiths with heartstones. A line from Selwyn's letter floated to mind. He'd said the *Vesh* of Lake Meera weren't behind the *Idar* murders, but how sure was he? My scalp prickled as I followed that thought to its inevitable conclusion. What would Alastair do if he found the monster haunting the lake towns was not *Tekari* after all, but one of our own kind? "I can't believe they'd bother," I said. "There wouldn't be anything left by now."

"Heartstones? No. They'll have collected the last of those

before the bodies were cold. But *Vesh* will take anything that can turn a profit. Armor, weapons, anything they can sell or smuggle."

"You really don't like them, do you?"

"They're parasites who feed off the shed blood of better men and women. No, I don't like *Vesh*."

We landed a few minutes later in the courtyard of a high stone house on a hill overlooking Hatch Ford.

"Who lives here?" I asked as Alastair helped me down.

"The unmitigated enthusiasm that goes by the name Lord Hatch," he said under his breath as a balding, potbellied man burst from the house, waving his arms and shouting *"Hallo!"* "You may want to brace yourself," Alastair added.

Lord Hatch stopped in front of us, panting and beaming. "The servants—saw a dragon coming. My dear sir—what an unexpected pleasure!"

"Good to see you again, Your Lordship. Forgive us for not sending word ahead."

"Nonsense! I said you were welcome anytime and I meant it. But who is this?" he asked, turning to me. "Not your new bride? Well! You are very welcome too, my dear. And you, noble Akarra. Thank the gods we're meeting under better circumstances, eh? What brings you to Harborough Hatch?"

"We're traveling to Lake Meera," Alastair said. "I hoped we might stay the night here before we continue."

"But of course! I wouldn't see you lodging anywhere else in the county." He took the luggage I carried and silenced my protests with a grandfatherly *tush*. "Oh, and Akarra, if you happen to fly over the east pasture, do take your selection of mutton-on-the-hoof. With my gratitude. Now," he said as Akarra took to the sky, "if you two will follow me, we'll see if Hatch House can't offer suitable accommodation for the heroes of Arle."

OUR ARRIVAL COINCIDED WITH THE START OF A FEAST IN Lord Hatch's Great Hall. We passed the smoke-blackened archway on our way to the guest quarters. The smell of mead wafted out, strong and sweet, mixed with the dull roar of a hundred voices all speaking at once.

"It's become our custom every sennight since the Worm's passing," Lord Hatch said, waving away our apologies for taking him away from his other guests. "Viola and I open our hall to all the townsfolk in need to eat together and toast the fallen. You're welcome to join us." At the foot of the stairs he paused. "I know you must be tired, but it would mean a great deal to my people if they could raise their glasses tonight to flesh and blood, not to ghosts and memories."

Alastair looked at me. I shrugged. If there was a hot meal to be had, sleep could wait.

We parted with Lord Hatch at the door to the guest chamber with directions to meet in the Great Hall in half an hour. It wasn't time enough for what we truly needed—a long soak in a hot bath—but we made do with a quick soak in a lukewarm bath, which a stream of servants filled without so much as a word. After two days of flying without a wash, even that was heavenly. Clean, dry, and smelling less of dragon than I had for a long time, I dug through our luggage for the one dress I'd managed to squeeze next to my spare underthings. The fine cloth took up little space, but the convenience came at a price. Mama would weep to see me in such a wrinkled skirt. I smoothed out the silvery-blue material again and again as we headed down the winding steps to the Great Hall.

"Stop fussing," Alastair said. "You look fine."

I eyed his jerkin. "*You* can talk."

"You could've worn the hauberk."

"Not to dinner!"

"You're a Daired now, *khera*. It's practically expected."

"Those clothes smelled like dragon."

A smile flitted on the corner of his mouth, more noticeable now since he'd had a chance to shave. "I have it on good authority that some people find that smell appealing."

"Oh, hush."

We drew near the open doors to the Great Hall. The roar of conversation had ceased, replaced by the thrumming notes of a lute and a single voice singing a familiar song, one that made the tears start in my eyes and my blood run hot and cold all at once. Whether it was from sadness, or gladness, or perhaps even embarrassment, I couldn't tell; my feelings when it came to the Battle of North Fields and the War of the Worm had long since been mangled beyond recognition. We stopped on the threshold to listen.

And valiant Stephan of the Iron Helm,
And Captain Ellyn on her bloodred steed,
And Robben, and Stylo, and swift Lord Colm,
Rode proud and strong against the Worm.

With shattered spears and broken bows,
Their voices raised in bitter song,
Dared desperate deeds with desperate blows.
Yet naught could stand against the Worm.

The frost of fear lay o'er the land,
Servant and master trembled and said,
"Is this our doom drawn near at hand?
For who can stand against the Worm?"

Their words still echoed in the air,
Terror clutched their beating hearts,
When forth flew brave Lord Alastair:
"I will stand against the Worm."

On pearled wings of wind and flame,
His noble dragon bore him near,
Closer, and closer, and closer he came,
His sword raised high against the Worm.

But as his heartstone blade descended,
The beast with craft and lightning speed,
Reared, its nightmare sting extended—
And fell the man against the Worm.

From barb to flesh black poison pulsed,
No help, no healing, no hope remained,
As Arle's defender lay convulsed,
And there in triumph stood the Worm.

Yet from the hour of Alastair's fall,
His dragon sought o'er hill and vale
To find the maid who would dare all,
To turn the tides against the Worm.

Lady Aliza, clever and brave,
Hart's Run daughter and maiden fair,
Flew leagues to reach the Broodmother's cave
And learn the secrets of the Worm.

Through fire and blood the lady fought

Against fell creatures with word and wit,
'Til she had found what she had sought:
What'd cure the poison of the Worm.

Back from death the dragon bore
Fair Aliza to embattled Fields.
O'erlooking the scene of ruin and war,
Her heart grew cold to see the Worm.

"The brave Lord Daired need not die,"
Said she to Riders gathered near.
"His fate we still can yet defy,
If he but eats th' heart of the Worm."

Despair fell heavy as she spoke;
The spark of hope had nearly died,
When flame-haired Charis in war-torn cloak
Rode forth once more to face the Worm.

Lady Charis alone felt no fear,
This Rider with plaits of woven fire,
Her fellows' lament she did not hear,
For Alastair's sake she faced the Worm.

Her cry rang clear from hill to hill,
Resounding hoofbeats and ring of steel,
She drew with grim and unmatched skill
Her sword against the laughing Worm.

Perish she would, she knew it well,
Daughter of blood and fire and wrath;

To life and Arle she cried farewell
And struck—she struck the mighty Worm.

Its jaws encircling made her tomb,
The monster's darkness drank her flame.
Yet in her death she wrought its doom
For with one stroke she felled the Worm.

The spell died away with the last note and the room breathed again, rapt silence melting into applause. I turned to hide the wetness on my cheeks. That Henry Brandon's "Charissong" had spread after the battle was no surprise, but to hear our names here, in the mouths of strangers, in a place where evidence of the Worm lay like a scourge through the heart of the city and its people, stirred me deeply.

Lord Hatch sprang to his feet. "To the Riders!"

Next to him, a massive woman with straw-colored hair stood and raised her glass. "To the saviors of Arle!"

The Hall resounded with the echoes of the townspeople as they called out their own toasts, drinking to the health of the Riders, the Free Regiments, the Daireds and their dragons, the Brysneys, the king and queen consort and long-absent prince, and whomever else they could think of. Lord Hatch caught sight of us over the rim of his glass. "Ah! Excellent timing," he cried. "Come in, my friends, come in. We've laid places for you."

The Great Hall of Hatch House was a circular stone room with vaulted ceilings and heavy rafters. More than a hundred men and women clustered around long tables, some still cheering and toasting, some drinking in silence, and some intent on nothing but the food. There were few fine clothes to be found among them. The longer I looked, the more rags, patched elbows, lean cheeks, and cinched belts I picked out. Shame pricked at me like thorns. My family had never been destitute, but even a few weeks at House Pendragon had made my past life in Hart's Run seem pauperish by comparison. Yet here were people who seized upon Lord Hatch's generosity with famished hands, not for remembrance and camaraderie, but for survival. Wrinkles suddenly felt very trivial.

A hush seized the room as we crossed the Hall. Some guests stood to get a better look. A few of the thinnest faces glanced up, shrugged, and returned to their meals, but the rest began to murmur among themselves as Lord Hatch led us to the high table.

"My wife, Viola," he said, and took the hand of the blond woman. "Viola, the Daireds."

Up close, Lady Hatch gave the impression of someone who wrestled trolls for the fun of it, and probably won. "Lord Alastair! Lady Aliza! Welcome, welcome to Hatch House," she boomed. "Come, sit!"

I took the seat to her right. Alastair followed Lord Hatch to the opposite side of the table.

"Now, niceties. Let me see," Lady Hatch said to me. "What brings you so far north? Anything interesting?"

I paused in my attempt to fill my plate with every hot dish in reach, tamping down my disappointment. Lady Hatch had already finished her meal and seemed eager for the conversation I was in no mood to give. With one eye to the roast venison haunch in front of me, I plastered on a smile and answered. "We're traveling to Lake Meera, Your Ladyship."

"So late in the year?"

"My husband took a contract with Lord Selwyn."

She raised an eyebrow. "Niall Selwyn? Lord Sentinel of the Lake?"

"Aye." I managed a slice of venison. "Do you know him?"

"Only by reputation. William and I were with the townsfolk on the western wall, you see, but I heard Selwyn and his people fought well. His Rangers took the plain north of the city back from a troop of trolls and a pack of direwolves."

I looked at her in surprise. The stupor of exhaustion and an empty stomach lifted, replaced with hunger of a different kind. Curiosity had me in its claws again. "Lord Selwyn was *here*?"

"Indeed he was. Rode south at the head of the Lake Meera Rangers when word of the muster spread." She poured me a glass of mead. It was strong stuff, all burning sweetness down the back of my throat. "When the Worm moved on, Selwyn and his people stayed behind to fight the creatures that didn't follow it. Brave man. I can't imagine why he'd need a Rider in Lake Meera." She stroked her considerable chin. "If you don't mind my asking, why *did* he hire your husband and his dragon?"

"His letter said they've been finding dead *Idar* around the lakes. Someone's been killing them and cutting out their heartstones, and now a local girl has gone missing."

Lady Hatch frowned. "Murdered *Idar*, stolen heartstones, and a vanished human girl, and a *Tekari* is the first thing he suspects?"

"What else would it be?" I asked.

"Eh, fair point," she said, not realizing the question had not been rhetorical. "But about the girl. Is he certain she didn't get herself smuggled out on one of the lake ships? I hear there's good trade . . ." She stopped suddenly. "But never mind. One hears so many rumors about those northern folk. Whatever is plaguing them, I'm sure you and your husband will set all things to rights."

Her pause was telling. I heard, or imagined I heard, a great deal in it: curiosity, puzzlement, even a touch of suspicion, but she brushed it away with a smile that looked almost genuine. Almost.

I made a note to ask Alastair what he knew of smuggling in the northern lakes.

Lady Hatch raised her glass again. "Lady Aliza, I wish you both the best of luck, and—gracious me! I didn't expect to see you tonight, Margrey," she said as a stout blond girl with a baby on her hip approached the table and dipped into a curtsy.

"Ma'am."

Lady Hatch laid a hand on my arm. "Margrey, I'm sure you know who this is."

"Oh, aye. Milady Daired," the girl said, and then she stuck her chin in Alastair's direction. "Them Riders got us out of harm's way when that monster came through." The baby on her hip made a gurgling sound and stuck a finger in its nose. "And we just wanted to say . . . um, thank you, milady."

She curtsied again and backed away before I could make the requisite, albeit awkward and thoroughly confused, *you're welcome*. I looked at Lady Hatch. She smiled at my bewilderment and leaned close. "The townsfolk who couldn't fight sheltered here during the battle. Those two were some of the last to make it inside. Your husband and his dragon saved them from a pair of valkyries."

"Why on earth is she thanking *me*?"

"Because of the Daireds present you're the least daunting."

I looked down the table to where Alastair sat talking to Lord Hatch, blind to the small crowd of admirers gathering at a safe distance around him. The space seemed an unconscious thing, the natural drifting of the flock around the protective yet intimidating presence of the sheepdog. I cleared my throat. "I'm glad they're all right."

"As am I, my lady. As are we all."

Music drifted through the hall as the bard strummed the first few notes of a harvest hymn to Janna. The music seemed to be a signal; the crowd around Alastair thinned as the townsfolk gave up on the idea of speaking to Lord Daired and returned to the celebration.

"But the battle is over," Lady Hatch said, brightening. "It's our duty to look to the future, eh? Now tell me, have you ever visited Lake Meera before?"

I shook my head, mouth full.

"It's a curious place, the land around the lakes. You can't live between the Old Wilds and the Northern Wastes for generations without being changed by them, and Lake Meera . . ." She wagged a conspiratorial finger. "Well, you know what they say."

"Not really," I answered honestly.

"Truly? I thought everyone knew. Let me see, how does it go? *Take heed, all ye who'd walk her shore: the lake gives much, and takes much more.* Or something like that," she said. "I hear that the merfolk who live there are a fascinating people. Not to be trusted, of course, but then few *Idar* are."

I thought of the trolls and centaurs I'd seen fighting at the side of the Worm. *The Indifferent,* they called themselves, but their indifference was a double-edged sword, and too often used against us. I wondered whose side Selwyn's murdered *Idar* had taken in the War of the Worm. "Has Hatch Ford had trouble with *Idar* since the Worm died?"

"Not . . . *Idar.* No."

An invitation hung on her hesitation. "Other creatures?"

"In a manner of speaking. Right foul carrion birds, if you ask me, but of course *those* we've had—"

Lord Hatch's head jerked toward us and Lady Hatch stopped short. He wore a pleasant smile as he nodded to something Alastair was saying, but there was a warning in the look he shot his wife.

"No trouble," she added quickly. "Ah, listen to me rambling.

We're rebuilding, Lady Aliza, just like everyone else. Slowly but surely." She patted my hand. "I hope you visit again someday when our city is whole."

"I hope so too. But what did you mean, the—?"

"How long do you plan to stay in Hatch Ford, Lord Alastair?" Lady Hatch asked above the clatter of the banquet, the singing guests, and my question.

"Just long enough to resupply," Alastair replied. "We'll need stores before heading north."

"North? Not east to Selkie's Keep?" She looked surprised. "Surely you don't mean to cross the Widdermere."

"It's the fastest way to Lake Meera."

"Quite true, and what are the Old Wilds to a Daired and his dragon?" Lord Hatch said jovially. He clapped Alastair on the back. "Best of luck to you all, my lord. I look forward to hearing about your adventures when you return. In the meantime, consider our city at your disposal. Whatever you need from the market tomorrow is on the credit of Hatch House. No, no argument! I insist. It really is the least we can do."

"You're very kind," I said to Lady Hatch as Alastair made another attempt to dissuade her husband, "but we couldn't—Your Ladyship? Is everything all right?"

Lady Hatch was staring at Alastair. Her throat moved up and down and she shook her head as if trying to discourage an intrepid fly. "So sorry. It's nothing. Never mind. It . . . actually, no, it's *not* nothing. That heartstone your husband wears," she said, nodding to the sliver of green peeping out from his high collar. "I've never seen that color before. Where did you get it?"

"It was a gift," I said. *Daughter of blood and fire and wrath . . .* "From Charis Brysney."

Understanding dawned in her eyes and she sank back in her

chair. "The heartstone of the Greater Lindworm," she murmured. "Then it is true. We've heard such whispers, such stories already, I didn't dare believe them." With sudden earnestness she turned to me and clasped my hands. "Listen to me, please. Arle has never seen the like of that gem, and doubtless will never see it again. I can only guess what it means to you both, but please promise me something, my lady."

"What?"

"When you and your husband venture out tomorrow, make sure he keeps it well concealed."

CHAPTER 8

WHERE VULTURES GATHER

Later that night as we prepared for bed I told Alastair about Lady Hatch's warning. His reaction wasn't what I expected. "If someone wants to take this, they're welcome to try." He fished the Worm's heartstone out from its chain around his neck and held it up. "When Akarra's finished with them, I might even be merciful."

"Oh?"

The eiderdown let out a little *whoosh* as he sank onto it. "I may allow them to keep their head. *Khera*, of all places in Arle, Hatch Ford is probably the least dangerous place to be right now. The City Watch is on hourly patrols, Lord Hatch said there's a company of the Free Regiments still camped east of the city, and Akarra's just outside the gates. Stop worrying."

He might as well have asked a direwolf to take up embroidery, but for both our sakes I did my best to put it out of my mind. There were plenty other mysteries on hand to keep me occupied. "Lady Hatch said that people tell stories about Lake Meera."

He made a vague sound, feigning interest.

"She said the merfolk aren't to be trusted."

"Merfolk rarely are."

"Do you think we'll see many?"

He sighed. The scent of mead lingered on his breath, honey-sweet and sleepy. "Honestly, Aliza, it still amazes me."

"What?"

"That after Odei made you he had enough inquisitiveness left over for other creatures." That earned a gentle smack from a pillow, and he laughed. "There are worse faults. No, I haven't the faintest idea if we'll see the Lake Meera schools and I have no intention of losing sleep over it." He snatched the pillow from my hands and eased it under his head. "Neither should you."

I blew out the bedside lamp and curled up beside him. The Worm's heartstone peeped through the open collar of his nightshirt, glinting in the light of the dying fire. There was no reason to worry, I told myself. *None whatsoever . . .*

Only hovering on the edge of sleep, soothed by the sound of his breathing and the crackle of embers, did my brain make sense of what was truly troubling me. *"Right foul carrion birds,"* Lady Hatch had said. *"In a manner of speaking."*

I almost sat up in bed. A very *specific* manner of speaking. I didn't need to be a Daired to know the Eth word for *vulture.* All Arleans did. *Vesh.*

FOR THE FIRST TIME SINCE WE'D LEFT HOUSE PENDRAGON I slept soundly and, much to my amusement and his consternation, so did Alastair. The rising sun failed to rouse him, and I couldn't resist a smirk when I nudged him awake at half past nine. He grumbled something about *learning from you* before drifting off again with a snore. It was fully eleven by the time we hauled ourselves out of bed and headed outside to let Akarra know what had become of us.

She lay basking in the sun on the ridge east of Hatch House.

"By the looks on your faces and the lack of luggage I gather we don't plan on continuing today," she said.

"No," Alastair said, shielding his eyes against the glare. "First thing in the morning."

"Whatever happened to not wanting to fly in a blizzard?"

"We've made good time so far. We would've needed to stop for supplies before starting for the Old Wilds anyway, and Hatch Ford is better than some of those godsforsaken little villages on the edge of the Marshes."

"Yes, of course." She looked at him sidelong through half-closed eyelids. "Nothing to do with Lord Hatch's excellent cellar."

Alastair folded his arms and made a show of scanning the landscape.

Akarra laughed. "No shame in it, *khela*. His mead nearly leveled Ruthven last time and he's twice your size. But if it makes you feel better, I could use a rest too." She yawned. "When you see William again, thank him for the mutton. It was delicious."

"Are you staying close today?" I asked.

"I might go hunting this afternoon. *Proper* hunting. Penned sheep may fill my stomachs, but they're not much fun." She sniffed the wind. "There's a herd of red deer nearby. I think I may pay them a visit. You?"

"I'd like to speak to the magistrate before we get supplies," Alastair said. "I want to see how the repairs are going."

"Ah, yes. Let me know what he says."

We left Akarra to her basking and took the road that wound from Hatch House to the river. Unlike Shepherd's Vale and Claykeep, the wall around the eastern half of Hatch Ford was little more than an earthen berm topped with quickthorn. The streets too were wider, with shops and houses rising only one or two stories above the ground. Or they were in the living half of the city. The main road passed by the Ford. I slowed as we approached the docks, at once horrified and mesmerized by the sight. The western half of Hatch Ford spread like a rotting corpse on the opposite bank. Crossbeams jutted from the rubble like cracked and broken bones, and mud and water washed across the cobblestones like blood. The dark shapes of scavengers moved among the rubble.

Alastair touched my elbow. "The magistrate's house is this way."

I turned away from the ruin, peering down the street toward the bustle and dust cloud that spelled *marketplace* in universal letters. "Why don't you visit him and I'll get what we need from the market?" He looked doubtful, so I added, with my sweetest smile, "Something about Hatch Ford being the least dangerous place in Arle suddenly springs to mind, dearest."

He grunted. "I suppose I earned that."

"Aye, you did. I'll be fine."

"You have your dagger?"

I raised the folds of my shawl to show the sheath at my hip, which seemed to ease his mind. We parted at the corner. With Lady Hatch's warning echoing in my ears when I woke, I'd pinned my heartstone brooch beneath my dress, safe from prying eyes. It wasn't the heartstone of the Greater Lindworm, but lamia heartstones were rare enough to warrant unwanted attention, and with the mystery of the slain *Idar* still looming over us, I felt better keeping it hidden. This too was the first time since we'd left House Pendragon that neither riding clothes nor Alastair's, well, everything, could give away my identity, and I looked forward to the anonymity. Besides, there was something else I needed at the market, something I'd just as well he not know about. His teasing would be the end of me.

The vendors of Hatch Ford were quieter than their cousins in Claykeep. A pall hung over the main square of the city, as if the stones themselves were holding their breath, waiting for some sign that laughter and chatter were safe again. Stall after stall stood vacant, and the ones that weren't offered a meager spread. The haunches of badly salted beef hanging from the butcher's stall were lean and withered, and my nose stung with the smell, just a day or so short of spoilage. A handful of wrinkled apples sat at the bottom of a basket in front of the greengrocer, who looked as despondent as his wares. A fly circled the basket twice before buzzing away to find refuse better worth its time. At the baker's stall I bought all the bardsbread he had, hoping twelve of the hard, flat loaves would be enough to carry us across the Widdermere. The baker stuffed the bread into a sack and muttered an apology for the quality. I paid him six copper trills and asked him to point me to the best place to find beggar's balm.

The stall he directed me to wasn't well stocked, but it had what I needed. The woman behind the table gave me a sympathetic look as she brought out the stalks of beggar's balm, their whitish leaves dried and pressed flat. "Always keep some of this on hand nowadays," she said. "Some of the people hereabouts are glad of something to soothe their stomachs after seeing what they seen." I offered her three half-trills, but she waved the money away. "My gift, dear. You look as though you may need it."

"Thank you." Now that she'd mentioned it, I did feel a little queasy. The smell of the butcher's stall was more pervasive than I'd thought. I plucked a leaf and stuck it under my tongue as I wandered through the rest of the market, tucking the remaining stalks in the pages of my sketchbook. The leaf crumbled in my mouth, stale and tasting of burnt clover, but the herb hadn't lost its virtue and the queasiness lessened in minutes. I hoped it'd be as effective while flying. After all I'd done to avoid getting left behind, I wasn't about to let my weak stomach serve as Alastair's excuse to turn us around.

Only one corner of the market escaped the cloud that hung over the rest of the city. The clank of metal and the roar of a forge drew me like a fox to a marshlight, and I followed the sound to the edge of the market where a squat stone building overlooked the river. A man sat in the shade of the doorway sharpening his knife. His whetstone stopped halfway down his blade as I approached. "Looking for something, miss?"

"Is this the lithosmith's shop?"

"Aye, finest in Harborough Hatch." He bent his head again to his task, the stone rasping smoothly along the steel. "You got business with the master?"

Through a chink in the door I caught a familiar flash of blond hair and wondered what the lady of Hatch House was doing in a lithosmith's shop.

"Miss? You coming or going?"

There was one way to find out. "Coming, I think," I said and went inside.

It was a larger shop than the one in Trollhedge. Dark wood paneled the walls and glass-covered cases lined in velvet filled the room. Heartstones of all shades and sizes glittered in the lamplight, some by themselves, some in rich settings of silver or copper. The blond woman at the far side of the shop turned at the sound of the door. It was not Lady Hatch.

"Lady Daired!" Margrey leapt down from the stool where she'd stood, a feather duster in one hand, a small four-faced statuette in the other. There was a thud from a back room and she dropped the statuette on the stool. She looked around wildly. "Milady, what are you doing here?"

"I'm sorry, I thought you were Lady Hatch—"

A curtain swished on the other side of the shop and a man in the dark tunic and leather jerkin of a lithosmith emerged from the back room. "Lady Daired!" he cried. "I did hear right, didn't I?"

"Aye, sir," I said, puzzled by Margrey's intensified look of alarm.

"Well! If this isn't good fortune I don't know what is." He swept into a bow. "Erik Tully, master of the Hatch Ford lithosmiths and your humble servant. To what do I owe this pleasure?"

"Sorry for intruding," I said. "I . . . just needed to step in out of the sun for a moment."

He turned. "Margrey, fetch Lady Daired some water."

She jerked as if slapped, her eyes wide. "Master?"

"Now, please."

"That's not necessary," I started to say, but Margrey rushed from the room before I could stop her. "Thank you, sir, but I'm fine."

It was a lie. The queasiness had returned, and this time the beggar's balm couldn't soothe it. Margrey's expression stuck in my mind, gnawing a warning. A prickling started up the back of my neck as the lithosmith set the statuette on the ground and pulled out the stool by the mantelpiece.

Why did I come in here again?

"Here, my lady. Rest."

I stayed standing. Something about him was wrong. The closer he came the more I felt it. His clothes weren't merely black; they drank the light, leaching color from everything around him. Looking at them made my head ache. My eyes slid off that woven absence like oil from water. His posture felt wrong too. He walked with a slight hunch, shoulders raised on either side of his head as if trying to protect it.

I edged back. "Thank you, sir, but I should be going."

"But you've only just arrived!"

"My . . . husband's expecting me," I said firmly and turned to the door.

"Ah, yes, the famous Lord Daired. We've heard that family name so much of late, you know. If you must go, you must," he said, sounding crestfallen, "only—forgive me, I should like to give you something before you leave."

"Yes?"

"Merely a trifle, of course. A token, really."

I paused on the threshold. "What is it?"

"A greeting from an old friend." The room behind me shuddered. Laughter started at the very edges of my perception, silvery and shrill, like a knife vibrating in the soul-space between silence and screaming. "The Minister of the Ledger sends his regards," he said.

Very slowly, I lowered the latch. My other hand felt for my dagger. I couldn't bring myself to turn around. "*What* did you say?"

"So you do remember! He thought you might. Well, he *hoped* you might. You were one of the few to see him as he is, he told me, and I think it rather endeared you to him. We do get so tired of hiding sometimes, you know."

My tongue felt thick and wooden, my throat dry as sand. "Who are you?"

"A servant."

"Of whom?"

"Someone who will be very pleased to hear me tell of this meeting. Unlike some of my brothers, you see, I am a very *useful* servant. Did you get the minister's gift?"

"How do you know about that?" I whispered.

"It's common knowledge that Garhadi ale is a favorite of your husband's, isn't it? My friend hoped he would enjoy it."

"I . . . got rid of it."

"Oh, that is a pity. He'll be disappointed."

I squared my chin to the door. "Good."

"There she is!" Tully said. "'*Lady Aliza, clever and brave.*' For all the rest of his doggerel the 'Charissong' bard got that part right. I can see why the minister remembered you."

I spun around, but the lithosmith was no longer standing by the mantel.

"So tell me," he said in my ear, "*have you felt it?*"

I sprang away, smacking my elbow against the nearest heartstone casket. My arm throbbed. "Stay back!"

Tully pulled a key from his pocket and smiled. It was nothing like the minister's grin, that knife shard in the dark, teasing out riddles and dancing with false fire. This smile was far too human—and much worse. "I have no wish to harm you," he said as he locked the door. "Not yet, at least. That would quite defeat the purpose." Again I reached for my knife, but the sheath was empty. He held up my dagger. "Tut, tut. A Daired shouldn't be so careless with a blade. But of course, you're no Daired. For all your fine titles, not a drop of Fireborn blood runs in those veins."

I had to swallow twice before I could speak. "What do you want?"

"Your answer will do. Have you felt it? I must know."

"Felt what?"

"The war that is coming."

"It did come." My voice shook. "The war is over."

"Over? *Over?* Oh, you poor, naive thing! The war has only just begun."

"No. The Greater Lindworm is dead." My voice caught as flames danced again in the dark places of memory. "I watched it die. I watched it burn."

He rolled his eyes. "You disappoint me, Lady Daired. Yes, the Worm is dead. A clever person would wonder why it woke in the first place."

"Revenge," I said, and cast around for an escape route. The poker by the fireplace caught my eye. "The Riders killed its spawn."

"Ah, but what woke the Lesser Lindworm?"

I opened my mouth, but no answer came out. In truth, I had no answer.

He smiled again. "So you don't know? Well, it doesn't matter. War is coming. Even now the Oldkind choose sides, and sooner or later you and your people will join them. What choice my master offers is this: stand aside and live—or fight us and die. There is no—"

"Fight," I said before he could finish. "We'll fight. Whoever you are, and whoever you work for, we will fight you. Every Arlean, from the Drakaina down to the last hobgoblin."

"Courage without sense is stupidity, child. If you knew who you stood against, you would bend your knee today."

I edged toward the fireplace. "Then why don't you tell me?"

"The *Tekari* sense it. *Idar* too, even some *Shani*. They have sensed it for years, though most do not know its name, and those who do dare not speak it."

Just a few more steps. "But you do?"

"I am a messenger. I speak what I am given, and I am not given to revealing things my master wishes to keep hidden."

"You won't win."

"Don't you understand?" He closed the distance between us. "The war is won already! Your kingdom is weak. My brothers and I have spent a long time making it so." He laughed. Scales and talons raked my soul. "Little debts all around the kingdom, little favors, ensnaring the desperate, fomenting the discontents, encouraging the restless, gathering allies from the darkest of your Arlean legends. We feed the embers of the fire that will consume the very heart of your people. There are many ways to win a war, dear false Daired. One might say our master's victory here is merely a matter of settling accounts."

I backed into the stool on the hearth. My bag fell from my shoulder, spilling loaves of bardsbread and beggar's balm onto the stones and knocking the poker from its place next to the fireplace. Tully's smile split his face like an unscabbed wound.

"You'll soon see, my lady. You and all your people. There's nowhere left to run."

I drew up my last ounce of courage. "All right," I said, looking him full in the face. "I've answered your question. What else do you want from me?"

His eyes sparkled—and changed. Yellow boiled through the blue of his irises, bubbling up in shades of sulfur. His jerkin writhed with a life of its own, sending out coils of darkness that swelled around him and over him and *through* him . . .

Mikla save us.

Two voices spoke from his mouth: one bitter and human, one shrill and smooth, seething with hatred just below the surface. He raised my knife. "You carry something of great value to my master, Lady Daired, and the brotherhood has—"

Floorboards creaked behind him and Tully paused to look over his shoulder. I stooped and felt around blindly behind me. My hand closed over the stone statuette.

"Margrey?" Tully's human voice said. "What are you doing?"

"Sorry, Master," she said.

"No! Don't you da—"

I brought the statuette crashing down on his head.

Nothing happened.

I lifted the statuette again—and Tully collapsed. Margrey stood behind him, a glass bottle raised above her head. She leapt out of the way as he hit the ground and began to writhe. Roiling tendrils of darkness licked along his back, flailing like disembodied spider's legs before sinking back into his chest. He went still.

I clutched at the edge of the fireplace, staring at the body at our feet. *Thell. Oh Thell.* "Margrey—I didn't mean—he was—"

"Ghast-ridden. I know." She seized my arm. "He won't stay down long."

I looked at the figure on the floor. His chest didn't move.

"He's not dead," she said. "That creature won't let him get away so easily. Hurry! You shouldn't be here."

There was a pounding at the door. "Master Tully? Everything all right?" the guard asked, and Margrey went rigid. "Master Tully?" The door shook as he tried to open it, but the lock held firm. "Sir?" The guard swore. "I'm getting the Watch, sir!"

"Quickly!" Margrey said in my ear. "There's a window in the back. Come *on!*"

I glanced one last time at the dreadful thing on the hearth and ran after her.

The back room was cramped and littered with stone chips, the air hot and smoky from the fire blazing next to the window. Margrey clambered onto the workbench and set to work on the window bolts. "Hope you don't mind climbing, milady."

"Margrey, stop! Shouldn't we wait for the Watch?"

She shook her head as the first bolt shot free. "Master Tully and his *Vesh* own the Watch. You won't get help from them."

"Then the magistrate—"

"The magistrate don't see anything he's not paid to see, and the *Vesh* pay him lots." The last bolt slid loose. "Listen, please. I don't know what the master wants with you, but if it woke that creature inside him it won't be good. Best chance you have now is to get back to your dragon." She balanced on the windowsill and offered me her hand. "Coming?"

Shouts sounded in the front room, and the door shuddered as someone kicked it. I took her hand.

The lithosmith shop bordered the riverbank. We dropped from the window into a tangle of waterweed. Mud sucked at my feet, dragging me toward the river, but Margrey took me by the elbow and hauled me to higher ground. Something crashed inside the shop. We dodged behind the corner just as a woman thrust her head out of the window.

"Search the market, and send someone up to watch Hatch House," the woman said to one of the guards inside. "Lord Hatch don't hear about this, understand?"

"That's the captain of the Watch," Margrey said in my ear and pointed to the crumbling façade of the next building over. "Bakery. Over there. Quick!"

We slipped and slid along the bank to the abandoned bakery, Margrey trailing after me to smooth away our footprints in the mud. There was an empty outbuilding close to the river, and we crouched inside as men and women of the Watch poured from the front of the lithosmith shop. Some headed back east toward Hatch House, some spread out into the market. Two stayed to guard the door, and only then did I realize I'd left my dagger inside, clutched in Tully's death grip. "Can we get past them?" I whispered.

"Not now. Your dragon's up at the house, inn't she?"

"She's out hunting."

"Where's your husband?"

"With the magistrate."

Margrey risked a glance through the outbuilding's grimy window. "That'll be the next place the Watch goes. They'll keep him there as long as they can while Tully looks for you." She ducked as a barge passed on the far side of the river, its timbers groaning beneath the shouts of its crew and the answering shouts from the shore. Margrey cursed under her breath. "River's out too. Boatswain and the Watch are thicker than—well, they are thieves."

Escape first, answers later. "What do we do?"

"Hide. Most of the Watch only got a few hours' search in 'em. If they think looking for you will make them miss their dinners, they'll give up."

"And Tully?"

"There are a few places I know he won't look." The clatter of boots on cobblestones faded and she peeked around the edge of the door. "C'mon."

CHAPTER 9

GHASTRADI

The worm-eaten boards trembled beneath Margrey's hand as she fumbled with the lock of a house near the northern edge of the city. I squeezed into the hollow of a doorway and surveyed the street. Rubbish packed the winding lane between the city's outer berm and the foundations of the higher houses, making a twisted seam through the slum quarters of Hatch Ford. None of the Watch had followed us. For the twentieth time in the last hour I found myself thanking the gods for, among other things, Margrey's uncanny knowledge of the city's alleys.

Before she could manage the lock, the door opened from the inside and a woman peered out. She was a broad, solid woman, not old, but with weary eyes and too many wrinkles for her age. A silver pendant in the shape of Janna's beech leaf sigil hung on a chain around her neck. She gave Margrey a sour look. "You're early."

"Trouble at the shop," Margrey said. "Why did you lock the door? I told you not to."

"And leave us unprotected? In this quarter of the city?"

Margrey grunted something under her breath and pushed past her.

"The baby's sleeping!" the woman whispered.

"We'll be quiet."

The house had only three walls. The city berm formed the fourth, its sloping surface shored up with planks and bits of furniture. A peat fire smoldered on the hearth, coughing more smoke into the room than it did into the chimney. The older woman waved one hand to the propped-up plank that served as a table and lifted a kettle from its hook above the fire. "Sit if you like. Tea." It wasn't a request, simply a statement of existence. "Are you going to tell me what happened this time?" she asked as Margrey carried three battered mugs to the table. "And why you dragged this girl into it?"

"Her name's Aliza," Margrey said before I could answer, and she shook her head with a frantic look before I could add *Daired.* "Aliza, my sister, Myrra."

Myrra brushed aside my unthinking curtsy. "Her mother on most days. What's gone wrong today, Maggie?"

"It's Tully," Margrey said. "The creature inside him woke up."

Myrra sighed deeply. "The creature you've imagined, you mean."

"For the last time, I didn't imagine it! The ghast is real. I saw it today. So did Aliza."

The sisters turned to me. "It's true. I think," I said, sifting through my mental notes of the *Chronicle of Foes.* There hadn't been much on ghasts beyond the obvious: yellow eyes and split voice, and even those entries had been faded almost beyond legibility. "*Something* had gotten ahold of him. There's no other explanation."

She gave me a narrow-eyed look. "You saw this ghast thing?"

"We saw a shadow—"

"There," Myrra interrupted. "That's all it was."

"It went *through* him, Myrra. It moved with a mind of its own,"

Margrey said. "And Tully—" A stirring sound came from beyond the curtained-off corner of the room, and the two looked up in alarm. When no cries followed, Margrey continued in a whisper. "He spoke with two voices."

"The *ghastradi* are old wives' tales. Everyone knows that."

"Din't you always say there's truth under the surface of those stories?"

"*Didn't.* And perhaps I did, but this? Shadow monsters on your back, pulling your soul strings like a puppeteer? If there ever were such creatures, they died out in Arle centuries ago." She sniffed. "You said Tully picked up that—whatever it is—months back. He—"

I gripped Margrey's arm. "How long ago?" I asked. "Where did he find his ghast?"

"Dunno. He went on business last summer to the Garhad Islands, but he was gone for a long time. Could've gone anywhere. When he came back that creature was with him."

"How did you know he was ghast-ridden?"

"I seen his eyes turn once, back at the beginning. All the stories say that's the sign."

"*Saw.* Yet she stayed on, you'll notice," Myrra said. "You can't expect me to believe it just sat around all this time biding its time. And if it really were a monster riding him, why didn't you leave?"

"You know why."

Myrra drew up to her full height and folded her arms. "No, you've never actually told me. Why?"

Margrey glanced in my direction. "Now ain't the time for this," she hissed.

"Now is a perfect time for it, begging your friend's pardon. A little honesty is a trifle in exchange for the belief you're asking of us. Why'd you stay?"

Margrey shrugged. "It was work, aright? Decent work."

"Decent work with a ghost-ridden master?"

"I told you, the ghost were asleep. Until today it was just Tully. He was fair. He never asked questions, not about Dinah, or you, or anything." She gestured to the sagging floors and crumbling walls around us. "Never even asked where I lived. He din't beat me."

"Neither would lots of other shopkeepers."

"They wouldn't take me."

"You mean they wouldn't take on the fool who'd gone and gotten herself with the magistrate's bast—child."

"Myrra. Don't."

"Pieter would've taken you on," she said. "You know he would've."

"Dinah and me aren't some charity offering to your gods," Margrey said in a quiet voice. "Stop trying."

Myrra rested her hands on the table, her shoulders slumped, head bowed. Margrey stared at the fire. I studied the grain of the plank in front of me with a concentration that said *I won't remember any of this if you don't want me to* and hoped the sisters would forgive me. The bundle in the curtained-off corner stirred again, the sound of tiny breathing layered over the rustle of blankets. At last Myrra sighed. "Fine. Do as you will, Margrey; you always have. But I still need an answer. If the ghost was asleep all this time, why did it wake today?"

"I was there," I said.

"You?" Myrra turned to me with a nearsighted scowl, as if she'd only just noticed the stranger in her sister's kitchen, not as an accessory to Margrey's story, but as a person. "You're not from Hatch Ford, are you?"

"Hart's Run."

"Girl like you go around waking lots of ghasts? Regular country pastime, hm?"

"I've never seen a ghast before in my life."

"You say this thing talked to you. What'd it want?"

I crossed my arms, feeling the hard edges of the brooch beneath my dress. "I wish I knew."

"Myrra, it tried to attack her," Margrey said. "It had a knife!"

Watch shouts drifted in from outside, accompanied by the tramp of boots on the paved streets above the slum quarter. Margrey stiffened. I watched understanding dawn in Myrra's eyes as she listened, and processed her sister's words, and put the pieces together. "Oh, dear gods. Margrey, what have you done?"

"We only . . . knocked him unconscious."

"*Margrey!*"

"No. Your sister didn't touch him," I said quickly. "It was me. She just helped me escape."

"Foolish, foolish girl. Both of you!"

"We had no choice," Margrey said. "He was coming after her and—"

"You had every choice! Now you have no choice. Ghast or no ghast, you turned against your master, and you attacked a citizen of Hatch Ford, Miss Aliza. There are consequences for that." Myrra started toward the door. "I'm sorry."

Margrey sprang to her feet and blocked her path. "Don't! Please. Shame me all you want. Toss me to the Watch, or back to the magistrate, or in the river for all I care, but don't bring Aliza into this."

"The laws are clear, Margrey."

"Aye, and you've never once let me forget it, but this inn't—this isn't about the rules. It's about what's right. *Please*, Myrra," she said. Their gazes locked. The room and everything in it seemed to hold its breath.

There was a booming knock at the door. "Watch business!" a man cried. "Open up."

Myrra came alive. She shoved Margrey and me toward the curtained corner, hissing for us to keep quiet. Behind the curtain was a cramped room with a sloping ceiling, and we crouched shoulder to shoulder behind a rough-hewn cradle, its occupant still cooing peacefully beneath its blanket. Myrra opened the door. Through holes in the curtain I could make out a young man's silhouette on the threshold dressed in the uniform of the City Watch, complete with helm and crossbow. The helm looked several sizes too big.

"What's this, then?" Myrra said.

"Sorry to bother you, miss, it's—"

"It's Madam Fitzwarren to you, young man."

"Er, madam. Sorry. I'm, ah, searching for a lady."

"I suggest you investigate establishments on the other side of the city."

He cleared his throat. "A particular lady, Madam Fitzwarren. Last seen at Master Tully's lithosmith shop."

"And is there any *particular* reason you're looking for this *particular* lady?"

"A misunderstanding, ma'am. Master Tully, um, wishes to see it resolved. The lady rushed out before their, er, business was concluded."

"Taking valuable heartstones with her, I presume."

"Beg your pardon?"

"The lady stole something, didn't she?" she said, her voice at once triumphant and disappointed. "Why else would the entire Watch be looking for her?"

"No, ma'am. Nothing was taken."

"Oh." Myrra's voice sounded far away. "Well. Best of luck."

The watchman would not give up. "You haven't seen the lady?"

"I see many people in this city, young man. It might help if you provided more description than 'a lady.'"

"Oh. Right. Dark hair, gray dress."

"That's it?"

"Shortish dark hair. Light gray dress. That's all I was told."

"Half the women in the north quarter could fit that description. Now, if you would be so good as to remove your foot from my threshold, young man, I will be most exceedingly obliged," Myrra said in a voice that could have curdled new milk.

"Please, Madam Fitzwarren! Her husband's looking for her too, and he's not a man we can disappoint. It's—it's Lord Alastair Daired."

Hinges squealed as Myrra flung the door open again. "*I beg your pardon?*"

"He and Lady Daired and his dragon are guests at Hatch House. Lord Daired went to visit the magistrate and his wife went to the market, but now no one can find her and the magistrate thinks Lord Daired will blame us and . . . and . . ."

"Good gods, boy, pull yourself together," Myrra said. "He's not going to have his dragon raze the city because his wife is flighty and our Watch is incompetent. I've told you all I know, so you'd best keep looking."

"Oh. All right. Um, thank you for your time, Madam Fitzwarren."

Myrra stood in the doorway for a long minute. "Just out of curiosity, young man, what's this lady's name?" she called suddenly.

"Lady Aliza, I think," came the faint answer. "Aliza Daired."

The door shut. The room grew dim and smoky again as Margrey pushed aside the curtain. The motion drew out a happy gurgle from the bundle in the cradle, who'd at last decided to throw in her lot with the waking world. Margrey picked up her daughter and held her close to her chest. Myrra looked up at me with an unfathomable expression. "So. You're one of them."

"I'm not a Rider, if that's what you mean," I said. "But yes, I am a Daired."

"She's married to one," Margrey added quickly. "Sister, she din't have anything to do with what happened here."

The gaze Myrra leveled at me might've kindled green wood. "Perhaps. Perhaps not. I suppose you'll be wanting to get back to your husband."

I shook my head, shifting uncomfortably beneath the accusation in those eyes. "I need to get to Hatch House first. If Tully's people are searching the city, I'll be safer there."

"The *Vesh* will be on the lookout too," Margrey said.

"I don't want to run into either of them before we meet Alastair."

"Of course not. Which is why you'll both stay here while I go find Lord Daired," Myrra said. "Lady Daired, you wouldn't make it three streets before someone spotted you, and Margrey, the *Vesh* will recognize you as Tully's help, so unless you both want to wait and strike out for Hatch House in the morning you'll let me find Lord Daired and bring him back here. Besides," she said, standing, "someone needs to look after the baby. I won't be long."

She swept out of the house without a backward glance.

Margrey shut the door after her and sagged onto a stool. "I'm so sorry, Aliza."

"Whatever for?"

"My sister don't much hold with Rider-folk anymore. Her husband tried to protect their street when the Worm came through and the Riders—well, they weren't there. Got himself hurt pretty bad. She still don't know if he'll ever walk again." The baby began crying. "Would you mind?"

"What?"

She pushed the blankets into my arms. "Hold her. I need to eat before I feed her."

I stared at the bundle on my lap. Tiny hands grasped the air, searching for milk, warmth, and comfort from the hugeness of the world. She was so *small*. I dared not move, hardly dared breathe, struck with the sudden and irrational fear that I might somehow drop her, or break her, or do something else unforgivably stupid. I sat stiffer than a gargoyle and just as reassuring as she wailed on my knees, her round little face screwing up into something at once too simple and too complex to be called an expression. It was nothing but raw need, primal and piteous.

Her cry pierced me like a needle, drawing memories after it like thread: memories of holding another bundle like this one in twelve-year-old arms, Mama sitting in the bed, smiling but exhausted, Papa grasping her hand and trying not to cry, Anjey and Mari and Leyda all jostling for a turn to introduce themselves to our new baby sister. "*Katarina Bentaine*," Mama had said. "*Mouthful, isn't it? We'll call her Rina.*"

I blinked and looked away.

Margrey had dug out a chunk of stale bread from a basket near the washtub and was chewing thoughtfully, glancing every few seconds out the crack around the door. I heard the sound of commotion at the end of the street.

"Why are you doing all this?" I asked.

"Hm?"

"Why are you helping me? I dragged you into this, not the other way around. You never had to leave that back room."

"And let that ghast hurt you? Not likely."

"He was your master."

"Erik Tully was my master. That thing he became today, that weren't." Crumbs scattered from the front of her dress as she unbuttoned the first few buttons and rolled up her homespun tucker. I handed her the baby and the crying ceased as she began to nurse.

"I don't know how to thank you."

"What, for taking the baby?" She smiled. "Look, I seen Lady Hatch talking to you at the high table last night. Guessing she told you what happened to us. It's a long way from here to Hatch House, and it ain't easy to run when you're dodging horses and stampeding townsfolk and holding a baby. A pair of valkyries near got us at the front gates. Your husband and his dragon swooped in just in time." The commotion in the street grew louder and Margrey squeezed my hand. "I don't got any money, but I pay my debts best I can."

"Right through here," Myrra said and pushed the door open.

The captain of the Watch strode into the room.

Margrey went rigid. More guards thronged around the doorway, including the young man in an overlarge helm who looked very confused. I sprang to my feet. *Myrra, no!*

"You're a difficult woman to find, Lady Daired," the captain said. "I'm glad we—"

"Aliza? Is she here?" Eth curses peppered the air. "For gods' sakes, let me through!"

Relief nearly brought me down into the nearest chair as Alastair shoved aside the guards and burst into the room. On seeing me alive, uninjured, and otherwise no worse for an after-noon's wanderings, he gasped something in Eth and hugged me tight enough to pick me up off the ground.

"*Thell*, you had me worried," he whispered. "They said you were missing, that you'd fallen in the river and . . . what happened?"

Over his shoulder the captain of the Watch gave me a tight-lipped smile. "I'll tell you later," I said in Alastair's ear. "Not here."

"You gave us all quite a fright there, Lady Daired," the captain said as Alastair set me down. "Hope you're not hurt?"

"I'm fine. Margrey was just showing me the city."

Margrey leaned out behind me and gave a little wave.

The captain's smile froze in place. "That was very kind of her."

"Yes. Thank you, both of you," Alastair said, first to Margrey, then to Myrra. He took my hand. "We should get back to Hatch House before Akarra sets something on fire for fretting."

I followed him out, mouthing one final *thank you* to Margrey.

Myrra gave Alastair a stiff, icy curtsy, favored me with a nod, and shut the door after us.

I WAITED UNTIL WE WERE SAFE IN LORD HATCH'S STUDY and out of earshot of the captain to tell Alastair and Lord and Lady Hatch what had happened. Lord Hatch groped for a de-canter on the sideboard when I spoke of Tully's transformation. Alastair sat by the fire, his face fixed and impassive, his sword in its scabbard resting on his knees. Of the three of them, Lady Hatch was the only one who didn't seem to be taken by surprise.

"Lady Viola, you warned me about the *Vesh* last night," I said. "Did you know Master Tully was a *ghastradi*?"

Lord Hatch winced at the word.

"I had no idea," she said.

"Have you ever seen a haunting in Hatch Ford before?" Alastair asked.

"Certainly not! We've had our fair share of *Tekari*, of course, but never those creatures. I thought they died out in Arle a long time ago."

"Why warn us then?" I asked her.

"I thought . . . well, to be perfectly frank, your heartstones are well known, and as much as I hate to admit it, there are some bad sorts among the *Vesh*," she said. "No matter how we try to control it, it's been chaos in our streets since the Worm passed, and I couldn't bear to think that one of them might try to . . . to . . . oh dear . . ."

Her husband patted her hand. "Be assured, Lord Alastair, we plan to do everything in our power to make this right. First thing in the morning I'll have a word with the magistrate and the captain of the Watch. I want to speak to every *Vesh* Master Tully had dealings with to see if they knew about this."

"You won't get very far," I said. "Tully owns the Watch."

"I'm sorry?"

"He pays off the magistrate too, I think."

"Are you certain?"

"I heard the captain talking with her guards. There's some kind of arrangement."

Lord Hatch shuffled to his desk and sat. His fingers tapped out a nervous rhythm on the wood. "Yes. Well. That is, er, unfortunate. I'm most terribly sorry. It will be addressed at once."

"Yes, it will be." Alastair rose. "Lord Hatch, do you have door wardens here?"

"One or two."

"Are they armed?"

"Of course."

"Have them meet us in the front of the house in five minutes."

"Sir?"

Alastair buckled his scabbard onto his sword belt and offered me his hand. "We're going to have a word with Master Tully."

VENDORS WERE CLOSING THEIR STALLS BY THE TIME WE arrived at the market. Those remaining glanced up in alarm at our procession, led by a glowering dragonrider and a pair of Lord Hatch's door wardens clutching crossbows and looking perplexed as we halted in front of the lithosmith shop. The guard from this morning had vanished. Alastair hammered on the doorpost. "Tully!" No one answered. He motioned for me to stand back and drew his sword.

The door wasn't locked. It wasn't even latched. He kicked it open. The shop was in shambles. Glass caskets lay shattered on the floor, their velvet linings torn and shredded, the heartstones missing. There was no sign of the lithosmith.

"What happened here?" one of the wardens asked. His face had gone the color of old dough.

"He ran," Alastair said grimly.

"There's a back room," I said, and the wardens went to investigate the curtained-off corner, their crossbows at the ready.

Alastair touched my shoulder. "I'm sorry, *khera*."

"I'd have been surprised if he'd stayed." I kicked aside the mangled lid of a heartstone case. "So what now?"

"Lord Hatch will sort it out with the magistrate and the Watch."

"I mean what do *we* do now?"

"We head north tomorrow morning like we planned."

"And leave all this?" My mind raced. "What if the magistrate doesn't want to cooperate? Or Tully comes back? Or—?"

"We have a contract with Lord Selwyn, Aliza. This city is Lord Hatch's concern, not ours." He sheathed his sword. "There are some things that can't be fixed with steel and dragonfire."

"Whatever happened to *tey iskaros?*"

"We do serve, but we serve where we're most needed. Right now, it's not here."

The wardens stepped out of the back room. "Nothing, milord. Emptied, all of it."

"Thank you. You can go," he said. "Tell Lord Hatch what we've found here."

Both men bowed and hurried out.

"We should get back too," Alastair said.

I followed him to the door. His logic made sense, but it still felt like we were leaving something important unfinished, though with Tully gone there really was nothing more we could do. While he might've paid off the Watch and the magistrate to turn a blind eye to his business dealings, I doubted they knew anything about a coming war or carried more greetings from the Shadow Minister of Els. I hoped.

Just as I reached the threshold, movement from the hearth caught my eye. My heart leapt into my throat. "Alastair. Wait."

The fireplace at the far end of the shop was cold and dead as it had been that morning, but the stool on the hearth had been righted and the bread and beggar's balm disposed of. My shawl and satchel sat folded on the stool. Above it, my dagger twisted slowly on a length of cord threaded through its hilt. The other end hung from the four-faced statuette on the mantelpiece, the cord wrapped tight around the outstretched arms of Thell.

CHAPTER 10

TROLL BRIDGE

We flew from Harborough Hatch at dawn the next morn-ing. Lord and Lady Hatch saw us off, our luggage filled to bursting with bread, hard cheese, dried fruit, and beggar's balm from their kitchens.

"The least we can do, truly," Lord Hatch said as he bowed fare-well. "Safe journeys."

Once we cleared the city Akarra turned into the wind, follow-ing the path of destruction leading from Hatch Ford into the hills of northern Harborough Hatch. We flew for a while in silence as my muscles grew reaccustomed to the saddle and my stomach to the business of not rebelling at every little dip and descent.

"What was it you said to Lady Hatch before we left?" Alastair asked as the roofs of Hatch Ford disappeared behind us.

I spat out the well-chewed beggar's balm beneath my tongue. "I suggested she have a word with Margrey about working at Hatch House." *Suggested* was a kinder term for what had actually transpired; I'd asked Lady Hatch after any open positions in the household and, on her affirmation, gently but firmly put forth Margrey's name. If I also mentioned it was the *particular* wish of

House Daired, and that my husband and I would consider it a personal kindness to the woman who had sheltered his wife from their corrupt City Watch . . . well, it was household business, after all. Alastair didn't need to know the details.

"You mean that blond girl with the baby?" he asked.

"Aye. She wanted to thank you, by the way. You saved her and her daughter in the Battle of Hatch Ford."

He pulled me close. "She kept you safe. I should be thanking her."

"Alastair, Aliza." Akarra's wind-battered voice drifted up to us. "Look."

She swooped low over the forested ridge. Below us spread the ruined field where the Worm had broken ground. The pit yawned in the sunlight like the mouth of the earth itself, still vomiting trickles of muddy water. I wondered when someone would be brave enough to try and close the hole, or if it even could be closed. No one knew how far beneath the surface the Greater Lindworm had slumbered and I doubted anyone was in a hurry to find out. The Worm had been the stuff of myth for generations. With its passing still fresh in our minds, people weren't about to start poking and prodding the dark places in the earth, tempting more legendary creatures to come ravening into the daylight. *Old, deep things . . .*

I fixed my eyes on the horizon. It did no good to dwell on questions without answers, to waste time fretting over riddles meant to madden. Harborough Hatch and everything that had happened there was behind us: let it stay there. No matter how much the creature within Tully wished otherwise, the war was over, and we had other monsters to hunt now. Ahead lay new adventures, and new mysteries, and—

Rain clouds.

The sky grew gray as midday approached, and not long after we'd eaten lunch it began to rain. First only a faint drizzle, it strengthened to a downpour within hours, lashing my face and turning my cloak into a soggy second skin. Akarra landed at the first sign of shelter, the lights of the village on the northern border of Harborough Hatch hardly visible through the rain. The townsfolk were welcoming, and though our plans to fly across the Widdermere in the morning met with raised eyebrows, they didn't try to dissuade us. A few of the older folk pointed out the settlements scattered around the edge of the Marshes on a map that hung on the wall of the public house, recommending we find lodging there if we couldn't make it across the Widdermere in a single day.

The next day the rain had stopped, replaced by thick, wet fog. Akarra's wings churned it like cream as we took to the sky and I was glad of her warmth. Hunkered close to the saddle, with my fire-dried cloak pulled tight around me and Alastair's arms wrapped even tighter around that, it was bearable. Not pleasant—it could never be pleasant—but for the first time in a long time I was no longer consumed with daydreams of solid ground. It helped that I couldn't see the ground even if I wanted to. We flew over a sea of white pierced every once in a while by the tops of tall pines. Watching grew dull after the first few hours, so we gave conversation a valiant effort, though we had to shout.

"Your mother met your father *how?*"

"He saw her theater troupe performing in Edonarle," I yelled, the wind whipping my words over my shoulder. "Mama said he asked her to marry him that same night."

Akarra shook beneath us and it took me a moment to realize she was laughing. Alastair held out a little longer. "What play?"

"*The Lay of Saint Ellia.*"

"She must've made a lovely Ellia."

"She was the sea-serpent."

This time he laughed too. "Next time we visit Merybourne Manor we'll have to ask for a performance."

Are you sure you're ready for that? I wanted to say, but just then Akarra's wings billowed like sails as she caught an updraft and rose, then nosed sharply downward, wingtips slicing through the tendrils of fog as we plunged toward the earth. My stomach lurched. Her wings shot out and we came to a hover. The ground swam into view only a few hundred feet beneath us.

"What is it?" Alastair asked.

"The wind changed," Akarra said. "And *khela,* I smell something up ahead."

"Danger?"

"I don't know."

"It must be close to noon. *Reqet.*"

Three minutes later I stood on damp earth, one hand on Akarra's foreleg, one pressed over my mouth, willing myself not to be sick. Alastair rubbed my back and said a few sharp words to Akarra in Eth, but she wasn't listening. She stared hard into the mist.

"I'm fine," I said. "Really. It just took me by surprise. What was it you smelled, Akarra?"

"I can't tell yet, but I'm going to find out." She rose into the air, and the fog swallowed her in minutes.

I looked around. The ground underfoot was spongy and the grass stems poking through the lichen-covered sod were rough and reedy. Sedges grew in clumps and on low hillocks as far as I could see, which wasn't far. Clouds hung heavy over the marshlands, filtering the late afternoon sun into a flat, gray light. The shadow of a bird drifted through the lowest clouds, vanishing and reappearing every few minutes with the rasping caw of a crow. I smelled rot and damp peat. Unpleasant, but nothing about that was alarming. Water gurgled somewhere ahead of us. "Where are we?" I asked.

"The southern stretch of the Widdermere," Alastair said. "That water you hear is the River Rushless."

I tried to conjure up a map of Arle in my mind as he dug out a loaf of bread and a slice of cheese from the panniers. Most maps at Merybourne Manor showed everything north of Harborough Hatch as a vague greenish-gray patch, crossed by the blue line of the River Rushless and a dark, forbidding scribble that was Rushless Wood. I took the bread and cheese from Alastair and started toward the sound of water.

"What are you doing?"

"Looking for the river," I said.

"We shouldn't wander."

"Just to the bank. I need to stretch my legs."

He peered one last time in the direction Akarra had disappeared before releasing his scabbard from its harness and joining me. "Just to the bank."

It was farther than I expected. The sound of the river took on an odd quality in the dead air. We arrived at the Rushless a few minutes later, our boots muddy and my knees damp from an encounter with a patch of slippery moss.

"There. We found your river." Alastair planted one foot on the bank and the other on a boulder sticking out from the shallows. "Not much to look at."

True to its name, the River Rushless flowed sluggishly in its weed-choked bed. It didn't look deeper than my shoulder, but it was very wide. I was glad we wouldn't have to ford it. I plucked a flat stone from the ground and tried skimming it along the surface. It skipped once before sinking with a half-hearted *plop*.

"Alastair, Aliza," Akarra called from somewhere to our left. "Come. Quickly!"

My skin prickled at the urgency in her tone. We followed her voice along the bank and found her perched on the arch of an ancient bridge, its paving stones crumbling, its pilings trailing long strands of green waterweed. With one wingtip she pointed to the opposite bank, where a boulder blocked the mouth of the bridge.

"There."

Alastair edged toward the boulder. I came behind him, feeling for my dagger as he tapped the rock-like thing with the point of his sword. Nothing happened. He stepped back.

The troll had fallen backward, its head facing the northeast bank. Akarra snaked the tip of her tail beneath its shoulders and lifted it up. The creature's tusked face bore a look of stupid surprise. A gash ran along its neck, slicing its throat open from ear to ear, and thick, brownish-green blood covered its shoulders and stained the ground beneath. Not fresh, but not very old either. Whatever had killed the troll had done it within the last day or two. And they'd left another mark. The troll's chest was cut open, ribs like shards of granite sticking out at broken angles. Nausea roiled inside me as I realized what had happened. The killer or killers had removed the creature's heart.

I thought suddenly of Master Trennan, of his feeling that something had followed him from Lake Meera, and goose bumps rose along my arms. I moved closer to Alastair and looked around. There was no sign of a battle. There was hardly the sign of a struggle. "Could a *ghastradi* have done this?" I whispered. For some reason it felt wrong to speak louder.

"You're thinking of Tully?" Alastair asked, and I nodded. "He couldn't have gotten here in time. This troll has only been dead a day."

"Did this Tully say anything specifically about *Idar*, Aliza?" Akarra asked.

I racked my brain, fighting through the shadow fear had cast over my memory of the lithosmith's shop. I saw the glint of yellow, the twist of his smile, felt the smooth stone head of the statue in my hand. "He said war is coming and the—" I looked down at the troll. "And that the Oldkind are already choosing sides."

Alastair bent down and closed the troll's eyes. "Perhaps it chose wrong." His voice was flat and grim as the river.

There was a splash from the mists to our left. Akarra's head jerked toward the sound, a growl in her throat. "There's something else," she hissed. Dragonfire accented each syllable as she extended her wing. "*Myet av-bakhan*, Alastair," she said. "And you too, Aliza."

We stepped around the dead troll, avoiding the blood-slicked stones. Beyond the bridge the hummocks grew higher and the sedges grew thicker. Rivulets of muddy water braided through the grasses on their way to meet the Rushless. I looked closer. Not muddy water. *Bloody* water. Alarm sang through me like ten thousand lute strings pulled too tight.

We heard it before we saw it: the wet, labored sound of a creature close to death. A centaur sprawled in a mossy pool of water beyond the last hill, her foreleg badly broken. An arrow protruded from her flank and another from her chest, right above a bell-shaped patch of white hair. One of her horns had been snapped off near the root and more blood stained what would've once been a magnificent mane of chestnut hair. She raised her head as we approached. Brown as her coat, with a horizontal pupil like a goat's, her eyes leapt from Alastair's sword to the crest on his shoulder, then to Akarra, then to me. Her head sank onto the peat.

"*Ket*," she said.

It was the Eth name of Thell-Unmaker. Alastair and Akarra looked at each other.

"*Ket!*" the centaur said again.

Akarra replied in a strange language; Cymrog, I guessed, the centaur tongue. The centaur's lips pulled backward into a sneer, but she nodded.

"Your Daired. He is a good son of Thell?" the centaur asked Akarra in labored Arlean. "Tell him to kill me."

"Who did this to you?" Alastair asked.

"Serve your bloody god, *hwe-ha-drach*. Kill me."

"I serve Mikla before Thell, centaur. Tell us who did this," he said, wading into the pool with sword drawn, "and I'll end your pain."

A dreadful sound bubbled up from the centaur's throat. "Your mate does not share your gods, *hwe-ha-drach*." Her gaze turned to me, and I saw neither malice nor hatred in those eyes, but only a deep, lasting bitterness. "A daughter of Janna, I think. She is afraid." Blood leaked from the corner of her mouth. "She is wise to fear."

"Help us find who did this to you," I said hoarsely. "We can avenge you."

Once more that wet, whinnying laugh. "Mate of the *hwe-ha-drach*, mirth hurts me. Do not make me laugh again. *You* want to find what creature took my life? Two humans and a *drachgma* avenge one of the Cymroi?"

"The troll too," Alastair said. "Whatever killed it removed its heartstone."

The centaur looked away. "The stone-son was dead before I came."

"Was it *Tekari*?" I asked.

"Neither *Tekari* nor *Idar* nor *Shani* did this."

Alastair and I looked at each other. "A human?" he said. "Or *ghastradi?*"

Her eyes grew wide at the word, her sides working like bellows to keep life in her broken body. "You speak of what you do not know. This was something old, old, so old it has no name in your tongue or mine. I do not know it. *Ket* take me, I do not know!"

Alastair made a motion and Akarra moved closer, resting one wingtip on my shoulder. "Is it nearby?" he asked.

"It may be beyond the next hill. It may be in Edonarle by now," she said, her voice growing weaker with each word. "I faced the creature when the sun rose this morning. We fought, and I saw it as it struck me, flashing like lightning in the darkness: hatred, hunger, a great void yearning to be filled, and then—nothing. I saw nothing more. I knew nothing more." The centaur's eyes wandered to the far edge of the pool, where a crossbow lay in the sedge. Again her lips drew back, and in that shattered smile was a touch of pride. "It killed me, but first it felt my arrow's sting. I die whole." Her breathing grew shallow. "*Ket.*"

Alastair placed the point of his sword on her blood-matted side, just above her heart. "Aliza, look away."

He didn't need to ask twice.

WE FLEW FROM THE TROLL BRIDGE IN SILENCE. A COL-umn of smoke twisted into the mists behind us, turning the light the evil yellow of an old bruise. Akarra had laid the troll's corpse out next to the centaur and burned the *Idar* together. They weren't *Shani*, but they weren't *Tekari* either, and after coming to such an end we couldn't deny them the dignity of a pyre. There was little else we could do.

Questions clawed at me as we plunged into the sea of mist that stood over the Widdermere Marshes, dark questions with even darker answers. *If it was neither human nor Oldkind, what else could it be?*

"I'm sorry, Aliza," Alastair said, his lips close to my ear.

I reeled myself back from my dreadful calculations. "For what?"

He rested his chin on my shoulder, his cheek warming mine where his words could not. "The centaur. I'm sorry you had to see that."

I'd turned away from the actual deathblow, but I'd seen the results. I'd expected an expression of peace, or perhaps relief, but she'd died with eyes and mouth open, teeth baring a challenge to the world. Alastair had seen it too, I knew. His movements while cleaning his sword had been slower than usual, as if weighed down by what he had done. I leaned into him. "She was in pain and you couldn't have saved her. You did the right thing."

"I hope so."

"When we return from Lake Meera, we must tell the Nest-mothers what we saw." Akarra's voice drifted up to us. "The Vehryshi too. They may know something the Cymroi do not."

"Or they may only have more questions," Alastair said. "Akarra, do you remember how far it is to the nearest town?"

"No."

More pressing fears lurched to life at the word, drowning out the general unease our encounter with the *Idar* had inspired. It would be dark soon, and if we couldn't find a village to spend the night, we'd have to keep flying. No one suggested we make camp. In the dark and damp of the Widdermere Marshes, with some-thing that was neither human nor Oldkind hunting in the mists, I doubted even Akarra could rest easy.

Silence wrapped around us once again, broken only by the rushing wind, the steady beat of her wings, and the cry of the oc-casional crow. As the mists above us grew rosy, then purple with the sunset, I began watching the ground, sifting the islets and hill-ocks for signs of a human dwelling: a lantern, a plume of smoke, anything. Once I nearly cheered at a flash of blue flame between the reeds, but it dimmed and went out before bobbing to life a few hundred feet away, dancing out of reach of a dog-like creature. My heart sank. It was a fox chasing a will-o'-the-wisp and its marsh-light, nothing more.

A dark shape skimmed the marsh below us. Another followed it, then a third, black-plumed and glossy. For a second I thought they were birds; ravens, perhaps, or the crows I'd been hearing all day, but they were larger than any bird I'd ever seen. Another shape flapped into my peripheral vision. I turned to look. Alastair's hand tightened around my arm.

"Don't scream," he whispered. "We see them."

The shriek of terror lay stillborn on my tongue. Night was falling, we were miles away from the nearest village, and we had just earned ourselves an escort of valkyries.

CHAPTER 11

WIDDERMERE MARSH HALL

Alastair leaned low over Akarra's shoulder and spoke a few words in Eth. She didn't reply, but her muscles tensed beneath us and her wings beat a little faster. He tightened his grip around my waist. "The harbinger's toying with us. Listen, Aliza. They've seen my sword, so they know what I am. Once we've landed they're going to come after me. If Akarra and I can keep them distracted, they won't look for you. You need to stay low and keep out of sight."

I thought of his stiff sword arm and counted what valkyries I could see. There were nearly a dozen in front of us and I heard more wings flapping behind. *Too many for him.* My pulse thundered in my ears.

"Ready?"

No. No, I'm not ready! I was never ready for this! I wanted to scream, but my cold fingers curled around Akarra's spikes anyway. I gripped the saddle between my knees and nodded.

"REQET!" he cried.

Akarra folded her wings and dove. With a shriek like talons across slate, the harbinger of valkyries followed.

We hit the ground hard. I tasted blood as I bit down on my

tongue, but there was no time for pain. I threw myself from the saddle and landed hard in a pool of stagnant water. Feathers and leathery wings beat the air above my head.

A flash. The sky boiled around us as Akarra flamed, her dragonfire burning bright and hot as lightning.

Move! I rolled, knees sliding in the algae-slicked mud. Something snagged the edge of my cloak. Blindly I swatted it away but it sprang back, stinging my hand. I crawled beneath the thorn bush, held my breath, and watched.

The curve of the waxing moon peeped through the ceiling of mists, painting the scene in the colors of dead daylight. Akarra reared, spitting another column of fire into the hovering harbinger. Flames swallowed three valkyries at once. Their charred bodies plummeted to the earth not far from where I hid.

Alastair fought with his back to her, his sword flashing in the moonlight. Every stroke I watched with fists clenched, biting my tongue, living each new terror with him. *Thrust.* Feathers scattered in a spray of blood, black against the moonlight. A valkyrie crumpled at his feet. Another dove. He ducked, spun, and drove his sword upward into the creature's exposed breast. It let out a gurgling squawk, flapped sideways, and did not rise again. *Thrust.* Two more fell. With each kill the silver glint of Alastair's sword grew dimmer, bathed in the monsters' blood.

And still they kept coming.

One after the other they dropped from the sky. Feathery bodies piled about him and Akarra, some beheaded, some still smoking, and yet there never seemed to be any fewer. They dove like a steady rain, chanting taunts in Valk.

Alastair's strokes slowed. Each new attack forced him closer to Akarra, who was fighting with tooth and talon and dragonfire to keep the main body of the harbinger away from him, but she couldn't take them all, and he was weakening. She saw it, and I saw it, and so did the valkyries. One of them dove beneath Akarra's tail and snagged Alastair's gauntlet, dragging his sword arm above his head and reaching for his exposed throat.

"Alastair!"

I forgot my promise, forgot reason, forgot everything. Before I knew what I was doing I was out from under the bush with dagger drawn.

The harbinger shrieked their delight in a dozen carrion voices and checked their flight in my direction.

"ALIZA, NO!" Alastair roared. He twisted away from the first valkyrie just as a second swooped low and buried its claws deep into his side.

His scream plunged like a red-hot iron through my heart. Somewhere inside I knew it was a bad idea, that I had made a terrible mistake and was very soon going to pay for it in blood, but there was no time for fear. *They're vulnerable from above—or is it below? Oh gods, which is it?* Feathery bodies hurtled toward me, claws open, eyes flashing with malice and hatred and bloodlust. I raised the knife—

And watched, horrified, as the sweat-slicked hilt slipped from my trembling fingers.

Something snarled behind me.

The foremost valkyrie squawked and tried to check its flight, but a dark shape sailed over my head and met it in midair, bringing it to the ground with a splash and the crunch of bones. The rest of the harbinger drew back, hissing in Valk as the dark shape divided. The smaller, human-shaped shadow brandished a sword. Alastair cheered weakly as the strange Rider put the blade to good use, hacking through the closest valkyries and sending the others flapping away.

Akarra gave chase. Flames seared the clouds and more valkyries fell burning, screeching, from the sky. After another minute, the flames and the cries faded. All was quiet.

My head spun. I knelt and felt for my fallen dagger. A bitter bile taste filled my mouth as I touched the hilt and I wretched, shoulders shaking as I emptied my stomach into the mud. The smell of blood and vomit, charred feathers and rotting peat stung my nose and I sat back on my heels, gasping. Alastair's scream still rang in my ears.

Wind stirred the grasses around me, combing away the stench of the battle, and slowly, brokenly, I came back to myself. My head cleared. The echo of his scream faded and other sounds bled into my consciousness. Water trickled through the roots of the sedges. A night bird piped its trilling song somewhere in the distance. Three humans panted in unison. Three humans, and something much larger than a human. I pulled myself to my feet.

"You all right?" a woman called.

"Aye," I said as Alastair muttered, "Yes."

The Rider laughed and wiped her sword on her knee. "I was talking to Magany. Suppose it doesn't hurt that you fools are still here too."

A new voice spoke out of the mist and darkness to my right. It was a round, resonant voice and gave the impression of fangs and fur. "Careful, dear. Let's not make enemies too quickly." A pair of glowing eyes came into view, as steady and unblinking as a stoorcat's. "Didn't I see a dragon here a moment ago?"

"She'll be back," Alastair said. "Aliza?"

I sheathed my knife with shaking hands and edged away from the creature.

"Are you hurt?" he asked quietly when I reached him.

"No. But *Thell*, Alastair, you are—" I reached for his injured side. He pushed my hand away before I could see how much damage the talons had done.

"Later." Louder he said, "Who are you?"

An enormous, panther-like creature padded out into the pale light of the moon. It was a female beoryn, slim, lithe, and deadly. Her black fur drank the moonlight. Her snout, and the fangs that came with it, was level with my shoulder.

"We, my poor, lost Rider, are the closest things to friends you'll find out here. *Bhraheg*, introduce yourself," she said to her Rider.

"Johanna Mauntell," the Rider said. "This is Magany, and you're a Daired." She raised her sword and pointed at me. The moonlight glowed off the milk-white skin of her bare arms. Stripes and whorls of blue woad ran down her chin to her chest, disappearing beneath the wolf pelt she wore over her shoulders. "You are not a Rider."

"My wife," Alastair said, touching four fingers to his forehead with an effort. "Alastair and Aliza Daired. We owe you our thanks."

"*Tch*. Don't bother. They're your gods, dragonrider, not mine."

Akarra landed behind us with a splash. "*Khela*, what's this?"

"Introductions, I believe."

"You're in the Old Wilds now," Johanna said without taking her eyes off Alastair. Neither of them had sheathed their swords. "You should know this is beoryn territory."

"We're only passing through."

She snorted. "That's what everyone says."

A second beoryn and its Rider bounded into the clearing, spraying marsh water all over us as they slid to a halt.

"What did I miss?" a young man asked.

"Nothing good," Johanna said, sheathing her sword at last.

"Daired, Daired's wife, dragon, this is the man you're looking for."

"I'm—wait, what?" the young man said.

The silver beoryn beneath him sighed. "You're Lydon Tam of Widdermere Marsh Hall, Rider of Thummerrum, who is altogether wiser, wittier, and better looking than you," he muttered, and glared at Magany, "and who is wondering why he wasn't invited to the battle."

"Yes, what happened here?" Lydon Tam swung off his beoryn and nudged the nearest valkyrie carcass with the toe of his boot. Unlike Johanna, he wore armor.

Akarra explained our encounter with the harbinger. By the time she finished, Alastair was leaning heavily on my arm. "We were hoping to make it to the nearest village," I said. "Can you tell us how far it is?"

"You won't find one anywhere in this quarter of the Widdermere. Nearest is half a day's hard riding due east. But if you're looking for a place to spend the night, we have room at the Hall." Lydon's grin flashed in the moonlight. "My parents won't mind."

"How far is it?" Alastair asked.

"Ten minutes' ride."

The breath hissed between his teeth and I felt the tension in his body as he staggered forward. Whatever damage the valkyries had done had left him in no shape to fly. Even riding while Akarra walked would be a challenge, but we didn't have much choice. I helped him onto Akarra's back. "Lead the way."

THE LONG, LOW EDIFICE OF WIDDERMERE MARSH HALL rose out of the sedges as if it had grown from the marsh. The Hall sat on stone pillars above the water, covered in dark moss and slick with brittlewort. We sloshed up the steps, Lydon and Thummerrum bringing up the rear, our panniers carried between them. "I'd invite you in, dragon," Lydon told Akarra, "but it's small and, well, wood."

Akarra told him she preferred sleeping outside anyway, whispered to me that she wouldn't go far, and bid us goodnight.

Inside the Hall was smoky and dim. Lanterns hung at irregular intervals from the raftered ceiling. There were no rooms, only sections draped off from the main chamber with animal pelts. A peat fire burned fitfully in a stone hearth in the middle of the Hall. The only windows were high, narrow slits under the eaves, which did little in the way of dispelling the smoke. Even indoors the moldering smell of the bog was inescapable.

"Tams!" Lydon called, banging his fist against the doorjamb. "Wake up! We have guests!"

A minute later the pelt at the end of the Hall drew back and a man and woman peered out, both dressed in nightclothes, their Rider's plaits in disarray. The woman came to her senses first. She rushed forward and smacked Lydon on the side of the head. "What in *Thell's* name were you doing out so late, young man? Don't tell me you were hunting marshlights again."

"We were hunting marshlights again," Johanna said. "Have you got any of the duck left, Prudence? I'm starving."

Prudence Tam tossed her head in the direction of the fire, muttering a phrase in Beorspeak. She turned to us. "Well? Who are you?"

"Lady Tam, my name is Aliza Daired and this is my husband—"

"He's hurt," she said. "How?"

"Valkyries."

"Bad luck." Her eyes raked the dragon crest on his shoulder. "Ah. Well, we'll get you sorted. Dragonrider, are you? Don't get many of those around here. Roland, get some water," she called to her husband. "And Lydon, fetch the good bearskins. Come over here and sit down, Master Daired."

I saw Alastair to a pile of furs near the fire before following Roland Tam to the pump outside the door. He was a slight, bearded man with a receding hairline that made his blond Rider's plait hang like an overlooked ear of corn from the back of his head. "Sir, do you have any hush in the house?" I asked.

He looked at me blankly.

"Grows on a vine, has small purple flowers?"

He shook his head.

I tried again. "Passiflora? Honey?"

"Afraid not."

"Oil of the Saint Marten flower?"

He brightened and backed away, returning with a small jug of oil and a few clean cloths. I thanked him and hurried back to the fire, where his wife was admiring the gashes in Alastair's breastplate. "My, you did take quite the talon, didn't you? I'd ask you what you and the *nakla* were doing out this way at such an hour, but we might be better off saving those questions for tomorrow."

"They were coordinated," Alastair said. His voice was controlled, but I heard the pain he tried to conceal as he eased out of his hauberk. "The valkyries. They took turns."

"Marsh valkyries cooperating?" Prudence said. "That's singular. They're usually at each other's throats as much as they're at ours. How many?"

"Three, four dozen."

At the other side of the Hall, Lydon stopped pulling down bear pelts. Johanna and her beoryn looked up from the end of the fire pit, the remains of a waterfowl carcass hanging from Magany's jaws.

"That's not a harbinger," Roland said at last. "That's every valkyrie in the southern Widdermere."

"They were *all* hunting you?" Lydon asked, but his mother waved her hand.

"Enough questions. Master Daired is injured and needs to rest. Roland, fetch some *mrumhgath* and more water." She knelt beside him and rolled up her sleeves. "Let's take a look."

I helped Alastair raise the chain mail and tunic. Blood stained the cloth, though less than I feared. Three violent purple welts crossed his torso. The tips of the valkyrie's talons had pierced the mail just below his armpit. The punctures still bled but the edges weren't ragged and they didn't look deep. Ugly, but not life-threatening. His jaw tightened as I checked for broken bones. "Just bruised," he said.

"Aye, but badly. You're going to be sore tomorrow."

"I'm amazed it wasn't worse, given what it did to your armor," Prudence said as she took the little box her husband handed her. The smell of moldy onions smothered the pleasant scent of the Saint Marten oil. "You're lucky, young master. A few inches deeper and we wouldn't be having this conversation. You owe your armorer a word of thanks."

She flicked open the lid of the box, and I took a deep breath through my mouth. At full strength the oniony smell made my eyes water. "Lady Prudence, what is that?" I asked.

"*Mrumhgath*. Swordsalve, in Arlean. Saint Marten's oil is fine for easing the pain, but nothing cleans wounds like *mrumhgath*."

I decided not to quibble. Something was better than nothing and, remembering what had happened to Anjey after the gryphon attack in North Fields, I didn't want to leave those wounds untreated a moment longer. I tore a length of cloth from the pile Master Tam had deposited beside me, daubed it with oil of the Saint Marten flower, and reached for the box. "May I?"

"What?"

"Aliza's an herbmaster, Lady Prudence," Alastair said. "She knows what she's doing."

"Oh, what you will." She handed me the box and stood. "If you need us, we'll be over there. Roland and I are light sleepers, so call if you think he's about to die."

Lydon hurried over and dumped a bundle of furs next to us. "Don't mind Mother," he said as the pelt to his parents' sleeping quarters fluttered shut. "She's not used to *nakla*. Have you got everything you need?"

"Yes, thank you."

"Good. Sleep well, then." He started toward the opposite end of the Hall. "Johanna? Magany? Are you coming?"

Again Johanna looked up from the fire. "You go. I'm not tired," she said and went back to sucking the marrow from one of the duck bones.

With a crunch Magany swallowed the rest of the carcass and stood. "Come along, dear. Can't you see the dragonriders want their privacy?"

Johanna growled and tossed the bone into the fire, wiping her hands on her breeches. In a single motion she seized Magany's ruff and swung onto her back. "Fine. Goodnight, Daired, Daired's wife. Best hope the waterbeetles don't bite. You might not wake up if they do."

The three padded to the end of the Hall and disappeared behind another bear pelt. A moment later the lanterns closest to them went out, leaving us in the only pool of light in the Hall. I inspected the swordsalve. Thick, brownish paste filled the little box. My nose burned. "Does anything else hurt?" I asked.

"My sword arm," he said.

"The same?"

"Worse now."

I washed my hands in the basin Roland had left by the fire, then cleaned his injuries with the swordsalve, forcing back queasiness as the wounds ran red, then clear. Alastair sat upright with his arm raised over his head, grasping a fistful of bearskin as I worked. It was the only outward sign of pain he gave.

"Tighter," he said as I wrapped bandages soaked in Saint Marten's oil around his torso.

I pulled the fabric as tight as it would go and tied off the strips. "That's the best I can do. I don't know if I can mix anything for your arm."

"I don't think anyone can." His voice came muted, hollow, as if he pushed the words through some great barrier. His expression was carefully blank.

The *pitter-patter* of water droplets drew my gaze to the floor. A pool of muddy water spread around my feet, dripping off my soaked and filthy clothes. I peeled away the damp leather plates, then my boots, and then, figuring we were long past *nakla* notions of propriety here, my tunic and trousers as well. I knelt next to the basin in my shift and daubed away the mud, thanking Janna that our spare clothes had stayed dry during the battle. Clean, or at least less dirty, I lay down next to Alastair.

"I'm sorry, I should've saved some water for you," I said.

"A bath is the last thing on my mind right now."

"You might change your mind if you knew what you smelled like. This marsh mud *stinks*."

"What did you expect, moorflowers?"

The harshness of his tone caught me off guard. "Of course not, but this—"

"If you didn't want to smell like blood and sweat and marsh mud, you should've stayed at Pendragon."

A clump of burning peat collapsed in on itself, shooting sparks into the air. From the end of the lodge, Roland and Prudence snored in concert. I sat up. "Alastair, what's wrong?"

"I told you to stay hidden. You broke your promise."

My earlier guilt flooded back with the taste of bile and blood. I parted the sleek black hairs on the pelt draped over my knees and watched them spring back into place. It was that or meet his eye, and I could not meet his eye. "Yes," I said quietly, "I did."

The crackle of the fire filled the silence.

"That's it? That's all you're going to say?" he said.

"What else can I say? I broke my promise and I'm sorry."

"What you did out there—what you *tried* to do—could've gotten us both killed. I need a better explanation than that."

Shame and anger twisted a noose around my voice and set it out to hang. How to account for what had gone through my mind in the instant before I'd left my hiding place? It was not a feeling; there'd been no time for feelings. Conviction was too weak a word. What was it called, that dreadful certainty of action, that flash of clarity in the midst of madness assuring me that whatever enemies rained down on us, he would no longer face them alone?

Mistake, came the answer from inside me. *It's called a mistake.*

"Do you think you need to prove yourself?" He sought my gaze. "Is that what this is really about? Because you don't. Not to me."

"I know."

"Then why'd you do it?"

"I couldn't watch you fighting alone."

"You can't leap into the fray whenever I'm in danger."

I stuck out my chin. "Why not?"

"This is no time for glibness, Aliza! You—but no." He turned away. In those fire-flecked seconds, the quiet was frightening. "I was wrong. I shouldn't have let you come."

"Don't say that."

"It's true. I see that now. Bravery alone doesn't win battles. Strategy and experience do, and you have neither. You don't understand the battlefield."

"I do—"

"You've seen two battles. Two. I've been fighting *Tekari* since I was twelve. There is always more at stake when Riders fight than just our lives, Aliza, and if we must die so others will live, then it's not your place to stop us."

"Not my place? Not my *place?*"

"It's never your responsibility to protect me. I bear the sword, not you."

I shoved the poker deep into the embers. "Fine, I made a mistake. All right? I admit it. But don't you ever tell me I don't have the right to protect my husband." I felt for the brooch among my clothes and tossed it onto the pelt in front of him. "You bear the sword, yes. Well, I bear your heartstone. This isn't about what a Rider should or shouldn't do for a *nakla*. This is about what I will do for the man I love, and if my leaping into the fray will save your life, then don't ask me not to do it."

"But it didn't."

"What?"

"It didn't help. You couldn't even keep hold of your dagger."

My face burned. "I can't do *nothing!*"

"You're going to have to learn."

I'd tasted anger on his behalf before: among the lamias, during my disastrous interview with the Drakaina, and when I'd seen what the poison of the Worm had done to him, but never before had I felt such fury. This was pure, instinctive, unreasoning, an animal cry against the arrow-tipped words driven straight into my heart. *Nothing.* Learn to do nothing, say nothing, because when the swords were drawn, I was nothing. A reckless, foolish *nakla*, now and forever. I couldn't bring myself to speak.

The smoldering peat threw his features into sharp contrast, each unforgiving shadow edged in gold as he stared at the hearthstone in front of him. "Say you do leap into the fray," he said at last in a hushed voice. "Say I let you. Tonight, or tomorrow, or next week, or next year: someday your luck is going to run out. The next time you stand between me and a diving valkyrie there might not be a mysterious beoryn Rider on hand to save you, and gods help me, I'll die a thousand deaths before I let that happen. I will not bury you."

"No more than I'll bury you, *dearest*." I spat out each word like a mouthful of rotten fruit.

"You may not get that choice."

I turned away, my words spent. He could tend the rest of his injuries by himself.

MUD CLOGGED MY DREAMS, SUCKING ME DOWN INTO suffocating darkness. I tried to run, to what and from what I had no idea, but it held me fast. Crow shapes hovered above my head, shouting taunts in Valk and Beorspeak and Eth, grasping for me with iron-tipped claws.

"*Little bird.*"

I sat up, clutching the bearskin to my chest. The Hall was cold and dark. The fire had burned to ashes and the light coming in through the high slits of windows was moonlight, not sunlight. Alastair snored next to me, his arm flung over his head.

A hand slid across my mouth. "Don't scream, little bird. It's only me," Johanna said in my ear. Shock was the only thing that stopped me from biting her fingers. Shock, and the point of a knife as it slipped beneath my jaw. "Don't make a sound," she said. "I won't hurt you, but we don't want company. Understand?"

I nodded.

"Good. Now, come with me. *Quietly.*" Johanna released her hand but not the dagger and I stood, her blade following my every movement. "Outside."

She prodded me onto the porch that ran around the Hall. Wind stirred the grasses around us. Mist lay like a thick white blanket over the marshes, but the sky was clear and the moon hung near the horizon. In its light the stripes of woad looked black against Johanna's pallid skin. She had the same wolf pelt draped over her shoulders and her scabbard at her side. I pulled away when she lowered her knife. "What do you want?"

She gave me a long look. "You're not one of us."

"Really? I hadn't noticed."

"You come in a Rider's clothes, on a Rider's mount, interfering in Riders' business, yet you are not. Why are you really here?"

"We told you. We're going to Lake Meera—"

"Not the dragonrider. You. Why are *you* here?"

"Because I chose to be." Anger from last night, filtered through troubled dreams and exacerbated by my aching *everything*, conspired to make my head pound. I rubbed my temples. "Lady Johanna, you haven't answered my question. What do you want from me?"

"I'm no lady."

"Johanna then."

"*Shh!*" She whirled around and faced the marshes, head cocked, hand on her sword. "Can you hear it, little bird? Listen!"

I forgot about answering. I forgot my anger too. It was the first time I had seen her back. Someone had carved a sigil in the skin below her shoulder blades, but this was no sigil of the fourfold faith. Deep lines spread across her back in a tree of scars, running from white to red near the tip of each branch. Some of them looked newer than the others.

The bleeding tree. Henry Brandon had sung of a symbol like that in Midwinter tales that had kept me awake for nights on end, staring at the ceiling and pretending I wasn't scared. *The Bleeding Tree of Rushless Wood.*

"Madness, madness, and such ancient hate," Johanna moaned. She clutched her head. "*Ach!* There's something hunting in my mists, something old and foul and so very hungry. Oh, little bird, what have you brought upon us?"

"What are you talking about? I haven't brought anything—"

She spun around, teeth bared. Her canines were filed long and sharp. "Don't lie!"

"Johanna, I'm not lying! I don't know what's out there."

"A *nakla* wouldn't understand. Couldn't. You're not from our world. Magany!" Her beoryn appeared next to the stairs and Johanna leapt onto Magany's back.

I watched until they disappeared into the mists before sinking to the edge of the porch. My knees had gone quite watery. *What just happened?*

"Yes, she is always like that."

I jumped as Lydon Tam peeked out from around a piling below the porch. "Master Tam! What, ah, are you doing down there?" I asked warily.

"Keeping a weather eye. Johanna didn't hurt you, did she?"

"She . . . no."

He swung up onto the porch and sat next to me. There was a minute of uncomfortable silence, broken only by the tap of his heels against the piling. "You're wondering if she's entirely human, aren't you?" he said suddenly without looking at me.

I blinked. That was not what I'd been wondering at all, but gods help me, I wondered it now. "I suppose."

"Yes, she's human, or as much as any Mauntell can be. By the look on your face I'm guessing you don't know a lot about the Mauntells."

"Last night was the first time I'd ever heard the name."

"I shouldn't be surprised. You southerners have your folktales; we've got ours. Though I think ours are darker."

"Who are the Mauntells?"

"The guardians of Rushless Wood."

My skin prickled. "You mean that mark on her back—?"

"Is the sigil of the Wood, yes. Family Mauntell has lived in Rushless Wood for longer than anyone can remember. It's an old family with old blood, and not all of it human." His solemn expression seemed odd and out of place on his boyish face. "Do you know how many *Tekari* live in Rushless Wood, Lady Daired?"

"I've no idea."

"None. And very few *Idar* or *Shani*. Do you know why? The Wood is safe from the Oldkind because that family is the most dangerous thing within its borders."

"Your mother would not approve of this kind of talk, Lydon," a deep voice said, and Thummerrum stepped out of the shadows beneath the Hall. "You know she wouldn't."

"I'm not going to lie to our guest, *bhraheg*."

"Nor should you, but these are family matters and with all due respect"—Thummerrum bowed to me—"Lady Daired is not family."

"No," Lydon said, seeing my reaction to the word *family*, "you needn't worry. I'm no Mauntell, and neither are my parents. Johanna is their foster daughter."

Thummerrum sighed and settled his massive chin on the edge of the steps. "Why do I even bother?"

"She ran from the Rushless Wood when she was a child," Lydon said. "Our beoryns found her wandering along the borders

of the Widdermere and brought her to my parents, who took her
in and trained her up as a Rider. She bonded with Embardoben
and Hurrummell's eldest cub and, well, she's been living with us
ever since."

"Did her family give her those scars?"

"We think so."

"Some of them looked new."

This time Thummerrum answered. "Once a year, in the weeks
leading up to the Long Night, she returns to the Wood. Why
she goes and what she does there we don't know. Johanna does
not speak of it, and if my sister knows, she will not tell us," he
said. "Magany doesn't accompany her. Johanna returns with fresh
scars."

"We've learned not to ask questions," Lydon said.

"And we have talked long enough on the subject as it is. Lydon,
you should—what is it?"

Lydon had started to his feet and was staring out across the
mists. The gray light around us had taken on the dead tinge of
not-quite-dawn and my breath ghosted in front of my face. I hadn't
realized how cold it had gotten. The noise of distant splashing
drifted toward us.

Thummerrum tilted his head. "I know that gait, Lydon," he
said. "Magany's scared."

A moment later Johanna and her beoryn hurtled out of the
mist, sliding to a stop at the foot of the stairs. They were both
breathing hard. Magany spoke to Thummerrum in Beorspeak as
Johanna flew up the steps. Her face was streaked with mud and
her eyes were so wide I could see the whites all around the pupil.

"Johanna?" Lydon reached for her. "What's going on?"

She eluded his grasp and drew her sword. Marsh water dripped
from the naked steel as she advanced on me.

"Johanna? What're you—" I stumbled back as she raised her sword. "Johanna!"

There was a dreadful *clang* as Lydon threw himself between us. "What in *Thell's* name do you think you're doing?" he cried, blocking her blade with his own.

"She brought this on us!" Johanna cried. "She and her dragon-rider!"

"What are you talking about?"

"The harbinger! They're coming back, Lydon. All of them."

CHAPTER 12

THE MANY USES OF HEAVY OBJECTS

Lydon lowered his sword. "You're sure?"

"Yes," Magany said from below. "We saw them coming a mile beyond the Broken Sedge. Valkyries and gods know what else. They're not going fast, but they're headed in this direction and they're not stopping."

"Wake Prudence and Roland and the dragonrider. We have ten minutes." Johanna stepped back and sheathed her sword as Thummerrum went inside. "Maybe." She leapt onto her beoryn and they loped off around the corner of the Hall.

Lydon turned to me. "What did she mean, you brought this on us?"

I opened my mouth to deny it, but a sudden idea stopped me. *Something we brought.* We'd brought nothing with us beyond the necessities—but what if it was something we hadn't meant to bring at all? With no other answers it was worth a try. "Come with me. I need to show you something."

Inside, Thummerrum stood with his head thrust through the curtain that guarded the elder Tams' quarters. As he informed them of the advancing *Tekari* I dug through our panniers until I found the mysterious silver box. I unwrapped it and set it on the pile of furs, telling Lydon briefly how we'd acquired it. "You don't know what's inside?" he asked.

"No one could open it. Do you think it's something the *Tekari* want?"

"I have no idea. Thummerrum?" His beoryn padded over, followed by two larger beoryns and a worried Roland and Prudence Tam.

Their approach woke Alastair. He blinked and sat up at once. "What's going on?"

"The harbinger you escaped last night is returning, young master," Prudence said. "They'll be here soon."

Alastair swore and leapt to his feet, wincing at the reminder of his injuries. Silently I helped him with his armor as the beoryns nosed the box.

"Can you tell what it is?" Lydon asked.

The slim, grayish beoryn grunted. "It's a box. Made of silver," she said.

"Nothing more?"

"Should it be?" said the other beoryn, a massive tawny male. "Embardoben, Thummerrum, come. The enemy approaches. There's no time for idle musings."

What slender tendrils of, not hope exactly, but a kind of desperate expectation, wilted inside me as the Tams and their beoryns retreated to the far end of the Hall to arm themselves. Alastair tightened his sword-belt with his good hand. Fear had washed the remnants of my anger clean away, leaving only a terrible sense of helplessness. I saw his weakened arm and bruised side and thought of dozens of valkyries descending to finish the job and knew that there was nothing I could do to stop it.

"Will you be all right?" I asked. *Please say you'll be all right.*

"I've fought with worse injuries."

"Akarra's not far," I said, as much to comfort me as him. "She'll come back."

"Pray she'll come in time. Aliza, listen to me. Bar the door and don't come out for anything. Not until you hear me or Akarra tell you it's safe."

"I will. I *will*," I said again at his look. "You have my word."

He pulled me close and kissed my forehead.

"Young master, you don't think you could summon your dragon before they get here, do you?" Roland asked Alastair as he joined them at the door.

"I'll try, but I don't know how far she's gone. She . . ."

The door thudded shut before I could hear the rest. My hands moved of their own accord, fastening the locks and hefting a heavy plank across the door. As I dressed I tried not to imagine what Alastair and the others were doing outside, but the harder I tried, the more I imagined, and the worse the images got. For a minute I paced around the fire pit, fiddling with my dagger. Alastair's whistled summons for Akarra were soon lost among the shouts of the Tams as they spotted the approaching *Tekari*, and I heard the rasp of swords being drawn from scabbards as they took their positions around the Hall.

Akarra, come back, come back, come back! If she'd nested within a mile of the Hall, surely she'd hear the sound of battle even if she hadn't heard Alastair's whistle. The Riders would only have to hold them off for a few minutes. Just long enough for her to fly to their rescue.

Claws scrabbled against the front wall, talons raking wood. I backed away as the door shook with a valkyrie's effort to break it down, but the crossbeam held, and after a minute the valkyrie fell away with a squawk. Alastair grunted. The squawking fell silent.

What if next time it doesn't? Out from under immediate threat, I pulled Henry's notebook from my pocket and riffled through the pages until I found the passage about valkyries. "'The killing blow to a valkyrie comes best from above,'" I read under my breath, and looked around. A gallery ran around the upper half of the Hall beneath the narrow windows. I tucked the notebook away and scrambled up the stairs, balancing on the moss-streaked boards as I made for the nearest window. The windowsill was scarcely wide enough to fit my hand, let alone my head, and I craned my neck and tried to see what was happening on the ground. The tawny flank of Master Roland's beoryn flashed to the right. Johanna was a dark shadow to the left, hacking at the diving valkyries and shrieking her battle cry in a strange tongue. I didn't see Alastair.

A face flitted in front of the window, white, bulbous, and fanged.

I screamed and fell back. A nixie squeezed through the window gap, followed by another, and another, until seven crammed onto the windowsill. They crouched beneath their translucent dragonfly wings, chattering to one another in Galeg and pointing at me, mouths open and grinning, each lined with needle-sharp teeth the length of my little finger.

How do you fight a gale? My mind raced; I turned just enough to see the Hall below me without losing sight of the nixies. A heap of peaty ashes sat in the fire pit, cold and dead. I swore. The nixies hopped closer to the edge of the sill, following my every movement with fourteen pairs of faceted eyes.

"What do you want?" I asked, hoping at least one of the nixies spoke Arlean. For good measure I repeated it in Low Gnomic.

One of the smaller nixies leaned out over the sill and said something in Galeg that made its fellows laugh.

"I don't speak Galeg."

"Nor good we speak Arle," the nixie said. "Want we what?"

"Yes, what is it you want?" I asked again.

"Want we what? Blood. Much blood, hot to drink!"

A second nixie looked over the first's shoulder. "And fun, all having!"

"Chase!" hissed another.

"Hunt! Long hunt, many prey!" said the first.

"Why are you hunting us?"

The other nixies looked at the smallest, who seemed to be the leader of their little gale. "Hotfire you dragons, not welcome."

I stood. *Slowly, slowly.* "We're only passing through. We're not here to harm you."

"Ah, but harm all *you* we will." The leader rose on double-jointed legs and spread its wings behind it. The teeth-baring grin returned. "Run you now?"

"No."

"Now?"

"No!"

The other nixies followed their leader. Some rose a few inches into the air, their wings moving as fast as a hummingbird's. All grinned at me. All chorused the single word, "Now?"

Don't run. Don't run. Run, and they'll swarm. Swarm, and they'll kill you. Sketches from the *Chronicle* crowded into my head with images of Riders who'd fallen afoul of a gale, their cheeks torn open, teeth broken, ears missing, eyes plucked from their sockets. *Or you'll wish they had.* They hovered in front of my face as I backed toward the stairs, each step steady and deliberate. A drop of sweat slid down my nose and fell trembling from my chin. My calves burned from the effort of moving slowly. "Why are you fighting alongside the valkyries?" I asked.

"Bird-brothers find fun sport!"

"Don't valkyries eat nixies?"

The small nixie spat. Its spittle struck the board next to my boot, sizzling on the damp wood. "Like them, no, but they eat brothers now no. Haark forbid it."

My hands shook. "Who's Haark?"

"Old, old wise bird-brother!" The second nixie flitted ahead of the leader. "Us give good chase, good blood, good hate, all fun!"

The first nixie hissed something in Galeg and the second retreated. The sounds of battle from outside grew louder as I reached the bottom of the stairs. "I'm not your enemy."

"All not-us folk make enemy!"

"I can prove it. I-I have a gift for you."

The leader's eyes narrowed. "Gift?"

"A treasure."

"What treasure?"

"Come see." I backed toward the middle of the Hall, toward the fire pit and the pile of furs. The gale followed, whispering to each other in Galeg. Without taking my eyes off the nixies I pointed to the silver box. "It's there."

The first nixie flew past me and landed on the lid. "This what?"

"Open it and see."

"Tell you first. Inside what?"

"Humans can't look." Inspiration struck. "Only the strongest of the Oldkind can open it."

A greedy light shone in those faceted eyes. "Strong we, yes!"

"Take it! It's yours."

The nixie tapped the silver with one fist, its head cocked to listen. The second nixie flew to its side. "Only box?"

The leader frowned. "Open it only me. Back."

"Back, you. Open it *me*."

A third nixie flew forward. "Open it all."

"Strongest!"

I felt for the corner of the bearskin.

"Open all, open *now*!" another demanded and, seizing the edge of the lid, tried to force it open. The lid didn't budge. The other nixies laughed and the leader shoved the struggling nixie out of the way, but it had no more luck than the first. It piped something shrill in Galeg. The remaining nixies surrounded the box. "Wait," the first nixie said. "Wait . . . *now*—!"

I flung the bearskin over the gale. The nixies shrieked and clawed at the pelt, but the hide was thick and even their teeth couldn't pierce it. My hands trembled as I rolled together the ends of the bearskin and cast around for something to tie it with. A length of cord hung by the door. Not wishing to turn my back on the nixies, even trapped as they were, I hauled the bearskin bundle to the wall to collect it. The nixie's shrieks grew louder, punctuated by a metallic *thunk* as the box tumbled around inside.

"I'm nobody's prey, thank you very much," I muttered as I tied the sack shut and covered it with another pelt. Only when it was secure did I collapse against the nearest wall, allowing myself a shaky smile. *Ha!* Seven *Tekari* caught, no blood spilled, and I hadn't broken my promise. If atonement could be made for my mistake in the marsh, perhaps it would start here.

A roar shook the lodge, crackling with fury and dragonfire, and the nixies' screeching turned into a wail. I sprinted up the stairs two at a time to see Akarra's return.

The first true rays of dawn shed a rosy light over the battlefield. Akarra wheeled against the brightening sky, chasing the last of the harbinger away from the Hall. Columns of smoke already billowed up from piles of charred valkyrie corpses. Lydon and Johanna and their beoryns were finishing off a few that hadn't died, and next to them, on foot but alive and unharmed, was Alastair. My heart nearly burst with relief.

The wooden beams above me creaked. "They *failed*," croaked a voice from the eaves. It was a deep, feathery voice, ancient and full of malice. My breath caught and I drew back into a shadow. "My children failed me."

"There will be other opportunities," another voice said—or rather, two voices spoke at once, familiar and not familiar, filling me with old fears and new horrors. My mind clouded with swirling images, red and piercing green and a shock of blond hair belonging to someone long dead. *Impossible.* It was impossible. "There will always be other opportunities, brother. This was only a test. But now, retreat. The battle here is lost and we have other work to do."

The beams creaked again as if something heavy had taken to the air.

"Aliza?" Alastair called as he banged on the door. "Aliza, it's over."

In a daze I headed downstairs. It couldn't be. *Tristan Wydrick is dead.*

But that voice . . . I knew that voice.

It took two tries to wrestle the plank from its place in front of the door. The beam landed heavily on the floor, missing the sack of nixies by inches. Alastair stood on the threshold, his sword bloody, his armor spattered with mud, grinning from ear to ear, and I forgot the voices on the roof and the horror they inspired. It was all I could do not to throw my arms around him. Praise rose to my lips, thanks for his protection, or perhaps congratulations on his battle prowess, but I only managed a stupid, "You won!"

His smile widened. "Yes, we won."

The Tams and their beoryns followed Alastair into the lodge. Johanna and Magany stayed outside. Alastair leaned close to me as Lydon and his parents tended to their weapons. "How quickly can you be ready to go? I want to put as much distance between us and the battlefield before dark in case other harbingers catch the scent."

"Give me a minute, I have—*careful!*"

He looked at the bearskin he'd been about to kick aside, then back at me. The Tams raised their heads from their weapons.

"Sorry," I said. "I, um, seem to have caught a gale of nixies."

"You *what?*" more than one voice said together.

"Under that bearskin."

Prudence and Roland watched with swords drawn as Alastair edged toward the bundle, more cautiously this time. He nudged it with the toe of his boot. The gale, which had fallen silent when they first heard Akarra's roar, shrieked all at once, spitting curses in Galeg.

Alastair threw back his head and laughed. So did Roland and Lydon. Even Prudence cracked a smile. "How many, Lady Daired?" she asked.

"Seven."

Lydon bent down to inspect the knots. "How did you manage it?"

I told them how I'd captured the gale. The nixies' argument over the box amused the beoryns to no end. "Petty creatures, gale-folk," said the silver male, whose name was Hurrummell. "What do you plan to do with them, young mistress?"

"I haven't thought that far yet."

"Let us take care of them," Embardoben said. "Unless you want to keep the box?"

Alastair and I looked at each other. Gift it might've been,

but we were still no closer to discovering the giver, and as yet it'd proved nothing beyond its use in capturing nixies. "It's no trouble to leave it. We didn't mean to bring it anyway," I said. "Are you sure you want it here?"

"It won't stay long. We'll have Johanna and Magany take the lot to the Dead Reaches at sunset," Prudence said with a grim smile. "Your gale friends won't be fit to trouble anyone after a night out there, and if your strange box is still around in the morning, well, let it stay there. Now—not to be rude, but when do you plan on leaving?"

"As soon as possible."

"Ah. Good. Not that we wouldn't welcome you to stay, but Ben's right," she said, resting a hand on Embardoben's flank. "Something tells me you shouldn't linger here. The harbingers have never shown such single-mindedness before. They may try again if you stay much longer in the Widdermere, and if not valkyries then some other *Tekari*. Others among the Oldkind may look for a chance to try their teeth and talons against Daired steel. However," she said as Lydon tossed the sack of nixies over his shoulder and carried it outside, "since that won't happen in the next fifteen minutes and I'm sure you'll all be leagues away before the *Tekari* can sort themselves out, first: breakfast."

WE ATE QUICKLY, HUNCHED AROUND THE REKINDLED fire pit with bowls of porridge, bacon burned to flaky black cinders, and mugs of bitter tea. The food all had the same marsh water tang, but I didn't mind. I hadn't realized how hungry I was for something that wasn't travelers' fare until I'd scraped the bottom of my second bowl of porridge.

Johanna did not join us. When I asked where she was, Lydon shrugged and said she was on patrol. As we ate, Alastair told the

Tams about the dead centaur and slaughtered troll we'd found at the border of the marshes. "Do you have any ideas about what could've killed them?" he asked.

"That doesn't sound like anything we've seen in the Widdermere," Prudence said. "We don't get many Rangers out this way and even fewer *Vesh*. Certainly none so stupid as to go through all that trouble and danger for a single heartstone."

"Sorry we can't help you," Roland added.

"Seems to me the *Tekari* have all gone mad since the waking of the Worm," Hurrummell said. "We never made it as far south as Hart's Run, but we saw our share of horrors in Hatch Ford. *Tekari* running unchecked through the city, plucking children from the streets, slaying *Shani* at will." He shook his head. "Be vigilant, Master Daired. The Worm may be dead but fell things are still moving in the dark corners of Arle."

His words had the weight of premonition. "How far is it to the next town?" I asked.

"Six or seven hours northeast as the beoryn runs. Little town at the foothills of the Langloch Mountains called Lykaina."

Alastair stopped with his last slice of bacon halfway to his mouth. "Lykaina?"

I'd heard enough of the various creature tongues to recognize the root of the name, even if I didn't understand the rest. *Lyka*, the native tongue of direwolves, wulvers, and, if Henry could be believed, the mythical lunehound. Lykaina. *Wolf town.*

"That's the name. You can bet they'll be happy to see a dragonrider there too. Foothills east of the mountains is direwolf territory," Roland said before turning to help Lydon with an armful of dried peat.

As they were occupied with stoking the fire, Alastair leaned close to me. "We should go," he said in an undertone. "Now. We've lingered too long already. We need to get to this Lykaina before dark. I don't want to be in direwolf territory any longer than absolutely necessary."

Knowing the circumstances in which he'd first met the Brysneys, I understood he had reason to fear direwolves more than most. Tristan Wydrick's betrayal had left a young Alastair to take on a pack alone, and if it weren't for the intervention of Cedric and Charis Brysney, Alastair would not have survived the encounter. He'd carried from that day not only a lasting hatred for direwolves, but also, as I'd noticed during our time at Pendragon, a keen desire to avoid even ordinary dogs. In any case, I didn't disagree with him. I had no wish to linger any longer than he did in known *Tekari* land.

"Tams, thank you for everything you've done," he said as we rose. "We won't trespass on your hospitality any longer."

"Bah, it was nothing." Prudence touched four fingers to her forehead. "Nothing any decent Rider wouldn't do for another. Mikla watch over you, young master, and Thell take your enemies."

They saw us out to the front of the lodge, where Akarra waited next to the smoldering pile of valkyrie corpses. We bid the Tams and their beoryns goodbye and set off, Akarra's wings stirring the smoky air as we turned northwest, toward the northern mountains and direwolf country.

CHAPTER 13

THE INDIFFERENT

Akarra flew close to the ground for the rest of the morning. A weak sun poured through rents in the clouds and burned away the mist, and for the first time I saw the true extent of the Widdermere. It spread in pools of silver and green for leagues in all directions.

It was three hours before we spotted the first signs of the edge, where the greenish-gray of bogweed melted into the hardier browns and yellows of autumn grasses. Trees dotted the landscape below us, first in clusters of twos and threes, then in small stands, then in groves as we continued north.

"Is this Rushless Wood?" I shouted over the wind as the dark line of forest loomed ahead.

"The Wood is back west," Alastair said. "You can't see it from here." He called to Akarra in Eth. Her rumbled response sent us tilting toward the earth, and I clung to the saddle.

"Why are we landing?"

He didn't answer until we were on the ground. "We need to eat and Akarra needs to rest her wings."

"Do we have to do it here?"

"We're at the very edge of the marshes. I'd rather land here than in direwolf territory."

"Don't worry, Aliza," Akarra said, "I'm not going anywhere until you two are safe in Castle Selwyn."

Alastair settled down on the grass next to her, broke open a stale loaf of bardsbread, and offered me half. I looked down at my hands. Dirt lined the beds of my fingernails. Thick black muck mottled the backs of my hands, washed away only where drops of sweat had slid over them. I didn't want to know what I smelled like. I turned down the bread and picked my way through the sedges to the pool at the bottom of the hill.

"What are you doing?" Alastair asked.

"Washing my hands."

"Washing in that water's not going to get you much cleaner."

"It's better than nothing. I'm *wearing* the Widdermere—" I straightened. "Alastair."

"What?"

"Come here."

He was at my side in an instant. I pointed to the small, whitish shape floating on the surface of the water. At first glance it looked like a duck, but it wasn't a duck. Then, for one terrible moment I thought it might be a hobgoblin, but it wasn't a hobgoblin either. A pearly substance spread in slow ripples on the surface of the water around the floating thing. Akarra drew it to the shore with one wing.

"*Thell,*" Alastair swore.

It was a dead will-o'-the-wisp. I'd flipped past renderings in the *Chronicle* and my sister Mari's bestiary, but I'd never seen one up close before. I knelt next to its tiny body, mud and stink and dirty hands forgotten. Though the resemblance to Tobble Turn-of-the-Leaves or any other hobgoblin grew less pronounced up close, I couldn't shake the nightmarish image of my friend's body spread out on the water. Will-o'-the-wisps were *Idar*, mischievous creatures, but mostly harmless to humans and almost impossible to catch. This one was no larger than a goose, with a smooth, flat face, and long, needle-thin fingers, on which would've danced the flickering flame of its marshlight when it was alive. Its eyes were open and staring. Phosphorescent blood stained its skin, which gaped open at the chest.

Its heart was missing.

"Same as the troll?" Akarra asked.

Alastair nodded and knelt next to the water. He examined the will-o'-the-wisp's body without touching it. "This is more recent," he said at last. "Whatever did this did it today. Maybe only a few hours ago."

I tore my eyes away from the stunned expression on the creature's face. Tears blurred silver blood and green marsh water until I could see nothing but broken streaks of anger, fear, and helplessness. The troll and the centaur I could understand; they were *Idar* in name and practice and often dangerous to both humans and *Shani*, but will-o'-the-wisps were *Idar* in name only. The only danger they posed was to foxes, and even then only to stupid ones. "*Why?*" I asked. "There's nothing to gain from this, and no one needed protecting. Why would anyone do this, Alastair?" I asked.

"I don't know."

"You're both missing the most important question," Akarra said, her voice low. "This thing, whatever it is, has been keeping pace with us. Possibly even from Pendragon."

Alastair straightened with a fierce frown. "You think it's Selwyn's monster?"

"Master Trennan did say he thought something followed him," I said.

"And if it is the same killer, *khela*, then it cannot be a land-bound creature," Akarra said.

A new shadow fell over Alastair's features. It was fleeting, just a slight widening of his eyes, but I recognized it. *Fear.* I felt it too, like a trickle of ice water down the small of my back. If Akarra was right, this changed everything. The creature we came to hunt was now hunting us. I looked again at the will-o'-the-wisp. *Taunting us, more like.*

I thought of the feathery voices and the creaking roof at Widdermere Marsh Hall. Quickly as I could I told Alastair and Akarra what I'd heard, leaving out nothing but the impossible. In my memory, the second voice no longer sounded like Wydrick.

"You're sure it was a valkyrie?" Alastair asked when I'd finished. Whether consciously or unconsciously his hand had moved to his sword hilt.

"No, I'm *not* sure, but it called the valkyries of the harbinger that attacked you its children. And the nixies I trapped said something about"—I racked my mind—"a creature called *Haark*. It was something old and wise and had united the *Tekari* of the Marshes."

"United them against who?" Akarra asked.

"Who else?" I stared down at the mutilated body at our feet. "Us."

"Not the *Idar*?"

For that I had no answer.

"Come," said Alastair after a dark silence. "We need to keep moving. No matter where this monster is, it's our duty to deliver its head to Lord Selwyn. But"—he touched my shoulder—"I won't start the hunt until you're safe in the castle—Aliza?"

Dimly I heard him, but I could not bring myself to move, or to look away from the will-o'-the-wisp. "Akarra, can you burn him?" I whispered.

"I'm sorry, Aliza. Will-o'-the-wisps are water-born. Dragonfire would only make things messy."

"Then I want to bury him."

"We don't have time," Alastair said, not unkindly. "It's not safe here."

"It's not safe anywhere anymore." I raised my gaze to meet his. "Besides, you gave the troll and centaur a pyre. This creature . . . I can't just leave him here."

"Aliza—"

"Please. It won't take long."

He looked at Akarra, but she was busy scanning the sky. He rubbed his forehead, leaving a streak of marsh mud along his temple. In different circumstances the sight would've made me smile, but now was no time for that. "Fine. But *quickly*."

He stowed the remains of our lunch while I set about giving the creature a decent burial. With nothing to dig with except my hands, I could only carve out a shallow hole on the bank of the marsh pool. Flies buzzed around my head as I worked. There were no stones for a cairn, only more mud. I smoothed a mound over its body and tried not to think of the pointlessness of it all. Giving the will-o'-the-wisp a grave hadn't stopped whatever creature had killed it, but I felt a little better knowing that small body, still so like Tobble in my mind's eye, wouldn't be left to rot out under the sun.

I stooped to wash my hands on the far side of the pool where the film of silver blood had not yet spread over the surface of the water. As I shook my hands dry, a reflection rippled out from the opposite bank. I looked up, and my heart skipped a beat.

A centaur stood at the edge of the pool, a crossbow the size of a small sapling in his hand, an iron-tipped bolt on the string and aimed at my head.

Alastair and Akarra saw it at the same moment. Akarra snarled and leapt into the water between us, teeth and talons bared. Alastair snatched my arm and dragged me away from the water. The centaur said something in Cymrog and Akarra replied in the same language. He lowered his crossbow.

"What does he want?" Alastair asked.

"He said Aliza buried the *hwooghre*," Akarra said carefully. "The will-o'-the-wisp. He wants to know why."

"Tell him . . ." *Tell him it looked like my friend? Tell him it was human pity, far too little and long too late? Tell him it was a* nakla's *desperate attempt not to feel useless?* "Tell him it was the right thing to do," I said.

There was a long silence after Akarra translated. Over her wing I watched the centaur's long, gaunt face, wishing I better understood their physiognomy. His expression was impossible to read. At last he said a few words in Cymrog, punctuated with a stamp of his rear hoof.

"He wants to speak with you, Aliza."

"What?" Alastair and I said together.

"And only you."

"Why?"

"Because you're the first *nakla* he's seen in years and he wants to ask you something."

"He can ask her now," Alastair growled. "Through you. From over there."

I pushed his hand away from his sword. "If he'll leave his crossbow there and come to us, I'll talk to him."

"This is not the time," Alastair argued.

"Two minutes. I want to know what he has to say," I said firmly. Akarra didn't wait for him to agree before translating my request. In truth the idea terrified me, but my curiosity was stronger. The fact that he hadn't killed us on sight meant he was curious too. "He might know something about what's killing *Idar*, Alastair. And look, he's leaving the bow."

Without taking his eyes from Akarra the centaur knelt on his foreknees and placed the crossbow on the ground. He rose slowly and waded into the pool, hands raised. The water came up to his hocks, staining his mottled legs with the greenish tinge of water-weed.

"*Khera*, I won't leave you alone with him," Alastair whispered.

"Good, because I'd rather not be left alone with him, but please at least pretend you're not contemplating taking his head at the first opportunity."

"I make no promises," he muttered.

The centaur reached the bank, stepping carefully around the will-o'-the-wisp's grave. Water streamed down his legs and filled his hoofprints as he came toward us. He lowered his hands and said in heavily accented Arlean, "Lady."

"You wanted to speak to me?"

"I'll say nothing in the hearing of the *hwe-ha-drach* or his *drachgma*."

I pointed to the nearest hill. "Will you talk there?"

"If the *hwe-ha-drach* stays here."

"If I must," Alastair said after a pause. "But you will not touch her, centaur," he said as we passed. "Do you understand?"

The centaur walked past him as if he hadn't heard.

I followed him toward the grassy knoll I'd chosen. It was within sight of Alastair and Akarra, if not quite within earshot. "What did you want to ask me?"

"Your kindness to the little water-runner was too late. Late, but not in vain." He turned suddenly and studied me with eyes the color of dead leaves. "The *hwooghre* are not friendly to your race."

"Will-o'-the-wisps don't hunt humans. They're not our enemies."

"Am I your enemy, Lady?"

"That's up to you."

Again his front hoof pawed the ground. "How do you find yourself in the company of a *hwe-ha-drach*?"

"If you mean the man, he's my husband."

"Then that belongs to him, yes?" He stretched one long-nailed finger to the heartstone brooch I wore.

I looked down in surprise. "Aye. He gave it to me, but—"

"And you gave yours to him?"

"Yes."

"Did you carve your *ghuach-hwel* from the heart of a friend or an enemy?"

I frowned, sifting his words for every possible meaning and finding only dangerous answers. "Mine was a gift. And what do you mean, from the heart of a friend?"

He peered at me. "Is this willful ignorance, Lady, or do you truly not know? Your people must have realized by now that the *Tekari* aren't the only creatures that bear inside them your precious hearts of bloodstone."

I didn't know what to say. No Arlean would ever dream of wearing the heartstone of a *Shani*, even if that *Shani* had died a natural death, but how could I explain that to a centaur, particularly as most lithosmiths were happy to sell *Idar* heartstones, centaurs' among them?

"You humans wear proudly that which you know nothing about. I don't understand it. I never have." He shook his head. "Explain this to me. You, who are no bloodstained Rider, tell me why you hold to this custom. Why do you treasure the sign of slaughter? Why do you keep death so close to your hearts?"

"It's . . . tradition," I said, realizing as I did that it was no answer.

He snorted again. "Be cautious, mate of the *hwe-ha-drach*. Thoughtless traditions can breed subtle evils, and where death is honored more death will follow." He turned and began walking down the far side of the hummock. "If you cannot answer my question, I have nothing more to say to you."

"Wait!" The other centaur's words burned in my mind, now underlined in the silver blood of a will-o'-the-wisp. *"This was something old, old, so old it has no name in your tongue or mine . . ."* I scrambled after him, slipped on a patch of mud, and slid to a halt only a foot from his front hooves. "Centaur, wait," I panted.

He stopped and looked down with an expression of frank disdain. "I am called Qiryn."

"Qiryn, then. The will-o'-the-wisp. Do you know what killed it?"

"I don't know who would kill a *hwooghre* and I don't care. It was cruel and thoughtless, but the water-runners are not of my blood. Its life was not mine to guard." He turned to go.

"The same creature killed a centaur on the other side of the marsh."

"*What?*"

"At the troll bridge. It killed the troll and cut out its heart, then shot a centaur and left her for dead." I didn't add that Alastair was the one to deliver the actual deathblow. "We think the same thing that killed—"

He spun to face me. "Her name! Did she tell you her name?"

"No."

"What did she look like?"

"She was chestnut, and she had a white patch on her chest." I touched my lower stomach. "Here. Shaped like a bell."

Qiryn threw back his head and reared, uttering a wordless

cry. He came down hard, clutching his horns in his hands. "Ah, Cyrsha! *Nymmer-hwi mhel ghoorha!*" he moaned in Cymrog. "You saw her die, Lady? Without a doubt, Cyrsha is dead?"

I nodded.

"*Ach!*"

"I'm sorry," I said. "We gave her a pyre."

Qiryn's sides heaved. "Then you did her honor, human though you are. We'll not forget it, but now you must go. Leave the marshes, you and your mate and your *drachgma*. The Cymroi are going hunting, and when we hunt, even a *drachgma* will not wish to be in our way. We will find this thing that killed Cyrsha and the *hwooghre* and the stone-son and its broken body will feed the carrion birds for weeks to come." He looked up. "Leave this place, Lady. Go. Now!"

With that he galloped down the opposite side of the hill, bellowing a summons in Cymrog that made my blood tingle and the hair stand up on the back of my neck. I hurried down the slope.

"What happened? Where is he going?" Alastair asked. One of Akarra's wingtips rested on his shoulder. I wondered how long she'd been holding him back.

"I told him about what we found at the troll bridge. He's marshaling the rest of the centaurs to hunt down whatever killed her." The fear I hadn't realized I'd been suppressing gave me the strength to vault onto Akarra's back faster than I ever had before, dragging Alastair up after me. "We need to get out of here."

THAT FEAR CONDENSED AS WE FLEW, HARDENING INTO A knot in the pit of my stomach. Every few minutes I found myself searching the sky for some sign of the monster following us: dark wings with blood-encrusted feathers, or shadows like a shell hiding something long dead, or some other terrible monster

I as yet had no notion of. But the sky stayed clear and bright. Hours passed and we didn't see anything larger than a sparrow. Gradually my fear settled, Alastair's arms around me an anchor to everything safe and sane and good amid the madness of the marshes.

As the sun started lengthening behind us we caught our first glimpse of the eastern mountains. Not long after their gray peaks came into view Akarra turned north, flying parallel to the mountains for several hours before nosing east again. Foothills rose beneath us. Dark firs covered the craggy slopes, casting long shadows onto the cliffs to our right.

"There's a town up ahead," Akarra shouted a few minutes later. The tip of her tail skimmed the tops of the trees, sending needles flying in our wake. "Looks big enough to spend the night." No sooner had she said it than we passed through a clearing and saw for ourselves. It was a large town, well situated at the top of a hill and encircled by a massive stone wall. Thatched and gabled roofs peeped over the edge of the wall. *Lykaina.*

Movement from the ground caught my eye and I gasped. "Alastair, look."

His grip tightened around my waist. "I know."

A pack of wolves ran below us, leaping over fallen tree trunks and hurtling over boulders like a silent gray wave. The smallest was the size of Lord Merybourne's prize sighthound. The largest was the size of a mule.

"Akarra," he said, "we're being tracked."

She banked west. I doubled over the saddlebow as she caught an updraft and climbed, following the curve of the hill toward the town. The pack bounded after us with preternatural speed, their howls growing frantic as we drew closer to the wall. And then they weren't wolves anymore. I nearly lost my seat from surprise as the first creature in the pack leapt into the air, its body writhing, and fell back to the ground on two human legs. With a loping gait it closed the distance between us as Akarra's claws touched the top of the wall.

"Hoooo there!" he howled up. Fine gray hair covered him from foot to forehead, and though he looked human enough from a distance, he had a little too much jaw and a few too many fangs to be mistaken for one up close.

"Wulvers are *Shani*, aren't they?" I asked Alastair in a whisper.

"So they say."

The wulver below stared up at us with unblinking silver-gray eyes, his hands and the claws that came with them resting on the wall. The rest of the pack gathered around their leader in their wolf-forms, tongues lolling from their mouths, watching us with heads cocked to one side.

Akarra spread her wings to keep her balance. "What do you want, wulver?"

"The gate is that w-w-way," he said, pointing south. A doggish growl accented his *w*'s. "W-what are you doing up there?"

"I don't like being followed," she snarled.

"But w-we come to w-welcome you! W-welcome, w-w-w-welcome!" he cried, and the rest of the howling joined in, leaping and yipping their greeting in Lyka.

Akarra looked over her shoulder. "I'd rather land at the gate than try to find an empty street."

"Fine," Alastair said. "Just—don't turn your back on them, all right?"

She sailed off the top of the wall. The howling followed us around the edge of town to the place where the gate stood shut and barred, but the first wulver bounded forward before we could fly away, holding out a hairy hand. "W-wait!" He lifted a silver chain from around his neck and fitted the key it held to the lock on the sally port. "W-wulvers always guard the gates of w-wolf towns."

We slid from Akarra's back and collected our panniers as the wulver unlocked the smaller door left of the main gate. Alastair watched him with narrowed eyes, one hand near his sword.

"Good lodging at the W-Wolf's Bane," the wulver said. "Best not be outside the w-walls after dark." He glanced at Akarra, who was studying the crags east of the town. "The direwolf packs w-will find you."

"Akarra?" Alastair said when she didn't turn.

"Hm?"

"I think he means you."

She grunted. "I'll see if the cantor has room in the abbey garden. Sleep well, *khela*, Aliza. Look for me in the morning."

The wulver watched, his wolfish jaw slack with admiration as she leapt into the air and soared over the wall. We bid him and the rest of the howling an awkward goodnight and entered Lykaina. The sally port thudded shut behind us.

A WOODEN DIREWOLF SAT ON PROUD HAUNCHES NEXT to the door of the inn called the Wolf's Bane, snarling its welcome to travelers. Inside was clean and spacious, or would have been, if it hadn't doubled as the local tavern. Half the town crowded into its front parlor. Several took note of our clothes and Alastair's weapons and hurried to introduce themselves, bowing and claiming a blood relation to one famous family of Riders or another. Most seemed under the impression that Alastair knew every Rider in the kingdom, and several were disappointed when he told them, with little attempt at courtesy, that he had no idea who the Brothers Browbeard were, that no, he'd never heard of a Rider from Lesser Eastwich called Corryn Trenowyth, and could someone please direct us to the innkeeper?

When we at last tracked the innkeeper down, it took almost ten minutes to draw him out of his game of ninechess, and another fifteen minutes as the servants prepared the room and we were able to shut ourselves away from the noise and crowd. Tucked away at the end of a narrow hall on the third floor of the inn, the room made up for a sloping ceiling and stuffy furnishings with a goose-down bed, a fire crackling in the grate, and—thank the gods—a freshly filled bath.

It was glorious to wash away the mud and stink and fear of the marshes, the warmth of the water loosening the knot in my stomach even as it loosened the knots in my muscles. Alastair took his turn in the tub as I dressed. Steam wreathed his face and the water lapped the welts on his chest. When I said I would go find some food, he mumbled something I interpreted as agreement and sank up to his chin in the water with a groan, rubbing his right shoulder.

The common room was even busier than before. I couldn't find the innkeeper at all, but on hearing my interest in dinner a serving girl directed me to the back of the inn. "Kitchen's back that way, miss. Cook'll set you up with a tray if you can pay."

The cook was happy to part with two bowls of jackrabbit stew and a loaf of raisin bread for a few copper half-trills, but there her hospitality ended. Wine or beer wasn't to be had unless we were the magistrate or town cantor, she said, and saving my reverence, I didn't look like either. She heaved a put-upon sigh as I dawdled by the door.

"Anything *else*?"

"You don't happen to have any hush or ashwine root, do you?"

"Not sure about that ashwine business, but we got plenty of

herbs drying out in the cold shed. Help yourself"—she waved a floury hand toward the back door—"if you must."

Slatted boards warped by the weather left gaps in the walls the width of my finger, painting stripes of moonlight across the bundles of herbs hanging from the ceiling of the shed. There was no ashwine but I did find a basket of hush as well as a handful of the woody, ropy herb Uncle Gregory called hallowsweed. I gathered up the dried stalks and returned with the tray to our room.

Alastair hadn't left the bath. His head hung over the edge, eyes closed, his Rider's plait swinging free and dripping water all over the floor. I set the tray on the nightstand, knelt next to him, and whispered, "The inn's on fire."

His eyes snapped open. In one motion he seized me by the shoulders and dragged me, laughing, into the tub with him. "I'm a light sleeper, *khera*," he growled in my ear. "You should know that by now."

"Yes, yes, I'll remember. Now let me go!" He released me and I climbed out, wringing my sleeves and trying to maintain a stern expression. "You shouldn't strain your side like that."

"Some things are worth the pain," he said with a little smile.

"Does it hurt?"

"Not as much as before. That swordsalve worked."

"I found hallowsweed downstairs. It might ease it some more. Now come out of there before the stew gets cold." I set the bowls on the table as he heaved himself out of the bath, splashing water everywhere. "There are towels by the fire."

There was a moment of dripping silence. "It can be dangerous, you know."

"What?"

"Wearing wet clothes for too long." He wrapped an arm around my waist and kissed my neck. "Easy to . . . catch cold."

I rolled my eyes. "Tell that to the man who pulled me into his bath."

"He doesn't regret it."

I smiled and kissed him lightly before pulling away. "He's about to."

"*Khera*, please. It's been too long."

"You'll survive," I said, rummaging through our luggage for dry clothes. "Besides, you're hurt, I'm tired, and—"

A cloth-wrapped parcel tumbled from the pannier and hit the floor with a metallic thunk. Alastair swore. Little shivers of dread needled through me as I stared at the floor.

The silver box had found us again.

CHAPTER 14

WOLVES OF THE OLD WILDS

Neither of us slept well. We found Akarra in the abbey garden at dawn the next morning, chatting with the cantor as he prepared the grounds for Martenmas. She sobered when we showed her the silver box.

"Strange." She lowered her head so she could see it better and gave the lid an experimental tug with her wingtips. It did not budge. "*Very* strange."

"It was in the bearskin with the nixies. And no," I said, anticipating her next question, "no one took it out. I swear it."

"Well, someone must have," Alastair said. "Johanna, maybe? We don't know where she went after the battle."

"No, Lydon had the bearskin, not Johanna. And I'm telling you, no one opened it! We would've noticed if a gale of angry nixies had been set free."

Akarra rested a wing on my shoulder. "Aliza, Aliza, calm down. There's an explanation, and we will find it, but right now we need to keep moving. We'd best not lose daylight here. We've still got the mountains to cross."

I shied away from the box as Alastair picked it up, wondering why it seemed to bother him so little. "Fine. But we're leaving *that* here."

"Why?"

"Just . . . please, Alastair. Leave it."

He frowned but did as I asked. The cantor had no qualms taking it off our hands, and after thanking us he pottered off toward the abbey, turning the box over and muttering under his breath.

We set off. The hills outside of the town sloped steeply upward. The arms of the forest fell away beneath us, giving way to sharp crags, which left me with the impression that we were flying over rows and rows of broken teeth. Dreadful as that image was, I was glad of the shift in landscape. The days of our journey from Pendragon had begun to blur together, each a windswept cycle of crowded inns and the squeak of leather and the mealy taste of bardsbread and dull misty marshlands beneath us, accompanied always by the smell of sweat and dragon. Here at least the mountains provided some interesting views. Even better, the sky had stayed clear, with neither hint nor sight of whatever it was that had pursued us in the Widdermere.

We landed in a mountain meadow for lunch. Steely peaks the color of a gryphon's heartstone rose high all around us. Snow dusted their slopes, and while the sun shone over the little clearing, the wind was cold. I was happy I'd donned my fur-lined cloak before we'd left Lykaina.

"How's your side?" I asked Alastair as we packed away what remained of our hasty meal.

"Better."

"Worth the smell?"

He made a face and I laughed. The compress of crushed hallowsweed I'd prepared in Lykaina had seeped through his armor, enveloping him in a pungent cloud that smelled of cut grass and sour earth.

"You're lucky I respect your skills or I would've scraped it off before we'd passed—Aliza, your nose!"

I touched my nose and stared dumbly at the blood on my fingers. "What in the world?"

"Oh, bad luck," Akarra said. "It's the mountains. Thin air."

I fumbled in the pouch at my hip for a handkerchief as I tilted my head back. "Well, blast," I muttered. It came out more like "*bladth*."

"I'll fly as low as I can, but we'll have to keep climbing for a little while before we reach the pass to Lake Langloch," she said as Alastair helped me mount. "It's on the other side of the range."

"How mudch farther to Castle Selwyn?" I said through the handkerchief.

"Two days. We'll spend the night near the Langloch and make it to Lake Meera by the next evening."

Several minutes later I pulled the handkerchief away and felt my nose. It'd stopped bleeding, but I tucked the square of linen into my cuff in case it started up again. *Just two more days*, I told myself. Two days until we could sleep in the same bed more than one night in a row, and eat real meals and wear clothes that stayed clean and enjoy the feeling of muscles that didn't ache every moment. Two days to the safety of Castle Selwyn.

Two days until the real hunt begins. The corollary dampened my excitement. I was a fool to think clear skies today meant an end of our danger. Whatever had slain the *Idar*, whatever had killed the girl from Lake Meera, whatever had cut out the heartstones of the creatures in the Widdermere, that monster was still out there. I gripped Alastair's arm a little tighter, wondering suddenly if this creature planned to reveal itself before we reached Castle Selwyn.

If it had been keeping pace with us, there was nothing to prevent a confrontation here in the wilds, without the protection of the castle walls. And if it did, I would once more be a liability.

As if you were ever anything else.

I shoved that thought aside, but the guilt remained.

MY NOSE DIDN'T BLEED AGAIN, BUT DIZZINESS CONTINued to plague me each time Akarra banked. Alastair leaned forward as we climbed, pressing us almost flat against her back as she zigzagged up the mountain face. I'd just made up my mind to ask if we could rest for a bit when we flew over the summit of the pass and I forgot all about landing.

Before us, spread out in the narrow valley between mountain ranges, shone the wide silver ribbon of the Langloch. The late afternoon sun sparkled over the rippling waters, reflecting the blue and dappled gray of the sky. We landed as the sun dipped below the western edge of the mountains, filling the valley with cool blue shadow. Lights flickered to life on the walls of the nearest town on the shores of the lake, a fishing settlement that Alastair said went by the name Langdred. After assuring a handful of fisherman that their boats were in no danger of going up in flames if she stayed, Akarra bid us goodnight and settled in a rocky hollow near the docks.

Our arrival ignited a storm of whispers as we wound our way through the marketplace, reminding me of the furor Alastair had created when he first arrived in Hart's Run. I smiled as we entered an inn called the Selkie's Stoop. At least he didn't resort to kicking his admirers across the garden anymore.

It was warm inside the inn, almost stifling, and our cloaks came off the instant we crossed the threshold. "Room for the night?" A red-faced woman with a snub nose and an air of being always in a hurry appeared at my elbow. "Supper's extra and—oh, begging your pardon, milord." She started and curtsied at the sight of the Daired crest. "And lady. Er, never mind that. Supper's included. Only a silver."

The room she showed us to was cozy if unremarkable, and after washing and changing, we headed back downstairs. A fire the size of a full-grown wyvern blazed at one end of the common room. Patrons hunched around the tables mostly gave us vague glances as we entered and returned to their conversations. One or two gave us longer looks, but they too turned away after a few seconds.

Several minutes later the innkeeper reappeared. "Here you are, milord, milady," she said, leading us to a table and setting down a basket of bread and a flagon of wine. She poured us each a glass. "Compliments of the, uh, cook. Best vintage you'll find in Langdred."

The flagon twitched in her hand as the front door swung open with a bang, admitting two more men and a petite woman, whose flaming, Charis-red hair drew my attention at once. All three of them joined a cloaked man at the farthest table and spoke in low tones.

"Supper'll be right out," the innkeeper said before bustling away.

Alastair took a sip and grimaced at her retreating back. "Barton would *weep* to hear that called a good vintage. I hope Lord Selwyn keeps a better cellar."

"Aye, let's hope." I raised my glass.

A motion from the red-haired woman caught my eye. She leaned forward, lips parted, watching us with the unblinking intensity of a cat. The instant our eyes met she turned away, but it wasn't enough to hide the shrewd light that gleamed there, nor the way her companions tried not to sneak glances in our direction and failed. The cloaked man had thrown back his hood, revealing a nose like a hawk's and cheekbones sharp enough to cast shadows. He smiled a little as Alastair drank, and cold dread settled in the pit of my stomach.

I looked down at the cup in my hand. Beneath the bouquet I caught the smell of musty cupboards and old cheese. I set it down.

"Alastair, don't drink the wine," I said.

He froze, the glass on his lips. "Why?"

"It's got valerian in it," I whispered, fighting back the now-familiar taste of panic. "Someone wants us to sleep."

"Who?"

Without turning my head, I nodded toward the end of the table.

He wiped his mouth with the back of his hand. The other crept toward the buckles that held his scabbard in place. "How long do I have?" he asked quietly.

I checked to see how much he'd drunk. Whoever had added the valerian had done a poor job of disguising it, but that made it all the more potent, and I had no idea what else they had added. "A few minutes before you start to feel it. Maybe more." *Maybe less.*

"It'll do." He'd locked eyes with the hawk-nosed man. The four had given up the pretense of talking together. All of them were watching us now, and the last remnants of conversation dried up as Alastair stood. "Aliza, go upstairs."

"Oh, I think not." The hawk-nosed man extended his arms to the rest of the inn. "All right, enough charade. Anyone who doesn't have a good reason to be here tonight, go find someplace else to finish your pints."

Half a dozen guests scuttled out the door, eyes bent to the floor, intent on pretending we didn't exist. The door thudded shut after them. The red-haired woman bolted it and stood on the threshold with a dagger in her hand and a smirk on her lips. Her other two companions spread out around the common room. None but the woman held weapons, but with shoulders that spanned the width of the door and expressions as surly as they were stupid, they didn't need to. Trolls might've made less effective doorkeepers.

Alastair reached behind him and pulled me close. "What do you want?" he asked.

"Only a moment of your time. We have a business matter to discuss," the hawk-nosed man said. He sighed as Alastair undid his scabbard's harness. "There's no need for this to get uncivilized."

"Let my wife go and we can talk."

"Certainly not. Our business is with her just as much as it is with you."

"Do you know who we are?" Alastair said through clenched teeth.

"Of course I do, and goodness me, I've forgotten my manners." He bowed. "I am Master Rookwood, king of the Langdred vultures and acquirer of rare and precious heartstones."

Alastair scanned the room. I turned with him, my back to his, marking the position of each *Vesh*. "Do you expect us to be impressed?" I asked, hoping I sounded braver than I felt.

"Not at all, my lady. Contrary to what some may believe, a famous name is not always an asset. I'd be quite the hopeless thief if everyone *knew* me, wouldn't I?"

"What's your business with us?"

"A simple exchange, nothing more. I want the heartstones you bear. You both want to walk out of here alive."

"If you touch us, I'll take your head," Alastair said, but his voice was already growing thick.

Rookwood sat and rested his feet on the tabletop. "If you manage that, I'll confess myself astonished and see to it that Madam

Knagg never mixes our sleeping draught again. Truth be told, I'm impressed your wife recognized it. In your forthcoming absence I hope she'll be as sensible as she is wood-wise."

The door to the kitchen creaked open. A serving maid saw the *Vesh* gathered around the room, gasped, and slammed the door shut behind her.

Alastair drew his sword.

Rookwood rolled his eyes. "As I said, there's no need to get uncivilized."

"If you don't let us go now, there will be," Alastair said.

"Look, this really isn't that complicated. Just hand over the heartstones and all will be well."

"No," we said together.

The *Vesh* laughed. Rookwood pretended to wipe a tear from his eye. "Your loyalty to each other is touching, truly. Unfortunately I don't have all night, and if at all possible I'd like to avoid soiling Madam Knagg's floor. The heartstones. Now, please."

"My dragon—"

"Isn't here. Yes, we've noticed." Rookwood stood. "You see, that's the real trouble with your kind. Take the dragon from the Daired and what's left? A fool, his pride, and his pointy stick. I'm not afraid of you."

"Not yet," Alastair said, and lunged.

Rookwood drew his own sword and parried the thrust with ease, catching Alastair by the throat as he stumbled forward. "Such a beautiful piece, you know. You shouldn't keep it hidden." He shoved him away, the chain with my heartstone in his hand. Alastair fell.

I stared, stricken by the sight, not of Rookwood with the gem, but of Alastair sprawled on the floor. Again I saw the cots crowding the North Fields lodge and smelled the stench of the dead and dying and heard their pleas. Again I saw my husband broken, wordless, weak.

He'd hurt Alastair.

Rookwood had continued speaking. "I know people who will thank you for this, young man. *Powerful* people." He kicked his sword away before Alastair could pick it up. "No need to get rude. Now, let's see if your pretty wife is more reasonable, shall we?" He smiled at me. "You will be reasonable, my sweet, won't you?"

He had hurt Alastair.

Before the other *Vesh* could cry a warning, before Rookwood could bring his sword up to defend himself, before I was even sure of what I was doing, my knife was in my hand, and this time I didn't drop it. Blade met the resistance of flesh, then bone. A dreadful jarring sensation ran up my arm but I held on, striking upward blindly, furiously, until the last resistance gave way.

For an instant there was total silence, broken by a small, damp *thud*.

He would not hurt Alastair again.

I emerged from the red mist of rage as Rookwood dropped his sword, mouth open in a silent scream. His right palm was slashed open and two fingers hung at an agonized angle. A third was missing altogether. Blood poured from the wounds. The dagger was sharper than I remembered.

"You *bitch!* You filthy, ghast-ridden *cow!*" Rookwood screamed. "Rhian, kill them!"

He whirled to see the woman, Rhian, pressed against the wall, Alastair leaning heavily on the doorjamb with his sword against her throat. "Drop—the—knife," he growled.

She did. Evidently as slow as they were massive, the other men blinked from Rhian to Rookwood and back again, seeking direction. Rhian shook her head, wincing as the blade bit into her skin.

I picked up Alastair's heartstone from where it had fallen. "You're done here, Rookwood," I said. "Take your people and go. We'll make your apologies to Madam Knagg."

Rookwood clutched his mutilated hand to his chest, his face purple with rage. Then, without the slightest change in expression, he began to laugh.

It was a high, dangerous laugh, punctuated by the splash of blood as it dripped to the floor. "Oh, my lady. You have many apologies to make, yes, but not to Madam Knagg." He backed away. *"You have no idea what you've done."*

I raised my shaking knife. "Nor do you."

"I yield, I yield. Come, friends," Rookwood said, gritting his teeth. The veins in his temples beat an excruciating tattoo and beads of sweat stood out on his forehead. "No more hunting here tonight."

The rest of the *Vesh* made a hasty retreat, Rhian backing out last. Alastair followed her every step with his sword, her dagger in his other hand. I shoved Rookwood in the same direction. "Get out."

"For your sake, woman, pray we don't meet again," he rasped, and he disappeared into the darkness outside.

My knife clattered to the floor as I barred and bolted the door behind him. Alastair slumped against the doorjamb. I grasped his shoulder. "Are you all right?" I asked.

"Help me—room."

Somehow I managed to half carry, half drag him up the stairs. Fear of the *Vesh* still held the rest of the inn in its grip; we didn't see the innkeeper, or the servants, or any other guests as we made our way to our room. Alastair collapsed on the bed as I locked and barricaded the door with the chest of drawers, fear giving me strength I didn't expect.

"'liza—"

"Shh. It'll wear off in a little while. Just sleep."

"*Dangerous . . .*" His eyes closed before he could finish. His breathing steadied.

I looked at the front of my shirt, now splattered with Rookwood's blood, and the green heartstone clutched in my lap. "I know," I whispered, and this time it was true.

I VOMITED TWICE INTO THE CHAMBER POT WHILE Alastair slept off the effects of the draught. Never before had I felt like this, not even when I'd killed the gryphon in the Witherwood. My arm ached with the memory of the contact, when blade met bone and blade won. Knowing it had probably spared us both from a worse alternative didn't save the remains of my breakfast, or my lunch. Exhausted but unable to sleep, I paced the room as I waited for Alastair to wake. I scrubbed the blood from my clothes, my hands, and my face, and paced. I set our luggage by the door, and paced. One pannier tipped forward as I passed, spilling Alastair's spare shirt onto the floor. I bent to pick it up, then, when it refused to stay, kicked it upright again. My toe connected with something hard. I tugged aside his shirt and froze.

That's not possible. Fresh horror seized me, cold and clammy like marsh water, and yet for some reason surprise eluded me.

It was the silver box.

I retched again, stuffed the cursed thing back into the pannier, gulped down water to cool my burning throat, and continued pacing.

"Aliza?"

I stopped midstride and rushed to the bed. "Oh, thank Janna. How are you feeling?"

"I'm all right." His voice was thick and his eyes took a moment to focus on my face. "What happened?"

"The *Vesh* tried to steal—"

"No, I remember that." He pushed himself upright and traced the dried tear tracks on my cheeks. "I mean what happened to you?"

"Nothing. We're safe, and so is this." I held out my heartstone on its broken chain. His fist tightened around it briefly before he tucked it into a pouch at his belt.

"Rookwood didn't hurt you, did he?"

"He didn't get a chance."

He glanced at the spatters of blood on my shirtfront. "Then I didn't imagine that part."

"No, you didn't," I said. "Please, let's not talk about it. Alastair, we need to get out of here."

"Agreed." He looked out the window. Clouds covered the moon. "It's dark enough. We'll go out the back and circle around to the north. That'll be the quickest way to get to Akarra."

"Can you call for her?"

"It's too far and the city's too noisy. We have to risk it."

"What if the *Vesh* are watching the inn?"

"It'll be more dangerous to stay. Keep your knife ready."

A TRAIL OF BLOOD LED AWAY FROM THE SELKIE'S STOOP, dark against the pale pavement. *Rookwood will need more than honey and hush to stanch that wound,* I thought with a twinge, first of pride, then of disgust as I remembered what we'd left inside on the floor of the common room: a finger in a puddle of congealing blood, payment in kind for Madam Knagg's drugged supper.

We crept out a side door into an alley next to the inn, weapons drawn, tensing at each nighttime sound and expecting to find *Vesh* hidden in every shadow. A stray cat narrowly missed a beheading as it ran in front of Alastair, but the alley hid neither Rookwood nor his associates. My heart nearly burst with relief when we reached the docks, and beyond them the comforting shape of Akarra in the dark.

After hearing what had happened it was all Alastair could do to prevent her from descending on the town in a rage, following the scent of Rookwood's blood to the place he hid, and showing him what it meant to underestimate a Daired and his dragon. Part of me even wanted her to. It was Alastair who stopped us both.

"No. We leave them," he said. "We leave right now and get to Castle Selwyn as quickly as possible."

"But *khela*, they almost—"

"I know what they tried to do, Akarra!" He took a deep breath. "I know. They deserve it. But we can't. Not now."

She snorted a short burst of dragonfire and looked away.

"We could at least get answers," I tried. "Rookwood said someone wanted our heartstones. We could . . ." I shifted, tasting the awfulness of the words I was about to say. "We could . . . *make* him tell us."

He shot me a sharp glance. I studied the ground. "That would take too much time," he said after a moment.

"If we found out who's behind this, it would be worth it."

"You don't know that."

"We need answers, Alastair."

"We *need* to make sure you're safe."

"Yes, but—"

"You think I don't want to hunt these *Vesh* down? You think I don't want to take the rest of Rookwood's fingers for what he tried to do? Well, I do, Aliza, but I can't."

"Why not?"

"Because I won't put you in harm's way again. I can't—don't you understand that? You wanted to come. This is the cost. I won't start this hunt until you're safe in Castle Selwyn, not for the *Vesh*, not for this monster, not even for answers." I opened my mouth, but he fixed me with a look of such frozen fury the words died on my tongue. "You knew the terms, Aliza. Don't fight me on this."

He mounted without another word. I climbed up after him, still too stunned to speak, and Akarra set off from the shore with a fiery sigh, leaving Langdred untouched behind us.

The moon had set behind the clouds by the time we reached the northern shore. Faced with the possibility of flying in starless darkness, we all agreed to spend the rest of the night in the nearby woods. Stupid with exhaustion, and fear, and the lingering sickness in the pit of my stomach, I wrapped my cloak around me and curled up at Akarra's side. Her wing blocked out the sight of the lights on the far side of the lake, yet even in the dark, with miles of water and an angry dragon and an even angrier Daired standing between Rookwood and vengeance, I couldn't shake the feeling that someone was watching us.

"ALIZA."

I opened my eyes. Akarra leaned over me, her eyebrows drawn together in dragonish concern. "What's wrong?" I muttered.

"It's Alastair. You need to speak with him. He's been doing that since dawn."

I looked where she pointed. Alastair sat on a boulder near the shore staring at the lake, his sword lying naked across his knees. Every few seconds he ran the stone in his hand against the blade, eking from the steel a cold, silvery song.

"He won't talk to me," she said.

I stood with a grimace, my limbs stiff and cold from sleeping on the stones. It took effort to walk without hobbling, but I picked my way across the shore to where he sat. His only acknowledgment of my presence was the slow ring of stone on steel.

"I thought forge-wight swords didn't need sharpening," I said at last.

He stopped and looked at the stone in his hand as if he was seeing it for the first time. "They don't."

"What's wrong?"

"We should go," he said, but he didn't move, and neither did I.

"Alastair, what is it?"

"I'm sorry about last night," he said quietly. "I shouldn't have said those things."

Aye, you shouldn't have, a voice inside me crowed, but I smothered it. Because in the end, no matter his manner, no matter his tone, he was right. This was what I'd agreed to. But I couldn't bring myself to say that either.

"I was wrong about the *Vesh*," he continued. "Rookwood won't be the last to come after our heartstones."

"Maybe not. Probably not." I sat on a boulder beside him. "That's not why you're here though, and I'm not flying again until you tell me what's bothering you."

"And if I choose not to?"

"Then I suppose we'll be sitting here for a long time."

He said nothing, studying the place where the blue of the lake met the icy white of the mountains. I waited.

"It's not getting any better."

I looked at his right hand resting against the flat of his sword. In the morning light his skin looked pale, a sickly pinkish-gray instead of the normal golden-brown. Old scars crisscrossing his fingers stood out against the unnatural pallor, threads of white and purple weaving the reminder of battles long past.

"Your poultices help—a little. Hot water helps—a little. But it always comes back."

"The pain?"

"The weakness. The Worm's poison made me weak. It's *making* me weak. Rookwood was right." His voice fell. "Without Akarra I'm nothing but a fool."

My heart ached at his resigned tone. "You're *not* a fool."

"Aren't I? Even you thought so once."

It was a jab I didn't expect. Time and love had softened the memory of those angry words we'd poured out on that hill over-looking Edan Rose, but I hadn't forgotten, and apparently he hadn't either. "I never called you a fool."

"Only a hypocrite."

"And I was wrong, Alastair."

"How? How were you wrong?" He stood and touched the crest on his hauberk. "When people see me they're not supposed to see a man; they're supposed to see Edan Daired's heir and Mikla's Shield-bearer and the defender of the kingdom. It's what I am. It's *all* I am." He let his hand fall. "Except I'm not. I can't protect you. I can't even protect myself anymore."

"What happened back there wasn't your fault."

"I could have stopped it."

"Alastair, don't."

"I *should* have stopped it. I should've suspected something."

"Why, because it's been two full days since someone's tried to kill us? Those *Vesh* knew their work. They've probably had lots of practice drugging travelers who come through carrying valuable heartstones."

"They didn't fool you."

"They very nearly did." I frowned. "But what does it matter? We got away."

His lips curled as if in a smile, though there was no humor in it. He did not look at me. "Rookwood will remember."

"He'll remember that he failed."

"He'll remember the heir to House Daired sprawled on the floor of some half-trill tavern, too stupid and weak to keep ahold of his sword."

Understanding dawned slowly. I pressed my lips together. "Is that what this is about?"

"I don't lose battles, Aliza."

"You mean you don't know how to lose."

"No, and I don't want to. We win, or we die. My father taught me that. It's our way. It's always been our way."

"Perhaps it shouldn't be." There was a time for a gentle hand, for sympathy and soothing words. Now was not that time. "Listen, Alastair. How many Daireds have there been since the Fireborn?"

"What?"

"Just tell me."

"Thousands. I don't know."

"Do you honestly think not one of them ever lost a battle?"

"Of course not."

"And lived?"

He frowned.

"You told me Edan lost three times before he earned Aur'eth's loyalty." I thought of the mural at Pendragon. "And what about Niaveth? She couldn't save her friends. She failed, she lived, and the saints' story survived because of her. The *Shani* are the *Shani* because of her. You don't think she shamed your family, do you?"

He let the stone fall. "Is this your attempt at encouragement?"

"Is it working?"

"I don't know."

I touched his scarred hand and wove my fingers with his. "You are more than your name, Alastair."

For a minute the only sound was the gentle lapping of waves, the wind spiraling leaves away from the trees behind us, and the soft rhythm of Akarra's bellows' breath at our backs.

"We should go," he said at last, sheathing his sword.

The selfish corner of my heart wished he'd say something to assure me that my words had gotten through, that something I'd said had made sense, but he gave me nothing. I wondered as we set off if perhaps it was because I had nothing to give.

WE FLEW IN SILENCE. WHAT HAD HAPPENED AT LANG-loch weighed heavily on all three of us, the ghost of the *Vesh* and the silver box adding unwanted members to our traveling party. Alastair had paled when I told him about the box, and even Akarra had looked shocked. We debated for a minute whether we ought to try leaving it once more, but in the end there was no argument. It had found us twice before; undoubtedly it would find us a third time. So Alastair had wrapped it up again and stowed it at the bottom of our luggage, muttering something that sounded like a prayer.

In the end it was another nosebleed that helped lift the shadow of Langdred from us. The wind swallowed Akarra's apology, but Alastair chuckled as he helped me stanch the blood with my crumpled handkerchief.

"You really are earth-born, aren't you? I've never met anyone with less talent for flying," he said in my ear.

Yes, and I'd like to see you mix a bellboil draught sometime, I thought, but hampered by the handkerchief, I settled on a sharp jab with my elbow. It only made him laugh harder.

"Look!" Akarra called. "Aliza, Alastair, look."

We crested the last snow-capped mountain pass. Before us spread the blue-black waters of Lake Meera and there, glimmering with a thousand lights at the northernmost tip of the lake, sat the splendid edifice of Castle Selwyn. We had arrived.

CHAPTER 15

THE HOUSE OF SNOW AND STONE

The first stars were appearing over the mountain peaks as Akarra started her descent toward the castle, which rose like a buttressed and turreted icicle from the brow of a cliff overlooking the lake. To the east, an inlet curved around the castle's promontory and a long quay divided the waters as they flowed inland. The torches of a town glimmered along both eastern and western shores, but Castle Selwyn sat apart at the mouth of the lake, a lonely fortress of light in the gathering sea of night.

We landed in an empty courtyard. No grooms loitered by the gate leading to the stables; no guards stood at the door. Though lanterns burned in almost every window the castle was strangely quiet.

"Where is everyone?" Akarra asked as we dismounted.

"Do you think they knew we were coming?" I asked. If Master Trennan's gyrfalcon had somehow been waylaid, Lord Selwyn wouldn't have known to expect us. Trennan was probably still on the road.

Alastair shrugged and knocked. The door swallowed the sound with a hundred mahogany mouths, the carved faces of merfolk and sirens grimacing at us from their places on the lintel.

"Maybe they're all in bed," I said.

"It's too early for that." He reached for the doorknob, a great silver merman's head crowned in waterweeds.

"What are you doing?"

"I'm not standing out here all night," he said, and twisted the knob. It was open.

"Let me know when you find someone, *khela*," Akarra said. She peered east over the courtyard wall. "This place doesn't feel right."

Like the courtyard, the foyer was empty. I turned around a few times in the middle of the floor to take it in. Everything about the interior of Castle Selwyn was elongated: tall but narrow, with staircases and balconies and pillared galleries stacked one on top of the other, branching into towers like needles at the very summit.

"Hello?" Alastair called. "Lord Selwyn?"

No one answered. I looked around. A half-dozen doorways led from the foyer, some paneled in wood or carved like the front door, some hung with tapestries, some showing glimpses of firelight or long corridors beyond. One was plainer than the rest, a simple stone arch leading into an unadorned hallway. I started down it.

"Where are you going?" Alastair asked, hurrying after me.

"Kitchens."

"Aliza, we should wait for Selwyn—"

"Oh come on, Alastair. Not to *eat*. If no one's there, then we'll know to start worrying."

He hesitated beneath the arch. "Are you sure this goes to the kitchens?"

"Not at all, but if I'm wrong, you can choose the next place we look," I said.

I was wrong. The corridor twisted around the outside of the castle, the windows on our left throwing shards of moonlight on the floor in the dim space between torches. The hall ended in an alcove with neither doors nor windows, merely a wooden bench against the wall. A single painting hung above the bench—but what a painting it was! It was a portrait of a man and woman, undoubtedly Lord and Lady Selwyn, nearly as tall as me and done in the same masterful style as the portraits at House Pendragon. The gaudiness of its gilt frame seemed almost a pity. A Tornay deserved something less distracting. I found myself staring at the depiction of Lady Selwyn. If Tornay had painted faithfully, the mistress of the castle was an unusually beautiful woman.

Alastair took my arm. "My turn?"

"Aye, your turn."

He smiled, but tension wreathed his eyes and his hand on my arm suddenly seemed protective rather than conciliatory. "I don't like this."

"Who are you?" came a voice from behind us.

I yelped as Alastair's fingers dug into my arm. We spun around. An old woman dressed in the plain livery of a household servant stood in the corridor. The corridor that had, just a moment before, been empty.

"Who are you?" she said again.

"Alastair and Aliza Daired," Alastair answered. He did not relax his grip on my arm. "Lord Selwyn commissioned us—"

"You should not have come."

"Excuse me?"

"Lord Selwyn should not have sent for you. Go home."

"Where is he?"

"Did you not hear me? Go home!"

"Madam, you must know I can't do that," he said coldly. "Where is he?"

She turned away. "If you will not leave, then look to the lake, but know that you waste your steel here. You cannot protect us."

"Is Lord Selwyn at the lake now?"

"Yes."

She watched us in silence as we started back along the winding hall. When I looked over my shoulder, she was gone.

AKARRA HAD NOT LEFT THE COURTYARD. SHE PACED along the east wall, sniffing the wind. When we told her about the old woman and what she'd said, she agreed to investigate the lake at once. "I thought I'd noticed something over on the eastern shore. There's a commotion."

Neither she nor Alastair suggested I stay behind in the castle.

We flew east over the quay and the castle promontory. A lantern hung from the end of the quay, its rays piercing the nighttime mists rising from the lake, and soon we could see for ourselves the tumult onshore. Torches bobbed by the water's edge, and the sound of shouting and splashing reached our ears as Akarra landed on the beach at the edge of the circle of light. The shouts ceased. In the silence, a voice cried out. "Who goes there?"

Alastair announced us and a second man, one with long silver hair, stepped forward. I recognized him immediately. He even wore the same wheel-and-trident pin as his portrait. "Lord Daired! Thank the gods," Lord Selwyn said. "And . . ." His expression went carefully blank. "Ah. I see you brought Lady Daired. Well. Yes. I'm so glad you've arrived."

"One of your servants told us to come here," Alastair said. "What's going on?"

Selwyn beckoned us over to the shore. "Bad business, my lord. Come see."

The crowd parted to let us pass, and I caught everything from suspicion to disappointment on their faces as they took in the sight of their first Daireds. One bearded man even sneered.

"I told you about the girl who went missing, didn't I?" Selwyn
said.

"Yes."

"We found her."

A girl's body lay on the stones at the water's edge, her hair tangled with waterweeds, her dress ragged and torn. Her face and
neck were swollen to a nightmarish size, the skin mottled green
and livid. Eyes that might've once been blue stared at something we
could not see, their surface now clouded by water and decay. Her
flesh looked one careless touch away from falling off her bones. I
covered my mouth as Alastair crouched next to the corpse.

"When did you find her?"

"Brigsley-Baine did." Selwyn nodded to a short, plump woman
in the robes of a cantor hovering at the front of the crowd. "Not a
half hour ago."

"That's right, Your Lordship," Cantor Brigsley-Baine said. "I
was out for my nightly stroll when I heard splashing from the lake.
Merfolk don't usually come this close to town, so I went to see
what was the matter. A few of them were towing poor Isolde's
body there. They pushed it up on the shore and swam away."

I looked out across the lake. Dark shapes floated a hundred
yards from shore. When they saw us, they ducked underwater
and disappeared.

The townsfolk backed away to let Akarra through. She leaned
close to examine the body. "How long had she been missing?"

"A few weeks."

"No bites or claw marks, *khela*," Akarra muttered. "And no de-
fensive wounds I can see."

And no heart removed, I thought.

Alastair nodded. "Lord Selwyn, Cantor Brigsley-Baine, do you
know how she died?"

"We think drowning, my lord," the cantor said, "but the Lake Meera merfolk have never been malicious before. We can't imagine why they'd wish to harm her. Isolde was a sweet girl, and she knew better than to provoke the water-folk."

Akarra reached out with one wingtip and touched the girl's cheek. Her head lolled to the side—a horrible sight I felt confident I'd be seeing again in my nightmares for weeks to come—but something about the motion seemed odd too. Akarra nodded. "There. It wasn't drowning. Her neck was broken."

The cantor gasped, and she and a number of others made the fourfold gesture as if to ward away the evil that had touched their shores. Selwyn straightened and addressed the townsfolk. "Friends, go home. You can do nothing more tonight."

"Sir, what about her body?" the cantor said.

"The girl served my house for many years," Selwyn said. "She had no family but us. Castle Selwyn will see to it she gets a proper pyre."

With grave mutters and the quiet shuffle of feet the bulk of the crowd dispersed, taking their torches with them. Most that remained wore the navy livery of the castle. A man with the four-cornered hat of a magistrate came forward and plucked Selwyn's elbow. "My lord, a word?" Selwyn drew the magistrate aside, taking care to stay in the light of the torches. I listened to the two men as Alastair continued to study the corpse. "The guildmasters will not be happy to hear of this," the magistrate said.

"I'd hope not."

"Of course, sir, but there are already whispers among the dock-hands about the earlier, er, misfortune with the *Idar*. If the rumors of an unknown monster spread beyond the lake, trade will be affected. It's all we can do to keep the ships coming in as it is. The *right* ships," he said, with a brief glance over his shoulder. I followed his gaze and saw he referred to the bearded man—the same one who had sneered. He was speaking with the cantor.

Selwyn looked off into the shoreward darkness. His fingers tugged at the edge of his surcoat. "I'm aware of that, Polton, but what would you have me do? Gag every dockhand?"

"No, sir. I'm merely suggesting circumspection. Perhaps avoid mentioning Mermish involvement in Isolde's, ah, discovery, until we're more certain of our position with the merfolk. If this *Idar* business has turned the lake denizens against us, a dead chambermaid may be the least of our worries."

"Why do you say that?"

"Well, for one, the merfolk may not be willing to keep the channels clear when the ice sets in, and with the channels blocked—"

"This wasn't the doing of the merfolk, Magistrate," Akarra cut in.

Both men looked at her. "It wasn't?" the magistrate asked.

"If they'd killed her, they wouldn't have waited so long to push her body ashore," she said.

"She's right. This is something different." Alastair stood. "I don't think she was killed near here at all."

"You see?" Selwyn said. "Your guildmasters have nothing to worry about. Lord Daired has everything in hand."

"Well." The magistrate sniffed. "I suppose."

"Tell your dockhands there is a dragon in residence at Castle Selwyn. That will quell the gossip for a while," Selwyn said.

"It might, I grant, but—"

"For gods' sakes, go *home*, Polton." A new voice spoke from behind us. It was the bearded man, who I now noticed wore the red cloak of a Ranger. He had a hint of a Noordish accent. "That's what His Lordship is trying to say."

Magistrate Polton huffed and turned on his heel.

"Goodnight, Lord Selwyn. Lord and Lady Daired," the cantor said, and she followed the magistrate toward town, leaving the Ranger with us.

"I'm so sorry to welcome you this way, Lord Daired," Selwyn said, though he didn't look at us as he spoke. His eyes were still fixed at some invisible point in the darkness beyond the beach. At a cough from the bearded man he made a vague motion in his direction. "This is my, ah, friend, Captain Owin Rhys of the Lake Meera Free Regiment. I've invited him to stay on at the castle in your friend Master Gorecrow's absence."

"Theold isn't here?" Alastair asked.

"No, though I can't imagine what kept him. I expected him days ago."

Rhys gave Alastair a theatrical bow. "In the meantime, I trust you won't turn away the assistance of a poor Ranger, humble though it may be."

"We can discuss the details of your contracts later," Selwyn cut in before Alastair could reply. "Come. We really must return to the castle. Rhys, give me your cloak."

"What?"

"Your cloak, man."

"Why?"

"We need to carry her body up to the castle."

"Absolutely not!"

"Lord Selwyn, I'd like to take care of the pyre," Akarra said. "Here. Tonight. There's no need to take her all the way up to the castle."

He gave her a sharp look. "Are you sure?"

"You said she had no family?"

"No. But she had friends who may wish to say goodbye. She had been a chambermaid in the castle for years."

"They won't want to see her like this."

He glanced at the bloated corpse, then looked away. "All right. Do what you must. Lord and Lady Daired, the castle is this way."

"Go," Alastair said. "We'll follow."

"You—oh, very well, but you'd be wise not to linger. And watch your step on the cliff stair. It can be treacherous in the dark."

Akarra lowered her head as Selwyn's retinue started up the path to the castle. "Can you burn her body?" I asked when they were out of earshot.

"It will take some time, but yes, I can. She's not water-born. But that's not the only reason I want to stay. I want to try to speak to the merfolk. They may be more willing to talk about what happened if there are no humans around." She helped Alastair remove the panniers but nudged us toward the castle before he could unbuckle her saddle. "I don't mind leaving it on for one night. You have enough to carry." Voices rose and fell from somewhere along the path. The distance muddled the words, but Selwyn's irritated tone was unmistakable. "There," she said. "You'd better go keep things civil."

THE PATH TO CASTLE SELWYN WOUND ALONG THE SHORE and past the lantern-lit quay before angling upward along the brow of the cliff. We went slowly, heeding Selwyn's warning. Dirt and gravel gave way to stone steps. Moss made the risers slippery, and if it weren't for the moon, the stairs might've been almost impossible to navigate. At least the wall bordering the cliffside of the path gave the illusion of security.

Selwyn's return had breathed life back into the castle, and we passed two footmen with torches near the gate that bordered the castle grounds. They relieved us of our panniers and gave us directions to the Lake Hall, where they said our host had just gone in to dinner, but I heard nothing beyond the word *dinner*. We hurried inside.

The Lake Hall would've been hard to miss. Doors three times the height of a troll stood propped open with blocks of marble, each carved in the shape of a merman brandishing a trident. Inside, windows along the southernmost wall provided a breathtaking view of the lake and the moonlit mountains beyond. Delicious smells wafted toward us from a table beneath the window: roast waterfowl and sweet boiled pumpkins and stewed tomatoes and a dozen other dishes I couldn't name. Only three places had been set around the table. Rhys lounged at one end, idly spinning a pearl-handled fork on a plate already streaked with gravy. Selwyn paced in front of the windows. He stopped when we entered. "Ah, good. Your dragon was able to provide a pyre for the poor girl then, Lord Daired?"

"Akarra is seeing to her, yes," Alastair said.

"Excellent." A door opened at the end of the Hall, admitting a handful of servants carrying chairs, plates, and cutlery. They set them out and disappeared as quickly as they'd come. "Sit, please," Selwyn said. "You must forgive the lack of formality. Rhys and I had just sat down to dinner when the alarm went up from the lake and I didn't have time to order places for you. I wasn't certain when you'd arrive."

"Are you expecting someone else, Lord Selwyn?" I asked, taking the seat between Rhys and the empty chair on Selwyn's right. The plate before it was untouched.

"My wife will be joining us shortly," he said. "Now please, eat! Enjoy yourselves. You've traveled a long way and I'm sure tonight has been more eventful than you were anticipating."

He didn't need to ask us twice. I spooned out a small mountain of stewed pumpkin onto my plate, realizing as I did how much I missed eating with utensils.

"I must confess I'm surprised to see you here, Lady Daired," Rhys said. "I understand you were—are—a *nakla*."

"Hm?" I managed to tear my attention from the food long enough to answer his question. "Oh. Yes."

"Is it true what they say about the Battle of North Fields? Did you really wheedle the cure for lindworm venom out of a coven of lamias?"

I set down my spoon. His question stretched before me like the rest of my life, and I wondered how many more conversations with strangers I'd have to start from the bottom of that pit in Cloven Cairn. "Yes, I did," I said, willing myself to remain calm.

"Ye gods. For once the bards are right: you must be the bravest woman in Arle."

"No," I said quietly, and thought of red hair and brandished steel and the tears on her bloodstained cheek, "not the bravest." I cleared my throat. "Captain Rhys, can you tell me anything about the maid who died?"

"And you came all this way just to join your husband on a contract?" he continued, ignoring my question.

"Well, yes."

"Pardon my inquisitiveness, but why?"

Perhaps because I'm tired of people like you equating nakla *with helpless.* "I'm a healer. I hoped I could help."

"Ah. A much worthier motivation." He raised his glass. "Your good health."

"Thank you—I'm sorry, worthier than what?"

"You haven't heard what they say of Lady Selwyn?"

I shook my head.

"Well, *well!* If that's the case, I won't spoil the surprise. You'll see soon enough," he said, and smiled.

It was hardly more than an upward tilt of the corner of his

mouth, but it brought a cunning light into his eyes that I couldn't help but notice. Owin Rhys of the Lake Meera Rangers had the smile of a man who would trust his life to the power of his charm, or failing that, to a quick knife in the dark, no questions asked. I wondered as he turned back to his food how many times he'd been on either side of that hypothetical knife. Faint scars showed beneath his close-cropped hair and across his forehead, some with the ragged edges suggestive of a *Tekari*'s talons, some much cleaner. A few looked rather new.

"Captain Rhys, do you know what killed Isolde?" I tried again.

"The maid? No idea."

"Did you know her?"

"I'd seen her around the market at Morianton once or twice."

His dismissive tone hinted that line of inquiry was sure to be cold. I changed tactics. "What do you know about the slain *Idar*?"

He shrugged over a mouthful of fish. "No more than the rest of the townsfolk, my lady. Lord Selwyn had the bodies cleaned up before an hour had passed. Couldn't have them bleeding out on the beaches now, could he?" he added with a wink.

What is that supposed to mean? I wanted to ask, but at that moment a door opened near the wall of windows and a figure slipped inside. If I'd not been facing Rhys, I would've missed it, so quietly did it open, but the motion drew my eye, and seeing the person it admitted, I forgot even my disgust with the captain.

Growing up with Anjey, I thought myself inured against a certain degree of beauty. I'd thought wrong. Even her portrait had lied. The woman who entered the Lake Hall left light and loveliness dancing in her wake. The artist in me fumbled for pencils, charcoals, anything to capture the delicate lines of her face, her expression of sweet melancholy, or the way the candlelight reflected off the waves of her hair, so black it was almost blue, so shiny it looked wet. She came closer and I gave up. If Guildmaster Tornay could not do justice to this woman's beauty, neither could I.

Selwyn sprang to his feet. "There you are, my dear! I was beginning to worry." Alastair stood and bowed. I found myself curtsying as she took the seat next to mine. "Lord and Lady Daired," Selwyn said, "allow me to introduce my wife, Lady Cordelia Selwyn."

She didn't look at either of us, fixing instead her enormous, unblinking eyes on her husband. "Niall, Mòrag said the child has been found. Is it true?"

"Yes, but let's not dwell on that now, my sweet—"

"She is dead?"

"Yes."

"The merfolk pushed her body ashore near Morianton," Rhys offered. It earned only a thunderous glare from Selwyn. Lady Cordelia didn't acknowledge him.

"I will mourn her." She lowered her head. The air grew still, as if the room itself waited for its mistress's permission to breathe again. Her lips moved but no sound came out as she touched four fingers to her forehead, lips, and heart. Then, as if nothing had happened, she raised her head and turned to me with a smile so honest and innocent it would have made all the bards of Arle weep for joy. She laid a hand on mine. Her skin was milk-white and cool to the touch. "We did not expect you."

"I'm sorry, Lady Selwyn, I hoped you—"

"You are *most* welcome."

"*Ahem.*"

I jumped in my chair. The old woman from the portrait hall had appeared silently behind us. She set a covered plate in front of Cordelia and scowled at the sight of her lady's hand on mine. Cordelia withdrew it.

"Will my lady be requiring anything else?" the woman asked, her tone suited more to a governess chiding an unruly pupil than a servant asking leave of their mistress.

"No, Mòrag."

"Very good, my lady." She uncovered the plate and left as silently as she'd come.

"Castle housekeeper, Lady Daired," Selwyn said. "Strange old bat, Madam Mòrag, but harmless. Pay her no mind."

Alastair said something in response but I didn't hear, at once mesmerized and disgusted by the sight of Cordelia's meal. Beneath the cover, nestled on a bed of blood-soaked snow, was a raw fish. As if it was the most casual thing in the world, she decapitated the fish with her knife and pulled out the backbone. One by one she tore the ribs from the spine, sucked the flesh from the bones, and left them in a neat pile by her napkin.

"How was your journey?" she asked in between bites.

I swallowed, then swallowed again. "It was, um, memorable."

"They say those not born to the blood of the Riders find the sky an unpleasant place," Cordelia said.

"Aye, that's what made it memorable."

She picked the scales from the remnants of her fish, piling a tiny midden of bones and fins in the puddle of melting snow. "Did you fly the entire way?"

"We did."

"You didn't come through Rushless Wood, I hope," Rhys interjected. His smile faded when he saw my face. "Great gods, you did?"

"We flew over the marshes."

"Over the Widdermere? Lord Daired, you're a braver man than I thought," he said in a louder voice. "You couldn't get me to fly over that accursed swamp for all the dragons in the world. Unnatural things live there."

Selwyn laughed. The sound echoed around the Hall, loud yet somehow hollow. "Yes, we've all heard these bedtime tales. *Beware the monsters that lurk between the Wood and the Widdermere!* Children's fantasies and ballad fodder for half-trill tavern bards. Really, is there nothing to talk about but monsters tonight?" he asked. "We've had enough of that for one day. I'd hoped—yes, Mòrag?"

I stopped myself from jumping this time, but only just. The housekeeper stood at the end of the table again.

"A matter has arisen in the wheelworks that requires your attention, sir," she said.

"What is it now?"

"Fyri didn't tell me, sir. She merely asked that you join her in the pump house."

Selwyn sipped his wine.

"It's a matter of some urgency, my lord."

Cordelia pushed back her chair.

"No, no, darling. Don't trouble yourself," Selwyn said as he stood. "Forgive me, friends, but it seems I must attend to this. Enjoy the rest of your meal. Madam Mòrag will show you to the guest chambers when you're finished. Lord Daired, we'll finalize the details of your contract tomorrow morning. We'll no more talk of death until then. Goodnight." He excused himself with a bow.

No one but me seemed to notice the way Cordelia twisted her napkin in her lap as she watched her husband leave. Her other hand traced, over and over, the smooth contours and shifting colors of her pearl-handled knife.

CHAPTER 16

MERFOLK AND STRANGE MAGIC

It was a relief to leave the Lake Hall after dinner, and not only to escape the sight of the fish carcass. The undercurrent running beneath the surface of the meal left me on edge. It had danced around the fringes of our conversation, weaving through Selwyn's every word and hiding in every shadow, but I couldn't place it.

A tight-lipped Mòrag led us to the guest wing. "These will be your chambers while you're with us." She paused in front of a door decorated with the wheel-and-trident crest and cast a cold eye over my attire. "The chambermaids will collect any clothes you would like laundered. If you don't require anything else, I'll bid you goodnight."

She left before we had a chance to answer.

"Odd woman," Alastair said.

"Oh, never mind her. Alastair, *look!*"

The chamber occupied one entire tower overlooking the quayside of the lake. Pillars carved to look like tree branches supported the upper balconies, their beams twining and delicate. Our panniers sat by the side of a canopied bed large enough to fit a family of four, but those features paled before the magnificent bath in the center of the room. A series of complicated copper tubes, the like of which I'd only ever seen in mechanical drawings in Uncle Gregory's library, hung over the far side. *Plumbing*, he'd called it, and he'd cited the bathhouses in Edonarle as some of the finest in the kingdom. I guessed he'd never been to Lake Meera. Steam hovered over the surface of the water. Alastair and I looked at each other.

Never before had so many layers been shed so fast.

I slid into the water. The shock of the heat was no less pleasant than it was bracing and I welcomed the sting as it worked through my muscles and loosened knots in my neck and shoulders. I shook my hair free from its pinnings and sat on the stone bench that ran along the inside of the bath. The steam had the faint tang of old eggs, but compared with the stink of the marshes and the clinging stench of sweat-soaked leather, old eggs were an improvement.

Alastair sank onto the bench next to me with a sigh. "So, *khera*, we made it to the castle."

"Aye, we did."

"Is it what you expected?"

I gave him a sideways glance. There was no hint of sarcasm in his tone, no shadow of accusation or of our prior arguments on the topic. Still, I moved carefully, as much aware of my own latent anger as his disapproval. Safe for the first time in a week, with a full stomach and the prospect of sleeping in a real bed tonight, I had no intention of spoiling this moment of hard-won calm. "I don't know what I expected."

He let that pass without comment, to my relief. "What do you make of the Selwyns?"

"Honestly? I'm not sure yet." I said. "But did you notice how nervous he was on the beach?"

"I did. It was the first time he'd seen a dead body."

I turned to face him fully. "Are you sure?"

"I know the look."

But it wasn't the body he'd been looking at. I tucked that thought away and leaned back against the rim of the bath. There'd be time enough to parse out Lord Selwyn's motivations in the next few days. "Well, whatever it was, one thing's certain: I'll never be able to look at fish the same way again."

He smiled. "You should have dinner with the magistrate of Clawmouth."

"He likes raw fish too?"

"Eels. And he has the table manners of a troll." A faint gurgle came from the pipes and a few drops of water fell into the bath, the *plinking* sound they made loud in the stillness of the room. Alastair watched the ripples as he rubbed his shoulder. "I'm worried about Theold, Aliza. Master Gorecrow," he said at my puzzled look. "He should have been here days ago. Selwyn can't think what would've delayed him."

"Have you ever known him to be late to a contract before?"

"Never."

"And you've known him a long time?"

"We met on a contract near Selkie's Keep many years ago. Me, Theold, his beoryn Chirrorim, and . . . Charis."

He didn't offer any other details. I didn't ask, simply entwined my fingers with his under the water, and for a long while we sat in silence, immersed in our own thoughts. Isolde's bloated face swam to the forefront of my mind, overlaid with Madam Mòrag's muttered warnings and Cordelia's haunting stare.

The water lapped the wall at my back as Alastair shifted.

"You know, *khera*, Selwyn was right," he said in a soft voice.

"Hm?"

"We've had enough death for one day."

"Aye." *We've had enough death for a lifetime.*

"So let's not think of it. Not tonight. Let tonight be for living."

His lips brushed my shoulder, and I smiled. Fears and worries and anger had its place, but he was right. Not here and not tonight. Despite my teasing on the road, I wondered if he knew how much I'd missed his touch. "Did you have anything particular in mind?"

He slipped an arm around my waist and lifted me onto his lap in an easy motion. "I should think that would be obvious."

"I'm afraid you're going to have to be quite specific, Lord Alastair."

"*Tey iskaros,* my lady."

He rested his forehead against mine, a sensuous growl in the back of his throat as I brushed my fingers over the scars along his shoulder blades. Crescent and crosshatch, talon gash and old burns and *gods is he beautiful when he looks at me like that.*

He drew back, though his grip remained firm on my hips. "Aliza?"

"Hm?"

Need burned in those dark eyes, and not just physical need, though there was plenty of that. This was desire that went deeper than mere lovemaking, a plea that had nothing to do with our bodies. *Whatever monsters we face here,* it whispered, *whatever madness we stumble upon tomorrow—tell me you trust me.*

But he only said, "I'm glad you came with me."

"Me too," I whispered, and kissed him.

I'D LOST SOMETHING IMPORTANT. BLINDLY I GROPED through mist and fog and the smoke of a pyre that was consuming the countryside. Faces grinned out at me from the smoke, monstrous, bloated faces I knew but wished I didn't. I fell to my knees, feeling the ground. *Rina? Rina, sweetheart, where are you?* Stones cut my fingers, but there was no blood as the gashes peeled back, revealing bone and shriveled muscle. Black water dripped from my hands, her hands, *whose hands?* I looked down.

There!

The mist rolled away from Rina's body. She sat up, her throat hanging open like a demented second smile. There were funeral bells in her voice. *Aliza? Where were you?*

This wasn't right. I'd found her, hadn't I? *But too late. Always too late.* Tears choked me. *Dearest, I'm sorry.*

I don't want your apologies. You were supposed to watch me, but you forgot. You forgot, and you let me die.

No!

I drew my hands up to claw away that horrible expression from her face, because that wasn't my sister and she was wrong and I couldn't bear it—

I woke in a cold sweat, my heart racing, a terrible pressure on my chest. Seeing the unfamiliar canopy above only made it worse, and for one wild moment I was truly lost. I squeezed my eyes shut. *Just a dream. Janna preserve me, it's just a dream.* It took all my will to focus on the litany, to calm my galloping heart and force my mind back into the waking world. *Breathe.* Quietly in, quietly out, just as I had seen Alastair doing during his morning exercises. *It's all right. Breathe.* Slowly reality crept back in and the nightmare crawled back to its place in the dark corner of my mind where it knew I would not follow. *Breathe.* There were horrors enough here already; I need add none of mine.

A minute later I opened my eyes. A bar of sunlight fell like a gallows' lash across the pillow. Next to me the mattress dipped and the light grew brighter as Alastair pushed back the curtain around the bed. I squinted in the sudden brightness.

"Do you hear that?" he said.

"What?"

"Listen."

"'S bells. Come back to bed."

"Those aren't bells."

I propped myself up on my elbow. The sunlight drove the last terrors of the nightmare from my mind and the pressure on my chest eased. "Sounds like bells to me."

"There's something else. Voices." He leapt up and threw on a tunic. "From the lake." A door opposite the bathing pool led to a balcony overlooking Lake Meera. He pushed it open.

I bolted upright. It had always puzzled me why bards so often wrote verses in praise of Mermish choirs, knowing the danger it took to get close enough to hear them. Now I understood. It was not music that spilled from the lake. It was the love and sorrow and laughter and pain of a hundred souls, breaking like waves over some eternal stone and cresting together to greet the rising sun, and what was danger compared to all of that? I was on my feet and at Alastair's side before my conscious mind had given up its place in bed.

Lake Meera spread before us. Mountain slopes walled the valley in on either side, black and bare, rising upward into snowy peaks. Far below the stony spear of the castle quay shone white against the dark waves. Akarra sat at the end of the quay. The water around her frothed with movement, accenting the Mermish song with the occasional splash. Alastair and I dressed in a hurry.

My breath came in white clouds as we made our way to the cliff path. Mist pooled in the hollows of the hills beyond the castle walls, little puddles of cloud pouring down the mountainside toward the cliff, arrested here and there by piles of fallen stone and what looked like the ruins of an old abbey. The path to the quay wasn't so treacherous in the daylight, but we still had to mind our steps. Through a gap in the cliff wall near the ruins I could see the black waves breaking over the rocks almost a hundred feet below. The lake steamed in the cold air.

"Good morning!" Akarra called when she saw us. The quay was high and narrow, only three or four strides across, and her perch looked precarious. She had to extend her wings for balance as she crouched at the end. The Mermish song dissolved into splashes as the merfolk who'd been speaking with her dove beneath the water. "I hoped you'd be up. They'll be back. They're not fond of humans, but they're curious about you."

I leaned over the edge of the quay. It was a fair drop to the surface of the lake, and even close to shore the water was deep. The stone pilings beneath us sank straight down and out of sight, lost in murky darkness.

"Did you learn anything?" Alastair asked Akarra.

"Not from the merfolk. This is the first I've been able to call them, but I did speak with some of the townsfolk again. That cantor said that last night was the first time anyone from Morianton had seen Selwyn since the slain *Idar* were found. They thought he'd already holed himself up in his castle for the winter."

"Is that unusual?" Alastair asked.

"Before the Worm came he'd been helping the miller build a pump house like the one under the castle. Something about using the hot springs to run the mill. Since the slayings and Isolde's disappearance, he hasn't visited once. They've had to abandon it. What did you learn last night?"

We told her about our dinner in the Lake Hall. Halfway through my description of Cordelia's meal the water stirred beneath the quay and Akarra stopped me.

"*Shh.* Watch."

Faces rose out of the depths, blubberous, alien faces with all-black eyes and fringes of waterweed trailing from their necks. Two mermen clutched tridents of jagged flint, dark against the silvery-green of their skin, and with these they gestured first to Akarra, then to us, as if debating whether we were worth the trouble of surfacing.

"Can you hear what they're saying?" I asked Akarra.

She tilted her head toward the water. "Something about '*on the honor of my . . .*' either '*roe-bearer*' or '*shoalmother.*' *Shoalmother,* I think. The other one's questioning it. My Mermish is a bit rusty."

The arguing mermen drew back as a third drifted up between them, larger than both. This one bore no trident, but through the waving waterweed on his head I glimpsed the spikes of a crown. Without a ripple he surfaced, the gills along his neck sealing as nostril slits opened above his mouth. Milky lids closed over his eyes as he raised one hand: webbed, pale green, and bloodless. He nodded first to Akarra, then to Alastair. "Those of the deep greet those of the heights," he said. The words were Arlean, but behind them I felt the weight of unfathomable waters, dark and cold and mysterious.

Alastair knelt beside me. "Those of the heights greet those of the deep."

"I know of no cause of war between us, dragonrider. We welcome you to our shores."

"Nor do I. Thank you, sire."

The king turned unblinking eyes on me. "Roe-bearer of the Daired, I presume?"

"My wife," Alastair said.

I wondered if I'd forever be known to *Idar* by some variation of *dragonrider's mate.* "Aliza Daired, sire."

"Hm." The waterweed that formed his beard trembled. "She is weak and thin. She'll not last the winter. You'd best take others if you want a healthy spawning."

My cheeks burned, but Akarra intervened before I could say something we'd all regret. "Your waters are still clear, Your Deepness. When do you expect the ice this year?"

"Not for several weeks. Winter will come late to the north this year, but it will be a hard one. What brings you to Ommeera so close to the snows?"

"Lord Selwyn invited us," Akarra said. "He wants us to find whatever it was that killed that girl."

"Where did your people find her body, sire?" Alastair asked.

"My seneschal's roe-bearers found it drifting near the *uroo* beds by the western wall." He waved a hand toward the opposite shore. "It had been in the water a long time. We could not allow it to pollute the *uroo*."

Akarra spoke a phrase in Mermish and the king shook his head.

"It's been more than forty tides since I've spoken with the land-folk of the castle, and this is the first I have heard of a monster hunting *Idar* along our shores. The lord sentinel should have summoned us from the first. It troubles me that he did not." One of the guards beneath him extended his trident and the king ducked beneath the water. A moment later he resurfaced. "I must take counsel on this matter. May you ride on swift currents, Family Daired, and may the waters of Ourobauro ever break on your enemies' shoals," he said and dove into the darkness. The two guards followed, keeping well apart from each other.

"Interesting," Akarra said.

Alastair sat back on his heels. "I like these merfolk."

I smacked his shoulder. "He told you to get another wife!"

"Compared to the merfolk at Selkie's Keep, that's genteel. They just drown you."

"The merfolk of the lakes aren't fighting off drakens and other sea monsters every day," Akarra said. "They can afford to be nicer." She raised her head. "We'll talk more on this later, *khela*. We have company."

We turned to see a maid hurrying down the quay. "So—sorry," she panted. "Lord Selwyn is asking for you, Lord Daired. He has your contract ready in his study. And breakfast is laid out in the Lake Hall, milady."

Akarra spread her wings. "Alastair, Aliza, I'm going to visit the village on the western shore. Maybe someone on land saw something," she said. With a sweep of her wings she was airborne.

The maid, whose name was Bretta, led us back to the castle. I parted with Alastair in the front hall after securing his promise that he'd let me know if Selwyn shared any new information.

I followed Bretta into the Lake Hall. Save for the food and the furnishings, the long room was empty. The table had been cleared of the silver candelabras and pearl-handled utensils and was now set simply with plain dishes. Platters of cold smoked fish, bowls of fruit, chilled eggs and fresh toast, steaming porridge, and pitchers of cream filled one end. I gave the fish a wide berth.

Bretta hovered on the other side of the table as I picked up a ladle for the porridge. "Er, can I help you with anything, milady?"

"Thank you, I'm all right."

"Oh." She didn't leave. "It's just that Madam Mòrag said it's not right for a lady to serve and I don't want her catching me here—" She reached for the ladle.

"Really, it's all right," I said, but it was too late. She raised the ladle before I could bring my bowl underneath, upsetting the whole thing. Hot porridge splattered across the tablecloth and onto my skirt. "Bretta!"

She dropped the ladle. "Oh gods! Lady Daired, I'm so sorry—I didn't mean—"

"I *said* it was fine!"

She covered her face and burst into tears.

"Bretta? Bretta, it's all right," I said. "Please don't cry." Her only answer was to sink to the floor, shoulders shaking with sobs. *Well done, Aliza.* I hurried around the table and knelt next to her. "Don't worry about it, please. It's only porridge."

"It's not that, milady. It's just . . . just . . . *everything!*" She drew in a shaky breath and looked up. "You saw her, didn't you? The menservants say you were there when they pulled her out of the lake."

"Aye," I said gently.

"Then Isolde's really dead?"

"Yes. I'm sorry."

She wiped her cheek with the heel of her hand. "I knew. I knew the night she didn't come back to the castle."

I felt a swell of sympathy for the girl. "Were you close?"

"We were f-friends. Isolde was friends with everyone." She twisted the edge of her apron in her lap and sniffed. A tear dripped off the end of her nose.

"If you don't mind me asking, where was she going that night?"

"To light the lantern at the end of Long Quay. One of us house-folk does it every day at sundown. And Isolde . . ." Again her face screwed up, and she clutched at my sleeve. "Oh, milady, don't you see? *She* wasn't supposed to be out there that night!"

"What on earth is going on here?" Mòrag's voice cut through the air like shards of ice. "Miss Wrenson? What are you doing?"

Bretta scrambled to her feet as the housekeeper rounded the end of the table. "Nothing, ma'am."

"I see." Mòrag's gaze wandered from the ruined tablecloth to the porridge stains on my dress to Bretta's tear-streaked face. "I believe you have duties to attend to in the kitchen, young lady."

Bretta rushed out.

"I apologize for her unseemly behavior, Lady Daired," Mòrag said as I stood.

"She just lost her friend. She has every right to mourn."

"Not in front of His Lordship's guests."

"I don't mind."

"Was she responsible for this mess?"

"No, that was me," I said.

She knew I was lying; I could tell. She pursed her lips. "Very well. If you leave your clothes by the door to your chambers, a maid will come around shortly to collect them for cleaning. And my lady?" she said as I started for the door, dripping porridge. "There are napkins on the table."

THINKING OF ISOLDE'S BLOATED CORPSE MADE ME queasy again as I made my way back to the guest tower. After changing into my last clean outfit, I riffled through our luggage for any spare beggar's balm, but the panniers yielded nothing beyond socks and a pair of trousers. I felt the hard edge of the silver box at the bottom and withdrew my hand quickly.

A metallic *thunk* from the bath made me jump. With the hiss of steam the largest pipe trembled, releasing a torrent of water and filling the air with the stench of rotten eggs. With one hand over my mouth I swept up my shawl, dumped my dirty clothes in a heap by the door, and went off in search of fresh air.

The hall outside echoed with the clang of pipes moving somewhere inside the walls, and with nothing better to hold my attention, I followed it. At the foot of the stairs the noise died away, swallowed by the vaulted silence of the castle. It was only when I passed the entrance to the front hall that something about that struck me as strange: not so much that I'd lost the clanging sound but that there was nothing to take its place. Castle Selwyn was too quiet. I thought of Merybourne Manor and House Pendragon, unable to stop the pang of homesickness; even on uneventful days both estates thronged with life and bustle. By comparison Castle Selwyn was little more than a shell. A beautiful shell, but a shell nonetheless. What few servants I encountered in the corridors scuttled away before I could speak to them, like navy-clad mice fleeing before an invisible cat.

Or perhaps just a very stealthy cat. I paused in front of a familiar unadorned archway. There *had* to be a rational explanation for the way Mòrag appeared and disappeared as she did.

A minute later I stood in front of the portrait of Lord and Lady Selwyn. The alcove was narrow, only a few strides across, and the windows on the outside wall were high and barred by intricate iron scrollwork. She couldn't have come and gone that way. I felt around the walls, the floor, and the bench beneath the painting. All stone and wood, solid and unyielding. That left the portrait. On closer inspection I saw no artist's mark, but I'd sell my finest charcoals if it wasn't a Tornay. The colors were rich and vibrant and the brushwork exquisite, every detail painted with energy and attention. Selwyn stood behind his wife, his long silver hair swept back from a face I had to admit handsome, a proud, possessive light in those pale gray eyes. One hand rested on Cordelia's shoulder. *He* she'd captured to perfection. It was Cordelia's face that seemed off. The likeness was remarkable, of course, and even as an image her beauty defied description—but there was something missing in her expression, some subtle difference between the portrait and the real thing.

The comparison gnawed at me as I examined the frame, tracing the grain of the wood, following the carved gambols of merfolk and selkies, sirens and other creatures of the sea. *Where would a clever person put—?*

A lever disguised as a merman's trident sank beneath my touch. I nearly fell off the bench as the painting swung out on silent hinges. Warm air rushed out, and I smiled. The Daireds hadn't been the only family to build secret passages throughout their home. A hallway branched beyond the painting, narrow and windowless. The right-hand corridor followed the lines of the outer wall back toward the main hall, but my eye was drawn at once to the left-hand passage. It led straight down, following a spiral staircase into darkness.

Dozens of reasons why I should absolutely not investigate further crowded thick and fast into my mind. It was dark. It could be dangerous. I could fall down those stairs and break a leg and no one would find me for days, and there might not be anything down there of interest to justify it.

But then again, there might be.

Lanterns burned on hooks on either side of the alcove. I glanced behind me and, seeing no one, detached a lantern and started down the stairs.

The passage twisted a long way into the depths of the castle. It grew warmer with every step and by the time I reached the bottom my forehead was bathed in sweat. There was a strong smell here too, but homier and more pleasant than the stench from the pipes, less like rotten eggs and more like woodsmoke. Arches rose above me, their tops lost in darkness. The floor alternated between tiles and uncut stone and I measured each step carefully, unsure what I might stumble across.

Detritus of all sorts littered the cavern, for a cavern it was, I decided, skirting a toppled wheel the size of a cart horse. Chains lay strewn about between fallen beams twice as wide as me. Light from somewhere on my right sent red shadows leaping against the walls. I heard rushing water and a strange voice, metallic and accented with fire.

"Blast it all for a hammer that *works!*"

Ahead of me spread the dark waters of the hot spring, roiling and bubbling as a great wheel churned its depths. Pulleys groaned and pipes clanged. A masked and armored forge-wight stood next to the open mouth of a furnace, muttering curses over a broken mallet.

"Hello?"

The forge-wight jumped and spun around. The head of the mallet flew from her hand and landed in the spring. "Who are you? No, what are you doing here? Oh, never mind—quick, don't let it get away!" She pointed with one gauntleted hand as the mallet head floated past me. I stooped to snatch it, but the waters caught it and sent it bobbing out of my reach. It danced on the surface of the spring before swirling out of sight. The forge-wight swore.

"I'm so sorry," I said, mortified.

"Bah. It was a worthless mallet anyway. Who are you?"

"Aliza Daired."

"Yes, yes, Niall mentioned something about guests last night. What are you doing down here? Did he send you down with another one of his projects?"

"No. I'm just, ah, exploring."

"Oh." She bent back to her work.

I sat on an overturned cart. *Wheels, pulleys, pipes, and a pump house to send hot water to the rest of the castle . . .* "You're Fyri, aren't you?"

"Know of anyone else who'd be working down here?"

I watched her for a minute before my curiosity got the better of me. "What are you working on?" I ventured.

Fyri straightened. "Listen, child, I'm very busy today. If you've a mechanical turn of mind, I'm sure Niall would be happy to show you the sketches he has of the wheelworks, but if you don't have a project for me, then you've no business down here. I can't be bothered to look after you."

"Actually, I do have some questions for—"

"I don't have time for *some*. You get one."

"Three," I tried.

The blue lights burning behind her mask dimmed. "Then you'll leave?"

"On my word."

"Fine." She shoved a lever forward and the great wheel behind her churned faster, its waterlogged timbers creaking and groaning. "Ask, if you must."

"The bathwater in our guest chamber smells like old eggs. Is it safe?"

"Oh, *does* it?" Fyri grumbled something in Eth and turned away. A complicated system of pulleys and pipes rose to her left. Faster than I could follow she twirled tiny wheels, disconnected half a dozen chains from their respective pulleys, and reattached them to others. She tilted her head, listened for a moment to the gurgling from the largest of the pipes, and brought her fist down hard on its side. The pipe coughed, then resumed a steady hum. "There. Flow misdirected from the kitchens. Begging your pardon. And yes, it's perfectly safe. Good for human skin if you can bear the smell."

I raised my voice to be heard over the splashing. "Fyri, do you know what creature's been killing *Idar* around the lake?"

"What?"

"Do you know what creature—?"

"No, I heard you. Who told you about that?"

"Selwyn did. That's why he invited us here. He thinks some new kind of *Tekari* has been slaying *Idar* in the region. He's afraid it attacked and killed one of the castle chambermaids a few weeks ago."

"Yes, I heard about that. Poor child." She turned back to her machinery. "I'm sorry to disappoint you, Lady Daired, but the world outside the wheelworks is none of my concern. I can't help you."

"She doesn't tell you because she doesn't know," a new voice said. I sprang to my feet. Fyri jumped too. Cordelia stood by the pile of chains, a lantern in her hand. She raised it so the light fell on my face, and as I looked at her, I realized what Tornay had missed in Cordelia's expression. *Melancholy.* The guildmaster had painted her looking too happy.

"Aliza, what are you doing down here?" Cordelia asked.

"Never mind her, Lady Selwyn. What're *you* doing down here?" Sparks flashed behind Fyri's mask. "His Lordship told you to keep out of the wheelworks!"

"His *Lordship* doesn't have to know." Cordelia took my arm. "We should go back to the castle. It's not safe down here." Over Fyri's protests and the groaning of the wheel, she whispered in my ear, "There's something I need to show you."

CHAPTER 17

DEEP WORDS, DARK WATERS

Cordelia led me up the stairs, holding up a hand to ward off my questions. "Wait until we're outside," she said as we climbed out the portrait door. "You shouldn't wander. Fyri means no harm, but she can be thoughtless. You might've fallen in the spring and drowned and she wouldn't have noticed until the wheels dredged up your body. What *were* you doing down there?"

"The water pumped into our room smelled bad." It was a half-truth at least. "I wanted to see why."

"Sulfur. The waters here are touched with it. Fyri must've opened the wrong pipes. I trust she made it right?"

"Aye, I think so."

She looked around. A manservant replacing burnt-out candles across the hall saw us and bowed. "I haven't showed you around our gardens yet, have I?" she said in a voice just loud enough for him to hear. "They're this way."

Outside the sun shone brightly but the wind blew cold. Evergreens shivered around the borders of the derelict garden and I pulled my shawl tight around my shoulders. Cordelia paced in front of the central fountain, its basin empty but for a few inches of leaf-choked water at the bottom.

"I'm sorry," she said. "Truly."

"For what?"

"For"—she waved a vague hand toward the castle—"this. For the shadows and secrets and questions I cannot answer. Niall made a mistake bringing you here. You should leave. Today, before nightfall."

"I'm sorry, Lady Cordelia, but we can't. Not if someone here is in danger."

She sank onto the lichen-encrusted edge of the fountain. "So there is truth in *tey iskaros*. Isn't that what you say? And please, Aliza. We women put on enough faces for the wider world. Let's not stand by such disguises with each other. You must call me Cordelia."

"Cordelia then. Please, tell me what's going on here. We only want to help."

She considered that for a moment. "What did my husband tell you about this creature that's been plaguing us?" she said at last.

I sat next to her and summarized what I could remember of his letter. She pursed her lips when I spoke of the mutilated trolls and missing livestock.

"The *Idar* were killed nearby, yes, but there is more than that at work here, Aliza. There is much my husband did not tell you." She glanced toward the castle. There was no one in sight. "Come. Quickly."

She led me out of the garden and set off down the path to Long Quay. A few shreds of fog lingered around the archways and crumbling pillars of the abbey on the cliff, the walls stained with pale streaks of bird dung. We stopped beneath the ruins. "We found this not long after Isolde disappeared," she said, pushing aside a pile of cut evergreen boughs on the abbey side of the path. A spar of rock broke through the turf at waist height. Strange marks covered its surface. I leaned closer.

"Is that writing?"

"It is."

The lines formed letters, but they were not in Arlean, Eth, nor any other language I recognized. "I can't read it."

"There is no true translation from Mermish to Arlean, but as close as I can make it the word means REPENT."

I looked up at her in surprise. "You speak Mermish?"

She gazed out across the lake. "I grew up south of here, at the mouth of the Langloch. My family fished off the coast of Selkie's Keep. If you do not speak the language, you do not share the waters. It is the same here."

I traced the words. The letters went deep. Whatever had carved them into the stone had strength far beyond a human's. I inspected the path beneath the writing, hoping to find a clue, a hint, *anything*, knowing even as I looked there'd be nothing to find. Weeks of weathering had erased all signs but the word REPENT, and even that made little sense. "What do you think it means?"

"I wish I could tell you."

"Would it have been significant to Isolde?"

She let down the branches to cover the word. "Mòrag said she never heard the girl speak anything other than Arlean."

Why Mermish? My gaze trailed down the path to the lake, where the glassy black waters lapped the pilings of the quay. Even if the merfolk of Lake Meera were friendlier than most, they were still *Idar*. If the Mermish king had lied, if they had known about the heartstone slayings, might they have wanted vengeance on the land-folk for their fellow *Idar*? I weighed that option, then discarded it. One of the merfolk might be strong enough to carve the words, but no merman or mermaid could survive long enough out of water to make it to the brow of the cliff, even with help. Writing the warning in Mermish had to mean something else. *If it wasn't for Isolde, who was it for?* I looked toward the lake. From the distance the jetty pierced the waves like a knife. *Had Isolde—? Hold on a moment.* I *could* see the quay from where we stood. A little to our left there was a gap in the wall, not wide, full of rubble and displaced stones. It was through the gap that I could see the quay. In fact, it was only here that I could see the quay, or any part of the lake close to the shore. The height of the wall blocked the sight everywhere else. I went closer to investigate. Moorflowers poked their heads between moss-covered rocks.

"Cordelia, how long has the wall been this way?"

"Years. Niall always meant to rebuild it, but everyone knows to be careful here."

Unless she didn't realize where she was. Selwyn had said it himself; the path was treacherous in the dark. Carefully I peered over the edge of the gap. Black waves crashed on the rocks below. "I think Isolde may have fallen here."

Cordelia pulled me back. "The child was not so clumsy. She would have had a lantern. She knew this path."

"Was there heavy fog the night she disappeared?"

"Well—yes. I suppose there was."

"I don't think she wandered off. Something would have driven her this way." I saw no other breaks in the cliff wall. Even in the dark this was the only place she could have fallen. "Something must have frightened her enough to make her run. She just ran in the wrong direction."

"You think this creature knew she'd fall?"

"Your husband is looking for a *Tekari*. That's what *Tekari* do." Flashes of Rina's face crowded thick and fast into my mind's eye. I shoved them away. "It would explain how she broke her neck, and why she was found in the water."

She nodded gravely. "I fear you may be right. But come." She touched my shoulder, her eyes fixed on the ruins of the abbey. "We should return. Someone will have noticed we're gone."

The climb back to the garden was harder. I wondered what Alastair had learned from Selwyn, if he learned anything at all. Selwyn had already lied to us once, or if not lied, he'd at least hidden the truth. I hoped there was no clause in Alastair's contract that required us to trust him. I certainly didn't.

Cordelia slipped her arm through mine as we crossed the garden. "Aliza, will you be honest with me?"

"Of course."

"I did not expect you to come. Is it a common thing for the wives of Daireds to accompany them on contracts like this?"

There was no accusation in her tone, though I half expected it. Those enormous eyes turned on me with nothing but sincere curiosity and, to my surprise, admiration. "Well, since I'm the first *nakla* Daired in generations and I'm standing here, I suppose it is," I said.

"Were you not frightened?"

"Yes. Often."

"Yet here you are." She shook her head. "You must love your husband very much."

"With all my heart."

"Why?"

The question, at once so unexpected and intimate, brought me to a standstill. "I'm sorry?"

"Why do you love your Daired, Aliza?"

"He's . . ." I struggled for a word to contain all I felt for Alastair. "He's a good man."

"Hm. *Goodness*. A strange word, that. What is goodness?" She plucked a pebble from the rim of the fountain. "This may be said to be a good stone simply for not being made of wood. It is what it is and gives no thought for what it is not." The pebble slipped between her fingers and fell into the water with a dull *plunk*. "But a stone cannot warm you. A stone cannot give you light." She shook her head. "The bards sing of you and your Daired, Aliza. Did you know?"

"Aye, I've heard the 'Charissong.'"

"The Battle of North Fields changed him."

"It changed everybody," I said quietly.

She turned away. "Niall fought, you know. He and the Lake Meera Regiment rode away to Harborough Hatch when word came of the Great Worm. He must have been very brave. He must have protected people." Her voice fell. "Should he not have a song?"

"Maybe he will someday. The people of Hatch Ford remember."

"And in their memories they will make him a good man, will they?"

The intensity of her question unnerved me. "I don't think I'm the right person to answer that, Cordelia."

"No. You're right, of course. Forgive my ramblings. Let it be enough that you have found your Daired." She smiled. It was a sad smile, like the first rime of frost on the petals of a rose. "Your child will be born into a fortunate house."

"Yes, it . . ." I stopped and stared at her as the weight of her words began to register. "My what?"

"You don't know?" The smile turned at once to astonishment. "You *don't* know! Oh! Aquouris gives life! Uoroura sustains!" She pressed the four fingers of her right hand to her lips, her heart, and then, without hesitation, to my navel. "Joy be yours, Aliza Daired. Yours and your child's."

Twenty lindworms might've burst from beneath the mountains all around us and forty dragons might've fallen burning from the sky. I wouldn't have noticed any of them.

Yours and the child you bear . . . the child you bear . . . the child.

Her words flitted like an unruly gale around me, their meaning swaying just out of reach.

"It is very early yet, but surely you've noticed your body changing?" she asked.

Dazed, I tried to remember the last time I'd bled. *One, two, three, four . . .* had it been more than six weeks? I couldn't remember exactly but now that I thought of it, it had certainly been before the wedding. My heart beat faster. *A child? Already?*

"No, I haven't."

"You've not felt ill? Mòrag says it is common to feel ill in the beginning." She frowned. "You've noticed nothing?"

Maybe it wasn't flying that upset me after all. "I guess I have."

"Let's go inside. You need rest and food." My stomach chose that moment to impersonate a tribe of galloping beoryns, and her eyes twinkled. "Didn't you have breakfast?"

"I . . . couldn't get it down."

"Our kitchens are at your disposal. Our cook will see that you get whatever you need."

What I need? What do I need?

I needed time. I needed space. I needed somewhere to sit quietly and allow this revelation to wash over me. I needed to breathe, to let terror and disbelief run their course, to reconcile myself to the weeks and months and years ahead. I needed Anjey at my side, and Gwyn squeezing my hand in delight, and Mama making an almighty fuss over how I was feeling and what to call the baby and when she and Papa could move into House Pendragon to look after their grandchild. I needed to see the look on Alastair's face.

But Cordelia was right. First I needed to eat. "Does your cook have any pickled cabbage?"

HE DID. UNDER NORMAL CIRCUMSTANCES I WOULDN'T have touched the stuff, but it conjured no thoughts of fish and stayed down, so I gave in, ate the bowlful, and felt better for it afterward. Cordelia sat with me in the alcove of the kitchen and watched with an abstracted smile. She did not eat. The ever-present Mòrag sidled over to clear away the empty dishes. When I asked after Alastair, she told us the men had left the castle shortly after we had, intending to make a full tour of the grounds with Akarra. She did not know when they'd return.

Cordelia stayed with me throughout the afternoon. My pensive mood must've been contagious; for hours we wandered the castle library, flipping through tales of saints and Riders, browsing her collection of Noordish love poetry, speaking only about trivial things, and otherwise sharing a companionable silence. She did not talk of children; I did not talk of the dead maid, or the murdered *Idar*, or the warning on the stone. Often I found my hand straying to my belly, imagining a little life tucked inside. *It can't be.* This was far too soon. *I would've known. I'm sure I would've known.*

Yet even as I tried to convince myself that it wasn't true, something assured me it was. My body had been ready for a child; it was the rest of me that rebelled. *I don't know how to be a mother!* My pulse quickened again and I felt the pressure descending on my chest, squeezing my lungs and sending panic shooting like ice water through my veins. *I can't do this. I can't—*

Alastair cradling a downy-haired bundle, his face alight with wonder as he looks down at our son or daughter, laughing, or crying, or both.

The image was so clear, I could almost see him sitting across from me with our child in his arms. The panic and the pressure ebbed. Not entirely, but it slowed the tide of rising terror enough for me to find my feet and remember at the last second that I could swim.

"Lady Cordelia?" Mòrag stood at the end of the table, hands clasped in front of her. I jumped and silently cursed her stealth. The old woman really *was* everywhere.

"Yes?" Cordelia said, unruffled.

"The head chambermaid needs a moment of your time in the Winter Parlor."

"Very well. Aliza, will you be all right?"

"Aye. Thank you for lunch."

She left, a smile still playing on her lips. Mòrag didn't follow.

"You should not have come here, Lady Daired," she said as the door closed after her mistress.

I blinked. "I'm sorry?"

"Lord Selwyn invited your husband and his dragon, not you."

So it was back to this. "Maybe so, but I am here, and I can't leave now."

"You can and you should. Travelers' caravans run from Morianton to Selkie's Keep every week. The next sets out tomorrow at dawn. You should go before the snows come."

I frowned. "Madam Mòrag, I'm not leaving my husband."

"Then he should go too."

"You know he can't."

She stuck out her chin, all bony angles and witch's whiskers. "You must find a way to persuade him."

"Why?" I demanded. For once I had no stomach for mysteries. "What's going on here?"

"It is none of your business. You are not a northerner. You're not even a Rider."

"No." I shut my book and stood. "That doesn't mean I don't care."

"Care? Why should *you* care?"

"Because I know what it's like to lose someone to the *Tekari*."

Of all the things I'd said, that was the first that seemed to strike her with any kind of feeling. "Isolde was just a child," she said. "Too kind for her own good. It was not even her turn to light the lantern that night. She should not have been out there. She did not deserve to die."

"Then you understand why we have to stay."

The flash of feeling disappeared. "Pursue this creature and you will ruin more lives than you think." Footsteps and voices echoed in the hall outside and Mòrag dipped into a scathing curtsy. "I've spoken my piece, Lady Daired, and I'll say no more. You cannot say I failed to warn you. Good evening."

THE HOUSEKEEPER'S WORDS LEFT MY MIND IN A TUMULT. My stomach followed and I rushed back to our chambers, praying I'd be spared another glimpse of the pickled cabbage. I was, and when my stomach settled, I sat before the fire in an attempt to put my racing thoughts in order. First Cordelia, then Mòrag. *We must leave, we can't leave.* Isolde running along the cliffside path alone, frightened, chased by something in the dark, something that had already killed and longed to kill again. The nightmare lurking inside me laughed. *Always in the dark. Darkness and fire and old debts left unpaid.* But whose? And why? *Cordelia, Mòrag, Isolde. She was just a child . . . just a child . . .*

A child.

The door opened behind me. "Aliza! There you are," Alastair said. "Dinner's ready."

His voice scattered the ghosts of the day like frost under the first light of dawn. I crossed the room and flung my arms around him, breathing in his comforting scent of smoke and sweat and dragons.

He returned the embrace, albeit confusedly. "Is everything all right?"

"I just missed you," I said with a sigh.

"Oh. Good. I, ah, missed you too." He kissed my forehead as I released him. "The contracts are finalized. Selwyn agreed to pay us fifty gold dragonbacks when this *Tekari* is dead."

Somewhere in the back of my brain I tucked away my shock at the enormous sum. "Did you find anything on the grounds?"

"Not so much as a blasted coney. We're going to have to quarter the area and comb through every blade of grass. I'm sure you'll hear more about it at dinner. Rhys wants to draw lots for the first patrol."

"Alastair, wait." I gathered my thoughts and took a deep breath. "Before we go, I need to tell you something."

"Yes?"

"You . . . may want to sit."

Alarm spread over his face. He did not sit. "What's wrong?"

"No, don't worry," I said quickly. "It's just that we may have to take our time flying home."

"Why's that?"

Instead of answering, I took his arm, drew him closer, and placed his hand on my stomach.

He looked at his hand, then at me, then back at his hand. The question hung in the air between us, asked in the sudden tension of his fingers as they brushed the curve of my belly and in the shock lighting in his eyes, which widened more and more as the truth dawned on him.

"Yes," I said.

"You're sure?"

"Well, I'd hate to be nauseated and not bleeding for some other reason. It's still early, but yes, I think I am."

For a long time we stood there, his hand on my stomach, finding no end of wonder and terror and amazement in each other's eyes.

"You're awfully calm," he said at last.

"Give me a few days. Right now I'm too scared to panic properly."

"Me too."

I smiled. "Some use we'll be to Selwyn."

"At the moment, *khera*, I say Niall Selwyn can take his fifty gold dragonbacks and go hang. We're going to have a *child*." He knelt, pressing his lips to our hands clasped over my stomach. *"Shai shurran'a Ah-Na-al Akhe'at, shai shurran'a Ahla-Na Lehal'i."*

And standing like that, trembling under the weight of this thing we'd done and the weight of all we still had to do, I began to think that maybe—just maybe—it would be all right. We were scared, unprepared, and inexperienced, yes, but we were scared and unprepared and inexperienced together. It had to count for something.

"You know, unless you want our child's second language to be Low Gnomic you really should start teaching me Eth."

There were tears in his eyes when he stood, and he laughed as we embraced. "You're not fluent already?"

"You're not the most attentive tutor. I'm guessing that was something to Odei and Janna."

"'All honor to He-Who-Begins; all honor to She-Who-Sustains.' What would your hobgoblin friends say?"

"Ghep thgud gnomi."

"Meaning?"

"'Thanks for the sprouts.'"

He laughed. "I'll remember that." He kissed my forehead again, then my lips. It was a long kiss, sweet and lingering. "We should go," he said after a minute. "They'll be waiting for us."

"Aye, we should," I said, but he didn't move. I leaned against his chest, enjoying the sound of his heartbeat, the warmth of his arms, and the simple joy of being loved. The ghost of a dead girl and the threats of an old woman and the shadow of a mysterious *Tekari* hovered outside our door, waiting to pounce as soon as we crossed the threshold; but in this little moment with nothing but each other, we were content. "Just not quite yet."

CHAPTER 18

A RECKONING

Alastair and I rose early, eager to share our news with Akarra. We found her perched on the garden wall on the lake side of the castle, surveying the dark water below. Her tail swung like a pendulum off the wall, and I sat as close to her as I could in an attempt to steal some of her warmth as Alastair began his morning exercises. For once he'd dressed sensibly, sacrificing freedom of movement for the freedom of not freezing to death. True to the Mermish king's predictions we'd not yet seen a flake of snow, but today's Martenmas celebration marked the official beginning of autumn and it was already growing cold. Or rather, colder. In the high mountain air even full sunlight had a hard time dispelling the white clouds that drifted out with every breath.

"Find anything interesting last night?" I asked Akarra.

She grunted.

I looked over at Alastair. "Is that Eth for yes or no?"

He grinned as she scratched beneath her chin with one wingtip. "I didn't see, hear, or smell a thing," she said. "And Selwyn didn't think to save the *Idar* bodies, so we've nothing to go on there except what he tells us. Which so far has been precious little."

"He didn't tell you about the carving?" I said.

Alastair looked up. Akarra turned from her study of the lake. "What carving?"

I told them about the markings on the boulder near the cliff path.

"No," Alastair said. "He failed to mention that."

"You're sure the word was *repent?*" Akarra asked.

"That's how Cordelia translated it."

"And where did you say it was?" Alastair asked.

"There's a gap in the cliff wall a few hundred yards down the path from the garden, near the ruins of the old abbey." I felt Alastair's eyes on me as his smile dimmed and knew all too well the question behind it, which I ignored. "Cordelia and I think that's where Isolde was when this creature appeared. It must have frightened her off the cliff. The warning was left on the rock opposite the gap."

Akarra stretched her wings. "I'm going to take a look. *Khela,* you should come too."

"Wait!" I said. "Before you go, I need to ask—the road from Lake Meera to Selkie's Keep. Do you think it's still open this time of year?" The words tumbled out in a rush.

Akarra gave me a curious look. "To Selkie's Keep? Why on earth do you want to know?"

I caught Alastair's eye and winked. "Oh, just wondering."

"Well, there must be post carriages in Morianton that make the trip throughout the autumn," she said, "but I don't see why that matters."

"There's a kingsroad out of Selkie's Keep straight to Harborough Hatch, isn't there?"

"Last time I looked."

"There's one from Hatch Ford to Pendragon too," Alastair

added, and while I felt confident we'd be having a discussion about wandering around the castle grounds sometime soon, for the moment his grin was back. "I'm sure they'd have room for a few extra passengers after we're done here."

"How long will that take?" I asked, making a show of calculating it on my fingers. Akarra watched us both, her horned eyebrows drawing together.

"Three weeks, if the weather holds," he said.

"What are you two *talking* about?" Akarra said. "Of course you won't be taking a carriage to Selkie's Keep when we're done here, and even if it does snow, it won't take me three weeks to fly home."

"About that . . ." I said. "Flying is going to be a problem."

"I know you don't like it, but it is the fastest way—"

"The baby doesn't like it either."

Her head whipped around so fast she lost her balance on the wall and had to throw out her wings to catch herself. "The *what?*"

It took several minutes for us to recover from our laughter. Once we did, we told her our news. Her eyes blazed with delight.

"My *khela*, a father! And Aliza, a mother! Yes, of course we must find you a carriage home if you don't want to fly." She bent down so her head was level with mine. "But you're sure? You mightn't have mistook it somehow?"

"I'd like to visit the Lambsley midwife when we get back to Pendragon, but for the time being yes, I'm fairly certain I'm pregnant."

Akarra threw back her head and trumpeted. Dragonfire seared away the morning mist and warmed my chilled limbs. "Oh, to see the look on Julienna's face," she crowed. "And Mar'esh! Lady Catriona will be thrilled, of course. A new Daired heir! The Nestmothers will need to be told, and—"

"Akarra, Akarra! Slow down," Alastair said. "Give us a little time before you announce it to the world. We're still trying to absorb it ourselves."

Her wings drooped and she looked abashed, or as abashed as a full-grown dragon in a state of high excitement can look. "I'm sorry. It's just—"

From somewhere beyond the castle walls, someone screamed.

Our moment shattered. The scream came from a human throat, but it was so shrill I couldn't tell if it was a man or woman. Akarra leapt into the air as Alastair reached for his sword and ran for the gate. After a second's debate I followed.

We didn't search long. An ashen Jen Trennan stood in front of the front gate, his livery travel stained and dusty from the road, clutching the reins of his horse in one trembling hand. He pointed to the wall beside the gate where a ram lay on the grass, its throat severed. Blood frosted in spatters along its dappled coat. One of its horns was broken, and painted in blood on the white wall were words in a language I couldn't read. It was the same language as on the stone on the cliff.

"Akarra, do you know what it says?" Alastair asked.

"*IR QUAROS ESH*," she said. "Mermish. It means 'There comes a reckoning.'"

I pulled Trennan away from the wall as Alastair inspected the ram. The boy gripped my arm as if I were a piling in stormy waters. "Oh, milady, I didn't—I just came from the pass—" he said. "I don't know how—"

"Did you see anyone, Master Trennan?" Akarra said. "On the road, near the castle, anywhere?"

"N-no."

"This ram wasn't killed here," Alastair said. "There's not enough blood on the ground, and the body's cold. It's been dead for hours."

"It's from Morianton," Akarra said.

I looked again at the creature, wondering how the Morianton rams differed from any other. "How do you know?"

"I recognize the missing horn. The cantor showed me the fold the other day."

Trennan gave a hiccupping sniffle. "W-was it her?"

"Who?"

"The c-creature in the mists. Did she k-kill it?"

"How do you know it's a *her*?" Alastair sheathed his sword and seized Trennan's shoulder. "Trennan, do you know what did this? Do you know what we're hunting?"

"No! I don't know anything!" he cried and covered his face.

"Lord Daired! What's going on?" Selwyn and Rhys burst from the gate, Rhys with a crossbow in one hand, Selwyn carrying an ornate sword that looked better suited to a mantelpiece than a battlefield. Cordelia followed them as far as the courtyard, but stopped at the sight of the slain sheep, her face white as salt. "We heard a scream," Selwyn said.

"It's a warning." Alastair pointed to the words.

Rhys lowered the crossbow. "Ye gods."

"What does it say?" Cordelia asked.

"Never mind, my love," Selwyn said. "You'd better go inside."

"Niall, what does it say?"

"I said go inside, please!"

I watched as she backed away, then turned and ran into the castle.

Selwyn lowered his sword with a sigh. "Forgive me, Lord Daired, but what *does* it say?"

Akarra translated again, but I was no longer listening. As gently as I could I disentangled myself from Trennan's grip, deposited him into Selwyn's care, and followed Cordelia. I found her standing by the windows in the Lake Hall.

"Cordelia?" I asked. "Are you all right?"

"I told you to leave," she said in an undertone. "Mòrag told you to leave. Why are you still here?"

"Because . . . because that's not what Daireds do."

"You're no Daired."

My face grew warm. *And no one in the kingdom will ever let me forget it.* "Maybe not," I said, "but I am stubborn, and there's more going on here than a *Tekari* hunt. Those words by the gate were in Mermish. *IR QUAROS ESH.* Akarra said it means 'There comes a reckoning.'"

She waved a dismissive hand. "She has the right idea, but her vocabulary is limited. 'Justice approaches' is a better translation."

I narrowed my eyes. "You don't seem surprised, Cordelia. Do you know what's out there?"

"Even if I did, there's nothing you can do. There's nothing anyone can do."

"I don't believe that."

"You should, because it's the truth. Please, Aliza. Go *home.* Take your family away from these cursed shores before the snows come. You may not get another chance."

"We can't leave while you're in danger."

"I'm not in danger."

"How can you say that? This thing's already killed humans, trolls, pixies, and now it's leaving bloody warnings on your doorstep. Do you really think it'll stop there?"

"No. It will not stop." The utter conviction with which she spoke the words sent chills down my spine. "It will never stop until it is satisfied."

"Satisfied with what?"

Cordelia looked at me. It may have been a trick of the light, or only my imagination, but it seemed for a moment that her eyes flashed even blacker. "Vengeance."

"So you *do* know what it is."

She turned away again.

I seized her arm. "Cordelia, this isn't a game! If you know what this *Tekari* wants, you must tell me now. Before anyone else gets hurt!"

She wrenched out of my grasp, eyes wild. "You don't think I would if I could? Do you think I wanted this, Aliza? *Any* of this? I didn't ask for it! I *never* asked for it! If I could prevent—" Her voice caught. "If I were to tell—" She stopped, fingers fluttering at her throat as if to tear away whatever kept her from speaking. Tears spilled over her cheeks and her hands fell to her sides. "Nouroudos help me, I cannot speak of it. If it were in my power, I would, but I . . . I cannot."

She swept up her skirts and ran from the hall.

I FOUND AKARRA AND ALASTAIR ALONE IN THE FRONT courtyard. Rhys had gone to bury the ram in the softer ground west of the castle and Selwyn had ushered the near-hysterical Trennan inside. Quickly I told them what Cordelia had said.

"'Repent' first, and now 'justice approaches'?" Akarra asked. "What kind of *Tekari* announces itself like that? And in Mermish too?" Her words held the crackle and heat of dragonfire. She spread her wings. "I need to speak with the king of the merfolk again."

We watched her until she disappeared beyond the castle's towers. "Was Cordelia telling the truth?" Alastair asked.

I crouched next to the gate, examining the ground where the ram had lain. The grass was thoroughly trampled, but aside from

Akarra's tracks the only footprints were those of humans. "She was telling someone's truth." *Her husband's? Mòrag's? Or someone else altogether?*

A cold wind sent the grass on either side of the road rippling in green and silver waves. Alastair sheathed his sword but left his scabbard on his hip. "Aliza, will you do me a favor?"

"Aye, what is it?"

"Stay inside today. Please."

Once I might have argued, might have tried to convince him of my ability to take care of myself in a confused attempt to disguise stubbornness for bravery, but not this time. The lines between courage, recklessness, and stupidity were fine ones, and after everything that had happened in the past few days I was prepared to tread a little more cautiously.

I nodded, reaching up to plant a swift kiss on his cheek before we parted: he to his patrol around the perimeter of the castle, me to my wanderings inside. Wandering, and contemplation, and the piecing together of clues, and—

"How could you let this happen?"

I drew back behind a corner just as Trennan and Rhys hurried out of the servants' hallway.

"You were supposed to protect the castle, not stand around while this thing paints *bleschang* warnings on the *bleschang* walls!" Trennan continued, his Noordish accent getting stronger as his voice rose. "And what have you done with my *bleschangenfelt* bird?"

"Jen, calm down," Rhys said. "Tatterdemalion is fine. She's with the falconer in Morianton."

"You were supposed to keep her with you!"

"Good gods, boy, make up your mind! Did you want me to protect the castle or the bird? I can't very well go fight this monster with that mass of feathers on my arm."

Trennan grunted.

"I kept my promise," Rhys said. "Your bird is fine and it's not my fault Selwyn doesn't trust me enough to tell me what's really going on. I can't go out and kill something I can't see. Lord Daired and his dragon have been more than willing to take up the hunt in the meantime."

"They're doing their *job*. You might learn a lesson or two. Grandfather would be ashamed of you," Trennan spat. "Coward."

"Pragmatist, actually. And anyway, I didn't think you'd be back so soon."

"I rode fast."

"You'd have been safer if you rode slow."

"Aye, but unlike you I still have a shred of honor."

Rhys laughed. "Your honor doesn't stop you from being a fool, boy. You should have stayed in Dragonsmoor."

"I couldn't leave Bret—" Trennan stopped.

"Aha! So there is a girl."

"Shut up."

"I knew you were seeing someone."

"She has nothing to do with this, Owin. I brought the Daireds and I came back. I've done my duty."

"Then you'll be happy to know that they've already found Isolde's body."

The air in the corridor crystallized, frozen to a point of thunderstruck silence. Even though I couldn't see his face I felt Trennan's horror. "She's dead?" he rasped.

"Broken neck," Rhys said. "The merfolk pushed her body ashore near Morianton a few days ago. I'd bet anything she took a tumble off the cliff that night she went missing."

There was a slumping sound. "Oh *Thell*."

"She didn't deserve that end, even I'll admit," Rhys said. "Some others I can think of, yes, but not that girl. It wasn't pretty."

"Does Bretta know?"

"Contrary to what you might think, I don't make it my business to dally with every chambermaid in the county," Rhys said. "I have no idea what your ladylove knows or doesn't know. You may—oh, why do I bother?"

Footsteps all but drowned out his last words as Trennan rushed away. A door banged somewhere in the distance.

"You can come out now, Lady Daired," Rhys called.

I gave a violent start and looked around, wondering what had betrayed me, and my heart sank as I glanced over my shoulder. The reflection of the window on the opposite wall showed the entirety of the adjacent hall, including me. *Blast.*

I stepped around the corner, head held high, daring him to mention the blistering blush that had taken up residence in my cheeks. "Captain Rhys."

He swept his cloak aside in a mock bow. "You've a mite of stealth, I'll give you that. I hope you heard something interesting. I'll bid you good morning."

"A moment, Captain."

"My lady?"

Subtlety had no place in dealing with a man like Rhys, and as I'd likely not get the chance again, I threw caution off the metaphorical cliff. I could hardly embarrass myself further. "Why are you here?"

"Well, as a matter of fact, I was just on my way to the privy when my cousin—"

"Not in this hallway. I mean *here*, serving in Master Gorecrow's place."

"Selwyn asked me here to protect the castle."

"You don't like him much," I observed.

"Now, my lady, whatever makes you think Niall Selwyn and I aren't just the *closest* of friends?"

I let his sarcasm thicken in the silence between us. It was answer enough.

"Oh, fine. Look, it's not that mysterious. I command the largest fighting force within sight of the castle. Selwyn controls trade on the lake. A mutual understanding is beneficial for everyone involved."

"If your regiment is so close, why did he bother inviting Riders at all?"

Rhys ran a hand through his hair. "Lady Daired, I'm not the man to plumb the dark and twisted recesses of Niall Selwyn's mind. He's a man used to fine things, and your husband and his dragon are fine warriors. I'm here to uphold my end of a bargain and that's all there is to it." He pushed past me. "Now begging your pardon, but I really do need to piss. Good morning."

THE DAY PASSED SLOWLY IN THE CONFINES OF THE CAStle. Whether they were frightened of confronting me or simply didn't care, none of the servants made any attempt to prevent my explorations. I passed the portrait hall several times but didn't step inside. Those dripping letters from this morning had stained my mind's eye scarlet and I didn't fancy a second trip in the dark.

Cordelia remained absent, though Mòrag appeared in the library around noon to summon me to lunch. She said nothing of her earlier warning, nor gave any other hints that anything was amiss. I ate by myself in a smaller dining room off the Lake Hall, in which a handful of navy-clad servants labored, scouring the floors, washing the windows, and setting the table for the Martenmas meal later that night. Yet for all the activity the castle stayed strangely quiet. The servants talked in whispers if they talked at all. I didn't see Trennan or Rhys again.

Mòrag served lunch with her usual alacrity, answering my questions in as few words as possible. *Yes,* Alastair and Rhys were dividing their patrol around the castle while Akarra covered the nearby area. *No,* Selwyn had not accompanied them. *Yes,* her mistress regretted she could not join me for lunch. *No,* she was not ill, merely resting. Her nature was delicate and the dead ram had disturbed her greatly.

Did she know anything more about it?

No.

It was the last word I got out of her before she swept up my dishes and hurried out of the room.

THE SUN WAS SETTING OVER THE WESTERN MOUNTAINS when the bell rang to summon us to Martenmas dinner. Alastair had returned from his patrol not long before, bringing Akarra's disappointing news. She hadn't been able to call even one of the merfolk, let alone the king. As he dressed he told me of their plans to visit Morianton in the morning, hoping to ask the local shepherds if they knew anything about the ram. He struggled to buckle his sword-belt with his unmaimed hand, but when I offered to help, he waved me away.

"Akarra thinks they'll talk to me. They don't seem to like dragons much."

"What, do they think she'll accidentally set fire to their roofs?"

"Not accidentally." He continued fiddling with his belt. "They seem to be under the impression that dragons destroy everyone and everything that doesn't give them the answers they're looking for."

"That's a pity, and—oh, for gods' sakes, let me," I said, and finished buckling his belt for him. "There. Honestly, if you don't want us to be late next time, just ask. Selwyn probably thinks we fell asleep."

But it was clear Selwyn wasn't thinking of us at all when we arrived in the Lake Hall. The largest beoryn I'd ever seen stood at the end of the table, his head bent close to Selwyn's. His fur was dusty and tracks outlined in mud led from the door to the place he stood. An empty war-saddle sat askew on his shoulders. There was no sign of his Rider.

"Chirrorim!" Alastair cried.

The beoryn swung his shaggy head around and fixed us with a stare that pierced me to the soul. Beoryns had no tears, and they didn't need them. In that single look I felt his heartbreak like physical pain.

"Alastair," Chirrorim rumbled. "I am glad to see you."

"Where's Theold?" Alastair asked.

"I'm sorry, my friend. Theold is dead."

CHAPTER 19

MARTENMAS

Alastair sank into his chair, his face pale. "What happened?"

"We left Selkie's Keep nearly a week ago," Chirrorim said. "We planned to cross at the mouth of the Langloch and join a caravan across the Winter Spear to Lake Meera, but the caravan was delayed. It was Mikla's will, I think; the village at the ford was attacked by a pack of direwolves the night after we arrived. As the only Riders nearby it was our duty to defend the village. Theold tried to hold the gate." Chirrorim lowered his head. "He fell five days ago. When the direwolves moved on, I built his pyre, burned his body, and continued by myself."

Alastair closed his eyes. His lips moved silently. When he looked up again, his face was hard as flint, his voice flat. "What were the packs doing so near the coast?"

"I wish I knew. They turned south after Theold fell. They didn't even try to savage the bodies."

"That's not usual direwolf behavior, is it?" Selwyn ventured.

Alastair shook his head.

"I pray the Riders stationed in Selkie's Keep are able to finish what Theold and I started," Chirrorim said. "But no more of this.

Theold was a faithful servant of Mikla and he will welcome him into the Fourfold Hall with open arms. It is not our calling to dwell on the dead, my friend," he said to Alastair. "Tell me instead what we fight here."

I watched Cordelia as Alastair and Selwyn took turns summarizing the deaths of the last few weeks. She moved the empty oyster shells around her plate without looking at them, her eyes fixed instead on a point beyond the table, on something I could not see.

Selwyn noticed her abstraction halfway through the final course and put a hand on her shoulder. "I'm so sorry, my sweet. This is no conversation for the dinner table. Lord Daired, Chirrorim, let's continue this discussion in my study. Captain Rhys, I trust you can manage the evening's patrol on your own?"

Rhys's response to that, if any, was lost in the scrape of wood on stone as the men pushed back their chairs and followed Selwyn out of the Lake Hall. Chirrorim padded behind them.

"Would my lady like to retire for the night?"

I should've expected Mòrag. The silence the men had left in their wake held too much frost for her not to be present. Cordelia shook her head. "No. It's early yet."

"Yes, but wouldn't my lady like—"

"It's Martenmas, Mòrag. I don't want to sleep. Aliza, will you sit with me?"

"Aye, if you like."

"And you, Mòrag. Come sit with us."

"I have things to attend to, child. The meal, the kitchens . . ."

"The servants can take care of them."

"My lady—"

"Please," Cordelia said. "Just for a little while."

Mòrag sighed. "Oh, very well."

We followed Cordelia into the library. Moonlight threw

strips of silver across the hearth where the remains of a fire still smoldered in the grate. Mòrag set another log on the fire and settled on a stool near the wood cradle with an air of someone keeping vigil. "Our men will talk through the night," Cordelia said to me as we curled up on the sofa opposite. "For once let's you and I not concern ourselves with their affairs. Do you sing?"

I looked up, surprised. "What?"

"Your mind is already far away. I asked if you sing."

I laughed. "Not at all."

"Then Mòrag must do it." The housekeeper made an extraordinary face at the suggestion, but Cordelia would not be deterred. She knelt next to Mòrag's stool. "Oh, please do. Sing for us 'The Lay of Saint Ellia.'"

"My lady, now is not the time for that."

"It's Martenmas. There is only one day of the year better suited to the tale."

"Then I will wait until Saint Ellia's Day to sing it," she said. Cordelia's face fell, and for an instant Mòrag's icy expression cracked, showing the waters below roiling with feeling. Hesitantly, almost reverently, she tucked an idle strand of hair behind Cordelia's ear. "I won't sing it, child, but if you wish I'll tell the story."

She brightened. "I would like that. Thank you, Mòrag."

"Let me see. It begins—"

"*Many years ago, in the dark of the world,*" Cordelia said.

"Yes. Many years ago, in the dark of the world, a daughter was born to the king of a monster-plagued isle. Rhydian was the king's name, and Arle the name of his kingdom."

Cordelia sat back on her heels and watched Mòrag's face, mouthing the familiar words along with her. Mòrag gave me a sidelong glance.

"Now generations had passed since Edan the Fireborn and Aur'eth the Flamespoken Sire had been called up to the gods, and the kingdom was once again in turmoil. The blood of the Fireborn had run thin in Edan's descendants, watered down by greed and corruption, and while they and their dragons lived safe in their fortresses of stone, the people of Arle suffered under the teeth and talons of the ancient monsters that plagued the land."

That was new. I thought of my assurance to Alastair on the Langloch beach of the honor of his ancestors and wondered what he would say to hear Mòrag's version of the tale. The song we'd grown up with didn't hold nearly so much indictment for House Daired as Mòrag's recitation.

"What kind of monsters, Mòrag?" Cordelia asked.

"All kinds. There were no *Shani* in those days, you see. Save for the sworn dragons of House Daired, every creature you met in the time of King Rhydian was as likely to kill you as look at you. It was—"

"Even gnomes?"

Mòrag blinked. "Well, yes, I suppose. Now, it was during the dark of the world that certain men and women went in search of other creatures that might become their allies, as Edan had once with the dragons. Many died in their attempts to bargain with valkyries and direwolves, but some were luckier and found comrades-in-arms among wyverns and beoryns. These warriors called themselves Riders and spread throughout Arle, protecting towns and villages under attack from the Oldkind."

I drew my knees to my chest and watched the firelight dance along the windows on either side of the chimney, trying to imagine those first battles. Blood had flowed on all sides, human and Old-kind alike. Dark of the world indeed.

"King Rhydian was neither a kind nor gentle man, but he was

a wise king and it troubled him deeply to see his people suffer. When his daughter was born, he made an oath to the people of Edonarle: by the time the Princess Ellia wed he would bring peace to the kingdom, no matter the cost."

"*No matter the cost,*" Cordelia echoed thoughtfully.

"Princess Ellia was a singular child, gifted with a silver tongue," Mòrag said. "The queen consort died in childbed, leaving King Rhydian to raise his daughter alone. He saw her gifts grow as she did and, though he raised her harshly and without affection, he marveled at her ability to make people listen, to turn the unyielding and soften the hardest of hearts."

Except his own. The thought came to me unbidden, the sad truth at the heart of Arle's oldest tragedy. Henry's master had sung of it once when I was a child at the Merybourne Midsummer bonfire. No one liked the improvisation and he never tried to change the verses again, but I'd never forgotten the lines he'd sung of the young Ellia: "*For all her fine words she could not convince her father to love her.*"

"By her eighteenth birthday he had devised a plan," Mòrag continued. "A treaty, he called it—"

"The Accord of Kinds," Cordelia finished.

"Indeed. On the eve of her eighteenth birthday the king summoned his daughter and presented her with the Great Task: bring the Accord of Kinds before as many of the Oldkind as she could find and offer them a truce if they would swear an alliance with the humans of Arle."

The hum of her words wrapped around me like a blanket. I sank back into the cushions, eyes half closed as she continued in a singsong voice.

"Now the princess was no fool. She agreed to his task on the condition that she would not go alone. King Rhydian saw the wisdom in this and summoned the new Riders from all corners of the kingdom to a tournament in Edonarle, to compete in contests of skill and courage and win the chance to serve as Ellia's guardians."

"*And there the princess first laid eyes upon Marten, and Marten upon Ellia,*" Cordelia sang softly, "*and in a single glance kindled a love such as there has never been before, nor ever will be again.*"

"As you say, my lady. It was there she first saw young Marten Hull, a Rider out of the Western Wastes, and his wyvern Jadewing Jeweltalon," Mòrag said. "Rider and wyvern both fought valiantly, defeating all who raised their swords against them and winning the honor of a place at Ellia's side. And as Marten—"

"Do you think it's true, Mòrag?" Cordelia asked. "Do you think he loved her at first sight?"

"What? Goodness me, of course not, child! That's an invention of the bards. There is no such thing as love at first sight."

"But was that not how it was for you, Aliza?"

I opened my eyes. "Sorry?"

"When you first saw Lord Daired? Did you not love him then?"

Only her expression of perfect credulousness kept me from laughing out loud. "Good gods, no. I didn't even like him until a few months ago."

"But then how—?"

"My lady, you asked me to tell the story," Mòrag said gently. "Will you let me tell the story?"

"Yes, Mòrag. I'm sorry."

Mòrag set another log on the fire and settled back on the stool. "As Marten climbed the steps to receive the blessing of the king, a great silver dragon descended into the tournament ring, bearing the only daughter and heir of House Daired. Niaveth Daired had heard of the king's challenge, but it was her dragon

Sanar who convinced her to fly south and join the fray. King Rhydian accepted the offer of her pledged sword and together Ellia, Niaveth, and Marten set out across the wilds of Arle to fulfill the king's task, or to perish in the attempt."

My eyelids drooped again as she told of their adventures among the Oldkind, of Ellia's successes with the creatures who would come to be called *Shani*, and of her flight from the creatures who refused the Accord—those who would become *Tekari*. Words bled into words, their meaning growing dim as sleep drew me down into warm darkness.

"So the three returned in triumph to Edonarle . . . great celebration among the people, for there was the rumor of marriage between Marten and their beloved princess . . ."

I imagined the towers of Edonarle, glowing white and red in the setting sun as the city welcomed back their brave princess. Royal heralds trumpeting their return . . . *this sofa really is quite comfortable* . . . crowds cheering, banners waving . . .

"But when Marten asked King Rhydian's blessing, the king refused, claiming the Task was yet undone . . . and so he sent his daughter and her guardians on one final journey across the southern sea . . ."

The glint of moonlit water and the crash of waves against creaking timbers . . .

". . . for even then the distant land of Els had a dark and doubtful reputation, and Rhydian wanted to know more of it . . ."

Els.

I opened my eyes. Cordelia still sat at Mòrag's feet, absorbed in the tale. The fire burned with quiet heat, sending specters of shadow quivering along the walls. The silhouettes of bare tree branches moved beyond the window as the moon set behind the castle's eastern ramparts.

"But the three found the High Citadel closed to them, and its guardian, the monstrous Sphinx of Els, waiting outside the gates. Niaveth's dragon fought the sphinx, but dragonfire could not defeat a desert creature and the noble Sanar was slain.

"The sphinx turned next to Ellia, but Marten stepped between the monster and his love. The battle was terrible. In the end Marten and his wyvern slew the sphinx, but his victory came at a great cost. Marten was mortally wounded, and while Ellia and Niaveth were able to flee with him to their ship, he did not survive the storm-tossed voyage back to Arle.

"They say Ellia looked out over the sea as she cradled Marten's body and placed a terrible curse on the Kingdom of Els. No one knows what she wished upon them, for if Niaveth heard her, she never spoke of it afterward. All that is known is that the High Citadel fell silent from that day forward."

More shadows crept along the windowpanes. *And so the Silent Kingdom was born* . . .

I jolted upright. Within the shadow I'd seen a flash of—*something*. Red and white, a face in the dark, fair-haired and smiling the sunken grin of a corpse.

"Lady Daired?"

"Did you see that?"

Mòrag and Cordelia looked at each other, then at me. "See what?" Cordelia asked.

I went to the window. An empty parapet ran beneath the sill. "I thought I saw something moving out there."

"You've been asleep for the last quarter hour, my lady," Mòrag said. "You must have dreamed it."

I touched the pane, my breath fogging against the glass, and prayed to every facet of the Fourfold God that she was right.

"Sit, Aliza," Cordelia said. "The story's not ov—"

"Lady Daired!"

I yelped. The scream severed my last worry-frayed nerve. "Mikla save us, what is Rhys playing at?" Mòrag muttered, but I was already halfway to the front hall.

Alastair, Selwyn, and Chirrorim were already there, Alastair with one hand on his sword hilt, Chirrorim's fur standing rigid along his spine and a growl in his throat. Rhys stood panting in the middle of the hall, the limp, towheaded figure of Jen Trennan in his arms. Several voices spoke at once, but Mòrag drowned them all out.

"Owin Rhys, what have you done to that boy?" she demanded.

"Found him—like this," Rhys panted.

"Is he dead?" Cordelia asked over Mòrag's shoulder. "Nouroudos save us, *is he dead?*"

"Not dead." Rhys's voice edged toward panic. "Found him outside the gates babbling something about forgiveness and then . . . *schetze*, I shouldn't have left him alone! Lady Daired, you're a healer, aren't you?"

"Aye—"

"Can you help him? Please, gods, say you can help him!"

"Take him into the library," I said. Rhys fairly charged off down the hall before I could finish. Alastair caught my eye and followed him. "Madam Mòrag, can you—?" I turned around, but she was already ushering Cordelia away.

"Go, Lady Daired," Selwyn said. "I'll bring you what you need."

My mind raced. *What would Uncle Gregory say?* "More wood. And blankets."

"What else?"

"I don't know yet." I followed the men into the library and helped Alastair pull the sofa closer to the fire. "Lay him down, Captain."

As soon as Trennan touched the cushions he curled into a ball, shaking from head to foot with silent sobs.

"What's wrong with him?" Chirrorim asked.

I knelt next to the sofa. "Master Trennan?" He shook his head, his fists clenched on either side of his face. Back and forth he rocked, a wordless whine in his throat. I tried to take his hand, then settled for patting his arm when he refused to unclench his fists. "Master Trennan, it's all right. You're safe now."

"Why was he asking for forgiveness?" Alastair asked Rhys. "Did he say whose?"

"No."

"And you saw nothing?" Chirrorim asked.

"Nothing *to* see," Rhys said. "Clouds are rolling in. It's black as pitch beyond the walls."

I felt Trennan's forehead. It was damp with sweat, though not of the feverish sort. "I don't think he's ill. Just badly frightened."

"By what?"

Rhys stopped his pacing. "The monster. He saw it, didn't he?"

"She didn't want me."

Every head turned to Trennan.

"Who didn't want you, boy?" Alastair asked. "Tell us what you saw."

Trennan squeezed his eyes shut and buried his face in his hands, still rocking. "She's not here for me. Not for my sins. Not for me . . ."

The words trailed off into sobs as the door opened behind us, admitting Selwyn with an armful of logs. "What you asked for, Lady Daired." He deposited the logs into the wood cradle and cast a glance over Trennan's prone form. "Will he live?"

"Aye, I think so."

"Good. Mòrag will attend you if you need anything else. In

the meantime, I'd appreciate it if you wouldn't mention this to the other servants. I don't want to start a panic. Chirrorim, Lord Daired, Captain Rhys, we'd best make the castle secure."

"I'm not leaving my wife," Alastair said.

"As you will," Selwyn said stiffly. "Rhys, with me." He swept out of the library.

I TENDED TRENNAN THROUGH THE NIGHT. MÒRAG DID not reappear, so at my request Alastair brought mint, hush, hot water, and blankets from the kitchens. When the tea I made failed to have any effect, I sent him back for some valerian, and after several draughts Trennan passed from his strange catalepsy into a fitful sleep.

Alastair sat with me on the opposite sofa as we watched him toss and tremble, muttering nonsense. "You should've gone with Selwyn," I said. "If this thing is close to the castle, he may need your help."

"Chirrorim can take care of the defenses. No one else is going outside tonight."

I looked at the boy on the sofa. The dark circles under his eyes were more pronounced now, and I fancied there were a few gray streaks in his hair that hadn't been there before. "Alastair," I said quietly, "before Rhys came in I thought I saw something at the window."

"What did you see?"

The face of a dead man. The words had the tang of impossibility even as I rehearsed them in my head. "It—never mind."

He put his arm around my shoulders. "Aliza, tell me."

"It was just a dream."

"It scared you, whatever it was."

"It did, but it's gone now." The log in the grate split with an ashy sigh, coughing sparks onto the hearth. "He wasn't there." *He isn't anywhere.*

"He?"

"Wydrick."

Alastair's expression went blank. "Tristan Wydrick is dead."

"I know."

"I drove my sword through his heart."

"Alastair, I know. It was just a dream." I tucked my feet beneath me and laid my head on his shoulder. "Forget I mentioned it."

We sat in silence for a few minutes. Exhaustion tugged at my eyelids but sleep was busy elsewhere, leaving me groping around in a tense twilight. The haze had just begun to settle when Alastair shifted.

"I do too," he said in an undertone.

"Hm?"

"See his face. That expression when I ran him through. He looked me right in the eye and then—Thell, I wish I could forget." He pressed his hand to his brow. "He was the first human I'd ever killed."

I turned so I could see his face. He'd never said as much—no Rider I'd ever met said as much—but I'd always assumed their blades had drunk more than just the blood of the *Tekari*. Enemies to the kingdom came from outside the Oldkind as well as within.

"You did the right thing," I managed, and wondered why the words felt so hollow.

"I only wish I'd done it sooner."

"You did it, though, and that's all that matters."

Trennan groaned and rolled in his sleep. His lips moved but no words came out, intelligible or otherwise. Sweat still shone on his forehead. I felt his pulse. Strong and steady, if faster than usual. I checked the remains of the draught in his cup, adjusted his blankets, and sat again. This malady, whatever it was, would have to run its course.

A sudden thought struck me. "The thing out there," I asked Alastair, "it can't hurt Akarra, can it?"

The crackling fire and the sound of Trennan's steadied breathing filled the silence that stretched just a few seconds beyond what was comforting. "No," he said. "No, I don't think so."

But he didn't sound as sure as he once had.

CHAPTER 20

GHOSTS OF THE ABBEY

Sunlight streamed through the high library windows, falling in dusty beams across the bookshelves and onto the figure on the opposite sofa. I sat up and nudged Alastair awake. "Good morning, Master Trennan," I said. The young man blinked and looked around. A touch of color came into his cheeks when his eyes landed on us. "How do you feel?" I asked gently.

"I'm, uh, not sure, milady. Why am I in the library?"

Between the two of us we explained what'd happened. "What did you see last night?" Alastair asked.

Trennan stared at the ground.

"Master Trennan—Jen, listen to me," I said. "As long as this monster is out there, no one's safe. Lord Alastair and the others can defeat it, but first they have to know what they're facing, and you're the only one who's seen it. Please. We need your help."

"You can really defeat her?" Trennan said, looking at Alastair.

"We can, and we will."

"Why do you call it *her?*" I asked.

"That's what it was." He wiped his nose on his sleeve. "At least, that's what it looked like. A lady in the mists."

"What were you doing outside the castle so late?"

"You don't understand. I had to." He covered his face. "That message on the wall yesterday, I thought it was about Isolde. I thought it was for me! So I went to the old abbey to ask forgiveness. I figured if your gods were angry, maybe they'd listen to me there."

"What did Isolde have to do with this?" I asked.

"Nothing! She wasn't supposed to be out there!" He looked up, his cheeks shiny with tears. "It was my job to light the lantern that night. It should've been *me* out on the rocks! Isolde only did it because she owed Bretta a favor, and Bretta and me . . . we . . . it should've been me."

"What did you see when you went to the abbey?" Alastair asked.

Trennan pulled the blanket tighter around his shoulders. "It was dark, but I took a lantern. I thought if I left a few copper trills by the old statue of the Fourfold God, this creature would leave us all alone, so I dropped the coins and said I was sorry. That's when a woman came out of the mists. Only it—it looked like Isolde. She was wearing a green dress though. Isolde didn't own a dress like that."

"Did she say anything to you?" I asked.

"S-she asked me what I was doing there. I told her. She laughed at me and said I was little and petty and she wasn't here for my sins. Then she—" His throat worked up and down. "Then she turned into something else. No, no, I don't remember! Please don't make me, milord!"

Again he covered his face, and this time no amount of coaxing would bring him out of his little ball of misery. I drew Alastair aside to give the boy a moment of privacy.

"A *Tekari* that can change its face?" I whispered. "Have you ever met one like that?"

"No," Alastair said. "And there's nothing like that spoken of in the *Chronicle* either. This is something new."

Or something very old. The centaur Cyrsha's words came back to me. Voices rose and fell in the hallway outside, followed by a thump and the patter of footsteps. *Maybe something that's never gone beyond the borders of the Old Wilds before.*

"Akarra and I need to visit Morianton today," he said. "I'll see if the cantor knows any *Tekari* lore from these parts. In the meantime—"

The door burst open and Bretta ran inside, chased by Rhys. Trennan bolted upright. "Is he all right?" she cried. "Is he going to live?"

"Yes, he'll live, little miss. No need to rouse the castle." Rhys rolled his eyes over Bretta's shoulder as she flung her arms around Trennan, who reddened considerably at the attention. "Oh, and your dragon is in the front courtyard, Lord Daired," Rhys added. "She wants to see you."

"Tell her I'll be there in a moment. Aliza, listen," Alastair said as Rhys went out. "I know you're going to go looking for answers as soon as I leave. No, don't argue. I won't try to stop you. Just promise me you won't go alone, and promise you'll take your dagger."

"I don't think a dagger will do much good."

He looked at me seriously. "Please, *khera.*"

"Yes, all right. I'll take it."

He caught my hand and squeezed it gently before releasing me. "Thank you."

We parted in the hall. I returned to our room and dug out my knife from the bottom of the panniers, strapped the sheath to my calf, and went in search of Cordelia. She wasn't in the Lake Hall, or with Mòrag in the kitchens. After almost an hour of searching I found her in the garden, half hidden by the clump of leafless bushes that enclosed the fountain.

"Good morning, Aliza," she said without raising her head. A film of ice crackled under her touch as she trailed her fingers over the water. "It's strange, isn't it? A reflection. You see, and yet you don't see."

"I'm sorry?"

"The water. It shows so many facets, but never the full truth of the thing. It hides as much as it reveals. Curious, isn't it?" She looked up. "How is Master Jen?"

"He had a bad fright, but he'll be fine. Bretta's taking care of him now."

"He thought we didn't know," she said with a sad smile. "He thought none of us knew about the two of them." I told her what Trennan had said about seeing Isolde's ghost. "Brave, foolish boy. He shouldn't have been outside after dark."

"Cordelia, I want you to take me to the abbey."

She looked up sharply. "Why?"

"If you won't—or can't—tell me what's going on, then perhaps you can show me. Trennan said he saw the creature near the abbey. I want to have a look."

"No! Aliza, no. It's . . . too dangerous."

"It'll be more dangerous the longer we sit here without answers. Besides, it's the middle of the morning. You said it yourself, Trennan was attacked because he was out at night." I drew up the edge of my skirt and showed her the dagger. "If something is there and wants to make itself unpleasant, we'll be ready."

Cordelia tilted her head at the sight of the knife. "You mean to go anyway, do you not?"

I lifted my chin. "Aye."

She closed her eyes and exhaled a long, silent breath. When she opened her eyes, her expression was troubled. "I'll take you to the abbey. But we must be careful."

My breath frosted in white clouds as we started down the cliff-side path and I was glad of my fur cloak. The sky arched a hard, icy blue above us, but fog drifted in pools close to the ground and limited our visibility. I thought it strange to see so much mist so high in the mountains so late in the year, but Cordelia said such things were common around the lakes. Stones slippery with dew and lichen made the path along the cliff treacherous even in daylight. A few minutes later we passed the pile of pine boughs covering the carving and Cordelia veered away from the cliff, deeper into the fog. The blue of the sky faded to a pearly white. Shadows loomed in the distance.

"What are you hoping to find?" Cordelia asked. The mist deadened her voice.

I inspected the heap of stones that'd once formed the entryway into the abbey garden. Moss carpeted the courtyard. "I don't know," I admitted. *Footprints? More warnings? Something the men might've missed?* The empty arches of the abbey rose a few yards ahead. Inside I could just make out the shape of benches, most broken or toppled, surrounding the dark figure of the four-faced statue in the center of the abbey. It listed a little on its dais. Gulls croaked from the roofless walls. "We'll know it when we see it, I'm sure."

"You shouldn't be doing this."

I paused beneath the entry arch. "If you want to tell me what you know, I'm ready to listen."

She bit her lip and didn't answer.

"Thought so. Then I'll keep looking."

Moss muffled her steps as she ran across the courtyard. "Aliza, please! Think of your child!"

"I won't be—" The word brought me up short. My hand drifted to my belly. The signs had been obvious, or should have been obvious—to me. But to a stranger? To someone who I'd just met? "How *did* you know?"

"What?"

"How did you know I was pregnant? You never saw me sick, and even I know my body hasn't changed that much yet."

"I just knew."

"Cordelia. I need the truth."

She came forward and touched four fingers to my navel. "Water . . . speaks to me. All waters, even those of the womb." Her other hand rested on her own stomach. "There are so many things I wish I could tell you, Aliza, and so many more that I can't, but you must believe me when I say I would never wish you or your child harm. Please, come back with me. We can't stay—"

She froze, staring at something beyond me.

"Cordelia?"

"No. You cannot be here. Not now!"

"Who?"

She pointed over my shoulder. I spun and stared into the fog swirling around the shadows in the abbey, around the benches and fallen pillars and the four-faced statue—

The statue moved.

Cordelia shrieked and ran. The statue-shape moved with a soft slither, stirring the fog into swirls and eddies as it made its way toward the place I stood.

"Who are you?" I cried. "Show yourself!"

"Don't worry, Aliza," the dark shape said. It had a woman's

voice, rough, purring, and familiar. "I intend to," she said, and Charis Brysney stepped out of the mists.

That's impossible. "You can't . . . you're *not* . . . Charis, I saw you die."

Bloodred lips curled in a smile that made me feel cold all over. Her hair hung in a lank, reddish-gold curtain around her face, which was sterner and prouder and more beautiful than I'd remembered. She wore a gown the color of pond scum, damp at the hem and stained with dirt. "So you did," she said. "Yet here I stand."

"What are you?"

"I am whatever I need to be."

"You're *dead*."

"Not to you. Not to your husband. Not to a hundred thousand hearts that now hold my name in high honor. As long as I'm remembered I will always live."

"What—what are you doing here?" My voice shook.

"I'm here for the same reason you are. I was invited." With the same careless grace Charis once had the creature sank onto a toppled column. Her feet were bare. A breeze ruffled her gown. I smelled rotting peat and the damp, clinging scent of gravemold. "But come. I've missed a great deal since the Battle of North Fields. You must tell me all."

"You're *not* Charis."

"I'm as much Charis Brysney as you are a true Daired, Aliza Bentaine. Perhaps neither of us are who we pretend to be."

I bent and drew my dagger. Without breaking eye contact with the creature, I edged toward the abbey gate. She watched me with an impassive gaze.

"I don't want you to be afraid of me, Aliza. I never did," she said. "I've always admired your courage, and Alastair would not love a woman whom he could not respect. Still, I must say I'm surprised he went all the way and married you."

"Why does that surprise you?" I couldn't help but ask.

"I forget you've known him for such a short time. You never met his father. Lord Erran was a good man, but strict. He would've never allowed his son to marry a *nakla*." Long, ragged nails tapped the stone beneath her. "If he'd only taken you for his lover, I might understand. Men are weak that way. But as his wife? As the mother of his children? I wonder."

"You shouldn't," I said firmly. But her words had found their mark.

"And perhaps you should."

"He loves me; I love him. We chose each other," I said, or tried to. My voice came as if from a great distance, weighed down by this new, nameless terror. "It's as simple as that."

"It's never as simple as that." She stood and came toward me. I took one step back for every step she took forward. "Has Alastair never spoken of Selkie's Keep? Or the stand we took against the feral gargoyles of the Isle of Dean? Or our last, desperate charge against the centaurs of the South Fens?"

"No, but—"

"Then you can never know the love of the battlefield. You can never understand what it means to trust someone so completely that he becomes a part of you, just as you become a part of him. Two swords, but one heart, one soul." She held out her hands. "There are many kinds of love, Aliza, but ours was the truest."

"I don't believe that."

Her laughter was as brittle as the crust of snow over a frozen battlefield. "Believe what you wish; it doesn't change the truth.

You are not the first woman Alastair Daired has ever loved, and I do not think you will be the last. For all your kindness, all your courage, you can never be what that man truly needs. You're not strong enough. You're not brave enough. You're not . . . enough."

I couldn't look away from those dead gray eyes. There was a rushing in my ears, and I felt again the scorch of dragonfire as I stood before Lady Catriona's dragon in the courtyard of the North Fields lodge, She'd said the same thing. *A nakla, now and forever. A stain on House Daired, diluting the Fireborn's bloodline with your weakness and neediness. A secret shame to the man you love . . .*

"No!" I shook my head, dispelling the voice that I realized, with a feeling akin to plunging headfirst into the icy waters of the lake, wasn't mine. "What are you? How do you know all this?"

The creature laughed. "You bear these words on your heart, Aliza Bentaine, and you always will. Your fears and doubts are written on your face. I just know how to read them."

"You're wrong!"

"I'm not. This compromise you have with Alastair, this balance you think you've struck—it can't last. You know it can't. He is wind and fire and you are mere earth. Either by smothering or scorching, one must destroy the other. Which will it be?" Again she smiled. "I think the choice will fall to you in the end."

"What choice?"

"How long are you willing to watch him burn?"

And suddenly the rushing in my ears was the sound of waves, and I smelled crushed moorflowers, and the pebbles crunching beneath my feet weren't part of the abbey garden at all, and we'd gone a lot farther from the ruins than I'd realized . . .

"NO! Aliza, *stop!*"

A hand seized my wrist at the same moment my foot found empty air. Cordelia yanked me back from the cliff's edge. I fell hard, stones and gravel digging into my palms and belly. The Charis-creature hissed.

"Back! Leave her alone!" Cordelia shouted. "You cannot be here!"

"I can," the lady in green said, in a voice that no longer sounded like Charis Brysney. It wavered and crackled, spitting venom. "I was invited."

"Return to the Wastes where you belong!"

"Not before I claim what is rightfully mine."

"Nothing here is yours, creature."

"Ah, but it is. I was drawn here, Lady of the Keep, drawn by a deep and dreadful wrong, and I will not leave these shores until I have seen vengeance."

"You will. I command you!"

I peered up at the shape in the thinning fog. Charis was gone. The thing that replaced her had a gray face, featureless but for a wide, lipless mouth, now open to show fangs stained with darkness. Its gaunt form was still wrapped in the putrid green robe.

"My quarrel is not with you, Lady of the Keep," it said, "but do not dare command me again."

Cordelia's eyes blazed. "Your quarrel is not with this woman either."

"Her? Why should you care what happens to her?"

"She is a guest in my house and under my protection. You will leave her alone."

The creature threw back its head and laughed. "Your protection? Your *protection*? Oh, my lady, you have no idea what has come to your shores," she said, looking up. Dark bird-shapes moved in the fog above us and I heard the rasp of crows. *Crows? Are those crows?* My mind felt slow, my wits thick. A knot tightened deep in my gut. My palms throbbed. "No, I will not interfere," the creature said after a pause. "I've made my bargain. She is not the one I came for." She pointed at me, grinning to show every glistening midnight fang. "In any case, this one's fate is beyond even me now."

The mist swirled over her like a damp cocoon before melting into the air, leaving nothing but swaying grasses and the distant ruins of the abbey.

CHAPTER 21

OLD WIVES' TALES

Cordelia helped me back to the castle without a word. I didn't ask why she'd abandoned me in the abbey, or how she knew what the creature wanted. Silence, or at least an opportunity to explain, was all I could offer her in return for saving my life. With the thrill of horror when my foot lost the cliff's edge still singing through every nerve, I couldn't think of much else.

"Aliza, I'm so sorry," she said as we crossed the garden. "Your hands."

I looked down. My palms were scraped and bleeding from my fall. Tears welled up as I picked bits of gravel and lichen from the torn skin.

"Mòrag will have ointments and wrappings in the kitchens. Come."

I pulled away from her. "I'm fine."

"But those cuts must be cleaned, bandaged . . ."

"I'll do it myself."

"Aliza, please. I'm—I'm sorry. I shouldn't have left you."

"Then why did you? You knew that creature, and it knew you. Cordelia, for gods' sakes, you have to tell me what's going on here!"

She pressed her hands to her mouth, chin trembling, and shook her head.

I pushed past her. She might not be guilty of bringing this haunting on the castle, but if she would not help, she was no longer innocent.

The upper halls were quiet. I shut the door to our chambers and leaned against it, pain nudging panic from the forefront of my mind. An ache was building in my stomach, knotting and twining with the sick red tendrils of anger, impossible to ignore anymore. *It's fine*, I thought and forced myself to take measured breaths. *This is a delayed reaction to nearly falling off a cliff. It has nothing to do with the baby.*

My hands stung and smarted as I washed them in the bath, but the abrasions weren't deep and the bleeding stopped after a few minutes. There was little in the way of rags in our stately chambers, so I made do. A silk pillowcase, shredded into strips with my knife, made for perfectly serviceable bandages. My conscience gasped at the first slash of the fabric, prickled at the second, and gave up after the third. The Selwyns had withheld too much from us already; they could not begrudge me a pillowcase. I tied off the last knot and stood.

The next moment I was on my hands and knees on the edge of the bath, gasping for breath as what felt like a valkyrie's talons closed around my insides. I felt hot, and cold, and a slow, deep pain, and then somewhere very close, the warm wetness of blood.

Again I attempted to stand. It took two tries. My legs shook and for a few moments I could feel nothing, see nothing, acknowledge nothing but the pain. It dulled as I straightened. Another few breaths and it disappeared altogether. A cautious step toward the bed and it didn't return, but the blood did not stop. I saw it staining my undershift when I visited the privy: not much, just enough to worry.

I groped for the door and edged out into the hall. "Hello?" I called. There was no answer. *It's all right. Everything is all right.* I repeated the words to myself as I went in search of Alastair, or a maid, or Mòrag, or anyone. A little blood and a lot of discomfort was only natural. That's what it meant to carry a child, didn't it? Blood and pain and prayers that it would all be worth it in the end, and *Thell, where is everyone?*

I'd just managed to make it to the bottom of the stairs when the pain returned. I collapsed in a heap next to the bannister, clutching the stone railing with freshly bloodied hands.

Somewhere in the distance a door opened and shut. Footsteps pattered toward me, mixing with the despairing drumbeat of my pulse in my ears. The footsteps stopped.

"Lady Daired?"

I saw Bretta's face through a haze of tears as more cramps tore through me. It was all I could do to sit up. "Alastair," I panted. "Lord Daired. Find—my husband."

"Aye, milady! Right away, but I can't just leave—"

"And a midwife," I said and closed my eyes. "I need—a midwife."

AKARRA HAD NEVER FLOWN SO SMOOTHLY. SHE LANDED on the slope outside the abbey of a little town on the eastern shore of Lake Meera with hardly a misplaced pebble, apologizing for every sudden movement. Alastair helped me out of the saddle as if I were glass. "Are you all right?" he asked for the tenth time.

"Aye. I think so." I could breathe again without cramping and no blood stained the saddle where I'd sat. "Is this Morianton?"

He nodded as the short, plump figure of the cantor trotted out from the abbey. "Don't worry. She'll know where to find the midwife." He strode forward to meet her. "Cantor Brigsley-Baine," he said.

"My lord, you're back so soon! Is something the matter?"

"We need a midwife," I said.

"You—oh! You poor dear. How far along are you?"

"Cantor, the midwife," Alastair said. "Now."

"Yes, yes. Certainly. Carle!" she cried, and a lanky young man in the robes of a subcantor tumbled out of the garden gate. "Run and fetch Madam Threshmore."

"Won't she be out?" the subcantor said.

"Ask around Alchemist's Alley; the chief goldsmith is due soon. Come now, my lady," she said, taking my arm. "Carle will bring Threshmore back here in a trice and there's not a better midwife north of Selkie's Keep. We'll make you comfortable in the meantime."

She led me into the abbey as I described, in as general terms as felt appropriate, my symptoms. I said nothing of my encounter with the Green Lady, wanting to speak first to Alastair. He followed, radiating worry that would have been infectious if I hadn't had enough of my own. I felt with each breath I was balancing on the knife blade between possible fates. *In.* No cramping, no warmth of blood. *Out.* What if next time there was? *In.* The midwife would see us to right; there was nothing to worry about. *Out.* Our child. This was our child. *Thell, take whatever you want, but not our child.*

It was quiet and cool inside the abbey. Lanterns burned on either side of the door, but besides that the only light came from the high windows, which threw the interior into a dim, holy twilight. It followed the typical design of fourfold architecture: square with a sunken floor in the center, its stone walls unadorned save for the tapestries hung out for Martenmas. In the center rose the four-faced statue of the Fourfold God. Low benches surrounded the dais, resting places for the devout as they contemplated the faceted nature of their deity. Or would have, if Morianton had any devotees. The abbey was empty.

"Just through here," Brigsley-Baine said. She led us through the door to the cantor's quarters. Austere stone gave way to the warmth of wood and a crackling fire and she gestured to the chair by the window, on the arm of which rested a sewing box and a section of a torn tapestry. "You sit and rest, dear. Lord Daired, make yourself comfortable. I'll fetch a pot of tea."

She bustled off. I did not sit.

"How's the pain?" Alastair asked, hovering at my side.

"Gone now." It was very nearly the truth. I folded my arms and stared out the window. "And I think the bleeding's stopped. I'm sorry for panicking."

He rested his hands on my shoulders and I leaned into him, swallowing the sudden sob that lodged in my throat. He pressed a kiss into my hair. "You're protecting our child," he murmured. "You've no reason to apologize."

Don't I? With one terror past, the first came flooding back, clammy, cold, and tinged green. I pulled away and faced him. "Alastair, I saw the monster."

"What are you talking about?"

Quietly I told him about what Cordelia and I had seen in the ruins of the abbey.

"This creature," he said when I finished, and in a much calmer voice than I expected, "she said Lord Selwyn invited her? You're sure?"

"It seems that way. And whatever he did, Cordelia knows about it."

"She knew and didn't tell you?"

"She didn't seem to be able to. It was very strange."

He frowned. "You think she's being threatened?"

"Perhaps. Or she's protecting someone. You haven't gotten anything more from Selwyn, have you?" I asked, and he shook his head. "What about the magistrate? Or this cantor?"

"What's that, dear?" Brigsley-Baine asked, backing in through the door to the abbey kitchen with a tea tray.

"Er, northern lore, Cantor," I said quickly. "We were wondering if you knew any."

"Of course! Why, I was just telling some of the stories to Lord Daired. Traders of all kinds come through Morianton on their way down the lakes, and godsfearing or not, you can't hold a candle to the superstition of sailor-folk. The crews all come tramping through here at one time or another asking how best to curry the favor of the Blessed." She chuckled. "Mind you, some of this town I'd be only too pleased to see the Unmaker take out of the world, but some are honest. I give them what prayers I can. In return they tell me of the world beyond the mountains."

"Have any of them spoken of a *Tekari* that can change its face?" I asked.

"No," she said carefully, "not that I can recall, but as I told Lord Daired there are . . . whisperings. Have been here as long as the town. They say there's a creature—or creatures, no one can ever agree on that point—that lives in the Northern Wastes, right on the shore of the Great Ice. They say it's an ancient spirit of vengeance, older than the Oldkind, so old its true name has been lost. The stories call it 'the Green Lady,' or sometimes 'Hag-of-the-Mists.'"

"The Green Lady?" I asked, at the same time Alastair said, "Vengeance against what?"

"Who knows? It's an old story parents use to frighten disobedient children." The door to the abbey proper opened and shut and we heard voices in the nave. "Madam Threshmore!" Brigsley-Baine greeted a thin, ancient woman with the hardened features of someone who knew well the delicate balance between life and death. The subcantor stood behind her.

"Nola, take the lad and this young man out," Threshmore said. Alastair gave me a meaningful look before the subcantor herded him out. "Aliza, is it?" she asked as she took my hand. Her skin was cool and papery, like old parchment. "Very early along, aren't ye?"

"I think so."

"Your first, eh? Leaf and Lightning, how well I remember it. Nervous as a filly, I was. Now, tell me what's happening."

I did. She listened without interrupting, her eyes never straying from mine. When I finished, she examined me, old fingers gently probing my abdomen.

"Ye *can* breathe, child," she said, glancing up.

I exhaled. She continued her examination, lips pursed, muttering under her breath.

"Should I be worried?" I asked after another agonizing minute of silence.

"As I said, ye're very early along. Mite astonishing ye realized ye were with child at all. Any more pains?"

"Not since we left the castle."

"I don't think ye need be fretting yet. I seen wimmen bring bairns into the world after a worse bleeding than this, and I seen them full nine months gone without a problem only to deliver the poor things without a breath o' life in them. Keep half a mind to the workings of your body and send word if anything changes. There's naught else I can be doing for ye."

"Then the baby is all right?"

"Now, now, I said no fretting. Little one's fine best I can tell."

I slumped against the windowsill. "Thank Janna."

"Aye, thank all the ruddy gods ye wish, but mind ye relieve that poor man in the next room." She nudged me toward the abbey proper. "Nine times o' ten the mother's fine. It's the father keen to wear the floorboards down with pacing."

Alastair was indeed pacing the floor in front of the fourfold statue when we went out. The tension rolled off him like mist off a mountain slope when Madam Threshmore announced her verdict. His bow when he thanked her would have been deep enough for the king himself.

"You're all right, *khera?*" he asked me as Brigsley-Baine showed the midwife out.

I clasped his outstretched hand. "I think so."

He closed his eyes and touched his forehead to mine, whispering something to Mikla in Eth. *Thank them indeed.*

As we separated, I turned to the statue. The people of Morianton might not have been the most zealous devotees of the fourfold faith, but there were signs before the dais that spoke of the town's gratitude. Simple things: an ear of corn, a bunch of moorflowers, a child's carving of a boat. Thanks for a good harvest, protection from the *Tekari*, safety on the lake. I knelt before the dais between Odei and Janna. *Creator and Provider.* Their veiled faces pointed north and east, outstretched hands bearing the lightning shard of creation and the beech leaf sigil. I had nothing on me but a few copper half-trills, which I set before Janna with a whispered promise for something more fitting when we returned to the abbey at Pendragon.

Alastair did the same, kneeling and touching the place between Odei and Mikla. "For your protection," he said softly and laid three gold dragonbacks at Mikla's feet.

"They hear you, my lord, my lady," Brigsley-Baine said from the door. She had a faraway look in her eye. "I'm certain they do. Listen well and you might hear them answer."

And if they did, could we bear it? For the first time in a long time I looked in the stone faces of my gods, not to admire the sculptor's skill or the artistry of depiction, but to see if they held any numinous echoes of the deities they honored. *Child of one, child of all.* Hadn't I heard the High Cantor at Edonarle say that once? Provider and Protector I could understand. Without Mikla there would be no means to provide, and without Janna there would be nothing worth protecting. *But what does Creator have to do with Unmaker?* My eyes wandered from Odei to Thell. Of the Four only Thell went unveiled, her watchful stone eyes bent south, her features worn smooth by the weight of years. She held nothing at all.

I glanced at Alastair. He too seemed absorbed in theological musings, for he'd not taken his eyes from Thell. I took his left hand, the ropy scars around his remaining fingers raised and cool to the touch.

"We should get back," I said. "Akarra will be worried about us."

"You're not staying for supper?" Brigsley-Baine asked.

Alastair thanked her but declined as evening was nearing and the sun would be setting soon. In our rush we'd left our cloaks in the castle, and I didn't fancy another flight in the winter dark. The cantor, though disappointed, said she quite understood and bid us farewell at the garden gate.

Akarra hadn't moved from her perch on the slope above the abbey. Her agitated presence had drawn a small crowd onto the main street of the town, and more faces peered out from windows or stooped in doorways to puzzle at her unexpected return. I wondered how fast it would take the news that the midwife had attended an overanxious Lady Daired to spread through Morianton. Remembering the nature of gossip in Hart's Run, I guessed it'd be a miracle if every town around the northern lakes didn't know by the time we'd finished our contract.

Akarra heaved a sigh that set the pebbles cracking in the heat when I told her what Madam Threshmore had said. *"Teh-nes an Nymasi,"* she breathed. "Thank the Four for that. Are you sure you can ride?"

"Well, she didn't say I couldn't and I'm certainly not walking in the dark," I said.

As we mounted, Alastair shared what the cantor had said about the legends of a vengeful spirit from the Wastes. When I spoke of my encounter in the ruined abbey, Akarra growled. "Selwyn knows more than he's telling. If this creature was invited, he knows who invited her."

Her voice was just loud enough to reach the fringes of the crowd. I glanced over my shoulder as the frightened scurry began, everyone intent on pretending they hadn't heard the hired dragon threaten their lord. *She didn't mean it like—*

My stomach dropped. Standing unmoved in the middle of the street, his Ranger's cloak swirling in the wind, eyes bright with malice, was Wydrick.

"Alastair . . ."

I blinked. The street was empty.

"What?" he asked, glancing back at me. Concern etched deep lines in his expression.

I swallowed and fought back the wave of nausea that had nothing to do with carrying a child. It was impossible. Tristan Wydrick was long dead. "Nothing."

THE LIGHTS OF CASTLE SELWYN TWINKLED OUT OVER the darkening waters as we crossed the eastern spear of Lake Meera. Halfway to the promontory Alastair leaned close. "Do you hear that?"

I listened. Over the sound of Akarra's wingbeats was the sound of bells. "Merfolk?"

He shouted something to Akarra in Eth.

"Yes, it's from the western shore," she said. "There's—can you see it? The schools are gathering."

Even as she spoke a cry drifted up from the surface of Lake Meera. Higher than the sound of bells it rang out, thin and keening and cold. First one voice, then two, it grew louder as others joined in. The waters roiled and foamed and dark waves flashed silver as fins hurtled toward the western shore. Shapeless dread curled once more inside me. This wasn't a song at all. The merfolk were screaming.

At a word from Alastair we banked west. The mountain sloped more gently along the sunset shore, easing toward the lake instead of plunging into its depths as it did near Long Quay. Pines grew thick along the edge. A sharp northern wind rustled the boughs and sent more dark clouds scuttling across the sky, carrying with it the shouts of the merfolk. Akarra slowed as we approached the beach, which was little more than a pebble-strewn shelf gnawed from the shore by the motion of the waves and walled in by piles of driftwood. She landed with a crunch of pebbles and sun-bleached sticks.

I slid out of the saddle. My stomach lurched, and I emptied it in the closest pile of driftwood. Draped over a waterlogged tree trunk was the body of a young mermaid, her eyes open, clouded, and staring. Silvery blood drenched the stones in a circle around her. The mermaid's chest was cut open, and though I didn't have the nerve to look closer, I'd bet anything her heart was missing.

CHAPTER 22

THE LAKE LAMENTS

Dozens of merfolk lashed their tails in the shallows, stretching webbed arms toward their slain sister. "What are they saying?" Alastair asked Akarra.

"They say her name was Lyii-Lyiishen, spawn-daughter of Lyii and Ooara-Lyiishen, and she'd only lived thirteen winters. They're..." She paused.

"They're what?"

"Calling down curses on the one that did this."

Alastair went to the shore. "Translate for me."

"*Khela*, don't. They're not in the listening mood. You'd best keep away from the water."

"I have to." He knelt on the stones just shy of the tide line. The merfolk fell silent. "My name is Alastair Daired, son of Erran, son of Seraphina, daughter of Pietyr, Blood of the Fireborn." More heads emerged from the water as Akarra translated. Eyes as fathomless as the deepest waters of the lake narrowed as Alastair drew his sword. He placed his hand on the flat. "By Mikla-Protector and Thell-Unmaker, I will find who did this. I swear it."

The pearled spikes of a crown broke the water at the center of the school, followed by the bearded face of the Mermish king. "Do not swear an idle oath, dragonmaster," the king said in Arlean. "The last time we spoke you said you would hunt down the creature that murdered *Idar*. That was many days ago, and now one of my school is dead. Is this what you have to show for your bond-price, Blood of the Fireborn?"

Alastair's throat worked up and down. "We are looking, sire. We have hunt—"

"You have hunted rumor and myth, not monsters," the king said. "Yes, my people have told me of your dragon's questions."

There was a rustle and snap of branches behind us. Rhys and Selwyn clambered over the driftwood barrier, Rhys with his sword, Selwyn carrying Rhys's crossbow. "What's going on?" Selwyn asked. "We heard the cries and saw your dragon . . ." He stopped when he saw the mermaid. His face went very white.

"It's back," Rhys whispered. "Sulfurous hells."

"There may be truth in those rumors, Your Deepness," Alastair said. "What do you know of a creature called the Green Lady?"

There were hisses from the merfolk who understood Arlean. Selwyn flinched.

"It has been generations since that creature has stirred from her haunt in the Northern Wastes," the king said. "What do you want with one of the Eldest, dragonmaster?"

"The cantor of Morianton said she was an ancient spirit of vengeance. Have you heard the story?"

The king's gills ruffled along the side of his neck. He shifted uneasily in the water. "Of course. We all have."

"We believe she was responsible for the death of Lord Selwyn's maid. Could she have done this as well?" He gestured to Lyii-Lyiishen.

The king bared his teeth. "Never. She is an ancient and pitiless spirit, a guardian of the Northern Wastes, but she has no quarrel with the Oldkind. Some have even called her our protector."

"If that's true, why would she lead Isolde to her death?" I asked. "Isolde was northern-born."

The king gave me a scornful glance. "I said she was *our* protector, not yours." The waterweed that formed his beard trembled and he turned back to Alastair. "Be certain of this, dragonmaster: it was not she who murdered the *Idar* of Ommeera. And if a human was responsible for this evil, know that the Hag-of-the-Mists will not rest until they are brought to justice. Now Lord Sentinel, Lord Daired, give us back the body of our Lyii-Lyiishen. We will return her to the depths with the dignity she deserves."

Akarra lifted the mermaid's broken body with her wings and carried it into the lake. The waves lapped at her belly as she placed it in the outstretched arms of the one the king had called her shoal-mother. The merwoman's wail carried across the water, a haunting lament without words, and the king and the others followed as she sank out of sight, leaving only the echoes of her cries in our ears.

There was a minute of terrible silence broken only by the slap of the water against the stones, its surface tinged silver with Lyii-Lyiishen's blood.

"This has gone on long enough." Alastair turned to Selwyn. "It ends today."

Selwyn stared at the naked steel in his hand. "My lord, what are you doing?"

"My duty. The Green Lady said she was invited here and I think you know why."

"I don't know what that creature wants!"

"You do know. I'm not going to ask again."

Selwyn looked wildly from Alastair to Rhys. "Owin? Owin, we had an agreement."

"I'm sorry, Selwyn, but Lord Daired is right." Rhys avoided his eye. "We need to know what's really going on here."

The crossbow in Selwyn's hands jerked up, then fell to his side. "As you will," he said through gritted teeth. "I think, or I'm *afraid* she thinks I stole—"

A twig cracked behind us and Selwyn stopped. I looked over my shoulder, expecting to see Chirrorim, or perhaps even Mòrag, but it was neither. Colors like cold flames licked through my mind's eye, giving meaning to that red cloak, the blond hair, and above it all, those green, green eyes.

Tristan Wydrick stood at the edge of the beach.

Not a ghost or a bad dream or a memory, but smiling and whole and very much alive.

Rhys's voice came dimly through the humming in my ears. "What are *you* doing here?" he asked the red-cloaked figure, but then Akarra's roar drowned out everything but her rage, and I felt fire, and hatred, and then, like a terrible tide, the warmth of blood.

Shouts rose around me. Wydrick swept his cloak aside and turned toward the woods. I caught fractured glimpses of something monstrous clinging to him, darkness like spider's limbs buried in his back, before a swirl of valkyrie feathers swept Wydrick and the not-thing up into the sky. Akarra flew after them, trailing dragonfire.

I sank down on the nearest log. "Alastair?"

He didn't move, didn't answer, staring at the place Wydrick had disappeared.

"What was that *thing*?" Rhys said. "And what was that Ranger doing here?"

"Alastair?" I said again.

"I don't understand."

"None of this makes *sense*."

"Who *was* that?"

"Selwyn, we need the truth."

Voices merged, and droned, and faded. My breath rattled in my throat, dry like the rasp of old bones. The Green Lady wasn't the only thing hunting the shores of Lake Meera. *Red and green, the green and the red.* Another *ghastradi*. Too many impossible things. This wasn't right. None of this was right . . .

You're bleeding.

I slid off the log. Blood stained the sun-bleached wood where I'd sat. The world snapped back into focus.

"Alastair!"

My scream broke Wydrick's spell. Strong arms wrapped around my shoulders and I gasped as Alastair helped me up.

"Khera?"

"It's happening again."

He swore. One arm beneath mine, he half led, half carried me toward the castle. I saw nothing else, heard nothing else, knew nothing else. All my senses turned inward, where a new battle raged. Terror upon terror condensed into a single refrain that beat like war drums in my head, knifing through consciousness even as pain knifed through my body. *Janna, please no. Not our child.*

"How long has she been bleeding?"

I came to myself in the main hall of the castle. Mòrag's chilly touch forced my eyelids open as she felt my forehead. "It happened before, this afternoon," Alastair said, his voice rough with panic. "The midwife said she was all right."

"Get her upstairs. I'll have a maid fetch Madam Threshmore."

He carried me up to our chambers and set me on the bed. I lay back gingerly, listening, as Madam Threshmore had said, to the quiet cries of my body. The pain had eased but I could still feel muscles tensing inside me, waiting for any excuse to contract.

"Alastair, if we lose—"

"No. Don't say it."

I didn't need to. The words were already pounding inside me with the relentlessness of thunder. Another spasm took hold of me and I felt more blood flowing, crimson and clotted and hot. I reached for Alastair's hand. "Tell Mòrag to hurry."

MADAM THRESHMORE DIDN'T ARRIVE UNTIL DUSK. SHE looked me over a second time, ordered clean rags and a pitcher of water, and helped me exchange my bloody dress for a shift. A few minutes later Mòrag reentered with water, cloths, and Cordelia in tow. Alastair paced in front of the balcony door; despite Madam Threshmore's insistence, he refused to leave this time.

The midwife directed Mòrag to soak the rags as she felt my abdomen. Her face was graver than before. Cordelia laid a hand on my forehead as the midwife continued to probe, murmuring words in Mermish. I caught the names *Aquouris* and *Uoroura*. She repeated them several times. It sounded like a plea.

I raised my head off the pillow. "Madam Threshmore?"

"Aye, child?"

"You said we were going to be all right."

"As best I could tell, mind. Ye seem to have had quite a shock."

Yes, a dead man smiled at us from his grave. Fresh cramps seized me. "What can I do?" I panted when they passed.

"Nothing to do, dear. Only rest. And pray, if ye believe it'll help."

The sun set, and rose, and set again. Pain and blood ebbed and flowed like some terrible tide. One minute I felt fine; the next I wanted nothing more than to curl up into a ball and weep. Alastair never left my side. Glassy-eyed and quiet, he did as Madam Threshmore told him. Neither of us slept well, but he hardly slept at all, dozing off next to me for a few minutes at a time before jolting awake, reaching for the knife at his belt.

Minutes melted into hours, hours into days. *Sleep, eat. Shuffle around the chamber. Clean up the bloody cloths. Wash. Rest, or try to.* It was all I could do. Listen to my body scream, and whimper, and scream again.

And then, silence.

I knew. Madam Threshmore told me anyway, that iron voice rusting even as she offered her condolences. I thanked her, and Alastair thanked her, and she left with Mòrag and Cordelia. He shut the door behind them. The chair nearest the door creaked as he collapsed into it, his head in his hands.

I threw on a dressing gown and slipped out onto the balcony, away from the echoes of the midwife's words, which hung in the air like some kind of foul insect. *Lost.* As if we could find our child if we looked hard enough. *No need to worry, my lady. He's hiding in the gargoyle peaks of Nordenheath. Don't fret, my lord. She's pitched a tent in the pastures of Pelagios.* Lost, only to be found again. Perhaps in some world, but not by us. Never by us.

Flakes of snow stung my face as I stepped into the wind. The lake was foam flecked and choppy beneath the stormy sky. Mountains stood guard around the valley like soldiers, dull and leaden and silent. No Mermish songs rode the crest of the wind. No winged shapes hovered against the roof of the sky. Not even the gulls' cries echoed over the lonely lake. The air was cold, gray, and empty. I went inside.

ALASTAIR DIDN'T STAY IN OUR CHAMBERS LONG. HE SAID he needed to run, to exercise, to spar with someone, to do anything but sit in silence. I watched from the balcony as he met Akarra in the garden. Her lament shook me even to my cold and empty core and I hurried inside, resisting the urge to cover my ears.

DAYS TUGGED AT THE REST OF THE CASTLE LIKE A RIVER from its bank. The water rushed on, but in the little cove called now it had no power over me.

Whatever the servants brought up to our chambers, I ate, if I remembered.

I stood at the window and watched the lack of birds.

I sat in the bath, knees drawn up to my chin, following every movement of the ripples as they broke against the walls and faded into nothing.

At night I lay at Alastair's side in a shroud of blankets and prayed for dreamless sleep. It was the only prayer I had left. The gods had nothing to say to me, and I had nothing to say to them.

WHISPERS FROM THE REST OF THE CASTLE TRAILED IN after every dinner tray. Rhys and Chirrorim took up the guardianship of the castle. On one of her visits to our chambers, Cordelia told us they patrolled the grounds from the safety of the outer walls, as Selwyn had forbidden anyone from leaving the castle in case the Green Lady returned. Cordelia talked, but she didn't try to get me to join in her conversation. Nor, to my relief, did she try to comfort me. Perhaps she sensed how hollow it would sound.

ONCE I DREAMED OF UNCLE GREGORY. IN WAVERING, watercolor strokes, I watched as he helped me to my feet after I'd fallen on the breakwater rocks outside of Edonarle. My knee had been badly skinned. Young me wailed when he took me to wash it in the ocean, and in my dream I heard his voice, calm and kind and patient. *Remember, Sweet Alyssum, saltwater will do any wound a world of good,* he said. *Hurts like the blazes, but cleans better than you can imagine.*

Yes, Uncle, I said. *But it won't bring our child back.*

"Lady Daired?"

I woke with a start. Mòrag stood in the doorway, a tray in her hands. I sat up, bleary-eyed, blinking at the depression in the mattress next to me. I hadn't felt Alastair leave.

"I believe he's in the garden." She set the tray on a table. "You need to eat, my lady. You hardly touched your meals yesterday, or the day before that."

"Where's Cordelia?"

"With His Lordship."

"Why didn't you send a servant?"

"Because they will not make sure you eat."

"I'm not hungry."

Silver clinked against china as she set out a tea service. "No. You're beyond that now."

She was right. I'd passed from hunger to a gnawing, bone-deep emptiness, desperate to be filled with something, with anything. But I couldn't think of a single thing I wanted to eat. I faced the wall. The tinkle of cutlery stopped and a cushion sighed as she sat. I closed my eyes. If she'd stay, she'd stay without me. Sleep, or at least its dark and thoughtless approximate, called me back.

"I'm not leaving, Lady Aliza. I need to talk with you."

"So talk."

"And I need you to *listen.*"

I opened my eyes.

"This can't continue. The longer you stay in here, the worse it'll get."

"I don't see how that should bother you."

"It probably shouldn't."

I rolled over. "Why are you here?"

"Because I've taken a vow to serve House Selwyn, young lady, and you are a guest of my master. I do whatever I need to do to protect those in this house."

Protection. Inside I sneered at the word. *Yours and Cordelia's and Alastair's and the gods themselves, and it still won't bring our child back.* "I mean, why do you care?"

"You've been a friend to Lady Cordelia."

I stared at her.

Gnarled fingers twined and untwined in her lap as she studied the tiles. It was a minute before she spoke again. "Because what you're feeling now," she said in a low voice, "that gaping wound inside your chest you think will never be whole again . . . that's not something I'd wish on my bitterest enemy." She looked up, and there, shining for an instant in those icicle eyes, I recognized a familiar pain. Hers was an old scar, scabbed over many times, while mine was a fresh wound still bleeding, but the shape was the same. She had the hollow stare of a woman whose womb had borne too many children and whose arms had held too few.

In that moment we two—an old housekeeper withered by grief and a young mother who would never hear her child's cry—we understood each other.

I hung my head. "Does it ever go away?"

"No. But you live."

"How?"

Mòrag stood. "You get out of bed. You eat something. You get dressed. You go downstairs and comfort your husband, and let him comfort you. You find a reason to do it again tomorrow. That's all you can do." She turned to go.

"Mòrag?" I asked in a small voice.

"Yes?"

"How many?"

Ages might've passed in the seconds it took for her to answer, and in the single word I felt the weight of worlds, of the lives and hearts of countless mothers like her. *Like us.*

"Five."

I forced the words past dry lips. "I'm . . . sorry."

"Yes, child, so am I. But you cannot—" She stopped. Her chin trembled, eyes fixed on the floor near the foot of the bed. "N-never mind. Eat your meal, child, and remember what I've said." She hurried out.

I looked down, searching for what had caught her gaze. There was nothing on the floor besides my riding boots, a handful of pillows I'd kicked off the bed, and, peeping through the open mouth of a crumpled pannier, a corner of the silver box.

CHAPTER 23

WATER AND BLOOD

For a long time after she left I sat there, buried in blankets.
There was too much I didn't understand. Fresh apathy beckoned
and offered escape, but this time I fought it, sifting my soul for some
shred of strength that could tip the scales against indifference.

"Find a reason," she'd said. Madness and mystery and the shadow
of monsters still hung over Castle Selwyn. If we could do nothing
else, we could find answers. We could finish what we started. No
one else would die on the shores of Lake Meera.

I got out of bed, ate the food Mòrag had brought, washed,
dressed, and went downstairs.

I FOUND ALASTAIR IN THE GARDEN. HE DIDN'T TURN AS
I approached, my footsteps muffled by moss and dead leaves. If I'd
been wearing iron-shod boots on a flat marble floor, I don't think
he would've heard me either. The defeat of a clump of whitethorn
growing in the corner of the garden consumed his attention, the
makeshift quarterstaff in his hands a blur as he lashed out at the
hedge. His Rider's plait hung limp and greasy down his back.
Akarra was nowhere to be seen.

317

"Alastair?"

The staff fell to his side. Slowly he faced me. The faint glisten of tear tracks, dried and remade and dried again, showed on his cheeks. A hundred leagues' distance crammed into the arm's length separating us, and the air took on the textured silence of a thousand things not spoken.

"You're back," he said at last. His voice was hoarse.

"I am."

"Are you . . . all right?"

"No."

"Me neither," he said as he pulled me into his arms. I buried my head in his shoulder, needing to cry, wanting to cry, but my eyes stayed dry.

"Where's Akarra?"

"Patrolling with Rhys." He released me and sank onto the rim of the fountain. "What now, Aliza? What do we do?"

"What we came to do."

"And what is that? I'm not even sure if I know anymore."

"We hunt down this monster."

He didn't raise his eyes. "Akarra couldn't find him," he said. "Tristan. She searched the whole time you were—while we were gone. Nearly burned the forest down looking, but there wasn't a trace of him. I don't understand. I killed him. Blood for blood, death for death, Mikla's way. He died on that battlefield for what he did to our families. I ran him through. I watched him fall. Aliza, he was *dead*."

I sat down beside him. "I believe you."

"So how can he be here?"

"I don't know. And right now, it doesn't matter. The king of the merfolk said the Green Lady wasn't responsible for the *Idar* murders, which means we're hunting two monsters." I was surprised at the sound of my own voice. It was hard, cold, and it didn't sound like a *nakla* anymore. "We start with the monster we know."

"We don't know anything about this Green Lady," he said.

"We know what she wants. Vengeance."

"But for what?"

"*Drawn by a deep and dreadful wrong.*" "Perhaps it's time we found out."

SELWYN SAT IN HIS STUDY, A MAP OF THE CASTLE AND surrounding villages spread on his desk. Cordelia stood at the window behind him, drumming a nervous rhythm on the windowsill. They both looked up as we entered. Selwyn's eyebrow lifted on seeing me, but he managed a curt nod. Cordelia clasped her hands together. For a second it looked as though she would say something to me, but then changed her mind, settling on a look of pity that I ignored. I didn't want her pity. I didn't want anyone's pity.

Selwyn cleared his throat. "Lady Daired. Well. I'm glad to see you," he said. "Lord Daired, while you're here I suggest we start—"

"No, Selwyn," Alastair said. "No more lies. Tell us what you stole."

He spoke in a voice of deadly calm. I snuck a glance at Selwyn, but he didn't seem to appreciate how close to fraying the thread of Alastair's patience was. *Choose your next words carefully, Your Lordship,* I thought.

"Stole?" Selwyn repeated.

"On the beach you said the Green Lady thought you stole something," I said. "That's the wrong that drew her to Lake Meera. Tell us what it is."

"I misspoke," he said, still addressing Alastair. "I haven't stolen anything."

Cordelia flinched. "Niall, please."

"Hush, dear."

She bit her lip and clutched the windowsill like an anchor against a storm.

"You're lying, Lord Selwyn," I said.

"Lady Daired, I understand you've been through a terrible ordeal and I'm sorry for your loss, but it's not a lie. In any case, what does it matter what this Green Lady thinks? A *Tekari* is a *Tekari*. Death and destruction are what they care about, not justice. She's still—"

"No, Niall!" Cordelia cried. "This has gone on long enough. People have *died*. You must tell them what you've done!"

"*I said be quiet!*"

The sound of flesh striking flesh was magnified in the quietness of the room.

For one breathless second Cordelia stared at her husband, trembling fingers raised to the red mark spreading across her cheek. I was too shocked to move.

"Oh—oh *Thell*." Selwyn fell to his knees and reached for her. "Cordelia, my love, I'm sorry. I didn't mean—"

She shoved him aside and ran from the room.

Selwyn stayed on his knees, head bowed, his shoulders rising and falling in an unsteady rhythm. At last he dragged himself upright and collapsed in his chair. His eyes were red and glassy.

"Lord Selwyn," Alastair said in a voice of ice and iron, "your hand is forfeit for what you've done."

Selwyn gripped his head and groaned. "You don't understand. This was not supposed to happen. None of this was supposed to happen."

I started to follow Cordelia as Alastair removed his hand from the hilt of his sword and sat across from him. "Talk."

"I can't . . ."

"If you wish to keep your hand, you will talk."

"All right." He sucked in a deep breath and straightened in his chair. "It's—it's Fyri."

I paused, the name holding me on the threshold.

"Who?" Alastair asked.

"The forge-wight who works the pump house below the castle. Many years ago she came to me after hearing about the wheel-works my father had built. She's of a mechanical mind and she wanted to improve on his system. I agreed. Lord Daired, I'm sure you appreciate a forge-wight's skill when it comes to metalworking. Fyri is a genius, and I owe her a great debt of gratitude. She keeps my family home in the good repair it deserves."

"Why would the Green Lady care that you have a forge-wight working for you?" I asked.

Selwyn shifted. "Fyri will not take wages. I've offered time and again but she always refuses. Here she has food and lodging, and the only thing she wants in return is the challenge of the craft."

"So the Green Lady thinks you've stolen . . . what, Fyri's labor?" I asked. "Does she know how Fyri feels about it?"

"How should I know?" he snapped. "I—apologies." He pressed a handkerchief to his brow. "About a month ago, after Fyri and I'd gone to inspect the miller's new pump house in Morianton, we found the first dead troll. Not long after that the Green Lady's haunting, if that's what you wish to call it, began. Heavier mists than usual. Marshlights hanging about the abbey ruins, even though we don't have any will-'o-the-wisps here. Then the pixies, and the second troll, and then that night with the maid . . . well, I believe you know the rest."

"If this forge-wight has been working for you so many years, why did the Green Lady wait so long to show herself?" Alastair said.

"You think I haven't been asking myself the same question, Lord Daired?"

"May we speak with Fyri?" I asked.

I may as well have asked Selwyn if I could set fire to the castle. He gave a violent start. "For what purpose?"

"If the Green Lady is here because of her, Fyri may know how to send her away. To right the wrong she came to avenge."

"Ah. I see. Well . . . unfortunately Fyri left this morning for Morianton to continue work on the miller's wheelworks. She didn't plan to return until tomorrow. They're anxious to make sure it works before the ice sets in. I'm sorry I can't help you any further, my lord, my lady. I've told you all I know." He stood. "I trust you can show yourselves out."

Alastair scowled, but together we left the room without another word. Selwyn locked the door after us.

"Do you believe him?" Alastair asked in the hallway.

"No. But Fyri can tell us the truth. And I don't think it should wait for tomorrow."

"Agreed. Akarra and I can find her in Morianton and be back before sunset, but I . . ." He trailed off.

"What?"

"I don't want to leave you alone," he said.

Instead of answering I leaned up and kissed him. "I'll be all right," I said, and hoped he didn't realize it was a lie.

THE BED WAS MADE AND OUR CHAMBERS HAD BEEN TIdied when I returned, deep in thought. The shadow of despair clawed at me as soon as I entered the room and it took real effort to keep from throwing myself back into bed and forgetting about everything beyond the tiny world of warmth and blankets. I sank into a stiffly embroidered armchair by the fire and glared into the fireplace as if the leaping flames were hiding the answers I sought.

The pieces were there, but still something didn't fit. Around and around Selwyn's story flitted through my mind, looping and tumbling like a drunken pixie. I thought of the cavern beneath the castle. Fyri's home among the wheelworks wasn't luxurious, but I'd also seen nothing to hold her back if she decided to leave. That much of Selwyn's story seemed true. Besides, Akarra had confirmed that Selwyn had been supervising the construction of the pump house at Morianton. It'd be easy enough to find out if Fyri had gone with him.

The pipes to the bath gurgled behind me.

But if Fyri's gone back there, wouldn't the Green Lady notice? If an enslaved forge-wight was the wrong she came to right, why not right it when she had the chance? Fyri had been free of the castle for a full day, free to go where she wished, or leave entirely. Surely the Green Lady would have seen that? Or if she saw and doubted, why not at least use the opportunity to get the truth from Fyri herself?

More gurgling, this time accompanied by the smell of rotten eggs. I glanced over my shoulder. The largest pipe trembled as water gushed into the pool, before slowing to a trickle, then a steady dripping. *Plink.* The smell of eggs faded. *Plink.* A few drops sent the surface of the water shivering. *Plink.* I turned back to the fire.

And sat bolt upright.

Fyri controlled the flow to these pipes. Last time that happened she'd accidentally misdirected the water from the kitchens.

Which meant that Selwyn had lied. Fyri was still in the castle.

I snatched up the nearest lamp and hurried out the door.

IT TOOK CAREFUL TIMING TO AVOID BEING SEEN BY THE servants as I made my way back to the secret passageway behind the portrait. The underground cavern hadn't changed since I'd last seen it. Nor had the clank of oiled chains and the low, rumbling mutter of the wheelmaster as she labored over a broken pulley. I stopped at the edge of the spring and raised my lantern, throwing light over the forge-wight's armored back.

"Fyri?"

She spun around. "Good gods, girl, don't sneak about like that! You're liable to get an anvil thrown at your head." The blue flame behind her mask dimmed as she peered across the water. "Daired, wasn't it? Liza-something? I told you, unless you're bringing me one of Niall's little projects I don't have the time for questions." The fire brightened and she held up an ingot, shining dull white in the light of the furnace. "Though I have plenty more watersilver if you were here about a project."

"I'm not. But you gave me three questions last time, and I still have one left. I need to know about the pump house you and Lord Selwyn are building in Morianton."

"Why? Has something gone wrong? Did they break something already?"

"No, it's—"

"It couldn't have been those wheel bands. It'd take a mad troll to snap them."

"It's nothing like that. We—"

"Did the builders use the quarter-inch spikes for the mill wheel? Please say they didn't. I *told* them to use half-inch."

"Fyri, I don't know anything about what they've done! I just need to know if you've gone back there recently."

"Oh." It must've been difficult to make that steel mask look forlorn, but she managed it. "Well, yes, I suppose. Niall's had business in the castle for the past few weeks, so I went out to help the

miller test the waters. He wasn't sure how deep they needed to be."
She tapped one finger against the anvil at her side. "Then, ah, is
that it?"

"Not quite." As quickly as I could I told her about the Green
Lady and Selwyn's account of her presence around the castle.

Fyri laughed. "This thing is worried about *me*? Leaf and Lightning, what's the world coming to? Creature's wasting her time. I'm
no slave. Next time I go to Morianton I'll make sure to leave a
great blazing message on the grass for her."

"Oh." My shoulders sagged. The answer had been close, close
enough to taste, and it had slipped through my fingers. "All right."

"Is that it?"

"Aye. Sorry for bothering you." I lowered the lantern and turned
toward the stairs. Selwyn had led us in circles. Now we were in the
same place we started, full of questions without answers—

A moment later I was back at the spring. "Hold on a moment." I
looked at the ingot she still held in one hand. It looked . . . familiar.
"*What* did you say about silver?"

"I thought Selwyn might've sent you down with one of his little challenges. That's what he did last time. Had the old woman
deliver the specifications. Too busy to come himself, she said," she
added with a sniff.

"Fyri, *specifications for what?*"

"Oh, just a trifle. A plain silver box. Not much to look at, but
then, I didn't have much time. They were in a great hurry."

My hand shook on the handle of the lantern. "This box. It's
about two hands wide? Has a lid but doesn't open?"

Fyri wagged a finger, and I had the impression she was smiling beneath her mask. "Ah, there was the challenge. Watersilver's
an invention of mine, you know. Push and pull and pry on it all

you like; if it's not underwater, it's not going to budge, and—Aliza?"

I was already halfway up the stairs.

I EMERGED FROM THE PORTRAIT HALLWAY INTO A CASTLE in tumult. Servants rushed to and fro, whispering to themselves and looking scared. I ran headlong into Bretta as she dashed out of the kitchens. "Bretta, what's going on?"

"The mistress, milady. She's gone!"

"What? Where?"

"Dunno, miss. I never seen the master in such a state! He and Lord Daired are out combing the grounds now. That Ranger and the beoryn are rounding everyone else up to search the castle."

I left her and hurtled up the stairs to our chambers two at a time. The unease that'd been nibbling away at my subconscious for the past few hours blossomed into full dread when I reached the top. The door to our room was ajar. Heart in my throat, I nudged it open.

"Madam Mòrag?"

Mòrag knelt next to the bed, her back to me, surrounded by our scattered luggage. She whipped around. White hair stuck out at untidy angles around her face as she labored to her feet, the silver box clasped in her hands. "Lady Daired, I can explain."

And then, like a wave, understanding washed over me. "*You* sent it to us, didn't you?"

She nodded.

"What is it?"

"Come," she said and sat on the edge of the bath. Her hands trembled, but her voice was steady. "My lady was right. Things have gone far enough. I'm breaking my oath to Lord Niall by showing you this, but for Cordelia's sake . . ." She plunged the silver box into the steaming water. "This is the secret folly of Niall Selwyn."

Ripples danced across the surface of the water. The lid shivered and beneath the broken shadows of light a pattern emerged. Silver wires rose up in the center in the wheel-and-trident sigil of Lake Meera, and Mòrag turned the wheel to the left. A *click* sounded within the box and she lifted it out of the water as the last of the watersilver pattern settled into place. She turned the wheel back to the right. Somewhere within a bolt shot home. The lid sprang open.

The box was empty.

Empty—save for a folded cloth at the bottom.

I sat back on my heels. "I don't understand."

Mòrag pulled it out and spread it on the edge of the bath. It was a small cap, furred but lightweight, the cloth hardly thicker than an onionskin and so black it was almost blue. Water splashed from Mòrag's hands onto the stone and the drops scuttled toward the skin as if running to embrace an old friend. "It is the symbol of his great secret," she said. "You recognize it, don't you?"

Distant memories of *Idar* lore drifted to mind, stories Henry had sung or Mari had recited for us on winter evenings. My face felt suddenly cold. *Sealskin.* "That's a selkie's cap," I said slowly.

"None of it was supposed to happen this way. He loved—loves—her so dearly. I thought she was happy."

I couldn't tear my gaze from the tiny circle of fabric, at once so little and yet so dreadfully much. "Cordelia isn't human, is she?"

"No."

"So when she said her family was from Selkie's Keep . . ."

"She meant it. She told you the truth, such as she could. He forbade her to speak of it. He forbade her to speak of many things." She dried her hands on her skirt. "It was a long time ago. I've been housekeeper to Family Selwyn for more than fifty years.

I all but raised young Niall and he—well, his happiness means a great deal to me. Not long after his father died he visited Selkie's Keep on business. I don't know everything that happened there, but a fortnight later he returned a husband, Cordelia in his arms."

Husband to a selkie? From what I'd heard the gentle, seal-like *Idar* of the coasts were shy creatures, relying on the human forms their sealskin caps concealed only in great need. "Did he steal her cap?"

Mòrag didn't answer right away, and that in itself was answer enough.

"He did, didn't he?"

"No! She gave it to him. Cordelia told me that much. She would not be bound to his silence if she'd not parted with the cap willingly. She liked the land. *Likes* the land. And she did love him. I've never doubted that. But now . . . oh gods, it's all gone to pieces now, hasn't it?" She sank onto the nearest chair. "They could've been happy. They *would* have been happy, if it weren't for the Great Worm. When Lord Niall was gone with the regiments, Cordelia started looking for her cap."

"Selwyn didn't give it back?"

"She never asked! She was Lady of the Keep, wife to the lord sentinel, with wealth, a title, everything he could give her. We protected her, provided for her—"

"And she still wanted to leave." I stood. "Madam Mòrag, none of this explains why you sent the box to us."

"When Lord Niall returned from Hatch Ford, I told him what Cordelia had done in looking for her cap. I'd never seen him so furious. They fought that night. The next morning, he had me commission Fyri to make the watersilver box and ordered me to send it somewhere safe, somewhere it couldn't be harmed, but far from Cordelia. I sent it away with the wedding presents for you and your husband and hoped that would be the last of it."

"Why us?"

"The Daireds are a noble house. I trusted you'd take care of it, even if you didn't understand what it was. I never thought the box would find its way back to her. And I had no idea the Green Lady would come."

Oh, Mòrag, Selwyn, what have you done? "I wish you'd told me sooner."

Mòrag's lips contracted as if smiling, though there was no mirth in her eyes. "Yes, I should've. I've been a fool, Lady Daired. I'll be the first to admit it, but what I did I did for love of Family Selwyn. I cannot regret that."

"Do you know where Cordelia is?"

"I wish it were that simple, child. Even if we find her, it may already be too late."

"What do you mean? Where is she?"

Perhaps it was the fear in my voice, or perhaps the weight of her guilt reached its final tipping point; with terrible suddenness she rose from her chair and snatched up the cap like some withered bird of prey. "Follow me," she said. "We don't have much time."

CHAPTER 24

FIRE AND ICE

Blue was deepening overhead when we emerged from the castle, the sky pricked with the first icy lights of the evening. Mist had already gathered around the ruins of the abbey, creeping toward the cliffside path with unnerving deliberateness.

"Where is she?"

"The water." Mòrag fought to catch her breath as we dashed out the garden gate. "She's going to try to go home."

"Into the *lake*? It's freezing!"

She pressed her lips together and ran. I raced after her. Melting frost soaked my slippers and drove numbing spears of cold into my legs with each step. The wind off the lake had a razor's edge, and we bled warmth as the sky bled daylight. A stitch started in my side as we flew down the cliffside path, arms outstretched to keep balance on the slippery stones.

Mòrag didn't cry out as she fell. I heard only the crunch of stone and a sharp intake of breath as she went down, sprawled on her back in front of me, one leg twisted beneath her.

"Mòrag!" I slid to her side. "Are you all right?"

She tried to move and gave up with a hiss of pain. I slipped an arm behind her shoulders, but she batted me away. "Get to the quay," she panted, pushing the sealskin cap into my hands. "Give this to Cordelia. Help make it right."

"Not until you're back in the castle."

"Don't be stupid, girl! There's no time!"

"I'm not leaving you for the Green Lady!"

"She won't come here," she said. "She doesn't care about me, or you, or anyone else. Lord Selwyn was the one who took it from Cordelia. He's the one she came for. Go!"

I took the cap and stuffed it in my pocket, then unclasped my cloak and tucked it around her. She seized my hand.

"And you mustn't let Selwyn know you have it. Even now he might . . . Until Cordelia has it, he mustn't know." She shoved me away. "Go!"

Blinded by a sudden wave of tears, I sucked in a breath, leapt to my feet, and ran.

THE PALE SPAR OF LONG QUAY BROKE THE SHIMMER OF starlight on the surface of the lake. Dark figures gathered at the end. I nearly ran into Akarra as she paced on the stones along the shore. "Aliza, what's—?"

"There's no time! Mòrag needs your help. She fell on the path. I think her leg's broken."

"You *left* her?"

"She wouldn't let me take her back to the castle," I said and told her about the cap as quickly as I could. "I'll get it to Cordelia. You need to help Mòrag."

"You're sure?"

"Aye."

With a rumble and crunch of gravel she spread her wings and took to the air. I ran as fast as I dared down the quay, sliding on the ice-rimed stones. A single lantern burned high on a piling at the end, and by its light I saw Cordelia standing at the edge, dressed only in her shift, toes curled over the lip of the pier. Her gown and shoes lay in a crumpled heap next to her. Selwyn and Alastair stood between us, but Cordelia held them back.

"Lord Daired, Niall, stay where you are," she cried. "If you move, I'll throw myself in."

"Lady Selwyn, please," Alastair tried, edging forward. "Whatever's going on here, jumping into the lake won't—"

"You don't understand! You couldn't possibly understand," she cried, sounding close to tears. "How could you? You and your Aliza. You *chose* each other. You'd do anything for her: brave any terror, risk any death, and she'd do the same for you! What do either of you know of cold love? What do you know of broken trust?"

Selwyn pushed in front of Alastair. "Darling, please be reasonable."

"No!" Her voice rose to a shriek. "Don't you see? I have to go *home*. I have to escape now, before—before . . . It's the only way the Green Lady will leave us alone. It's the only way to make this right!"

"Cordelia, stop this now. Your home is in the castle. Your home is with me!"

"My home was never with you!"

"What else do you want from me? What else can I give you?" Selwyn knelt on the quay. "Tell me! Anything you want, anything at all!"

"I want to see my family again."

"I *am* your family."

"You're not!" she shouted. "I didn't ask you to take me. I never asked for any of this. All these years, all this pretending. Something terrible is coming, Niall, and if you won't give me my freedom, I'll take it myself."

"You'll die in that water!"

"Then I'll die."

I reached Alastair and touched his arm as their voices rose. "Aliza?" he whispered. "What are you doing here?"

"Making it right." I felt for the cap in my pocket. The sealskin wrapped around my fingers, warm and comforting, as I tried to figure a way to get past Selwyn. "Tell us, Lord Selwyn," I said in a louder voice. "Admit what you did."

Waves battered the pilings beneath us and the wind tossed up spray like snowflakes, tearing the words from my lips. With it came a familiar smell, stinging my nose with the scent of gravemold. My heart skipped a beat.

"Oh, but Aliza, he *can't*."

The Green Lady glided toward us along the quay, glowing with a ghastly marshlight. Once again she wore Charis Brysney's face.

"Did you really think it would be so easy?" she said. "I'm surprised you haven't worked out what kind of man he—"

Alastair leapt forward and drove his sword into her heart.

The Green Lady stumbled. She looked down at the steel buried in her chest, looked up at Alastair, and laughed.

"I am one of the Eldest, dragonrider, a shadow of a shadow of the first darkness that fell upon this world, and even you cannot hurt me." With a flick of her wrist she twisted the hilt out of his grip and pulled the sword from her body. Inky nothingness dripped from the edge. Needle fangs shone in Charis's mouth, and then her face dissolved, swirling into the gaunt, spectral figure I'd seen in the abbey. Alastair fell back.

Only a nakla . . . *always unworthy . . . never enough . . .*

The Green Lady swung the sword lazily. "Come now, you're

all too easy!" She clucked her tongue as she held the blade aloft, pointing it at each of us in turn. "Such keen regrets to uncover. Such dark secrets to dig up. Such delicious, dangerous *lies*." She settled at last on Alastair. "Alastair Daired, pride of House Pendragon and heir to the Fireborn. Is that what you call yourself? Look at you! You are *weak*. You couldn't protect your wife, you couldn't save your child, and you will never, never be the man Erran Daired was."

A secret shame . . . poison to his noble bloodline . . . not enough . . .

Black hair flopped in an untidy braid down one shoulder and blood splattered her face, her throat torn by a gryphon's talons. Child's eyes darted from me to Alastair and back again, clouded and unseeing, my nightmares enfleshed. She spoke in my little sister's voice. "What about you, Aliza? You let me die. You forgot about me, and you let me die."

"Rina, no . . ."

"You want to be a healer, but you carry death in your body. You may try and try and try, but you will never bring a child into the world, and those you love will resent you for it before the end."

That's not true! Alastair cried, or perhaps I did. Did we? *Will he?* Marshlight drank the darkness around us. Cold washed over me, freezing body, mind, and will. I couldn't move, couldn't scream, couldn't escape. *I carry death in my body . . . I carry death . . . death . . .* The choice would fall to me in the end. *How long am I willing to watch him burn?*

The Green Lady slipped between us like smoke, Rina's features melting into a putrid mockery of Cordelia's beauty. Selwyn shrank against a piling as she approached. "And *you*. Oh, there are no words for what you've done, Niall of the Keep."

"You don't understand," he moaned. "I love her! She was going to leave me. She was going to leave!" He fell to his knees and covered his face with his hands. "No, not you! Get out of my mind!"

"I could not touch your mind if you were not guilty, Niall Selwyn, and I have waited a long time for this. The one who called me here told me there was a deep and dreadful wrong to avenge on the shores of Lake Meera, and he was right." She smiled and crouched next to him, stroking his hair with slimy fingers. "He did not tell me this vengeance would be so sweet."

"Get out get out *get out!*"

"You kidnapped a daughter of the sea. You betrayed the trust of an innocent selkie. You've kept her prisoner for all these years: as your wife, your plaything, your slave."

"But she *loved* me!"

"You lie," the Green Lady hissed. "There can be no love between *Idar* and humans. It is an abomination! You stole her cap. You stole her life. You are guilty."

"Get out of my head!"

"Not until you do what you must do," she said and pressed Alastair's sword into his hand. "Shorten your years for all those you stole from her. One little thrust—"

"Leave him alone!" Cordelia's voice cut through the icy air. My head cleared. The whispers faded. My fingers closed around the sealskin cap in my pocket. "He did wrong, but I'm the one he wronged, not you," Cordelia said, "and if I must, I will make it right."

"Pray, selkie, how will you do that?"

Cordelia backed up until her heels hung over the edge of the quay. "I-I'll return to the water. I'll go back where I belong."

"In your human form? Fool! You won't last two minutes."

"Long enough. I know the laws of the sea; I know the laws of your kind. It'll end what he started. You'll have no more hold over him or anyone else in his household."

The Green Lady made a sound in her throat that might've been a laugh. "Perhaps." She let one long nail slide along Selwyn's cheek as she took the sword from his hand. He shuddered and went rigid. "Then again, perhaps not," she said, facing Cordelia.

Which meant, for a few precious seconds, neither Selwyn nor the Green Lady were looking in my direction.

"Cordelia!" I cried and raised the cap.

Both Cordelia and the Green Lady saw it at the same moment. The shriek that went up from the Green Lady's throat rolled over the water, foul with the fury of a spoiled hunt. She whirled on me, the Cordelia mask falling away in flashes of marshlight and dripping darkness as she raised the sword.

"*NO!*"

Alastair threw himself forward. Dead green arms grappled against his living ones, the blade flashing between them as they struggled on the edge of the quay.

My scream came too late. They plunged over.

Black waters roiled beneath us and Alastair surfaced, but the Green Lady dragged him down again before he could seize the piling.

Cordelia tore her cap from my numb fingers, tugging me back even as my body made the decision to jump in after him. "No. Stay here," she said and pulled the cap down low on her head. The furry flaps lengthened, tumbling down around her shoulders and fluttering after her like a cape. Her arms grew long and flattened, her eyes turned black, and she dove off the quay as brown-gray fur closed over her face.

My mind churned to life again. *Rope. We need rope!* I seized Selwyn's shoulder as he stared at the place Cordelia had gone under. "Selwyn! Is there any rope nearby?"

"They're gone."

"No! They're not gone! They're coming back, but they need our help. Selwyn, look at me! *Is there any rope?*"

Slowly he shook his head.

I released him, casting my eye around for something, for anything to help haul them onto the pier. The little roofed enclosure that sheltered the lantern yielded nothing beyond spare wicks and a tinderbox. There was a splash, mixed with a barking cry from the lake. A seal's head bobbed a dozen yards from the quay, but Cordelia kept slipping under, webbed arms thrashing the water as she struggled to surface. Alastair clutched at her, his face ashen.

Fear brought an edge of clarity. *Rope. Cloth. Clothes?* I tore the cloak from Selwyn's shoulders and swept up Cordelia's fallen dress, looping them together and tying them fast to the nearest piling. The ends just reached the water. It might work. *It has to work.*

I looked up, and my heart plummeted. Cordelia and Alastair hadn't moved. Wavelets lapped at them, calmer than before. Alastair no longer struggled. Ice crystals lined his hair, shining in the starlight. His breath ghosted over the water, rapid and uneven, and my rational mind did the calculations even when the rest of me cried out against it. Alastair's armor was too heavy. He was dragging them both down. They weren't going to make it. *Unless . . .*

Don't be a fool. She was with Mòrag at the castle, and the castle was too far away. *She can't hear.* My voice wouldn't be loud enough, would never be enough . . .

"AKARRA! HELP!" I poured into those words my last drop of faith in the gods, in everything right and fair and just in the world, in everything I ever cherished, hoping it would be enough for a miracle. I screamed her name until I thought my lungs would burst. "*AKARRA!*"

Cordelia barked as Alastair slipped underwater.

And suddenly it wasn't me screaming anymore but a much

deeper voice bellowing Alastair's name as Akarra dove toward the lake in a glorious explosion of wings and dragonfire. Talons tore at the waves as she plunged in after them, clawing through the dark water. With a hiss and a sputter the column of dragonfire vanished, its absence leaving bright spots in front of my eyes. I crumpled to my knees. *Come back!*

More flames erupted from the lake. Akarra hurtled out of the water, her wings tossing up spray as she flew toward the quay, cradling two limp figures in her talons. I hauled up the makeshift rope and untied Selwyn's cloak as Akarra landed and set Cordelia and Alastair down on the stone. There was no sign of the Green Lady.

I rushed to them. Alastair's eyes were open and unblinking. His breath gurgled in his throat. "Alastair? Can you hear me?" I swore. "Alastair!"

He rolled to his side and vomited water onto the quay, then slumped back into my arms. His lips moved, but no sound came out. I struggled with the laces and buckles that fastened his armor, then gave up, drew his dagger from its sheath, and cut him free from the waterlogged leather. He held on to me as I pulled off everything but his breeches, his shivers shaking me almost as much as they did him. *Good.* If he could shiver, it meant he wasn't past saving. I wrapped us both in Selwyn's cloak and held him tight.

"You're safe," I said. "It's all right. You're safe."

"I k-n-n-now," he said in my ear. "Just p-p-please don't let g-g-go."

A leathery wing encircled us and Akarra drew us close. Her sides steamed in the cold air as Alastair hunkered next to her. She held my gaze over his shoulder.

"You heard," I whispered. A sob caught in my throat. "You heard."

She brought her head close to mine and touched my cheek with one wingtip. "I'll always hear."

"Is he all right?" a rough, barking voice asked.

Akarra and I turned. Cordelia stood at the end of the quay, naked but for the dripping sealskin cloak. She'd pushed her sealskin back from her face so it hung like a mantle around her shoulders, and she'd resumed her human appearance in every aspect save for her eyes. They'd stayed pure, fathomless black.

"I'll l-l-live," Alastair said. "Thank y-you."

The dark shape that was Niall Selwyn groaned and stirred, clasping his head in his hands. Cordelia looked at him, looked at her sealskin, looked at the lake. Scales flashed near the surface of the water. One or two webbed hands pointed to Cordelia's sealskin, the Mermish voices cresting with excitement before descending into shrieks as they noticed Selwyn crouched in front of her. A selkie on land needed no further explanation. They understood what he had done.

Cordelia tore her gaze from the water and knelt next to Selwyn. "Niall? Niall, do you hear me?" He clutched at her, and she smoothed his hair from his forehead. "Shh. The Green Lady is gone."

"I never meant to hurt you. I never meant for you to hate me. I thought you wanted to be here. Cordelia—love—please. I'm so sorry. Forgive me." He buried his head in the folds of her cloak. "Oh gods, forgive me!"

"I do."

He looked up. "Then you'll stay?"

"Niall, you know I can't," she said sadly. "This is not my world, and I cannot face the—no. I have to go home."

He uttered a despairing cry.

"That's not the only reason I need to leave," she said. "There are other things in the Wastes, old, dark, vengeful things, and the next might not toy with its victims so long. As long as I am land-bound you are in danger. If I return to the water, their kind won't torment you again. You have wronged me, Niall, but I cannot wish on you another creature like that. I want you to be free." She kissed his forehead. "I want us both to be free."

"I don't want to be free. I don't want any of this if I can't have you!"

Cordelia kissed him again, once on each cheek. "Then I'm sorry," she said and straightened. Her eyes met mine and she gave a small nod. "Aliza, Lord Alastair, I pray the favor of Aquouris and Uoroura, Nouroudos and Ourobauro go with you always. Thank you for all you've done here."

Selwyn staggered to his feet and reached for her. She raised her hand to his. For an instant their fingers intertwined, but before Selwyn could embrace her, she shook her head and lowered her arm. "Find someone who can love you as you deserve, Niall. That's the only prayer I have left for you."

"Cordelia, please."

"Goodbye."

She pulled the hood over her face. The sealskin flowed together, enveloping her in her true form as she dove into the starlit waters of Lake Meera, to the cold, silvery cheers of the merfolk below.

CHAPTER 25

LONG SHADOWS

We didn't linger to listen to the Mermish songs as they welcomed back the land-lost selkie. I supported Alastair up the cliff path, Akarra following overhead, carrying in her claws what remained of his armor. Selwyn refused to come. He hadn't moved from where Cordelia had left him, unseeing eyes staring at the water. After my third plea fell on grief-deafened ears, we gave up and headed back to the castle without him.

No servants met us at the door. Rhys stopped us by the garden gate, but he took in the sight of a shivering, half-naked Alastair, noted the heat shimmering around Akarra's open mouth, and let us pass without questions.

NIALL SELWYN DID NOT RETURN TO THE CASTLE.

Tending Alastair as he recovered and seeing to Mòrag's broken leg took up my attention for the rest of the night. Whispered rumors acquainted the servants with the details of what had happened on Long Quay, and by the next day the castle was in an uproar. Over the course of the morning Rhys and Chirrorim rounded up some of the braver servants to scour the shore from

Long Quay to the dead mermaid's beach, but they returned without success. Selwyn had disappeared. That evening the stableboy found his master's prize stallion missing.

"We ought to go after him," Rhys said after the stableboy slunk away, ushered out of the Lake Hall by Chirrorim. "Clearly the man's not in his right mind."

"Where do you suggest we start?" Alastair asked. He wore his bearskin cloak, clasped at the throat and tucked well around his shoulders. Since we'd returned to the castle he'd kept it close, even when sleeping, and in every room we entered he gravitated toward the fireplace. We'd eaten dinner at a small table pulled almost onto the hearth. "Do you have any idea where he's going?"

"How should I know?"

"You knew him."

"Not that well."

"I don't think he wants to be found," I said.

Rhys sprang to his feet. "Yes, it's all very well for *you*. You two can climb on your dragon tomorrow and leave all this behind you, but some of us have to live here. Lord Selwyn had no heir and no other family, which means that when word of his absence gets out, there'll be chaos in the lake towns." He paced along the hearth. "The magistrates will want to call for a new lord sentinel, and the lords from Langloch and the coast will want their share in the decision. The lord from Langdred has two sons. He may want to see his youngest set up in Castle Selwyn before the year is out. And that's not counting—"

"Captain, lest you forget, Selwyn's not actually dead," Alastair said.

"He may as well be. And anyway, it doesn't matter. If the local lords and magistrates won't fight for the position of lord sentinel, they'll fight to be steward of the castle until he gets back, which would give them the lordship anyway. Whoever holds the castle holds the lake. It's always been that way." He stopped, considering. "We could always *pretend*."

Alastair and I looked at each other.

"Yes, why not?" Rhys said. "No one but you witnessed what happened on the quay. If we spread the word that he's ill, we could buy a few weeks' time."

"I think you underestimate the intelligence of some of the townspeople," I said. *And the speed with which gossip travels*. With any luck, or perhaps lack of luck, word of Selwyn's disappearance had already reached Morianton and the surrounding villages. "Captain, why not just let the magistrates choose a steward?"

Rhys frowned. "Perhaps you're right. We're only guests here, after all, and—speaking of which, how much longer do you plan to stay? You won't want to get caught anywhere in the mountains when the snows come. I'd bet we'll see the first storm before the fortnight is out. We've gone too long without one already."

He spoke in the fast, friendly way that suggested he wanted nothing more than for us to take his advice and ask no more questions. I hid a humorless smile. He might as well have handed us a written invitation to stay.

"We'll return to Pendragon as soon as we're certain Castle Selwyn and the towns nearby are safe again," Alastair said. "In the meantime, we owe it to the cantor at Morianton to tell her what's happened."

"Unless you think she'll try to take over the castle herself?" I said.

"Brigsley-Baine?" Rhys said. "No, she's a decent sort. But she will tell the magistrate."

The fact that my sarcasm had passed without so much as a lifted eyebrow proved his mind was truly elsewhere. "With the stories the servants are already spreading I'd think it a miracle if they don't already know something happened," I told him.

"Aliza's right, Captain," Alastair said. "He was their lord. They deserve to know. To let them think otherwise is dishonorable."

"We—oh, very well. I'll ride out in the morning."

"Akarra and I will come with you."

Rhys agreed without much enthusiasm. After they set on a time and a meeting place he bid us goodnight and excused himself.

"Do you think he's going to try to run?" I asked after he'd gone.

"No," Alastair said carefully. "He's mercenary through and through. Whatever he's afraid of, he won't leave until he's sure it won't work out in his favor. I've seen his like before."

"What do you think he's hiding?"

"Something he didn't have to worry about when Selwyn was around," Alastair said with a thoughtful expression. "I'll keep an eye on him tomorrow."

I leaned back in my chair and stared at my unfinished food. The bread was burnt and the meat was cold, but that wasn't what I found unappealing. Nausea no longer plagued me, but in its place was another kind of emptiness, a sad, small hunger that no food could satisfy. Thoughts I'd pushed away since Cordelia's disappearance came creeping back, dark thoughts of dreamless sleep, of hollow sympathies and dead men walking and eyes too full for tears.

"I haven't forgotten, you know," Alastair said after a minute.

"Forgotten what?"

"Lyii-Lyiishen."

The unexpectedness brought me back from the edge of the mental precipice. "The mermaid?"

"I swore an oath. Our work here isn't done yet."

I thought of the Mermish king's warning of a hard winter

with a pang of homesickness. Exposing the Green Lady and her haunting of Castle Selwyn had only been half of the contract, and I had the dreadful feeling it would prove to be the easier half. The memory of the Wydrick-thing on the beach still made me shudder. "I know."

"Aliza," he said in a quiet voice, "I didn't ask before, but I'm asking you now. Stay here tomorrow."

Protests rose inside me, old, familiar complaints I'd clutched to my chest like poisonous jewels since the moment I'd taken the Daired name. One by one I held them up to my mind's eye and, for the first time, saw them clearly for what they were. Their luster had faded; their facets were chipped and broken. I tossed them aside in disgust. All that bravado, that recklessness, that desperation to prove myself: how empty and arrogant it seemed now. Alastair was right all those weeks ago. I'd seen the battlefield, but I'd never truly understood it. I'd never known loss like this.

"I won't go wandering the mountainside," I said, "but I can't do nothing."

My look must've told him the truth my voice refused to carry, because he didn't try to dissuade me. "I know. I wouldn't want you to, and we need to know what we're facing on the human side."

"Politics?"

"Politics. Find out what Mòrag and the servants have to say about the local magistrates."

I nodded. Bells chimed in the distance, marking the late hour. The crackle of the fire echoed around the empty room, casting the only light aside from the candlesticks on the table. In Selwyn's absence lights no longer burned at all hours and darkness had crept back into the corners of the castle, but it was a homely, domestic darkness, and it hid no evils. I thought of what awaited us tomorrow. If Alastair and Rhys wanted to catch the cantor and magistrate first thing in the morning, they'd—

I straightened in my chair. Those weren't bells.

"It's the merfolk," Alastair said.

We listened. The strains of a Mermish lament penetrated stone and glass, blood and bone, piercing me to the soul. Tears gathered in my eyes but I refused to let them fall. No words in Mermish, Eth, or any other language could fit the shape of what I felt. "It's for Lyii-Lyiishen, isn't it?" I asked. "They're still mourning her."

"Yes."

Another minute passed. The fire burned lower. The shadows lengthened.

"It doesn't ever end."

"Someday it will. Not today. Not tomorrow," he said. "Maybe not next week or next month or next year, but someday."

"Do you know for certain?"

He reached for my hand, but the table was too wide, and there were too many things between us. "We'll have another, Aliza."

"That doesn't change what happened."

"I know."

"And what if we don't have another child?" Desperate words tumbled from dry lips. "What if we can't? She said I carry death inside me. What if she's right?"

"She wasn't."

"How can we be sure?"

"*Khera*, stop. This is the Green Lady talking, not you."

"This *is* me. She only told me things I already knew."

"She wasn't telling us the truth. She told us whatever would hurt us most."

I stood and faced the fire, hugging my arms around my chest

as if by holding on hard enough I could somehow keep the pieces of my broken heart from splintering any further. "She chose well."

"No, she didn't. Aliza, it doesn't matter whether or not you can have children, and even if you can't, I would never resent you for it."

"How do you know?"

"Because I made a promise," he said in a quiet voice. "I gave you my word before our families and before the gods. You are my wife, now and forever, and I love you. There were no conditions."

The gentleness with which he said it broke down the last of my defenses, and that illusion of distance shattered. His words crossed every inch of the uncountable leagues between us and drew me back with him. Tears spilled over my cheeks, rolling like rain clouds over the desert inside. I buried my face in my hands, shoulders heaving, and wept.

I might've cried for a few moments; I might've cried for years. Time did not meddle in the business of grief.

After a while the sobs that shook my body steadied, then stilled, and a clean, exhausted calm drifted over me. The wound was still there, raw and ugly, but the bleeding had stopped, and my heart felt whole again, or as whole as it could be. Mòrag was right. *You do live.*

Alastair touched my arm. I looked up. His eyes too were wet. "Dance with me," he whispered.

"Why?"

"Because neither of us can stand on our own anymore."

"There's no music," I said, but my hand met his.

"Listen."

The Mermish lament was fainter now, the haunting melody weaving through the rhythm of our beating hearts. It was quiet, and distant, and it was enough. We moved together, graceless and awkward, weighed down by grief and fear and regret, but still moving, still alive. I leaned against his chest. The bearskin prickled against my cheek, drinking the last of my tears. My head felt light, but for the first time in days it was the lightness of clarity, not emptiness, and I knew what I wanted. I slid my hand under his tunic. He stopped dancing.

"It's been too long," I said, no longer caring that we were standing in the castle's Lake Hall, nor that any number of servants could enter unannounced at any moment. I knew only the raw, untempered need to be close to him, to feel in some tangible way that our lives hadn't ended. "Kiss me."

He did, long and deep. I fumbled with the pin that secured the cloak as he guided me backward. He ran his fingers through my hair, his other hand moving toward my skirt as my shoulders met the wall.

"*Alastair*," I whispered and he paused, his breath ragged against my cheek. "No, don't stop."

"This isn't—wise."

"I don't care." I tugged at the buckle of his sword-belt. "I don't care that we're in the Lake Hall. I don't care that the doors are unlocked. I don't care if the whole bloody kingdom barges in. I want you. I *need* you." I kissed him again. "Everything since we arrived has been complicated. Let this at least be simple."

He braced himself against the wall and put some space between us, studying me not with the hunger I wanted, but with concern. "The midwife told us to wait."

"What?"

"Madam Threshmore told us before she left. She said we should wait a week or two. To let you heal."

"I don't remember that."

"You said thank you and told her we'd do whatever she recommended."

"I . . . didn't know what I was saying."

"You were a long way away."

"It's been days. Surely that's long enough? I feel—" I paused. The blood had stopped some time earlier, but even then it was hard to say if my body had fully healed. A lost child and the terror of everything that had happened on Long Quay had blurred the lines between physical and emotional pain beyond recognition. "I'm all right."

"She said a week."

I leaned up and kissed his neck just below his ear, enjoying the small, desperate sound he made in his throat. He closed his eyes.

"At *least* a week. Aliza, please don't make this any more difficult than it already is."

"It doesn't have to be." The buckle of his sword-belt gave up under my fingers. It fell with a satisfying *clink*. "Do you really want to wait?"

"*Thell* no."

"Good."

"But," he pulled away, "I will if I have to."

I scowled up at him. "You do realize I'm in a position to make you regret this in the future."

"Quite a lot of me is regretting it right now," he said with a rueful smile. "I'm sorry, *khera*."

"I don't want you to be sorry. I want you to make love to me."

He sidestepped my attempt to kiss him and picked up his fallen sword-belt. "When we get back to Pendragon, I promise I'll make amends. *Thorough* amends," he added in my ear, the roughness of his voice sending a renewed shiver through me. "And after that we can talk about all the ways you'll make me pay for this."

I gave up. With exaggerated care I adjusted my skirts and the neckline of my dress. It was a little war and a playful one, but it stood as an island of normality amid the tempest-tossed seas of the last few days, and I clung to each moment, looking for ways to draw it out.

So I waited until we were on the threshold of the guest suite before turning to him and saying, "By the way, as you're so happy with the idea of sleeping alone, I believe you'll find the divan quite comfortable tonight."

ALASTAIR AND RHYS LEFT AT DAWN THE NEXT MORNING, Rhys picking his way along the eastern road to Morianton below Akarra, who flew just far enough behind to keep Rhys's horse from bolting at every flap of her wings, but close enough to keep the gelding moving at a brisk and terrified trot. I stayed close to the castle. Inquiries about the attitudes of the surrounding noblemen were best started with the person who, in all likelihood, had been alive longer than most of them.

Mòrag surveyed me over the rim of her teacup. Bretta had helped me brace and wrap her leg when we returned from Long Quay, and she now sat with it propped up on a chair by the kitchen fire where she could supervise the comings and goings of the maids. Her hair hung loose around her shoulders. It made her look softer, older, and frailer than before. Her tongue, however, had lost none of its sharpness. "Seventy-two northern winters I've lasted, child. A few broken bones aren't going to send me to my grave," she said when I asked how she was feeling. "I'll be fine. Did I see your husband and his dragon fly off toward Morianton this morning?"

"They've gone with Captain Rhys to tell the magistrate about Selwyn's disappearance."

"Lord Niall was a fool to run."

"Do you know where he went?"

"No idea. This castle was his life. If he left, it means he doesn't plan on returning. Nevertheless, I pray the gods grant him peace. He was—" She stopped and looked me over again. "No matter. Lady Daired, I really don't see why you're still here. The Green Lady is gone. Chirrorim is keeping watch on the castle, and Rhys could've delivered the news to the nearby towns without Lord Daired's help. You should be on your way home before the snows come."

"You're sure the Green Lady won't be back?"

There was an almost imperceptible pause before she answered. "Yes."

I cocked my head. "Why do I have the feeling you don't believe that?"

"Oh, I'm sure she won't be back to haunt the castle. I'm just not convinced she's dead."

"Well, that water was very cold and we didn't see her surface."

"A few minutes ago you said your husband stabbed her through the heart, yet she pulled it out and smiled."

I conceded. "She was—is—*alive* though, isn't she? She could swing Alastair's sword, so she must have substance. On the quay she called herself one of the Eldest. Do you know what she meant?"

"Stories have been around of a dark spirit of the Wastes from time immemorial, child. She must've thought the name fitting. And of course she's *alive*, though not like you or me. I'd wager she has more in common with ghasts and ghouls than humans and selkies. 'Frogs of the soul,' the bards would say, with one foot in both visible and invisible worlds. And frogs can live a long time underwater."

"That's not comforting."

"You never said you wanted comfort. And you haven't answered my question."

"You didn't ask me anything."

"Why are you still here?"

"It wasn't the Green Lady who killed those *Idar*."

Her mouth puckered in a whiskery frown. "Then who?"

"There was a creature on the beach where we found the dead mermaid," I said carefully. "He wore the face of a dead man Alastair and I knew once. It looked like a *ghastradi*."

"The ghast-ridden? *Here?* Mikla save us," she muttered, and for the first time looked truly unsettled. "For all our sakes I hope you're wrong."

"Maybe I am. I couldn't see it clearly, but there was something riding him."

"Ghasts don't ride corpses."

"I know. But whatever it is, we have to stop it." I pulled a stool next to hers and told her about the slain *Idar* we'd found in the Widdermere Marshes. She listened without comment. When I described our encounter with Qiryn, she set down her cup.

"A whole herd of centaurs hunting this thing and it slipped through the marshes unseen? That takes more than luck."

"I know."

"What exactly do your husband and his dragon intend to do when they find this creature? Chase it down and cut off its head and hope that does it in?"

"They'll keep it from killing again. Whatever that means. Whatever that takes."

She gave me a long look. I could almost see the scales in her eyes, weighing me out, evaluating each word, wavering between suspicion and trust, and coming at last to a decision. "And what do you plan to do while your dragonrider does his work?"

"Something useful." *Starting with this.* "Mòrag, what do you know about Captain Rhys?"

"Owin? Why?"

"He was very eager yesterday to keep us from telling the nearby towns about what happened to Selwyn."

She snorted. "You mean he didn't want Polton to find out. That's the magistrate of Morianton," she said, and I thought of the nervous man from the beach where we'd found Isolde's body. "There's been bad blood between those two for years. And no, before you ask, I don't know why. You'll have to find out for yourself."

I poured her another cup of tea. *No fear there, Mòrag.* That was exactly what I planned to do.

THE MEN RETURNED LATER THAN EXPECTED BRINGING news that, if it couldn't be called good, at least had a corner on interesting. Chirrorim and I met with them in the front courtyard, me coming from my interviews with the servants, him from his patrol of the castle grounds. Rumor had indeed already reached the eastern shore and Morianton was buzzing with news of Selwyn's disappearance. According to them, Magistrate Polton had gone nearly apoplectic. "He's sent out messengers to the nearby towns," Alastair said. "They're going to call for a gathering of some kind."

"A colloquy," Rhys said. With one hand he patted his horse's steaming neck; in the other he held aloft his cousin's irate gyrfalcon. The gelding shied and sidestepped to put a few more feet between him and Akarra. "Three days from now. Here, at the castle."

Akarra tapped her talons on the stone. The gelding laid his ears flat against his skull, eyes rolling. "Three days isn't much time. I don't think—oh, for gods' sakes, Rhys, will you tell your horse I'm not about to eat it?"

Chirrorim chuckled. Rhys ignored him.

"Three days is just long enough for all the parties to get here, but not enough for them to make many plans beyond that. It's calculated, it is. Polton will try and take the stewardship," he said, turning his horse toward the stables. "You watch."

"Any reason he shouldn't?" Alastair said. "He seemed like an honest man."

Rhys paused long enough to look over his shoulder, his face grave. "Connell Polton is straight as an arrow, Lord Daired."

"What's wrong with that?" I asked.

"The straight arrows are usually the ones that kill."

CHAPTER 26

THE COLLOQUY OF CASTLE SELWYN

The morning of the colloquy dawned stormy and gray.
Snow started soon after breakfast, which I'd taken charge of as
Mòrag recovered. She was in the Lake Hall, hobbling along on
makeshift crutches and barking orders to the maids as they rushed
to finish preparations for the colloquy.

The first embassy arrived just before noon, led by the magistrate of Morianton on a shiny black gelding. Three weary-looking
mules plodded behind him, bearing three equally weary travelers
bundled against the cold. Polton dismounted with a flourish. He
wore nothing but black from his boots to his long leather gloves,
and he seemed to take each snowflake that settled on him as a
personal insult.

"Polton, you've met the Daireds," Rhys said as the magistrate
and his retinue filed into the castle.

"An honor," Polton said. His face, which in full daylight looked
a bit like a prune, nevertheless gave the impression of, if not trust-
worthiness, then at least competence. He removed his gloves, then
took my hand and bowed. "I'm sorry we didn't get to speak much

355

when we, ah, first met, Lady Daired. I'm very glad to meet you in less grievous circumstances."

"Likewise, sir," I replied.

"Yes, yes. Polton, food's set out in the Lake Hall," Rhys said. "You'll want a good seat, I imagine."

Polton turned away with the expression of a man in possession of a brilliantly scathing reply and just enough self-control not to say it.

"Cantor Brigsley-Baine you know. This is Subcantor Carle and Mill-Master Dougal," Rhys said, and we greeted the rest of the Morianton embassy.

Brigsley-Baine expressed similar relief at meeting us in a place with no dead bodies. She did not mention our visit to the abbey, but I caught her glancing at my belly with pity in her eyes, and when she took my hand her grip was tight.

Her companion could be nothing but a miller. Master Dougal had a pleasant face, a white wisp of a beard, and years of flour ground into the seams of his clothing. He clutched his hat in both hands as he bowed, beaming at us without a word. The subcantor, on closer inspection, had the unremarkable appearance of a man who read the *Book of Honored Proverbs* for fun. I didn't need to see the rolls of parchment in his bag or the ink stains on his fingers to know he'd come in the role of clerk.

Others followed, their names blurring as the front hall filled with the chatter of the guards and lackeys. There was another magistrate from a town on the western shore of Lake Meera, a man with a drooping mustache and a bloodhound's baggy, bloodshot eyes. Behind him was the cantor of the same town, a person of indeterminate sex and unknown features, so buried was he, or she, in cloaks and hoods and furry stoles. A voice from deep within the furs said something that sounded like "Too cold in here."

Behind the swaddled bundle of cantor came the embassy from a town southeast of Morianton, led by, to my surprise, a Rider. Her single lock of silver hair twisted in a plait around her shaved head and she walked with the aid of an iron-tipped cane. She greeted Chirrorim in Beorspeak. He replied in the same language, sounding happier than he had since he'd arrived.

"Good to meet you, Magistrate Farrell," Alastair said when they finished exchanging pleasantries. "I didn't know there were any Riders in the lake towns."

"Former Rider, Lord Daired. My beoryn died in battle many years ago and I've since hung up the sword. Turns out there are as many wild beasts within civilized halls as there are on the battlefield. Stay wary, eh?" she said and clapped him on the shoulder. "See you inside."

A flurry of snow and a flustered Trennan announced the final embassy, this one consisting of no fewer than five guards, three clerks, a lost-looking groom, and a gaunt man in a gray cloak that billowed behind him like his own personal storm cloud.

"Where is Lord Daired? I must speak with Lord Daired!" he cried in a high, nasally voice that sounded as if he was fighting off a sneeze. He caught sight of Alastair and wafted—there was no other way to describe his manner of walking—toward us. "My lord! Is it true? Is Selwyn really gone? We heard such wild rumors flying about, and then that messenger from, ah, Polton—" He caught sight of Rhys at the door to the Lake Hall. "What is *he* doing here?"

"The captain was a guest of Lord Selwyn's when he disappeared," Alastair said. "He helped organize the colloquy."

With a wet sniff, the man I christened Damp Handkerchief swept aside the folds of his cloak and billowed into the Lake Hall.

"Well," I said softly as I took Alastair's arm. "This is bound to be interesting."

NORTHERN COLLOQUIES WERE THOROUGHLY PRACTICAL affairs. They dispensed with the ceremony as quickly as possible. Once everyone had found a seat at the long table in the Lake Hall, Rhys stood up and addressed us all. "Friends and neighbors, welcome. I trust you all know why we're here today. We have much to decide, but first we must—"

"Have a spot of lunch?" said an indistinct voice from within the Furry Bundle.

"—choose a master of the colloquy." He cleared his throat. "I put forth Lord Daired."

There were murmurs from the guests.

"No, Captain Rhys." Polton half stood and gave Alastair an apologetic bow. "Saving your honor, my lord, but these are local matters and you're not from Lake Meera."

"Exactly," Rhys said. "Lord Daired has no prejudice invested in our decision today. He'll choose fairly."

"Lord Daired, would you have any objections?" Cantor Brigsley-Baine asked.

"No, madam."

Polton sat with a faint *hrrrmph*.

"Any other objections?" Rhys asked.

Damp Handkerchief shifted in his seat. Furry Bundle, who'd removed one layer of furs but no more, made a noise that sounded vaguely negative. There were whispers from around the table, some of agreement, some of suspicion, but no one challenged him and no one else offered any other names.

"Excellent." Rhys signaled to Mòrag, who stood on her crutches next to the kitchen door. "In that case I believe it's time for lunch."

Servants streamed in, bearing steaming tureens and platters of broiled fish. Alastair leaned over to Rhys as they set out the food. "I would've appreciated some warning, Rhys. What exactly is the master of the colloquy supposed to do?"

"It's a simple role," Rhys said. "The magistrates will bicker for an hour or so before settling on two possibilities: send a petition to the king to appoint a new lord sentinel, or select a steward to maintain the castle and day-to-day duties of the lord sentinel. They'll choose the latter."

"You're sure?" I asked.

"A petition to the king won't get looked at for months and we all want this handled as soon as possible." He glanced down the table to where Bloodhound was already deep in debate with the silver-haired Rider. "And I can tell you now who it'll come down to: Lyra Farrell, Connell Polton, and Lord Langdred's youngest son."

"Who is?"

"Not here. His father's magistrate will fight for him though," he said, nodding to Damp Handkerchief. "I've met the boy. Lazy and conniving little snotpig, just like his father."

I thought of Rookwood, Madam Knagg, and the *Vesh* ambush we'd faced in Langdred and found myself similarly ill disposed toward any embassy from the southern lake town.

"Anyone you would recommend?" I asked in a low voice.

"Farrell would do well. She'd see to it that things are kept up in the castle and trade stays open on the lakes."

If I hadn't been watching him closely, I would've missed the sidelong glance he gave Alastair when he said it. But I was watching, and I didn't miss it.

"I'll keep that in mind," Alastair said. He hadn't missed it either.

AS SOON AS THE SERVANTS CLEARED THE LAST BOWLS away, the colloquy commenced.

"But I don't understand. Why is any of this necessary? Where has he *gone*?" Damp Handkerchief cried. "And what happened to Lady Cordelia?"

Polton rubbed his temples. "I told you in my letter, sir. We don't know where he's gone. And Lady Selwyn . . . well, Lady Selwyn is gone too."

"Your letter said she was a selkie," Farrell said. "Lord Daired, is that true?"

"Yes," he said, "and she's returned to the water. She won't be coming back."

Whispers rippled down the table.

"But what about these rumors we've heard of *Idar* slayings?" Damp Handkerchief asked. "I understood Selwyn commissioned you to catch the culprit, Lord Daired. What progress has been made there? Is the lake safe again?"

I looked at Alastair. Admitting we had fulfilled Lord Selwyn's request to find Isolde's killer—and found it was a creature that could not be killed—would do little to secure the trust of these people, and if we were to complete this contract and hunt down the second, *Idar*-slaying monster, then we would need that trust. We would need all the help we could get.

"We're close," Alastair said.

Damp Handkerchief pursed his lips and seemed about to speak again, but after a glimpse of Alastair's face, wisely decided not to press the matter.

"And the longer we dither here, the longer we keep His Lordship from the hunt," Polton added. "As for Selwyn, what's done is done. We must look ahead. Can we at least agree that the castle needs a steward?"

Next to me, Subcantor Carle lowered his spectacles and stopped scribbling notes. "Proper protocol demands we petition the king for a new lord sentinel, sir," he said.

"Only if it's proved the current lord sentinel is dead," Bloodhound protested. "I understand that's not the case. Lord and Lady Daired, we hear you were the last to see him before his, er, disappearance. Do you have any reason to believe he isn't alive?"

"No," I said. "He was alive when we left him, and he took his horse the next day."

Damp Handkerchief sniffled. "The man, ah, had no heirs? No family whatsoever?"

"None," Rhys said.

"Then yes, it's agreed we need a steward." Cantor Brigsley-Baine had to strain to see the rest of the table over the pitchers and candelabra in front of her. "The real question is, which of us is able? I know I certainly can't leave my abbey."

"You really could, you know," Subcantor Carle muttered, but no one but me seemed to hear him.

The mass of furs that was the southern cantor's head swayed slightly, which Furry Bundle's neighbors took as agreement. He or she could not leave his or her abbey either. I guessed it was a very warm abbey.

Damp Handkerchief dabbed his nose with a napkin. "As it so happens, my Lord Langdred's youngest son has shown considerable interest in the management of great estates such as this one—"

Farrell rolled her eyes. "His *considerable interest* drops off sharply once he's gotten past the wine cellars."

"That is a gross slander!"

"Oh, come off it. Langdred's youngest couldn't do sums if you held a dagger to his throat. He'd close all trade on the lake because one of the stevedores looked at him funny, and gods forbid he ever met the king of the merfolk. His Deepness would drown the boy in a heartbeat." Farrell sipped her wine. "And I for one would send him a thank-you present."

Red in the face and sputtering, Damp Handkerchief looked around the table as if hoping someone would correct Magistrate Farrell's assessment. No one did. A few heads bobbed in agreement. There were even one or two snickers. He slumped back in his chair.

"It's obvious, isn't it?" Bloodhound said. "The matter of the stewardship is one of practicality. You can't steward much of anything across a mountain range. Whoever we choose would have to stay close to the castle."

"Indeed, sir," Subcantor Carle said. "The household will need to be maintained in case Selwyn should return, or, in the event his death is proved, when the king appoints the new lord. The steward will also have to manage, to some degree, the flow of trade, and that is of course most easily done . . ." He trailed off as Brigsley-Baine dug her elbow into his side.

"Yes. Precisely," Bloodhound said. "Thank you, young man. The steward will need to live near the castle or, if at all possible, in it. Magistrates Polton and Farrell, your towns are closest. You're known to everyone here as fair and reasonable magistrates and honorable individuals." He paused, peering around the table as if daring someone to challenge that claim. Farrell watched him without expression. The briefest of smiles touched Polton's lips before he too turned to Bloodhound with a look of surprise. Ever so slightly, Rhys's knuckles whitened around his wine glass.

Bloodhound stood. "Lord Daired, I'd like to offer Magistrates Connell Polton and Lyra Farrell up for your consideration as candidates for the stewardship of Castle Selwyn and the position of lord sentinel. Or lady sentinel, as it may be."

"I'm honored, sir, but I must withdraw," Farrell said before Alastair could reply. "As much as I'd like to do right by Lord Selwyn, my townsfolk need me where I am." She tapped her cane, the iron-shod echo ringing through the hall. "I'm afraid I wouldn't be able to travel very often. I must decline."

"Oh, very well." Bloodhound sat. "Polton, are you up for it?"

"It would be a great and solemn honor."

"Does anyone else have any considerations?" Rhys said. "Any at all?"

Glass and silverware tinkled somewhere farther down the table. Furry Bundle hiccupped. Damp Handkerchief blew his nose. Beads of sweat stood out on Rhys's forehead. Polton smiled.

"I do," I said.

All eyes turned to me. Rhys leaned forward. "Yes, Lady Daired? You have a name?"

"Madam Mòrag."

Somewhere in the shadows near the kitchen door, a crutch clattered to the floor. Heads swiveled this way and that as those who didn't know Mòrag tried to figure out who this person was. I left the table and helped her pick up her fallen crutch. "What are you doing, you silly girl?" she said as I drew her into the light.

"The right thing," I whispered. Louder, I said, "Madam Mòrag has been the housekeeper of Castle Selwyn for years. She knows it better than anyone here." We stopped at the end of the table between Brigsley-Baine and Dougal. "Lord Daired, I'd like to offer Madam Mòrag as a candidate for the stewardship of Castle Selwyn."

Alastair smiled. "Madam Mòrag, do you have any objections?"

"I—well—Lord Daired, I'm not . . ." She looked around at the faces watching her with varying degrees of bewilderment, tightened her grip on her crutches, and straightened. "It would be an honor, sir."

Polton and Bloodhound exchanged a glance. Polton looked blank. Bloodhound only shrugged.

"Excellent!" Rhys cried. "Lord Daired, as master of the colloquy you have until sunset to make your decision. I believe we'll all be—"

"No need, Captain. I've made up my mind."

"Sir?"

"Magistrate Polton—"

Rhys's face fell.

"—and Madam Mòrag."

Brigsley-Baine tucked a strand of hair under her cap. "A joint stewardship, Lord Daired? That's rather irregular."

"But not without precedent, Cantor Brigsley-Baine!" Subcantor Carle said. He pulled a sheaf of notes from his pocket. "There are accounts going back as far as the time of High Cantor Idwalion. I read it only the other day. Before the Selwyns there were, let me see . . ."

"Yes, yes, Carle, we believe you," Brigsley-Baine said.

"Madam Mòrag will continue to manage the household," Alastair said. "Magistrate Polton will have responsibility of the lake trade. They will consult together as needed on any matters in which they share interest. Is this decision acceptable to the colloquy?"

A number of "ayes" and "yes, my lords" went up from around the table.

"Very well." Alastair raised his glass. "A toast, then. To Madam

Mòrag and Magistrate Polton, stewards of Castle Selwyn and Keepers of the Lake." The others stood and followed suit, raising their wine goblets to whichever of the two was closest. "Madam, Magistrate, your good health."

Mòrag blushed.

The toasts were drunk, blessings said, or in the case of Furry Bundle, muttered, and the colloquy of Castle Selwyn came to an end. Few lingered. We said goodbye to Furry Bundle and Bloodhound in the front hall. Damp Handkerchief and his retinue cut our farewells short as they hurried out after them, sniffling something about needing a word with the local tavern-master.

Magistrate Farrell chuckled as we watched them sort out their horses in the courtyard. "That man will need quite a few words with the tavern-master before he works up the courage to tell Langdred what we've decided," she said. "But it was fair." She touched her forehead. "Thank you both for what you've done here today. How long do you plan to stay in Lake Meera?"

"As long as it takes," Alastair said. "We've still a monster to slay."

"Yes, of course, and best of luck on the hunt. But a word of advice from a fellow Rider, my lord: find this creature before the snows blow in. Dragon or no dragon, you don't want to get caught in these mountains in a bad storm. We might not find you until spring."

"We'll be careful," he said.

"Good." Farrell tucked her cane beneath her arm and tied her cloak around her. "Wherever the gods take you, I hope they grant you every happiness along the way. Mikla grant that we meet each other again, and perhaps next time under better circumstances."

"Magistrate Farrell, may I have a word?" Chirrorim asked before she could signal the groom for her horse.

They moved into the courtyard together, switching to Beor-speak before they'd gone half a dozen steps. Alastair smiled as he shut the door behind them.

"What were they saying?" I asked.

"He asked if he could accompany her back to town. He wants to know how she adjusted after the death of her beoryn. Yes, Cantor?"

The embassy from Morianton still lingered at the mouth of the Lake Hall, where Mòrag and Polton were already deep in discussion. Rhys was nowhere to be seen, and Brigsley-Baine was waving us over. "Lord Daired, Master Dougal has a request to make before we leave."

Dougal stepped forward. He touched his forehead and made a series of complicated gestures that seemed to imitate something spinning. "He says he'd like to visit the forge-wight," Carle translated. "He has many questions for her. They're having trouble with the wheel at his mill again."

"That's a question for the steward," Alastair said. "Madam Mòrag?"

"Eh?" she said.

Carle repeated Dougal's question.

"Fyri? Oh. Aye, of course. Excuse me, Magistrate. If you'd follow me." Mòrag turned, and Brigsley-Baine, Carle, and the miller followed her in the direction of the portrait stair.

"I suppose I'd better start back without them," Polton said. "Bring up her precious wheelworks and that forge-wight will talk even Dougal's ears off his head. And Carle's going to want to know the history of everything, and . . ." He shuddered and pulled on his gloves. "Yes, I think I'd best be off. Lord Daired, thank you again. Lady Daired, it's been a pleasure."

The question that'd been hanging at the back of my mind surfaced as his foot crossed the threshold. "Before you go, Magistrate Polton, may I ask you something?"

"Of course," he said, pausing on the stoop.

"Why don't you like Captain Rhys?"

He raised an eyebrow. "Why would you think that, my lady?"

"No offense, sir, but neither of you are subtle about it."

"I suppose not." He sighed. "Well, I won't deny it. Owin Rhys loathes me, and the feeling is entirely mutual."

"But why?"

"Because for three years I've been trying to dismantle the smuggling operation he and his regiment have been running out of my town, and now that Selwyn's not here to protect him, I intend to finish the job."

"Rhys is a smuggler?" I said, but even as the words left my lips I wondered how I'd missed it. The charm, the nerves, the scars, the long-standing arrangement with Selwyn: it all made sense.

"Of anything and everything. False dragonbacks, heartstones, Noordish alchemical wares, Garhadi ale. You name it and Rhys has smuggled it. For years I've done all in my power to stop his game, but he and Selwyn had a deal of some kind, and without Selwyn's support I couldn't touch him." He smiled. It was a grim smile, neither vindictive nor angry, and just a tiny bit sad. "Of course, unless he is much stupider than I believe him to be, he's already followed Selwyn's example and fled. Ah, well. There'll be more than enough to handle with the rest of his regiment." Polton donned his cap and bowed. "I think you may want to check how many horses are in the stable before you retire for the night. Good evening."

A COLD WIND DROVE PELLETS OF SNOW THROUGH THE cracks at the bottom of the door, scattering hay across the floor, but inside it was warm, and dim, and full of the curious snuffling of a half-dozen horses. Light flickered below the stable door. I held my breath as the latch rose with a creak, and the door swung open just enough to allow a man inside. He wore a traveling pack and carried a shaded lantern. He hung the lantern on a peg and reached for the catch of the nearest stall door.

I struck a light. The lamp in my hand blazed to life. "If you're looking for speed, I'd go with the one on your left," I said. "That mare's a bit jumpy."

Rhys froze.

"Why did you wait so long to run, Captain?" Alastair asked. "You don't have much daylight left."

"I . . . what do you mean, run? I was just—"

"Don't bother. Polton told us."

For a moment it looked as though Rhys would continue the charade, but something—perhaps Alastair's hand on his knife—broke his resolve. With a sigh he let his pack fall to the ground. "Meddlesome old bastard."

"Conscientious civil servant," I said.

"You'd be surprised how often those lines cross, my lady."

The wind howled outside, sending more snow sifting through the cracks around the door. "Poor weather for riding," Alastair said.

"I'm an excellent horseman, Lord Daired, and I know these mountains well. Look, what do you want from me? If you think you're going to hand me over—"

"We're not going to hand you over to Polton," Alastair said.

The captain blinked. "You're not?"

"Call it a small mercy to a fellow warrior. But we do need something before you leave."

Rhys's relief was palpable. "Anything."

"That day we found the dead mermaid. Do you remember the man in the forest?"

"The one dressed as a Ranger? Aye, I remember."

"You recognized him. Where had you seen him before?"

"A Ranger that looked like that man in the woods came through Morianton a few weeks ago. Just before you arrived, actually. We get the odd Ranger now and again looking to join a regiment, but this one never approached me. I only saw him once or twice. Tell you the truth, I'd forgotten about him until we saw him on the beach."

"You're sure?" Alastair said.

"If it wasn't him, then they looked a damn sight alike."

Alastair turned away.

"Captain, this is going to sound mad," I said, "but this man . . . was he *alive?*"

Rhys stared at me. "Of course he was alive. What makes you ask such a thing?"

"And he was human?"

"Well, given that I couldn't spot a selkie at close range I wouldn't give my discernment on the matter a glowing recommendation, but yes, I believe so. Certainly flesh and blood."

Human. And alive. My mind raced. *Impossible.*

"Just out of curiosity, what's this man to you?" Rhys asked.

Quite suddenly I wished I had another lantern. I wished I had a dozen lanterns, and a bonfire, and the full light of day to keep this terror at bay. "No man, Captain Rhys. A *ghastradi.*"

"A *what?*"

"You should go," Alastair said, "before the storm gets worse. We won't follow you."

"Something I appreciate, but what do you mean, a *ghastradi?* A real one? Is my regiment in any danger?"

"They're not your regiment anymore."

"Well . . . yes, I suppose. But look, I can't just—"

"Go."

Rhys hesitated, one last protest still visible on his lips, but he reeled it in and picked up his traveling pack. "As you say, my lord."

I moved to Alastair's side as Rhys saddled the gelding, the speed with which he did it suggesting he'd had a good deal of practice sneaking out of stables at dusk.

"Alastair, how could it be him?" I whispered.

"I don't know."

"Then *Wydrick* killed the mermaid? And the other *Idar*? The actual Wydrick?"

"I don't know."

"But—"

"Aliza, I said I don't know."

Rhys led the gelding into the aisle. "I may not understand everything that's going on here, but I'm no fool. You let me go; that's worth more than a few questions about some Ranger in the woods."

"You have nothing else we need, Rhys," Alastair said.

"Begging your pardon, my lord, but that's not quite true. A man in my trade hears things. All sorts of things, from all parts of the world, and there's been a rumor of particular interest to some of my *Vesh* friends drifting around of late. A rumor involving two very rare, very precious heartstones."

Alastair and I looked up.

"I'm telling you this because despite my best efforts over the past few days I've grown to admire the two of you," Rhys said. "You're persistent if nothing else, and I think you deserve a warning. They say certain interested parties are willing to pay several thousand dragonbacks to whoever acquires the Daired heartstones."

"What interested parties?" My heart pounded as I thought of the inn, of Rookwood, of the feeling of my knife hitting bone. "Captain Rhys, *who wants them?*"

"I don't know, my lady. I'm a smuggler; I only pass things on. But by Midwinter I wager there won't be a heart-hound in Arle who isn't desperate to get ahold of your heartstones, and when the *Vesh* get desperate, unpleasant things tend to happen." He glanced at Alastair's empty scabbard. "If I were you, I wouldn't wait much longer to get a good sword."

"I don't plan to."

Rhys unbarred the stable door and swung into the saddle with a smart salute. "In that case, all I can do is wish you safe travels." He ducked to avoid the lintel as the gelding trotted outside. "Oh, and say goodbye to your dragon for me, will you, Lord Daired? I rather liked—"

The wind tore his last words away and swallowed the sound of hoofbeats as he rode off into the gathering storm.

CHAPTER 27

THE RANGER

We didn't stay in Castle Selwyn another night. Alastair and I agreed; with the Selwyns gone and the colloquy over, sleeping in an empty castle felt wrong. Mòrag was surprised at our decision but didn't try to stop us. She did insist, however, on paying Alastair's bond-price despite his protests that he'd not yet fulfilled his contract. "But you will, my lord, and saving your reverence, I'd rather not have to think of it again," she told him, and then of course he could not refuse. After counting out the promised dragonbacks from the cache in Selwyn's study, she saw us to the front gate, keeping pace on her makeshift crutches with a dignified wobble. When we told her about Rhys, she only shrugged. "If that man was chief of the smugglers in Morianton, I can understand why Polton wanted to arrest him. The trade has brought grief and corruption enough to that town, and Rhys walked too long on the edge of a precipice. He has only himself to blame for a fall. You're going to Morianton, then?"

Alastair nodded.

"There's decent lodging at the Wheel and Trident. How long will you stay?"

"Until we're certain this creature killing *Idar* cannot kill again," Alastair said. "Captain Rhys said there were sightings of the *ghastradi* in town."

"Then Mikla watch over you both. And since I doubt we'll ever see each other again, I suppose now would be the time to say it," she said. "You, ah, did right by Lady Cordelia. You—well, yes. Thank you for that."

Alastair touched his forehead and swung up onto Akarra's shoulders. "*Tey iskaros.*"

I stayed on the ground. "Thank you, Mòrag." And then, because she was a bitter, foolish old woman who had walked through darkness I couldn't fathom and still had compassion enough to pull me out of my own, I embraced her. She stiffened but did not pull away. "You were right," I whispered.

"About what?"

"You *do* live."

"Oh. Yes. Yes, you do. Now, off with you," she said as I released her, brushing from her cheeks what for the sake of her pride I decided were melted snowflakes. "You'd best get there before the storm gets any worse."

I managed one last look over my shoulder as Akarra banked east around the curve of the castle walls. Mòrag stood in the gateway. She touched her forehead, then her heart, nodded once, and went inside.

IT WAS LESS THAN TEN MINUTES' FLIGHT TO MORIANTON, but my cheeks were nearly frozen solid by the time we landed. The snow thickened as the sun set, stinging our faces like wasps. Even buried in our cloaks with heads bent close to Akarra's back to block out the wind, the cold slipped through, jabbing icy needles through bearskin and leather hauberk. Akarra spat tongues of dragonfire into the air as she flew. It warmed us a little but nothing like enough. Alastair started shivering the moment we left the castle, and he didn't stop until we were safe within the smoke-stained walls of the Wheel and Trident.

The innkeeper recognized him at once. "Ah, Master Daired! Didn't expect you again so soon."

"A room," Alastair said and tossed him a silver half-dragonback. "And for gods' sakes, something hot to drink."

After the grandeur of Castle Selwyn, the tiny, earthy room the innkeeper showed us to should have felt cramped, but it was hard to notice anything beyond the fire blazing in the grate. We shed our riding gear and sat for twenty minutes on the hearthrug until our limbs and faces had thawed enough to speak in full sentences.

"I want to visit the local smithy first thing in the morning," he said. "I need to see if they have any swords for sale."

"We should have asked Fyri before we left."

"That would take too long. I don't want to go another day with an empty scabbard."

I thought of his beautiful Orordrin-wrought blade now sunk in the depths of Lake Meera. "Maybe Akarra can ask the merfolk to bring back your sword."

He didn't smile. "These merfolk aren't *that* friendly, and that would take more time than we can afford."

No teasing tonight, then. "Alastair, how do you kill a ghast?"

He stared into the flames. "I wish I knew."

A knock at the door announced the innkeeper, who told us dinner was ready in the common room. After a last longing look at our cloaks still drying by the fire, we headed downstairs. It wasn't crowded. Half a dozen patrons huddled around a game of quartermarks in the middle of the room. A few others nursed drinks in quiet corners. Most seemed to have already met Alastair on his previous visits to Morianton, so save for the occasional nod from a newcomer, we ate our meal in peace. Wind howled outside and snow pelted the windows, a steady background din as unsettling as it was persistent.

"We're not planning to fly in this weather, are we?" I asked.

"Not if we can help it."

"Does Akarra mind?"

This time he did smile. "She was hatched in a nest of ice on the frozen peaks of Dragonsmoor. She loves the cold." The maid stopped at our table to clear away our dishes. "Miss?" he said and offered her another coin. "For the meal."

"'Salready been taken care of, Lordship."

"I'm sorry?"

"That man there paid for your meal," she said, nodding behind us. "With compliments, he says."

We turned. A man sat at a table in the darkest corner of the common room, his furred hood drawn up, battered boots on the table and a mug in his hand. When he saw us, he lowered his feet and pushed back his hood.

Alastair rose. My fingers closed around my dagger hilt.

Wydrick smiled and beckoned for us to join him.

I followed Alastair across like a sleepwalker caught in a familiar nightmare, wanting to run, to fight, and finding my limbs had betrayed me. Wydrick drew up two chairs and we sat, no doubt looking to the rest of the inn like nothing more than three friends meeting for a quiet drink after a long journey. If they'd known the truth, I imagined few would stay.

"*You*," Alastair said at last.

"I see you have the same way with words you always did," Wydrick said. He tipped back the last of his beer and wiped the foam from his upper lip. "Yes. Me."

Alastair drew his knife and rested it on the table. "Give me one reason I shouldn't kill you now."

"It'd make a terrible mess."

"A good reason."

"Because you already tried that." Wydrick unlaced the collar of his tunic and pulled it open. "Or did you forget?"

A wound gaped just above his left breast. The edges were raw and flayed-looking, and I didn't need to see his back to know there'd be an identical mark beneath his left shoulder blade. Where there should have been blood, tendrils of darkness roiled and writhed. The skin around the wound was the bruised yellow of a new corpse.

Alastair stared. "You were dead," he whispered.

"Possibly. I don't really remember much of those last few minutes," Wydrick said.

"I ran you through."

"Well, you missed."

"*Ghastradi*," Alastair hissed.

"Now that's not very polite," Wydrick said. "Didn't your father teach you manners?"

Alastair's fist tightened on the hilt of his knife, but I put a hand on his arm. "I thought ghasts didn't ride corpses," I said.

"I can't speak for the entire brotherhood, mind, but in my experience, they don't."

"Did you find yours on the battlefield?"

He laughed. It was a long, slow chuckle, building with the force of a wave and cresting over us with the mirth of madness. "Oh, Miss Aliza, my friend had reason to keep me alive long before the War of the Worm."

I gripped the edge of the table. That ghasts had been drawn out from the dark and evil corners of the world by the waking of the

Worm I was prepared to accept. *That Wydrick had been ghast-ridden before that, possibly even when we first met* . . . "Was that why you tried to kill my sister? That thing inside you wanted, what? Practice?"

He looked shocked. "You believe I wanted to *kill* Leyda? Don't think so badly of me, Aliza. I was doing the sniveling brat a great honor—"

The force of my slap stunned even me. Several patrons stopped talking and looked in our direction as Alastair pulled me back to my chair.

Wydrick stayed still for a moment, head turned aside, one hand on his cheek. "Be careful, my lady," he said in a quiet voice. "You'd best not wake him right now. He won't be so eager to answer your questions."

"Then choose your words about my little sister more carefully."

He lowered his hand. Yellow like sulfur boiled up through the green of his eyes, but he drew it back, his smirk laced with poison. "Noted."

"What did your ghast want with Leyda?" Alastair asked.

"Him? Oh, Ghethel didn't want anything to do with her. We tried, but even a strong ghast can't hold an unwilling heart, and in my eagerness I'd, ah, made her very unwilling. Pity too. Given her family connections she could have been useful. But that's not why you're here, is it?"

Alastair's throat worked up and down. "Lyii-Lyiishen," he said at last.

"Who?"

"The mermaid," I said. "Her name was Lyii-Lyiishen. You killed her. Why?"

"She was curious. I needed her heartstone." He shrugged. "It wasn't hard. She'd never been on land before. Didn't put up much of a fight."

"And the troll?" Alastair asked. "The will-o'-the-wisp? The centaur? You wanted their heartstones too?"

"That centaur, now. She did put up a fight." Wydrick pulled his tunic open even further to show another ill-closed wound in his side the size and shape of a crossbow bolt. Shadows moved inside the arrow hole, dripping darkness like blood. "I wish I could've stayed to see her end. Alas, other *Idar* calling, other heartstones to collect. Honestly, I'm surprised you only found the two. I'd arranged more than a dozen surprises on the road from Pendragon to Lake Meera, though strictly speaking, they weren't really for *you*."

Alastair was shaking in earnest now. The vein in his temple began to throb. "Why did you kill them?"

Wydrick smiled. "You still have no idea, do you? Suffice to say I offered them a choice; or rather, my master offered them a choice." He spread his hands. "They chose wrong."

"Why *Idar*?" I asked.

"Why do you think, Miss Aliza? They are the Indifferent. They've always needed to choose a side. All things will, even the Eldest." He eyed the empty scabbard at Alastair's hip. "I suppose I have you to thank for frightening away the Hag-of-the-Mists."

"That creature was responsible for the death of a child," Alastair said, straining to keep his voice even. "It nearly drove Lord Selwyn mad—"

"Yes, and he'd kept a selkie-wife for the better part of a decade. Don't pretend he didn't deserve it."

"He—"

"How did you know about the Selwyns?" I interrupted. "How did you know what she was?"

A glimmer of yellow shot through the green of his eyes and a new voice spoke, one that turned the air in my lungs to ice. "We know a great many things of the Oldkind, Miss Aliza. We know of creatures older than them, creatures stronger and more ancient than you can imagine. Why else do you think our master sent us to this wasteland but to summon allies for the coming war?" The yellow faded but didn't disappear entirely. "Though it wasn't as easy as he promised," Wydrick said in his human voice. "It took the refusal of many *Idar* to draw her from the Wastes."

The pieces at last fell into place. "You brought the Green Lady here with the promise of vengeance—for what *you'd* done?"

"Oh, I'm sure she would have liked that, Miss Aliza, but even for ten thousand slain *Idar* she would not dare dispense her wrath on us. No, she knows whom we serve too well for that. But we were not ungenerous. She came south to avenge a great wrong; well, we gave her what she wanted, though not perhaps what she expected. She needed vengeance for the *Idar*. We gave her Selwyn."

"And now she and Selwyn are gone," Alastair said, "and it's time for this to end." He rose, gripping the edge of the table. "Their heartstones. Why did you take them?"

"What, isn't that what Riders do? Hunt down the dangerous creatures of the world? Lay them open and take their heartstones as trophies?"

"Don't you *dare* call yourself a Rider." Alastair's voice rose. "Riders don't kill innocent creatures. Riders don't kill children!"

"I'm as much a Rider as you'll ever be," Wydrick said, and his eyes flashed yellow again. "Your family may have denied me my dragon, but no human in centuries has done what I've done. I've tamed the things that haunt your nightmares. You have your tempest-bringer, yes; I ride the sire of all valkyries. And we've been watching you, Fireborn. For a long time now, we've been watching. Listening. From air above and from earth below. We've heard your plans. We've seen your weakness. You, who've known hate, who've tasted the lifeblood of one of the Great *Tekari*, who bear so proudly the heartstone of the Daireds. Surely you didn't think there wouldn't be consequences?"

Alastair and I were both on our feet now, but Wydrick didn't move. His eyes were full yellow and smoldering with vicious delight.

"There is a war coming, a war of which the Battle of North Fields was only a foretaste. As the brotherghast in Hatch Ford told you—yes, I know of his ill-conceived attempt to sway you, Miss Aliza—you must also make your choice: stand aside and live. Fight us and die."

"You know our answer, monster," Alastair said through clenched teeth.

Wydrick's voice gave way to a strangled whine as the ghast inside him spoke again. "Soon! Soon you will see. The summons comes for the House of Edan Daired and old things will be called into account. The ledger will be brought forth. Debts must be paid!" He leaned forward, his nails raking furrows in the table as if trying to claw his way toward us. "The days of your house are numbered, Alastair. You will all fall before the end. Everyone you ever loved: your sister, your wife, your whole family. When the moment comes, you won't be able to protect them." He smiled suddenly and looked at me, speaking once more in his own voice. "Just like you were not able to protect your child."

Then he changed. Shadows seethed in shapeless mass behind his back, wrapping red and yellow and green in a cloak of living nightmare. The darkness deepened. I squeezed my eyes shut, and in that space between frantic heartbeats, quiet as the breath before a scream, I heard their voices together, slithering like windblown snow over the bones of the dead.

"When this war is over and all Arle kneels before our master, *then* you'll know I've won."

I opened my eyes. Wydrick and the ghast were gone. Alastair stood over his fallen chair, breathing hard, his knife in his hand. The common room was still and silent. One by one, all heads turned from the door. All eyes fixed on us.

"Did you hear it?" I asked Alastair.

"Yes."

"Er, begging your pardons, milord and lady," one of the quarter-mark players said, "but *what in Thell's name was that?*"

Alastair sheathed his dagger. I picked up the fallen chair. Shutters banged against the front of the inn and the wind howled in the chimney, making the fire sputter. Somewhere in the distance I heard a shriek overlaying the sounds of the storm, ancient and hate filled and familiar. A valkyrie's cry. And now, more than a cry. It was a challenge.

Alastair reached for my hand. I laced my fingers with his.

"Our next contract," I said.

ACKNOWLEDGMENTS

Thanks first belongs to God, who gives life and breath and makes all things possible.

Despite being unforgivably belated, I'd like to acknowledge Jane Austen and the masterpiece that is *Pride and Prejudice*, which inspired the original story of *Heartstone*. Ms. Austen, thank you. I am in your debt.

Thanks also to Thao Le, my wonderful agent; Priyanka Krishnan, editor extraordinaire; and the entire Voyager team who helped shape this story into everything it could be.

To Kelsey, Stephanie, Bailey, Colleen, Arleen, Leanna, Amanda, and the rest of my beta readers: you guys are incredible. Thank you for your honesty, your thoughtfulness, and for staying up late to read every draft I threw at you. I owe you all the coffees.

To the Nuhfers: thank you doesn't begin to cover it. Without your encouragement this story would not exist.

And lastly, to the Plaza Restaurant, for graciously putting up with the odd girl in the corner booth hammering away at her laptop until closing time, and for always having plenty of tea.

ABOUT THE AUTHOR

Elle Katharine White grew up in Buffalo, New York, where she learned valuable life skills like how to clear a snowy driveway in under twenty minutes and how to cheer for the perennial underdog. She now lives in Pennsylvania, where she drinks entirely too much tea and dreams of traveling the world.

www.ellekatharinewhite.com
Twitter: @elle_k_writes